I0730372

ABOUT THE AUTHOR

Lexie Winston has been an astronaut, rock star, princess and time traveller. In her dreams. But none of the dreams have lived up to what becoming an author has been like. She gets to live in a world of pure imagination, and her heroines get to do the things she's always wished she could.

When not writing books, Lexie is a mother of two gorgeous teenagers and the wife to a patient and understanding man. They live in Western Australia and are lorded over by a black toy poodle. She loves camping, reading and if her Kindle was stolen, her world would explode.

And you can find all links at

www.lexiewinston.com

ARDENT QUEEN

KINGDOM OF ARAMIS DUET

KINGDOMS SERIES
BOOK TWO

LEXIE WINSTON

ALSO BY LEXIE WINSTON

The Collectors Division

(Paranormal Reverse Harem Series)

Guardian

Guardian's Blood

Guardian Ascending

Collector's Division Omnibus

Neighpalm Industries Collective

(Enemies to Lovers Reverse Harem)

Abandoned Girl

Broken Girl

Tormented Girl

Wanted Girl

Cherished Girl

Loved Girl

Superficial Girl - Jacinta's Story Part 1

Superficial Girl - Jacinta's Story Part 2

Neighpalm Industries Collective 1-3

Neighpalm Industries Collective 4-6

Seductive Sins Collection

(Reverse Harem Series)

Glorious Gluttony

Gangs, Guns, and Glory

Glory Glory Hellelujah

Crowning Glory

What's the Story, Morning Glory?

(Seductive Sins Omnibus)

Galaxy Circus

(Sci-Fi Reverse Harem Series)

Apprentice

Stagehand

Whisperer

Mama - Galaxy Circus Novella

Performer

Ringmaster

Interlude

Spectacle

Ovation

A Night Most Wicked - Galaxy Circus Novella

Broken Promises

(Dark Poly Romance Series)

Secrets Kept

Lies Untold

Trust Broken

M.I.T.H.O.S

(Contemporary RH)

Spies Like Me

Spies Like Us

Storm View Stories

(Contemporary Standalone RH)

Ice Me Out

Kingdoms Series

(Paranormal RH)

Kingdom of Aramis Duet

Unwilling Queen

Ardent Queen

First published by Neighpalm Publishing in 2025

Copyright © Neighpalm Publishing 2025
The moral right of the author has been asserted.
All rights reserved. This publication (or any part of it) may not be reproduced or transmitted, copied, stored, distributed or otherwise made available by any person or entity, in any form (electronic, digital, optical, mechanical) or by any means (photocopying, recording, scanning or otherwise) without prior written permission from the publisher.
This is a work of fiction. Names, characters, businesses, places, events and incidents are either the products of the author's imagination or used in a fictitious manner. Any resemblance to actual persons, living or dead, or actual events is purely coincidental.

Title

Mobi format: 978-1-7636228-9-0
Print: 978-1-7638409-1-1

Cover design by Covers by Aura

Editing by Elemental Editing

Earlier at the ball

Gryffin

My tiger thrashes around inside me as I watch Colbie walk away. I could see how angry she was when she found out I was the tiger in the stables last night, but she didn't want to hear any of my excuses, and I don't blame her. No one at the breakfast table said anything to her this morning either.

He pushes hard, trying to force me to shift, but I grit my teeth and clench my fists, refusing to concede control to him. I have no idea what his fucking problem is. He has never shown so much interest in a shifter apart from Gem, and he was always happy to wait for our mate to appear before we even contemplated starting something with him, so this behavior is completely unexpected. He's acting like she's our mate, and it simply can't be possible. I should probably keep my distance, but it's going to be hard with us guarding her and teaching her how to control her shifts.

"There you are. I've been looking everywhere for you." A silky finger brushes across my shoulder, and I spin around to find Isla Tideman fluttering her eyelashes at me. My tiger snarls, and it's all I can do to stop it from escaping my mouth. "Now that you don't have to pay attention to the queen, I can have you all to myself."

She holds her hands up, waiting for me to lead her in a dance across the ballroom. It's the last thing I want to do.

"But it's my turn. I've been waiting for ages." The petulant voice comes from my side, and Gianna appears in my eyeline.

Isla loses her flirty grin and glares at her. "And you'll keep waiting, Gianna. Don't think I don't know what you've been doing with Liam. You're not exactly subtle about it. Stay away from Watch Team One. If anyone is going to be marked as their bond mate, it will be me."

"Like fuck it will. I have a relationship with all of them. I've been working with them at the watch while you've been nothing but useless eye candy doing luncheons and tea with your mother and her friends." Gianna pushes me out of the way and gets in Isla's face. Both of them are tall and willowy shifters, so different from Colbie's curvier, slightly shorter frame, and neither of them are backing down. Isla shoves Gianna and snarls, and I see fur sprout up her arms.

"Whoa. Easy girls. No one wants you shifting in the middle of the royal welcome dinner." Gem slides between the two women. "And neither of you can dance with our boy here. He is needed elsewhere. How about you head to opposite ends of the ballroom and cool down before you both get banned from future royal engagements, or worse, kicked out of the palace. Just because your parents live here doesn't mean you have to," Gem cautions, and reality seems to hit the girls.

Both of them look over to where my parents are watching with narrowed eyes, looking very unimpressed. Without saying a word, the girls slip into the crowd and disappear. I know exactly how they feel, because I want to do the same thing when that glare is leveled at me by my parents. Thankfully it doesn't happen very often.

"Thanks for the save," I tell my friend as my eyes sweep over his form. His suit fits him like a glove, and he looks fucking incredible. It's becoming harder to rein in my attraction to him, and I know he feels the same way. My tiger stops finally thrashing to get to Colbie, his attention turning to our immediate companion. He chuffs and rolls onto his stomach, exposing his belly, and I know he wants me to shift so Gem can run his hands all over him. I internally roll my eyes at his behavior. What is his problem? He's becoming a hussy.

Gem steps into my personal space, close enough that if I put my arms around him, we would be slow dancing, and I'm tempted. My hands twitch, and I start to reach for him. "Anytime. I'm not even sure how Gianna managed to attend. I know she lives with her parents, but she was banned from all royal functions. The thought of those nasty bitches' hands or mouths on you makes my phoenix scream with anger and want to burn them to ashes."

I frown, not surprised by his response one little bit. My tiger feels the same way about any female or male putting their hands on him, despite our previous need to go slowly, but that's all starting to become too hard.

"How did he feel when I danced with Colbie?" I ask, curious about how his animal reacts to our new queen.

He tilts his head to the side, and the flames in his eyes blaze higher, like his phoenix is paying attention to our conversation. "Not maiming jealous, but like he wanted to squish her between us and make her scream with pleasure."

I brush my hand over his back, and I feel him shiver beneath it. "Yes, my tiger felt the same way."

Gem pushes even farther into my space so our bodies rub together, his pelvis grazing mine. "Doesn't feel like only your tiger felt that way. How about you let me take care of that not so little problem?"

Feeling guilty about my reaction to him, I go to step away, but his hand snaps up and grabs my chin, not allowing me to move. His grip is just on this side of bruising. "Stop running, Gryffin," he hisses. "I respected your wishes for a long time now, but there is no sign of our mate, and do you really think it would be a problem for her if you and I started something? Hell, do you think your father would be upset if your mothers decided to have a sexual relationship with each other?"

I grimace at the thought of my parents doing anything sexual, but I know he's right. Even though my mothers don't have that kind of relationship, I know my father wouldn't care, and there are many bond groups who take pleasure with one another before their mate is marked. I'm also sick of resisting him. There's no difference between us being together and us having relationships with people outside of our bond until our mate appears.

He must see the moment I decide to give into the attraction, because the flames in his eyes blaze even higher, and he drops my chin, picks up my hand, and drags me out of the ballroom. He doesn't stop even when I hear Brodie call our names.

"Brodie," I start, but Gem hisses, his phoenix's agitation all too clear.

"I've waited too long to let the wolf distract us."

"What if it's important?"

"They can go without us long enough for me to wrap my lips around your cock and show you how good I can make you feel."

Just like that, all thoughts of my team members, the girls fighting over me, and the queen leave my mind, and my cock twitches behind my zipper.

The dark corridor we are in leads to the family wing, but we don't get as far as our suite. A small alcove off to the side is nice and private, and that's where Gem leads me, pushing me against the wall. He cages me in between him and the hard surface at my back. The only lighting in here is from the hallway and the flames burning blue and orange in his irises. Without another word, he kisses me, his lips conveying all the built-up sexual tension between us. I melt into him, our bodies molding so closely together you can't see where one starts and the other ends. I groan as his teeth scrape over my lip, his tongue pressing for entrance, and I give him free rein, allowing his mouth to devour mine. He tastes smoky and wild, and I can't get enough of him. I wrap my arms around his lean waist, pulling him closer to me, his hard length brushing over mine with delicious friction.

I gasp for breath, dazed when he finally pulls away,

my lips throbbing from his punishment. I know Gem is going to make me pay for making him wait so long before giving into this thing between us. When I gain control of myself, I find him smirking at me.

"Now don't you wish we were doing that all along?" He arches an eyebrow but doesn't wait for an answer. His hands slide to my belt buckle, and he makes quick work of popping the button on my pants, unzipping the fly before he slowly sinks to his knees in front of me. I moan as he slides his hand into my pants and pulls out my throbbing length, giving it a sharp tug.

My knees threaten to buckle from the heat of his hands wrapped around me, but I lock them just in time as he runs his tongue up my shaft before circling the tip, catching the bead of precum leaking from it.

"Fuck, Gem," I rasp, tangling my hands in his unruly curls while thrusting. He chuckles and lashes my length with his tongue, teasing me while rolling my balls with his other hand.

"Suck it," I beg. "Please."

"I should make you suffer for making me wait so long for what I've been craving. I spent so many lonely nights fisting my dick, imagining I was sinking my cock into you, but I can't wait any longer. Maybe after this, you won't deny what we have anymore." His voice is low and cruel, and I know he's still mad at me, and that will be my cross to bear. If he needs to punish me to get over his anger, then I will happily accept it.

My cock throbs with need, and I'm just about to plead again when he takes me deep into his hot, wet mouth. My head drops against the wall as I squeeze my eyes shut and resist the urge to fuck his mouth. I want to give him control, knowing he needs this after I denied him for so long.

The suction of his mouth is exquisite as he hollows his cheeks and draws back along my length before taking it even deeper. My tip touches the back of his throat, and he swallows around me. My spine tingles, and I grip his hair harder. He moans, and the vibrations caress my dick, drawing another deep rumble from my chest.

"Fuck, Gem, it feels so good. Such a good boy taking me deep," I praise, and I feel his whole body shudder beneath my hands. I tighten my grip in his hair and flex my hips forward, watching as my cock thrusts in and out of his wet heat. His nostrils flare, and tears well in his eyes as he gazes up at me with so much desire, it sends heat coursing through my body. I take control, thrusting in and out harder, fucking his mouth with abandon.

"Fucking look at you on your knees at my feet, taking me like the cock slut you are. My cock slut... So pretty with tears streaming down your face." I grit my teeth, holding back my release, and fuck his mouth harder than I would a woman's, knowing he can take my punishing pace. "I've waited so long to feel your lips around me, I can't wait to know what it feels like when I breach your ass and fill you with my cum."

He groans and slides his hands away from my balls, thrusting a finger deep into my ass and hitting that spot that sends me hurtling over the edge with a roar that brings my tiger to the surface. My fingers lengthen into claws, biting into Gem's scalp as I bury my cock deep in his throat, holding him in place as his finger continues to pound against my prostate as I fill his throat with my cum. The scent of blood tinges the air, but he doesn't fight me, drinking me down like a well-aged wine. He gazes up at me, his eyes burning with desire, but I can't help imagining what it would look like if a set of amethyst colored eyes were also looking up at me.

Annoyed at myself, I release him and pull my cock from his mouth before bending down and hauling him up, crushing my lips to his. I taste myself on his lips, and my spent cock throbs again.

A noise in the hallway has us both freezing and turning our attention to whoever is out there.

"I saw them come this way. If I hurry, I might catch up to them and convince them to make me the meat in their sandwich," I hear Gianna tell someone.

"You better hope you can. I'm not happy you got yourself kicked out of the watch. I had to beg that useless king to allow you to even come tonight, but I'm going to try to get you a position with the new queen, so instead of making snide comments about her dress, you should be kissing her ass so we can cement our position for the next forty years," the voice hisses, and I recognize it—Councilor Sophia Gardiner, Gianna and Liana's mother, and a pain in my father's ass.

"Ugh, she's such an ugly troll. Why did the goddess pick her? Why do we have to continue to have humans as our royals? If her mates don't show up, why can't the council push for the role to become hereditary? Then Gryffin would be king, and I can be his queen."

Gianna's voice is petulant, and Gem stiffens in my arms. What she's suggesting isn't something that hasn't been proposed by the council before, but it is considered slightly treasonous to question the goddess's decisions. The sound of flesh hitting flesh echoes into our secluded little nook, and I hear Gianna's cry of pain.

"Shut your mouth, you stupid girl. You don't know

who could be listening, and Gryffin wouldn't be king. Gretchin would be queen because she is the oldest. Unless you plan on seducing her—which I'm sure she would be open to—we would have no control over her. Moreover, we need to focus on manipulating the new queen, which is why I need you to befriend her. Tomorrow, we are going to join them for breakfast, and I want you and your sister there working your charm on her. Now go seduce those two men. If you distract them with your pussy, maybe they won't have their attention on the queen."

The voices fade away, and Gem relaxes against me, resting his head on my chest. "I didn't like the sound of that," he murmurs, snuggling his face against my shirt-covered chest. I smile and hold him tighter against my body, knowing this interlude is done.

"No, we should talk to Dad and the moms and let them know what we overheard so they aren't blindsided at breakfast tomorrow."

"We should warn Colbie too," Gem suggests as he pulls away from me, allowing me to straighten my clothes.

I shake my head. "Leave her be for now. She has enough to worry about without having to add the scheming of two manipulative females. My parents will put barriers in the council's way that will be insurmountable. They have had to deal with the majority of the schemes their whole term, so they won't allow it to continue during Colbie's." I give him a gentle kiss, resting my forehead against his. "To be continued," I promise him, and he smiles and nods.

"But promise me you won't retreat behind walls again," he requests, looking unsure.

"I promise, Gem. I was an idiot for denying you for so long. You know I love you, right?" I say, and his eyes blaze with shock, but then he smirks at me.

"Of course, how could you not?" He smacks a kiss on my lips before grabbing my hand and dragging me out of the cozy nook, heading back into the gritty realm of palace intrigue.

CHAPTER
TWO

Colbie

"I said that mark is Watch Team One's. You are my brother's bond's mate."

"Oh my god!" Violet squeals with excitement as Gretchin's answer reverberates in my ears, and I sway a little, grabbing hold of the counter to steady myself.

"I'm sorry, could you repeat that?" I stammer as my grip tightens on the vanity like it can keep me from losing my shit.

"Your tattoo matches the one on my brother and the rest of his bond," Gretchin repeats slowly, and Gracelin peers at me through the mirror with concern.

A whirlwind of emotions batters against my chest. Shock is the main one, but excitement and lust also swirl like a swarm of butterflies. "I thought royals weren't matched with a bond group."

"Well, normally they aren't," Gretchin replies, frowning.

"And there are only five members of Watch Team One," Violet points out, nibbling her lip, her eyebrows furrowed. "So that leaves one crown still free."

Gracelin gasps and looks at her sister with shock. "Holy fuck. All this time, Gryff hasn't been chasing a ghost."

Gretchin groans. "God, he's going to be insufferable now. He's never doubted what that damn witch told him."

Violet and I exchange a glance. "Would you like to share with those not in the know?" I wave at the two of us, feeling frustrated, but a weight in my stomach makes me think I know what they are going to say.

"You know, instead of us standing here while you're half naked, how about you change? Then, we can talk about it out there," Gretchin suggests, and I almost argue with her, but she's right. The three of them leave the bathroom, and I turn around to stare at the tattoo in the middle of my back, the feeling of déjà vu super strong. It's just like the one on Nox's chest, with a heart in the middle of the tree trunk and six elegant, swirling branches forming the canopy. There is no doubt this tree matches the one I got super up close and personal with only a few days ago, and I have a feeling that Gretchin and Gracelin are going to tell me why.

Huffing out a breath, I spin around and study myself closely, surprised by my reflection. Although it's been two days since my transformation, I really haven't taken the time to look at myself, and I'm surprised by what I see. My face and skin are flawless. In the past, being a baker with somewhat of a sweet tooth, my skin has been prone to occasional breakouts. Then there are the chicken pock scars on my cheek that I scratched in my sleep, becoming a constant reminder of that very uncomfortable week in my early teens, but now they are gone, and my skin glistens like I spend hours a day on my skincare routine. The most shocking change is my eyes. I always thought they were a pretty, unique color that set me apart from everyone, but now they are stunning with that shifter glow behind them. They look like sparkling amethysts on display in a jewelry shop.

My gaze drifts lower to study my unfamiliar body. The muffin top I was rocking from trying too many of my own creations has flattened and become defined, like the muscles are sitting just below the skin. My hips are still curvy, but they have lost the dimpled orange peel skin, as have my thighs and ass. The stretch marks on my breasts from a growth spurt when I was thirteen have also disappeared. I'm still pale, but now instead of appearing sick from spending all my time inside, everything is sleek, smooth, and glowing with a healthy sheen. Even my hair, which is usually tied back and unwashed, is glossy and thick. Sure, I've been pampered by the attendants, but this is just something more. I'm assuming it has to do with my new magic.

Unable to look at myself and all the changes any longer without tears prickling in my eyes, I hurry into my closet and peel off my bra, pulling on a tank top and shorts. Despite the rapidly cooling weather, my new shifter metabolism keeps me warm, or that's what Violet told me when I questioned her about the castle's heating.

My hand brushes across the pendant around my neck, and my thoughts go to the man who gave it to me. I have no doubt in my mind that Nox wasn't telling the truth. I'm hurt, but rationally, I only knew him for a few days. Although, when he discovered my big secret, I would think he would share his. Then again, maybe he was flustered. There is obviously a reason he lives in the human zone and disguises the fact that he is a shifter. Maybe he thought I would force him to return to the shifter zone. Hell, no wonder he drove away without a backward glance, and I haven't heard from him since.

A pang inside my chest makes me wince. I thought we had something special, but then I recall his comment about being the hit it and quit it type, and I guess I really shouldn't be surprised. He was just another person in my life who disappointed me. Brushing off the sense of melancholy, I step into my bedroom and brace myself for whatever I'm about to find out.

"Okay, let's talk about this tattoo." I wave absently at my back as I join the other three girls on my enormous bed. I have no idea why a queen needs such a big bed, but if I had to guess, I would say it has something to do with the royals having multiple mates. I feel a small throb inside me at the thought of sharing this bed with several men, and a few of the unattached male shifters I have met come to mind, but I quickly push those thoughts away. I need to focus on what the girls have to say.

"That tattoo matches my brother's bond group, which means instead of a whole heap of men being marked for you to choose from like royals in the past, you've been gifted a fully formed bond group who has been waiting for their destined mate," Gracelin explains gently, almost like she's waiting for me to freak out.

I swallow the lump in my throat, but before I can say anything, Violet bounces up and down, looking gleeful. "Oh, I can't wait to see Gianna's face when she discovers that Watch Team One is no longer a possibility."

"Your brother's bond group? Do you mean Brodie, Hunter, Liam, and Gem? They are my mates?" I can't hide my incredulous tone. Sure, I was super attracted to them, even before the royal marks appeared on my wrists, and I've felt a tug toward them every time I'm around them, but I knew I had no chance with them and was resigned to that despite my growing attraction once I was marked. A small flame of hope kindles inside me, but I don't allow it to flare higher just in case Gracelin is mistaken.

"Yes, that mark on your back matches theirs perfectly, and not only them…" Gretchin pauses for a moment like she's trying to gather her thoughts. "When the tattoos first appeared and the guys were matched, they were sent away for a few weeks, basically an all expenses paid vacation so they could bond. While they were on that trip, they stumbled drunkenly into an apothecary, looking for anise so they could get high, and the witch who ran the shop had a vision, telling them they had a sixth member and that their mate wouldn't reveal themself until their sixth member did."

"But that was almost ten years ago now, and no one has come forward with the same mark as the guys. Bond group members are usually the same age or within a few years of each other," Gracelin explains. "I think he must have died before he could join the bond group, and because they weren't bonded, they didn't feel it."

"But there are six consort crowns, so that can't be true. He must still be alive," Violet argues, and the sadness on Gracelin's face clears, her eyes brightening with hope.

"Shit, you're right."

"But why hasn't he come forward then?" Gretchin grumbles. "Only a shifter who isn't in their right mind would reject a bond." Her face falls, and she turns pale. "Oh God, what if he's feral or shift frozen?"

Both Violet and Gracelin also look sick, but I don't really have an idea what they are talking about. I know shifters aren't allowed to change humans because they can go feral, but I don't know exactly what that means, and I've never heard about shift frozen.

"Shift frozen? Can you explain that to me?"

Gretchin looks visibly shaken, but she runs a hand through her shorn locks and grimaces. "The reason shifters aren't allowed to change humans is because without the magic of a royal, the human is always feral. It's a population control thing, I think. Shifters would quickly outnumber humans if it wasn't controlled, but occasionally, a born shifter can turn feral as well. If they spend too much time in their shifted form or something tragic happens to them, their animal can take over, and they won't return to human form. They are not as dangerous as turned humans, but again, without the magic of a royal to force them to shift back, they are permanently lost to their animal."

"And you think this is what happened to their sixth member?" I ask carefully, feeling guilty that I haven't said anything about what I know.

"I mean, what other reason could there be?" Violet says. "Bond groups are kind of sacred for shifters."

"Are all shifters part of a bond group?" I ask, because I really need to know more. I spent all morning in lessons with the king and queens, but it was mostly learning about the council and not about shifters in general. I know I have more lessons scheduled tomorrow, but I have so many questions burning inside me now, and if I'm fated for this bond group, I need that information going forward. I also want to hear it from a firsthand source and not a secondhand one like the book Nox loaned me.

"No, not all shifters are fated for bond groups. Adam isn't part of a bond group, but he and I are fated mates." Gracelin pulls the collar of the tank she borrowed from me down, showing a gorgeous mark between her breasts, a combination of stars and moons, but unlike mine, which is black, hers is gold like the marks around my wrists. "We were marked for each other by the goddess, similar to a bond group, but some shifters don't get marks at all and end up mating whoever they want."

"No one knows how or why mates or bond groups are selected." Violet frowns, her eyes clouded with worry. "But bond groups usually receive their mark by their eighteenth birthday, and not many receive one after that. Their mate then receives their mark when the goddess deems the group ready, but it usually happens within a few years of the bond group forming. Watch Team One going almost ten years without a mate was unusual." I wonder if she's thinking about Talon. I know she likes him, and I saw them dancing at the ball while I was being introduced to people. Later, he introduced her to a group of men who must be his bond group. I almost stepped in because she looked overwhelmed, but Ember joined them, and Violet seemed to relax, so I let them be.

"And what about individual mates like Gracelin?" I ask, and Gretchin shrugs. "That can happen at any time, but usually before a shifter turns thirty. It would be awful if a shifter was in a relationship with someone and got married and then found out they were fated to another. Most shifters don't enter into serious relationships until after that age so they don't have to worry about broken hearts and the tragedy that would come with finding a partner and then losing that partner."

"That makes sense. Do you have a mate mark?" I ask her, but then I grimace. "Fuck, am I allowed to ask that?"

She giggles and pulls her collar down, showing me a black mark between her breasts. "Yes, but I haven't met them yet."

"How does that work?" I ask, leaning forward to get a closer look. Her marks are different from Gracelin's. Hers are a series of geometric designs.

"Like a bond group, I register the mark with the mark registry and then wait until someone else gets the same mark. It's been a year now. I'm hoping it happens soon, because I'm getting anxious," she admits.

Gracelin reaches out and gives her sister's hand a squeeze. "It will, and when it does, we won't see you for weeks. Mating is an intense process." She grins mischievously and winks at her sister who rolls her eyes.

"I remember. I'm just glad the rooms in the palace are soundproofed. None of us needed to hear what you and Adam got up to during those few weeks."

"Mating? It isn't just the marks and bam, you're together?" I have so much to learn, and my head throbs with all the information, and maybe from the sparkling wine I've been mainlining.

All three girls giggle like schoolboys, and Gracelin shakes her head. "No, when you are marked and meet your marked mate, there is an instant attraction, and you can't keep your hands off one another. You need to bite each other to seal the mating during sex, and if it's not during sex, then it usually occurs very quickly after it. Once that happens, the mark turns golden like mine, forever sealing you together." She points to a scar on her neck that I hadn't noticed. It's the perfect imprint of an animal bite. It's silvery and faded, but it's definitely there.

"You look like you got mauled by a bear," I remark, leaning forward to get a better look.

She bursts out laughing. "That's because I did. Adam is a bear."

"And he bites you in shifted form?" I ask, sounding horrified, and then something else pops into my mind, and I can't stop the flow of words. "Do you fuck in shifted form as well? I read a book that talked about knots and spurs and all sorts of things. Is that right?"

They all laugh again, Violet rolling off the bed with a thud, but Gretchin shakes her head and reaches down to give our friend a hand back up. "No fucking in shifted form—you aren't always mated to the same kind of animal—but you partially shift your mouth so you can seal the bond. As for knots and spurs, if you're mated to the same animal, then they can fuck in shifted form, and that's when those things come into play."

I sigh with relief, and some of the tension leaves my body. "Well, that's good, because could you imagine having to have sex with a six-headed hydra? Talk about a boner killer," I grumble.

"But you aren't just a hydra, are you?" Gracelin points out, and I shrug.

"No, I guess not, but I don't really understand that.

Your dad and moms talked about me being a dual shifter this morning, but it kind of went over my head, and I don't remember much after I shifted the first time."

"Shifting for the first time is disorienting for mythical shifters. Natural shifters have been doing it for as long as they can remember, so it doesn't really matter," she assures me.

"And you three are natural shifters, right?" I ask, and Gretchin nods.

"Yes. I'm a panther and Gracelin is a tiger." We all look at Violet, and she blushes and looks down at her hands. "What kind of shifter are you? Usually I can tell, but I have no idea with you."

"I'm a fairy," she mutters, and both Gracelin and Gretchin gasp.

"Seriously? That's super rare too! There are only small groups of fairy families, but they stick to one farming community. I've never met any of them, because they stick to their own."

"Yes, my mother is a fairy, and the fairy gene is guaranteed to pass to any female. For males, it can be a toss-up whether they inherit it or get the gene from their father. If their father is a fairy and their mother isn't, and they have a son, then that could be what he is. We don't advertise it because fairies were almost hunted to extinction by humans during the war. They would kill us and keep our wings as trophies, not to mention the rest of shifter society has always looked down on us because we don't shift into an animal." Violet's expression darkens. "My parents didn't even want me to go to college, and they only let me when I promised not to shift in front of anyone. They were worried that someone would try to mate me by force."

"How long has it been since you shifted?" Gretchin asks at the same time I exclaim, "You can be forcefully mated?"

"I haven't shifted all semester," she admits before turning her attention to my question. "Yeah, you can, but it will only ever be one-sided, and it causes agonizing pain for the individual who is bitten unless they return the bite. It's forbidden and punishable by death, but it still happens. Not all shifters are good people."

"It's punishable by death because that will cause the half mark to fade on the shifter who was bitten without consent, allowing them to live a normal life." Fury flashes in Gretchin's eyes. "But sometimes the person bitten without consent just gives in because the pain is so bad, and then the shifter is imprisoned, because when one mate dies, the other usually will as well."

We fall into an uneasy silence while I process everything they just told me. It's a lot, but it's been a good distraction from learning about my fated bonds.

"How can you stand it?" Gracelin asks Violet gently.

"I haven't felt comfortable in my skin for a long time. It's why I got a job with Colbie. I need the money, but the distraction also helps. I should probably take a trip home so I can shift, but I can't afford to miss any classes."

"Well, now that you're one of Colbie's advisors, you can use the same room she did when she shifted the first time." Gretchin gives the girl's hand a squeeze. "We'll go first thing tomorrow. I know it won't be the same as shifting in nature, but at least it's something."

"That would be great, thank you." Tears well in Violet's eyes, and I lunge forward to give her a hug. Gretchin and Gracelin join the pile, and Violet giggles. I feel a wave of relief. I don't like seeing her sad. It's like kicking a puppy.

We pull apart, and the three of them look at me, their expressions turning serious.

"How do you feel about everything you just learned?" Gracelin asks warily.

I huff out a breath that blows a strand of hair off my face. "I can't deny that I felt a weird pull toward those men even before I was this—" I gesture to the marks on my wrists. "I'd have to be blind not to be attracted, and even then, they smelled incredible. It's only gotten stronger since I walked through the palace doors. You need to remember, though, that I was human until a few days ago, and it's a lot to adjust to. I was having trouble finding one man, let alone six."

"So you're going to reject them?" Gretchin asks flatly, and I quickly shake my head.

"God no, but I would like a little time to wrap my head around this, and I'd like to get to know them without the bond getting in the way." Gretchin's eyes narrow like she wants to argue with me, but Gracelin puts her hand out and gives her sister's arm a squeeze.

"We can understand that, but you may not be able to help yourself. The bonds are designed to pull shifters toward one another. They will become painful with the need to seal them, and you can't be crowned without all six of your mates. We can give you a week, that seems fair. You'll be working with them on your shift every day and learning self-defense, but for their sake, we won't hold our tongues longer than that," she negotiates, and I agree with a nod.

"But what about the missing mate? If she can't find him, does that mean she won't be crowned? And if that occurs, then what happens to the magic?" Violet asks, worry in her voice.

The two sisters exchange a glance. "We don't know, but I doubt it's something good."

THREE

Colbie

The conversation changes after that, the subjects becoming lighter as they recognize I'm reaching my limit. Once they leave, I try to get some rest, but my mind whirls with everything I've learned. My thoughts keep returning to Nox and what I've discovered about him. I didn't mention him to the girls, but I'm going to have to come clean eventually.

He is most definitely the last member of Watch Team One's bond group. There can be no denying it. He is absolutely hiding the fact he's a shifter. If none of this had ever happened to me, I would have continued on thinking he was a reclusive human, but now I know he lied to me, despite learning my own secret, and I'm kind of hurt. I also wonder if he is still living at his cottage on the beach or if he took off. He can work from anywhere, and he knows who I am and that I know how to find him, so if I went to get him, would he still be there or disappeared? He probably thought I would force him to join shifter society.

It isn't like I wouldn't have figured it all out eventually, considering our pendants match. Maybe he thought the chances of me connecting his tattoo with a bond group were slim, and they probably would have been if that mark hadn't appeared on my own back. I certainly haven't seen any of Watch Team One's marks, though that might change in the coming days if they are going to help teach me to control my shift. We're probably going to end up naked around each other, which is going to make it even harder to resist the pull of the mark now that I know what it is. I wonder if all my clothes have the magical fabric that shifts with me. That would be very expensive, but I am the queen, so maybe I'll get lucky.

I also can't be crowned until all six crowns have a head to be put on, but the thought of forcing Nox back into shifter society when he obviously doesn't want to be a part of it makes me feel ill. I didn't get a choice, but I'd like him to have one. If that is the case, then what will happen next? Will there be no monarch, and is that such a bad thing? Wouldn't a council be just as useful as a ruling monarchy? Sure, they might not have the power to grant shifters the chance at choosing human mates or help a shifter if they get shift frozen, but I get the feeling those things aren't common anyway. It's definitely one of the questions I'm going to bring up with the king and queens tomorrow. There won't be any mate matches presenting themselves at the palace gates, so it will give me the opportunity to bring up the subject without clueing them into our new discovery.

My train of thought drifts once again to the bond group I am fated to be with. While they are all very attractive men, I don't know them well. Hell, I don't even know what kind of shifters all of them are. Gem informed me he was a phoenix shifter when he came to check on me this morning, and he has the power to heal. I know Hunter is a dragon and Gryffin is a white tiger, but I'm clueless about Brodie and Liam… and Liam is kind of an ass.

I'm not blind. I saw how they were watched by quite a few hungry females at the ball tonight. They are extremely appealing men, but that doesn't make a relationship. I'm nervous about doing shift training with them but excited as well. I want to know what kind of guys they are without the pressure of them knowing I'm their fated mate. I don't want them to treat me any differently.

My mind eventually settles, and I find myself drifting. My dreams, filled with flashes of light and teeth, keep me tossing and turning all night, making my sleep restless. Finally, I can't take it any longer, and when the sun starts to peak its head above the horizon, I throw the blankets back and take a shower, hoping it will clear my mind.

The shower helps, and I find myself staring at my closet at a loss for what to wear. All of the clothes are new and were apparently placed there by the same magic that activated the minute I stepped across the threshold—goddess magic. Although I didn't really want this position, I have to admit the perks are pretty damn good, but I'm still not sure about the dress code. I have meetings with the king and queens this morning and then self-defense and shifting training with Watch Team One in the afternoon. I can't imagine that I can train in a dress, but what are the protocols for meetings?

I eye a pair of capri leggings and a tank top longingly. They would be good for self-defense training. I'm still considering my choices when I hear Violet's voice.

"Colbie, are you ready for breakfast?"

I whirl around and find her standing in the doorway of my closet, looking at me with amusement. I look at what she's wearing, since she will be joining me for both my meeting and training sessions this afternoon, and sigh with relief as I take in an outfit very similar to what I was eyeing. "Oh, thank God. I wasn't sure if I had to wear a dress or if I could get away with training clothes."

She smirks at me, and I narrow my eyes. "I can get away with training clothes, but you are the queen, so you will need to wear a dress this morning, and then you can change before your training session," she informs me, grinning with an evil glint in her eye. How is she settling in as well as she is? I'm kind of jealous of how quickly she's adjusting, but I'm so glad she's here.

"Ugh, that sucks," I grumble and turn my attention to the hanging section of my closet. It's split into two sections—formal and informal—and it's the informal ones I start to look through.

"Heavy is the head that wears the crown," she teases behind me, and I throw up my middle finger. "Do you need me to get an attendant in here to help you?"

"God no. Although they are nice people, I don't need them doing things for me."

"Colbie," Violet says, and when I turn to look at her,

I see the sympathy in her eyes, and I have to stop myself from flinching. "You know it's okay to allow people to help you, right?"

I turn back to the dresses and pull out a soft jersey gown in sage green with silver embroidery on it. It has a sweetheart neckline and three-quarter sleeves. "What do you think?" I hold it up, ignoring her comment, and she pauses for a moment before nodding.

"Looks good." She leaves, taking the hint that I don't want to talk about it. Sure, I have a decent support system with Grampy and Granny, but Mom hasn't always been great. She is very much into keeping up appearances, and I often don't meet her expectations.

I brush away my thoughts and quickly get dressed, and the two of us head down for breakfast. Before the three girls left last night, I enforced the week's grace they are allowing me, but I feel nervous as we approach the doors of the dining room. I hear voices and know I am about to face my mates. A rush of excitement flows through me, followed closely by one of nerves. My stomach rolls, and I place my hand across it in hopes it will quell the feeling. Violet doesn't miss my action, and she gives my hand a squeeze.

"It's going to be fine, I promise. We won't say anything, and you will get to know them without the knowledge of the bond influencing them," she assures me.

"They won't know?" I ask, biting my lip.

"No, they will still feel the pull like you will, but they won't know for sure until you confirm the mark." She puts a hand on my arm as I go to enter the room and drops her voice, her lips set in a straight line and a furrow between her eyebrows. "But remember, Colbie, the mating marks are sacred to shifters. They may feel hurt when they find out you are hiding it from them," she warns me.

It's my turn to frown. I don't want to hurt them, but my human state of mind is still very much ruling my thoughts. There's also the subject of Nox and how I should tell them I know where their sixth is. If I don't tell them, I am betraying them, but if I tell them, I am betraying Nox. I'm completely torn and confused, but I can't hide. I am queen, and I need to make a tough decision. I'm sure it won't be the last time either.

Giving her a weak, reassuring smile, I allow her to open the door. There is no herald this morning to announce us, thank goodness, but when I enter the room, I feel a heavy sort of tension. Everyone at the table stands as I enter and nods their head. There is an instant pull in my chest, and I find myself looking at the opposite end of the table to the men I now know are my mates. The heady scents of frost, cedar and pine, smoke and whisky, sunshine and chocolate, coffee, and lime, mint, and rum all swirl through my senses, and I take a step toward the group.

"Ah, Colbie, good morning," King Lucas calls with a weak smile, jolting me out of my trance just in time. My animal keens inside as I turn my attention away from what she desires most. When I focus on the king, I see the tension in his body, and I realize that breakfast is a lot more crowded this morning.

"Please don't get up on my account," I tell everyone, and they return to their seats.

"Why don't you grab a seat, and I'll fix you a plate?" Violet murmurs, narrowing her eyes on the people at the table. Instead of arguing, I allow her to serve me, and I make my way across the large room to the table. I really did want a few more moments to distract myself, but I've noticed the table is much larger than yesterday, and it seats many more people than the previous morning's fairly relaxed breakfast.

Today, we're joined by the six council members, and some of them have even brought their families. This is not how I expected to spend my breakfast, but I force a smile onto my face as I take the chair next to Lucas.

"Ah, Your Majesty, so nice of you to join us this morning," Councilor Vallen Tideman calls passive-aggressively with a smirk on his face. "We were wondering if maybe you would sleep in after such a big night last night."

"No rest for the wicked, I'm afraid," I reply as one of the servers attending the table offers me coffee. I thank her as she pours some into the mug at my place setting. "Though I am surprised that so many people are joining me for breakfast." I smile serenely as Lucas mutters, "So were we," next to me.

"Oh, the council thought it might be nice for you to have some familiar faces this morning to answer any questions you might have," Councilor Sophia Gardiner, a petite, dark-haired woman with long hair and cold, almond-shaped eyes explains. "Especially since none of your mates have deigned to show themselves yet." One of the unknown girls at the table snickers, and I turn my attention to her.

"I'm sorry, I don't believe we've met," I say, recognizing her as one of the girls who made snide comments about my dress last night. Sophia waves at the two younger women who are spaced around the table. One is sitting between Gryffin and Liam, and she has her hand on the latter's arm and is batting her eyelashes. The other one is next to Hunter's brother, Talon, and she's acting similarly. Talon looks uncomfortable, and his sister, Ember, is glaring at the girl. Liam is smiling at the girl next to him, but he removes her hand from his arm in a subtle gesture when Gem, who is on his other side, elbows him in the side.

"Oh, these are my daughters, Gianna and Liana. I wanted to introduce them to you last night, but you disappeared rather early." The woman waves her hands. "I thought they might be able to help guide you in shifter society, and maybe Gianna could become one of your advisors. Having someone who is knowledgeable in shifter society by your side will be a great benefit, and she is currently between jobs."

Those names sound familiar, and when Violet places a plate in front of me with a grimace, it comes to me. These are the two girls she told me about. Gianna is the one who blew off my call about Archie, and Liana is the girl who bullies Violet.

"Well, that's a very kind offer, but at this stage, I have all the advisors I need." I wave to Gracelin and Violet, who takes her seat when Ember waves her to a spare one next to her.

Councilor Gardiner narrows her eyes on Violet before returning her attention to me. "Surely someone who is more familiar with the workings of upper-class society would be more beneficial for you."

I take a drink of my coffee, not removing my gaze from the woman. "Possibly, but you could also say I need the perspective of all shifter society, not just the elite, and I also need someone who is going to take the role seriously. I believe Gianna has already proven she's not capable of listening when it doesn't suit her."

That gets Gianna's attention, and she whirls around and glares at me as Sophia gasps, putting a hand against her chest while looking hurt.

"Why would you suggest such a thing?"

"Gianna was recently fired from the watch, correct?" I ask, and the councilwoman's lips thin, and her eyes go flat as she glares at General Bryson. I can also feel Gianna's own glare burning into my skin. She goes to say something, but her mother cuts her off with a sharp look.

"It was merely a miscommunication." She continues to glare at General Bryson, who doesn't even flinch under her gaze and glares back at her.

"Unfortunately, I don't believe that was the case, since I was the human she blew off," I announce as I take a bite of my food. Councilor Gardiner pales a little at this information. "I need someone who will have my best interest at heart, and at this stage, I don't believe Gianna does. Maybe we can revisit this at a later date, once she's proven she can be trusted," I add, trying to be diplomatic. I know that's never going to happen, though, since she rolls her eyes and turns her attention to Gryffin who is on her other side. Yeah, that's never going to happen.

"Very well," the woman concedes, but she's already calculating how she can get me to change my mind. Over my dead body, but maybe she's planning that too.

There's some awkward silence around the table as I eat. "Your Majesty, I don't believe you were introduced to my wife, Margot, last night." Councilor Andrew Mason is a smart-looking man, with dark, dirty blond hair and brown eyes, which currently twinkle with amusement as he smirks at Sophia before gesturing to the petite blonde woman sitting next to him.

This is the man Archie said is having an affair with one of our castle staff. I wonder if it's consensual or if she's being forced into it. I must do some investigating. If she's willing, then I'm not sure she is someone I want in my house. I hate women like that. She obviously knows he's married, and the councilor can definitely go. If he's going to cheat on his wife, then what's to say he's going to be loyal to his queen?

"It's a pleasure to meet you." I smile genuinely at the woman who gives me a regal but disdainful nod. Well, okay then. I guess she isn't a fan either. I wonder if they are mates or if they are an arranged pairing. Do shifters have arranged marriages?

"For God's sake, let the poor child eat. She's going to get enough of our hot air in the weeks to come," an older, gray-haired gentleman grumbles. He waves his coffee mug at one of the servers who hurries over to fill it. "Don't know why we had to come and disturb her this morning."

This is Councilor Emmett Coldicott, whom I was introduced to last night. I like him. Lucas told me that he has been on the council for the last four reigning rulers and is one of the longest serving members. He's also a former king himself. This puts him at over a hundred and sixty years of age, but he looks to be in his mid-fifties.

"The council doesn't usually join you for breakfast?" I ask Lucas under my breath as the attention turns away as Brodie starts a loud conversation, allowing me to lean over and talk to the king privately.

"God no. They are up your ass more than enough on a usual basis that you don't need them first thing in the morning as well."

"We were wondering why you were gracing us with your presence this morning, since breakfast is usually reserved for family," Mia comments casually, but her body is rigid with annoyance.

"Well, considering that Colbie has no family here yet and there are no signs of any potential mates, we thought she might like the company of people other than your family." This comes from the final male member of the council, Jonathan Altmore. "We wanted to show that she has the support of the council despite the fact that she hasn't been crowned yet." The tension at the table ratchets up even higher, and it's all I can do to eat my food. It feels like there was a small threat in those seemingly innocuous words.

"It's only been three days. Give them a chance to arrive. It's a big adjustment for anyone who gets marked. They will be here, I'm sure." This is from the final council member, Audrey Coldicott, a tall, statuesque female with a sharp dark bob. Yesterday, General Bryson informed me she was a general with the shifter army before him. She retired when the former queen was replaced by Lucas, and he was appointed. I asked if there was any bad blood, but he insisted there wasn't. She simply wanted more time to spend with her mates and her grandchildren. He informed me that she is a great asset to the council and can be trusted. She is also one of Emmett's mates

Apparently, it's up to me whether I keep these people on the council or replace them, and so far, I'm not keen on keeping most of them, but they seem to have forgotten that they are replaceable.

I wipe my mouth with my linen napkin and focus on the council members. "While that is very kind of you, I don't believe I will need your presence at breakfast every day. I am still taking advice from the king and queens, and should I need your input, I will ask you. I look forward to hearing your thoughts at our scheduled council meeting at the end of the week," I tell them firmly, and I see both Emmett's and Audrey's eyes sparkle with amusement, whereas the other four look angry that I have dismissed them so easily. When Councilman Tideman goes to argue, I don't let him get a word in. "After all, I am still making decisions on who I will keep on the council and who will be released from their positions, as is my right as the new ruler."

"Look here, missy! Until that crown is on your head, you have no say in who is on this council," Sophia hisses. "And that's not happening until six mates appear —if they ever do." I hear the threat in her voice, and so does everyone else at the table.

"Yes, I don't believe there is a precedent if that happens, so we will have to consult the archives. Can there even be a queen without mates?" Jonathan Altmore muses thoughtfully, but I see the glee in his eyes. Lucas and Layla exchange a loaded glance. It seems like they know more than they are saying. I will have to corner them later.

"Enough!" Lucas slams his hands on the table and stands up. "Colbie has been selected by the goddess Aramis to be the next queen. Who are you to question anything she does?"

"Calm down, Lord Lucas. We were merely stating

the facts. After all, it is a tumultuous time, what with missing shifter children and the upsurge in ferals. We want to make sure our leader is prepared and at full strength for the coming months," Councilor Altmore states, and I feel my brow wrinkle. Missing shifter children and upsurge in ferals? Lucas and the queens didn't mention anything like that in our meeting yesterday. A hand rests on my leg, giving it a squeeze, and Layla, who is on the other side of me, gives me a minute head shake. I see the promise of information in that gesture and allow my frown to smooth out, but before I can form a response, Emmett huffs.

"I don't know about you, but I believe that conversation should be left until we have finished our meal. It's not suitable in the aid of my digestion."

"Fine, but it will be discussed in great detail in our meeting later this week. I want to know what the queen is going to do about both issues," Sophia sneers. "So far, we've kept the information from the general shifter population, but that could change at any minute, and that wouldn't go down well if our people were to learn that the royal family has been keeping secrets." Everyone at the table hears her threat.

"Careful, Sophia. Your words could be considered treasonous. You swore an oath to the crown, and if word leaks of any of those things, you will be the first person we look to for answers," Bryson threatens, causing the sneer on her lips to drop.

I've kind of lost my appetite now, but I force myself to eat, knowing I have a long day ahead of me. Conversation picks up again, and I relax slightly once all the attention is off me.

"You handled that beautifully," Lucas says quietly. I

know shifter hearing is exceptional, but hopefully no one is paying us much attention. It seems like each of the councilors have been distracted by one of the others, like they all decided to help me out, which I appreciate.

"I'm not sure about that," I mutter, and Evie leans around Lucas, her eyes sparkling with mirth as she nods.

"Did you see Sophia's face when you put her and Gianna in their place? That was golden, and it will live rent free in my mind for the next couple of days. I hate that snake, and her daughters are just as bad. I pray to Aramis regularly that Gianna won't be marked for our boys."

"Didn't you choose them for your council?" I argue, and Mia leans a little closer from Layla's other side so we can keep this conversation as private as possible. "All four of us were new to high society. None of us knew what they were like when we agreed to keep the previous queen's council. We regretted that very quickly, but once they are sworn in, it's for the whole term of the reign. We couldn't get rid of them, and they've done nothing but throw roadblocks in our way for the past forty years."

"Actually, I think you should keep Emmett and Audrey. They are really wonderful and have the best interest in the shifters as a nation. The rest of them are only out for themselves," Layla suggests. "Ultimately, it is your decision, but it is one that needs to be made before you are crowned, so think carefully, okay?"

Before I can reply, our private conversation is interrupted.

"I believe you know our younger son, Brock," Councilor Tideman's wife says to me, her eyes bright and hopeful. She hasn't said anything until now, and I can't remember him telling me her name. Neither of their other children are here today, and at the mention of Brock's name, Vallen's whole body stiffens.

"Yes, I do. He and his partner own the business next to mine in the neutral zone," I reply casually.

"Can't you do something to appeal his ban?" she pleads, and I frown at her.

"You have no one to blame but your own husband for your son's actions. He's the one who gave him permission to bring my mother into the shifter zone despite the rules during royal succession," I reply, unable to hide my surprise.

Vallen glares at me. "That had nothing to do with me. Brock got his information wrong." Of course he would deny it just like I was told he would.

"I gave the ban, and it will stick. Brock should have known better. It is unfortunate, but there is nothing stopping you from going to visit him, Ashley." Lucas gives Vallen his own glare. "Maybe your office needs to be clearer with its communication in the future."

I can see how annoyed Vallen is, and when his wife starts to argue, he reaches for her hand and squeezes it so hard, she winces, but it stops her from speaking again. I can't wait to see the back of that man. He's reprehensible.

Conversation turns to more mundane things as everyone finishes their meal around me. I don't get to speak to any of Watch Team One at all, but I observe them and their interactions. They seem to ignore the councilors, answering their inquiries with short responses, and I watch with amusement as Gryffin fends off Gianna who is like a grabby octopus, constantly putting her hands on him. At one stage, Layla removes my knife from my hand with a knowing look, and I feel myself blush. Brodie, Gem, and Hunter talk with Hunter's siblings and Violet, and it's nice to see them include her like she's a friend.

I notice Talon's attentiveness toward her, and I have to wonder if I'm going to have a brokenhearted friend on my hands when his bond group gets their mate. I hope for her sake the goddess is kind and makes it happen sooner rather than later. I can see her growing more and more attracted as the minutes go by. Liana glares at her like she could blow up her brain with her mind. We will need to keep a close eye on that one as well. Maybe I should assign Violet a protection detail. It's something to discuss with Bryson.

I stand, knowing the former rulers are being patient but have been waiting long enough. "Shall we get started then? I'm sure you're going to overwhelm me again this morning, so we shouldn't put it off any longer," I say, and Lucas laughs, standing as well.

"Come on, Colbie, it won't be that bad, I promise," he tells me as the four rulers, Violet, and I make our way to the conference room we were in yesterday after bidding farewell to the remaining breakfast guests.

"I think you're telling me lies, Lucas, but I appreciate it," I retort with one last look at the men who I now know are my mates. All five of them watch us go, and Brodie gives me a wave and a wink.

"We'll see you for training this afternoon. Can't wait to see what you can do with your animal," he calls, and I nod in response.

"What is she? I bet she's a prey animal, right? Maybe an equine shifter?" Gianna asks loudly. "With that ass, I bet she's a donkey."

I don't hear what any of the others tell her, the door closing behind us as we leave, but I know we are keeping the nature of my creatures to ourselves for now. The less people who know, the better for now. Lucas thinks I will have a target on my back once people realize how strong I will be, and after the council's actions today, he may be right.

FOUR

Brodie

I watch as the new queen leaves, surrounded by Gryff's parents. My wolf feels longing and the persistent need to follow her. He pants after her like he's discovered a female in heat and wants to mount her. I've struggled to keep a handle on my shift since she first stepped into the palace, her scent driving my inner animal crazy. He's reacting like she's his mate. Maybe Liam is right. Our animals have waited too long for their mate to be marked and they've finally had enough, and now they are seeking comfort in the first attractive female to walk their way.

"What is she, Liam?" Gianna asks, and I drag my attention away from the pretty queen and back to our table.

"Yes, I must admit I'm curious as well. If she is a prey animal, then that doesn't bode well for her ability to keep our great kingdom safe." Councilor Altmore's eyes twinkle with excitement at the thought. "We should consult the archives today to see if there is a precedent for a ruler with a prey animal and no mates. Surely there is something we can do if this is the case."

"Careful, Jonathan. Those words sound treasonous," Emmett warns, a frown on his face.

"Why isn't she sharing her animal with us? Why is it a secret if she has nothing to hide?" Sophia argues, jumping into the conversation.

"Well, if I could hazard a guess, it would be because it's none of your damn business," Bryson growls at her, and she glares at him. There is definitely no love lost between those two, and it's even worse since he fired Gianna.

"Of course it's our business. We need to be able to run damage control with the people if she is weak and unsuitable to rule. We owe it to our kingdom," Councilor Mason argues. "It's the council's responsibility to keep our rulers in check."

"Pfft," Emmett scoffs. "You overestimate your importance, Andrew. We are here to help guide them, not make decisions for them, nor is it our position to speculate." The oldest council member leans forward, his eyes blazing with anger. "I would worry about your own security before worrying about our queen's. So far, none of you have realized that our own positions are on the line, and after that little performance, it would come as no surprise if she replaced us all."

His words finally register with the rest of the council, and they shift uncomfortably in their seats.

"But I want to know," Gianna whines, and I see the moment she pushes my bond mate too far. Liam shoves his chair back and wrenches his arm from her grasp.

"I won't be the one to tell you. I'm under strict

instructions to keep my mouth shut, and I won't jeopardize my career for you," he announces before storming out of the room. She gapes at him and starts to push her own chair back to chase after him.

"Sit down, Gianna," her mother orders, her teeth clenched.

"I can assure you that none of you need to be concerned about what animal our new queen shifts into. Once she is ready, she will be happy to show you," Gryffin, forever the princely diplomat, says calmly as Gianna drops back into the seat beside him. He wasn't there when she shifted, and I don't think any of us have told him what she is, but he trusts us.

"What about the fact that no mates have presented themselves? That's something we can worry about. She can't be crowned until that happens, so we are in limbo until such a time," Vallen argues.

"It isn't the first time that mates haven't appeared and been instantly chosen," Audrey points out. "When Emmett was king, it took weeks for him to decide on whom he was choosing for mates." She looks at her husband affectionately. "He was such a manwhore, he thoroughly explored all of his options."

He grins at her and shrugs unrepentantly. "I was going to spend the rest of my life with them, so I wanted to make sure I had the right combination. I didn't hear you complaining when I invited you to help me with the interview process." He leans back in his chair. "Ah, that was a fun time. So many eager and willing males and females, all vying for my attention. I would have been remiss if I made snap decisions."

We can tell by his tone that the interviews involved more than an exchange of words. My wolf growls inside my chest at the thought of Colbie "interviewing" anyone.

"Disgusting," Vallen grumbles loud enough for us to hear. We all know he has a problem with same sex relationships. Disavowing his son only proves it, and Emmett's mates are two females and two males, and Vallen has never been friendly with any of them. Luckily most of the shifter kingdom doesn't have the same prejudices.

"I don't know about everyone else, but I am thoroughly done with breakfast." Sable stands, followed by her husband, General Bryson, and their two younger children. "I have better things to do with my day than sit around in idle speculation. I have patients to attend to and an archive to visit."

"Don't go hiding any books from us, Sable. We will be down there later today to look over the histories of past kings and queens," Vallen warns her, and she glares at him.

"How dare you question my integrity? I was awarded the position of historian by the king when none of you wanted to take that role. I will see to it that you have the books you need, but I can assure you none of them contain the information you seek."

"Maybe the royal vault? It has books we don't have access to. We should demand the king and queens hand it over," Sophia suggests, looking to the more manipulative council members for support.

"Again, that sounds rather treasonous, Sophia. You don't get to demand for the king or queens to do anything," Audrey warns, scowling at her fellow councilor. "You are walking a fine line today."

"Agreed, and I will gladly arrest you if you keep up

this line of questioning and investigation," Bryson threatens. "Go ahead and keep pushing, I dare you." He turns his gaze to my group leader. "Gryffin, if you, your team, and Gretchin can join me, I'd like to go over the queen's security schedule with you," Bryson says, and I almost jump up and kiss the man for giving us an excuse to leave. I don't hesitate to follow their lead, pushing my chair back and getting to my feet.

"I'll go find Liam. Where should we meet you?" I ask the general as the rest of my team and Gretchin also get to their feet.

"The barracks, please. I'd like to supervise morning training now that all of our troops are back in the city for the coronation."

"Hopefully he hasn't gotten very far, but if I know him, he probably shifted and is running in the forest. We'll be there as soon as I can find him," I assure the general and hurry away before anyone can stop me.

I'm grateful to be out of that room. The council has always seemed slimy to me, except for the Coldicotts. I hope Colbie isn't considering keeping them, because they would make her life miserable. As I hurry through the palace in search of my bond mate, my mind returns to the pretty new queen. She handled herself with grace and dignity at breakfast, and I can't help but admire her. Her old life has been ripped away from her, and she's been shoved into a completely alien environment, not to mention the changes within her, and she's rolling with the punches admirably. I think if I were to suddenly find myself human, I would be rocking in the corner. Maybe I'll order some treats from her bakery to cheer her up… or maybe that would just make her sadder. I'll ask Gem, he's good with that kind of thing.

It was a smart idea for her to leave that pendant on so she doesn't have to deal with a whole other being inside her mind while she's finding her footing and waiting for her mates. I wonder where she got it from.

This afternoon, we will help her get control of her shift and learn to use her new body—or bodies, I guess. I couldn't believe it when I saw her shift from a hydra into a wolf. Mine almost burst out of my skin at the sight of her, and with the residual royal power saturating the room, I almost lost control like Archie did, but I held on by the skin of my teeth. My wolf wanted to nuzzle the pretty black wolf with purple eyes, then chase her through the forest and breed her.

I felt so fucking guilty that my animal was reacting to her like that. We were betraying our future mate, but I also couldn't help but want the same thing he did. My soul is conflicted, and it's causing a disconnect between my wolf and me. It's why I offered to find Liam. I really need to shift and run to get the scent of our queen out of our nostrils and get my wolf's brain firmly back into line.

I follow the bond connection out of the castle and into the forest, just like I suspected. I tug off my clothes, tossing them in the pile of Liam's obliterated scraps of cloth on the ground at the tree line. I guess he didn't wait to undress before he shifted. We must remember to grab all the scraps before we go back inside, otherwise Evie will take us to task.

I allow the shift to wash over me, smooth and pain-less and very much unlike Colbie's shifts. As a born shifter, I've been shifting longer than I can remember, and it feels as natural as breathing. My paws hit the leaf laden ground as I sniff the air, trying to figure out which way Liam went. I locate the giant pawprints his bear left behind, and I head in the same direction. Polar bears are fast despite their size, and I know I'm going to get a good workout trying to catch up with him.

I'm pretty sure I know where he's headed. There is a waterfall where we like to hang out during our down-time, and Liam likes the cave behind the rush of water. He's kind of claimed it as his den, and I know that's where I will find him. His bear has been unruly, I'm just glad he didn't go as far as biting Gianna while they were fucking. I don't resent him having sex with other females while we wait for our mate to be marked, but Gianna is dangerous. I wouldn't put it past her to force a mate bond with him, and it seems like his bear may have been close to crossing the line. That would have been a disaster for all involved.

The air is sharp against my fur as I race through the forest. The trees are losing their leaves as they prepare for the incoming winter, though there are still a number of deciduous varieties so the forest doesn't look dead. The rumbling of the waterfall gets louder as I grow closer, and Liam's frosty scent gets stronger, but as I reach the edge of the pool, I slide to a stop and sit down, considering my options.

The water is so clear in this pond that despite its depth, I can still see the rocky bottom and fish swim-ming around happily undisturbed. Normally during summer, it's a refreshing balm for the stifling hot days, but as we grow closer to winter, I know the water will become colder, and although it doesn't freeze over completely during winter due to the waterfall, the water is much cooler now than during the height of summer.

It's okay for Liam who enjoys swimming in the frigid

water, but for those of us with creatures that are a little bit more sensible, the thought of getting wet makes me pause. Maybe I can howl and get his attention. My gaze moves to the thunderous wall of water that sits between me and my destination. Who am I kidding? He won't hear anything over that despite his enhanced hearing. I'm going to have to go through it. That's what makes it such a great hiding place. There is no way to access it except through the towering wall of water. I feel my wolf's displeasure. He enjoys swimming in summer, but he also remembers how cold it is at this time of the year.

I walk farther along the bank of the pool, getting as close to the falls as I can so my time in the water is minimized. Unable to find an excuse to delay any longer, I plunge into the water, scattering fish. The cold just about steals our breath, but my wolf starts to paddle without delay, our destination clear in his mind. It doesn't take long before we approach the curtain of water. We get battered around a little as we swim through it, but my wolf stays on course and comes out the other side, blinking drops of water from his lashes and shaking his head to clear the water from our ears. Reaching the side of the pool, we scramble up onto the bank and flop down on our stomach, our sides heaving with exertion.

We push to our feet and shake our body furiously, sending droplets of water flying in all directions. I look around, my shifter sight not hindered at all by the dim light. Liam isn't in this front cavern, so he must have moved into the back section, which he has made cozy for himself. I head in that direction, and my wolf wrinkles his nose at the wet musky smell that reaches our nostrils. Liam is definitely in here somewhere, I can practically smell his desperation. Unlike his usual crisp, frosty scent, like fresh snow in a pine forest, this smells distressed and anxious.

I find him curled up in a pile of blankets. His head lifts, and he growls at me as I approach him, but he doesn't move. I get down on my belly and crawl toward him, nodding my head at him in submission until I get close enough to nuzzle his side. Liam's bear is as grumpy and unruly as he is, and you never know if he will smack you with one of his giant paws or smother you with a hug hard enough to crack ribs.

He doesn't react at all, though, and that's what worries me. He ignores us as we butt our head against his body, inviting him to play. In fact, he just rolls over and gives me his back, ignoring me completely with a large huff of air. I listen carefully to the sound of his heartbeat, and I can tell it's already starting to slow down. Damn it, the stupid bear is going to trigger a hibernation if he isn't careful. I'm sure polar bears don't actually hibernate, but he's been talking more and more about it recently, so I'm concerned he's going to give it a try in an attempt to block out his bear's need.

That isn't good. I allow my wolf form to flow away and wrinkle my nose as my bare ass finds the cold, dirt-covered floor. I look around and find one of the spare blankets he usually uses as a nest and pick it up, wrapping it around my waist before taking a seat.

"Hey, man, you can't sleep. You need to shift back. Bryson wants to go over the queen's protection detail with us and Gretchin, and he didn't say anything in front of the council, but I have a feeling he wants to talk about the ferals and the missing kids. We need to figure out a way to go into the human zone and search without causing any political drama. We've exhausted all options in the neutral and shifter zones."

I wait for him to reply. The sound of the nearby waterfall is still loud, but not as deafening as it was when we were closer. This chamber is down a small tunnel, and the rocks block out a lot of the noise.

When he doesn't respond, I nudge him with my foot, and he snarls and rolls, swiping at me with a giant paw. I yelp and jump backward. The damn lardass is fast.

"Hey, don't be an asshole. Fucking shift, man, so we can at least talk."

He snarls at me but gets up onto his paws, and I watch as he shifts into his human form and looks up at me, his eyes filled with turmoil.

"I need help, man."

CHAPTER
FIVE

Colbie

The palace corridors are quiet this early in the morning. It's a large structure broken up into separate wings. The main wing contains the kitchen, offices, ballrooms, dining rooms, and a variety of different rooms for social events and business, as well as the central shifting chamber where they took me to shift yesterday. The wing where my room is has the royal family living quarters. Along with Violet and I, Gracelin and her family, Gretchin, and Watch Team One, Lucas and his wives have suites. The wing on the opposite side is where the councilors and their families live, as well as General Bryson and his family. Talon's new bond group will be taking up residence as well once their final security clearance comes through. I don't actually like how close the council is, but apparently it's how it has always been.

I'm mulling over the awkward and uncomfortable breakfast interaction when we reach the same conference room we were in yesterday. We take seats around the table, and Lucas waves his hand in my direction.

"Right, let's start with any questions you may have this morning," he suggests, and I take a moment to gather my thoughts.

"I have so many, I don't know where to start. How about we talk about the breakfast debacle? There is no way I want to spend the next forty years dealing with that crap. What are my options?" I ask, referring to the incredibly painful interaction.

"It is your right as queen to choose a new council if you are inclined, and I have to say I don't blame you," Lucas explains. "Like Mia said, we were blindsided when the former royal refused to counsel us when she was forcibly retired against her wishes. We learned after we took over that she was constantly pushing to change to a hereditary crown, but thankfully, the council was too scared of the goddess to vote with her. They were mostly a new council back then. Vallen is the son of the king before her, and they came around to her way of thinking by the end of her reign and have been pushing hard for it during ours. We shut down so many of their suggestions."

"She didn't want to give up the role, despite the goddess's rules, so instead of helping us, she left us flailing. None of us are from what you would call high shifter society," Evie explains, and Violet gasps.

"Really?"

Evie gives her a smile of understanding. "Yes. Mia and I came from small shifter villages much like yours, but Layla lived in the city, and again wasn't from the acceptable social circles."

"My father is a professor at the university, and my

mother is a hairdresser. Both still live in the city in the house I grew up in. I tried to convince them to move into the palace, but they decided they were happier where they were. We still see them regularly. I'll introduce you to them next time they are here for a visit," she tells us.

"None of us are stupid, but we blindly trusted the council, thinking they had our best interests at heart, and while Emmett and Audrey do, the others made it clear very quickly that they are only out for their own gain, but by then, it was too late. We learned how to deal with them through sheer stubbornness."

"So how does it work? How do I appoint a new council?" I lean forward, eager to hear the answer.

"You can announce that the positions are open and ask for applications, or you can ask people you trust to be on your council."

Before I can ask Lucas another question, the door slams open, and Gracelin hurries in, taking a seat and breathing heavily like she's been running. "Sorry I'm late. Archie had a tantrum when he wasn't allowed to have breakfast with you. It took me this long to get him to calm down and off to school."

I smile as she speaks. "Does he go to school in the palace? Like, does he have tutors?"

She shakes her head, laughing. "No. He goes to one of the local elementary schools. The social interaction with other kids is good for him, since he gets spoiled by all the attention from his grandparents and the palace staff." She mockingly glares at her parents, but I can tell she isn't upset.

"Smartest kid in the whole school," Lucas boasts,

and I can't stop my own smile. He reminds me of my grandpa, except, you know, he looks forty and is hot.

"Now, did I hear you telling Colbie about those assholes on the council? I can't believe they crashed breakfast. I'm so glad Archie was hungry early this morning and had breakfast with his nanny. Could you imagine if he talked about Colbie being his sidepiece and said something to Councilor Mason while his wife was there?" Her cheeks pinken as she laughs awkwardly.

"I would have paid to see something like that." Lucas slaps his hand on the table, laughing whole-heartedly.

"We were just telling Colbie that she doesn't have to accept the council in its entirety or any at all really, but we suggested she keep Emmett and Audrey, since they do have the shifter nation as a whole in their best inter-est," Layla explains, and their daughter nods.

"Yes, both of them have been assets, even when they haven't always agreed with decisions you've made. The rest of them are a waste of space, only out for their own interests. I agree, you should get rid of them, and they certainly don't usually come for breakfast. That was them flexing their proverbial muscles."

"But I don't know any shifters. What if I get rid of them and the ones who apply are worse than the ones who are already in the positions?"

"Dad and the moms will guide you," she says, but then smirks. "Or you could ask all four of them to fill the vacant roles," she suggests, and I feel a glimmer of hope.

"I can do that?" I look at the four rulers who are staying suspiciously quiet on the subject.

"Yes…" Lucas sounds reluctant to answer, and then I realize something.

"Oh, you are probably looking forward to your retirement, right? I'm sure you have better things to do than spend the next forty years advising me." I feel a pang of disappointment, but I completely understand. I'll probably feel the same way when it's my turn to retire.

Mia scoffs. "Are you kidding? It doesn't look like either of our other two children are going to give us grandchildren anytime soon, and the thought of being idle makes my skin crawl, but we didn't want to influence you in any way. This needs to be a decision you make yourself. Personally, I would be happy to join the council, and it isn't uncommon. Emmett is a past king, and Audrey is one of his queens. The other three decided they were happy with their hobbies, but those two have always enjoyed the political intrigue that comes along with being on the council, and their vast knowledge and contacts are invaluable. They also coordinate the liaisons for the other kingdoms. You will meet them at the coronation. Each kingdom has an ambassador who lives in the palace. They are mostly figureheads, but they help with any problems we may have with any fae, witch, or vampire who visits our land."

"They weren't at the ball last night?" I ask, unable to recall being introduced to anyone other than shifters.

"No. Our retirement is also a chance for other kingdoms to appoint new ambassadors. They will be presented by the rulers at the coronation when they come to pay homage to the new shifter queen," Lucas answers, leaning back in his chair. "I, too, would be happy to be on the council if that is your wish." His eyes sparkle with excitement, even though he keeps his expression neutral.

Evie wrinkles her nose. "I mean, I guess we could be persuaded to join the council. What do you think, Layla? Ready to commit another forty years to the shifter nation?"

Layla sighs heavily. "I don't know if it would be a good idea for all four of us to be on the council. The public might consider it manipulation if all four of us are on it. I think Mia and Lucas should, and you should choose two others. Evie and I will always be around to give advice."

"Yay! That means you won't have to move out of the palace and our family can stay together," Gracelin cheers.

"Of course, I'm sorry, I never thought about it in that way. You and Gretchin will be staying since you will be my secretary and advisor, and her my body-guard, but your parents would have left. That was thoughtless of me. I don't like the idea of splitting a family apart," I apologize, thinking back to the snide remark from the council about me not having any family or mates yet that they know of—not that I would like my mother here, and I am super thankful she's still human. I wonder what happened to Lucas's family

She shakes her head. "It isn't a big deal. Their new home wasn't going to be too far away, but I know this will make Archie happy."

"What will the two of you do?" Violet asks the two queens, sounding curious.

"Nag Gracelin for more grandchildren." Evie grins at her daughter who rolls her eyes.

"It isn't like we're aren't actively trying," she grumbles, and Lucas grimaces while his wives laugh at him.

"Shifters don't conceive easily?" I ask, and Layla shakes her head.

"No. It took all of us almost twenty years to get pregnant with our three, and we haven't had any since."

"Supernaturals have long lives, so I think it's a way of keeping the balance. All supernatural races are the same. We were lucky to have Archie so soon," Gracelin explains.

"But General Bryson and Sable have three children who are closer in age. There's less than ten years between Hunter and the twins."

Mia smiles and nods, but there's an air of sadness to the smile. "Yes. Dragons have it a little easier. Dragon females lay eggs, unlike a normal shifter pregnancy, and they will incubate the eggs for a period of time. The children are born dragons but shift quickly, and they don't shift again before the age of mythical maturity. It keeps them from becoming menaces. Not all eggs are fertile though. Sable was incredibly lucky, but more often than not, it's heartbreaking for the dragon parents because the eggs never show any sign of life."

"What about bond group relationships with multiple mates? Will the female have a child for each mate?" Of course I'm curious given my new mate status, not that I've shared it with them yet. Gracelin smirks before quickly smothering it so her parents don't get suspicious.

"Ah, bond groups are a little different. For groups like ours, where there is one male and multiple females—"

"Which is very uncommon compared to multiple male groups," Evie interrupts Layla, who narrows her eyes at her. She winces and apologizes, gesturing for her to carry on.

"As I was saying, bond groups like ours only require the male to inseminate the female once, whereas other bond groups need all parties to participate in the insemination process to achieve a pregnancy."

"Let me get this right… I supposedly have six mates, and all of them need to participate if I want to have children?"

"Yes, all males need to make a deposit at the bank, so to speak, if you want to have a child." Mia struggles to contain her laughter as she confirms what they said. I feel my cheeks heat as I blush furiously at the thought.

Mia thankfully changes the subject before this becomes more uncomfortable than it is. "But having six mates is unheard of. I checked the historical records, and there has never been a ruler with so many. I'm not sure what it means, to be honest, and whether or not we should be worried about why the goddess deemed it right for you to have so many."

There's a pregnant pause as I see everyone mull over the implication in their minds. My own nerves cause butterflies to flutter in my stomach, but I ignore them for now. I have so much to learn.

I desperately try to come up with something else to talk about that doesn't revolve around me fucking all six of my mates at the same time. "I know shifters can't interbreed with humans, but what about interbreeding between kingdoms? Is that a thing?" I ask, voicing another question that has been nagging at me.

Everyone turns to Lucas. I get the feeling that I might have just asked a sensitive question. He sighs, and I can't help but feel a little guilty.

"Officially, no. Or as far as the humans are aware, there is no intermixing of the supernatural races, because that would lead to even more turmoil between us. Though wildly discouraged, there is intermixing between the species, but most individuals who end up pregnant from an interspecies relationship or choose to marry someone from another race end up being ostracized by their family, so there was a need to create a sanctuary for them to live and thrive without being persecuted. There is an unofficial fifth kingdom that exists for these outcasts. They are not ruled over by a goddess, and they are led by a royal family that has familial succession."

"What species are the children born from such unions?" I ask, unable to contain my curiosity despite not knowing if that's a polite way to ask this question.

"Most of them will take after one parent, but sometimes the more powerful traits from both parents will come through as well," Mia explains. "It's one of the main reasons they were shunned. Jealousy is a powerful motivator, and some of the crossbreeds are very powerful."

"Chaos Kingdom likes to pretend the rest of us don't exist. They are a kingdom of misfits who are happy to remain in their own little world. Their kingdom isn't on any official maps, but if you look at a map of the kingdoms, all of them are linked by the Mysola Desert. It's always been no-man's-land because nothing survives there—or that's what humans have been taught. In actuality, that's where the Chaos Kingdom is, and only the outer rim is desert to discourage visitors. All of the other kingdoms touch its borders, and there are ways for people to come and go, but they are known to very few. It discourages people from being tempted to visit. Works for both our population and theirs."

"Despite the fact that most of them are rejected and disowned by their families, the outcast kingdom is actually treated as a fun vacation destination because it's dedicated to indulging in your greatest desires and vices. It's kind of hypocritical to be honest, but it's how they make money. They have an amazing beach resort town, as well as a sinful central city with any kind of entertainment your heart could desire. If you want to party and have a good time, Trisa is the place to do it. The shifter nation has a floor of rooms in one of the hotels where it sends its bond group to… well… bond," Gracelin says, sounding excited. "It's where I became pregnant with Archie after a wild weekend with Adam. There's something about that place that lets all your troubles float away. It's awesome, and most of the younger generation doesn't abide by that interspecies breeding crap. Who cares who you love?"

I rub a hand across my face, my brain hurting from all the information I absorbed today. My gaze goes to my friend, and Violet looks as uneasy as I feel about this conversation—she won't meet my eyes. I will have to corner her sometime later and ask her for her input. I can see she isn't going to say anything for now.

"What is our relationship like with that kingdom?" I ask cautiously, not sure I can handle any more bombshells.

Layla waves a hand. "It's fine. We leave them be, and they leave us be. We do trade with them. The Chaos Kingdom is also a veritable goldmine for precious gems, and allowing them to control them keeps them out of trouble. Plus, I'm sure they've gathered enough black-mail material to make even the most aggressive person tame. We have a good relationship with the new king. His grandfather was an asshole though."

"Could the outcasts be the source of the ferals and also be responsible for Archie's kidnapping?" I ask, grasping for straws since we really don't have any good leads.

"No, I don't think so. They know that if we choose to invade, their odds aren't good," Lucas replies, but he rubs his chin thoughtfully. "I could probably reach out to my contact and ask him to check it out though."

"By contact, do you mean…" Before Layla can finish her question, there's a knock at the door, and one of the palace staff members wheels in a cart filled with coffee, tea, and a variety of snacks. Although breakfast wasn't all that long ago, my stomach rumbles at the sight of the pastry-laden gift from the kitchen. I must take a moment to pop in and talk to the kitchen staff and ask them if I can use it occasionally. Baking has always been a stress reliever for me, and I don't see my stress levels reducing anytime soon.

CHAPTER

SIX

Colbie

Once we've all partaken in the tasty offerings, I get the conversation back on track. As interesting as supernatural procreation is, I have more pressing issues at the moment.

"Okay, let's get back to the topic of the council. If you two don't want the roles, then would you care to make a suggestion?" I inquire, sure Lucas will let me know if he has any luck with the outcast kingdom.

"I think Sable would be a good addition. She is from high shifter society and would be a good asset. She has her hand in everything that is going on, not to mention she's the chief archivist for our kingdom, and she is a respected doctor as well," Gracelin suggests, and her parents agree.

"And I recommend you open up the final position for application, allowing anyone to apply. You never know, you might find an overlooked gem who will be a real asset." Layla smiles at Violet, who blushes prettily, looking down at her hands. She's right. Having her here with me has made everything a lot easier. It's like we've been friends forever, even though it's only been just over a week.

"Okay, that's settled. I can't wait to see their faces when we tell them their services are no longer needed. That means they will have to move out of the palace too, thank God." Gracelin is gleeful, like I told her that all her dreams are about to come true.

"You will advise them at the meeting on Friday, and we can send an announcement for applications at that time too," Layla says, and I murmur my agreement as I think about what I want to talk about next. "Soften the blow by offering them a generous severance package. Gracelin can draw something up for them."

Gracelin wrinkles her nose but murmurs her agreement. "I'm not sure they are going to be happy with anything we offer them, but I can try. There are a number of royal owned properties available to be gifted to them, and the best thing is, they aren't in the city. The farther away they are, the better, because they can't cause too much trouble from a distance." She makes a few notes, and I change the subject to something I overheard at breakfast.

"What did they mean about feral shifters and missing children?" The mood in the room instantly changes, and all five of them look troubled. "Archie wasn't the only one taken?"

Lucas shakes his head. "No, there are three other shifter children who disappeared without a trace. We've had watch teams search the shifter zone without any luck. As for the ferals, you know it's illegal to change a human without permission from the crown, right?"

"Yes. If a shifter happens to fall in love with a human, they need to petition the royal family to ask them if they can change the human," I reply. It's one of the things that you are taught early on in life.

"Yes. The monarch's magic will help the transition. Without it, the human will become feral. I think it's a way to create balance. Neither humans nor shifters want to risk someone becoming feral, so it really discourages random biting. It still happens, but it's way less frequent than it would be. Up until recently, it was never a problem, but in the recent months, there has been an increase in feral sightings, like someone is going around biting humans for fun. We have had to send the military or one of the watch teams in to deal with them."

"So is there nothing you can do about the ferals? Aren't you able to fix the ferals with the same magic you use when someone asks permission?"

There's a loaded silence as the four rulers exchange a glance, then Mia sighs. "The law says that a feral must be put out of their misery, and the shifter who bites them must be punished. If we rewarded people for going against the law, then there's nothing to discourage unsolicited changing."

"So are you saying that ferals can be rehabilitated, but you choose not to?" I ask, slightly horrified by the fact that they are punishing the victims.

Evie's eyes glisten with tears. "We don't know. We haven't actually tried. As far as we know, though, the royal magic has to be bestowed before the changing bite. Usually it happens when a shifter chooses a human to spend the rest of their life with. There are a lot of back-ground checks and mental health assessments that need to be passed before we will even consider granting permission, and then there is a small private ceremony where Lucas bestows his blessing to the couple before they retire privately to complete the mating ceremony."

"His blessing?" I look at the man in question.

"There's a ritual that you recite, and then you place your hand on the human's head and infuse them with your magic. It is instinctual, but the words are a spell of sorts. It turns them into a shifter, giving them an animal. The book is kept in the vault, and nobody can access it except for the royal in power. A drop of your blood will open the book."

"So nobody else can do this kind of magic or even tried after the shifter has already been changed without permission?" I push, leaning forward in interest. The four of them exchange a glance.

"I don't know. I don't know if anyone else has ever tried either. There is no record of it. We could ask Emmett and Audrey, they may know. They have been around a lot longer than we have," Lucas admits before scrubbing a hand over his face. When his gaze meets mine, I can see he's conflicted. "We think there is someone out there who is using the children who were kidnapped in an attempt to make it work. Once a child has shifted to their animal, they can't shift back without help from an adult. We think the stolen children are being used to change humans for some reason. Those poor children would be frightened and wouldn't hesitate to bite in self-defense if cornered, but it isn't going to work without the spell."

"Holy crap…" I sag back in my chair, reeling from that announcement. "But why?"

"That's the big question, isn't it? I would guess that someone was trying to build an army of shifters from the human population, but what's the point if they can't control them?" Mia's eyes blaze with anger.

"And we know the spell book is still in the vault?" Gracelin asks her father, who nods.

"Yes. It was the first thing I checked when Bryson suggested the theory."

"And you think that's why they took Archie? He has royal blood, so they thought maybe his bite might be more effective than the other children's."

"Yes, but thankfully they never got to test the theory. I'm almost certain they are wrong, since only the current ruler can wield that power. Archie and our children wouldn't have the power, but who knows what they would have done to him to force it." Lucas looks green, and tears well in Gracelin's eyes at the thought of her child being in so much danger.

"And there has been no sign of the other missing children?" I ask, and they look defeated.

Mia shakes her head. "No. We've had our troops and the watch team turn the shifter and neutral zones upside down."

"What about the human zone?"

Layla winces. "It's a difficult situation. For us to search in the human zone, we would have to give the human authorities a reason why we need to. While they know that humans are missing, we are reluctant to share our theories with them. It may give them the excuse they need to start another war with us. As much as we coexist peacefully now, there has always been a divide born from necessity and no small amount of wariness despite the war being so long ago. I'm not sure separating the races was the best idea, because the same issues of jealousy still exist, but I don't think we can allow it to stay in our hands any longer."

"It might be more well received for you to ask, because you were so recently human that they may still see you as one of them, but I don't think we can afford to wait. We need those children back, and we need to stop the influx of ferals," Evie remarks, and Lucas nods, his expression the most serious I've ever seen it.

"The human authorities are going to put two and two together soon, and when they realize that all the missing humans have been seen in the neutral zone, they are going to blame us, and we could be on the brink of war again."

My stomach lurches at the thought of war. "What about a tracking spell? Can we ask the witches for help?" I suggest. They explained that all four supernatural kingdoms have relationships, hence the ambassadors, but that they also tend not to get involved in each other's issues. "What if we asked the witch ambassador to help us?"

"Yes, I think that might be the direction we need to head in, but until you are crowned, we can't appeal to them for help. We are in limbo until your mates appear and the coronation is official." Mia bites her lip with worry, and I notice the other three rulers are also worried because none of my mates have presented themselves.

My attention drifts to Gracelin who is staring at me, and I wince internally. I know all I have to do is tell them about the mark on my back, and we can at least ease some of their concern, but call me selfish, because I still need a couple of days to wrap my head around this. If it happened the way it normally does, then I would be getting to know the marked men anyway before making my decision, just like Lucas did with his queens, so I keep my mouth shut for now.

CHAPTER
SEVEN

Colbie

The rest of the morning flies by, and it's almost lunchtime when I remember a question that has been in the back of my mind since I found out that Violet is a fairy shifter.

"What's the difference between a fairy shifter and a fae from the kingdom of Shayla?" I ask, interrupting Lucas who was telling me about the various trade agreements the shifters have with other kingdoms. "I always thought shifters were only animals."

Evie's eyebrows jump in surprise. "You know about fairy shifters? How?"

My eyes swing to Violet unbidden, and everyone's attention follows my gaze. She swallows nervously, playing with a strand of hair that has fallen into her face.

"You're a fairy?" Lucas sounds awed, and Violet shrugs uncomfortably.

"Yeah, but I had to promise my parents I would hide it when they agreed to let me attend university in the city."

"Ugh, it makes me so angry that even amongst our own people, there are still prejudices against the humanoid shifters," Mia growls, sounding much like the cat she contains within.

"Excuse me, you've lost me. Can someone explain what you mean? I thought you said you hid it because humans used to cut off fairies' wings?" I ask Violet who winces slightly. I'm starting to get frustrated with everything I don't know.

Layla rolls her eyes and huffs. "Some of the elite society shifters believe you are lesser if you don't have an animal form, so fairies and merpeople are often shunned or disadvantaged, which is complete and utter bullshit. They are all still shifters with two forms, theirs just isn't an animal."

"And there are also the assholes who believe any of the equine shifters are lesser as well, and that they are prey animals as opposed to predators. That's in spite of two of the equine species being magical and having powers, but they are also pretty, so how could they be scary? It's all really stupid, to be honest. Prejudiced assholes exist in all societies, Colbie. Humans most definitely don't have a patent on it." Gracelin sounds disgusted, and I feel my own anger rise in sympathy.

"Did you say mer?" I ask, trying to wrap my head around everything. "And magical equines? Is that why I am a pegasus?" I haven't really processed my three different forms yet. I am still coming to terms with being a hydra, let alone two others.

"Yes. The mer colonies keep to themselves and mostly live in the coastal region of the shifter section of Aramis."

I try to picture the map of Aramis. I thought only the human settlements abutted the sea, but the shifter territory that is coastal is actually much bigger, I just hadn't really paid attention.

"The difference between fae and fairy shifters is quite significant," Violet explains. "We are good with animals and plants, but we don't contain and control magic like fae do. They have powers that allow them to conjure, control the elements, and more. Mer are much the same as fairies, as in they are excellent at controlling marine creatures but don't have any inner magic either."

"They are fierce warriors in and out of the water though. Bryson has a couple of them in his army," Lucas adds. "I've always hated the stigma associated with mer and fairies. I've tried to include them in matters of the shifter nation, but I have been rebuked every time. There's too much bad blood over our kingdom's prejudiced history."

My brain is running a million miles an hour. "What if we invite one of them to be the final member of the council? Surely that would go a long way in proving that we want them to be a part of shifter society. Hell, we could invite one of each species. Would it matter if we had seven or eight council members instead of six?" I ask my advisors, who all wear looks of great pride that make me feel warm and fuzzy. My body heats, and I feel a wave of magic much like the first rush that flowed through me as I stepped through the doors of the palace. I shiver as the mark on my back warms, and it's all I can do not to wince with pain. What the fuck was that?

"Holy crap, what was that?" Violet is gasping, and pretty fairy wings have appeared behind her, fluttering like crazy. They are just like her namesake, a variety of purple hues, and are thin and translucent.

"Goddess magic," Lucas says with whispered reverence. "Obviously she approves of your choices, Colbie. Well done," he tells me, and I feel my cheeks heat with his praise.

"I knew you were going to be an amazing queen, and this just proves it." Evie beams at me. "You should definitely send invitations to them. Violet, do you know anyone who would be a good representative for the fairies?" She turns to my friend, whose eyes are glistening with unshed tears.

"You're serious, aren't you?" She looks at me with wonder.

"Of course. Why should they be excluded? They are shifters too. I'm just surprised no one has done it in the past. While we're at it, what about one of the equine shifters?"

Lucas snorts. "The previous queen was as speciesist as you could get. She doesn't even like the mythical shifters. I think jealousy played a huge part. She was a wolf and hated shifters who had access to magic she didn't. All of the current council members are natural shifters except Emmett, who is a griffin."

"Okay, well, my invitation will probably piss them off even more than when they find out they are being replaced. Gracelin, could you send invitations inviting the mer, fairies, and equines to put forward a member for council? They will still need to be approved by me. I'm not going to spend the next forty years dealing with an asshole, but ask them to send a few candidates to choose from. Talk to Violet for her recommendations, and maybe ask Bryson to speak to his mer personnel and see if they recommend anyone." I sigh and slump back. "At least we have one thing sorted. Now we need to focus on those missing kids and ferals. Can we send a covert group into the human zone to search for them? Is there any way we can get a tracking spell earlier? Is the former witch ambassador still here or have they returned to their kingdom yet?"

Mia shakes her head. "No. They left with the witch consortium after the retirement party."

"Is there any other way to track them? Do any of the mythical shifters have tracking abilities?" I ask, grasping at straws.

Lucas's face brightens. "Actually, there is a mythical that can track. I'm not sure why we didn't think of that in the first place."

"Unicorns!" Gracelin sighs. "I'm not sure if any of them will help us. The previous queen did a good job of pissing them off, as well as encouraging the prey animals are lesser mentality. They and the pegasus have remained distant through your rule for a reason. They know how to hold a grudge."

"Ugh," I groan, unable to hide my frustration. "Why can't one thing be easy?"

Lucas stands up and stretches his arms out wide. "I'm sure you sending an invitation for one of them to join the council will go a long way in trying to mend those bridges. I think we've done enough for the day. Why don't you have some lunch and do some shift training with Watch Team One? They'll also walk you through some basic self-defense, though they will go everywhere with you until your mates show up."

My gaze goes guiltily to Gracelin, and I only just control the grimace that wants to cross my face at her stubborn expression. I know she said she was going to keep quiet for me, but it doesn't feel right. I should be honest with the king and queens. They've been nothing but open and kind to me. I owe them that much.

"Yeah, about that… It turns out that none are going to show up," I announce, and the king and queens exchange a confused glance.

"Of course they will, sweetie. Sometimes it just takes time," Evie says gently, and I shake my head.

"No, you misunderstand. No one is going to show up because last night, we noticed that I have a bond mark on my back. Gretchin and Gracelin are familiar with the bond group I am matched with."

"Really? That's unusual. I can't think of a time in shifter history when that has ever happened." Lucas sounds partly intrigued and partly worried. "But the goddess bestows the marks, so she must be confident that you are a match for the bond group."

"This is exciting!" Evie claps her hands and bounces on her chair. "We can get you coronated straight away then, no having to wait for you to choose."

I wince internally, knowing that isn't going to happen until I come clean about Nox.

"Is it anyone we know? I can't think of any bond groups with six people in it." Layla turns her attention to her daughter. Gracelin is staring at me with wide, surprised eyes. I shrug. I don't want her to have to lie to her parents.

"Yeah, it's Gryff's mark," she tells them, and Layla gasps, putting a hand to her mouth as the four of them turn their attention back to me.

"How wonderful! Welcome to the family, Colbie." Evie reaches over and gives my hand a squeeze.

"They don't know yet," I warn them. "I wanted to take a couple of days to get to know them, but that doesn't seem fair."

Lucas grimaces. "Now that you wear their mark, they are going to find themselves drawn to you more and more. It's going to confuse the shit out of them when their animals insist on being close to you, but you have to do what is right for you. Don't be surprised if they can't keep their hands off you and vice versa."

"Hang on, there are only five shifters in that bond, but you have six crowns. The math doesn't add up." Mia frowns, but before I can admit to knowing the last member of Watch Team One's bond group, there is a furious knock at the door.

"Enter," Lucas calls as all of our attention turns to whoever is on the other side. The door flies open forcefully, and a uniformed attendant stands there, breathing heavily. He looks to be in military garb, and not the normal uniform of the palace staff.

"Your Majesty, come quickly. Something happened in the throne room—something you need to see right away." I'm not sure whom he is talking to. His eyes dart between me and Lucas as if he's unsure which one of us he should be addressing as well. Lucas pushes his chair back, and the rest of us follow suit.

"Report," he demands as we make our way out of the conference room. Gracelin and I exchange a glance, and she shrugs as we follow the guard and her parents through the palace, Violet keeping pace with us.

"What's in the throne room?" I hiss.

"I have no idea. Dad doesn't use it unless there is an official engagement with another kingdom or he's holding a grievance forum with the shifter nation. Though the crowns were moved there after the retirement party so maybe it;s something to do with them"

"What's a grievance forum?" I ask, trying to keep up with the princess. Apparently, though, I'm now a shifter that doesn't come with automatic fitness. I struggle to keep up with her, and Violet grabs me as I stumble, my coordination not any better than when I was human. I hear her snicker and glare at her playfully. Her wings are tucked away again now that the magic has dispersed.

"Once a month, Dad sets aside a day to hear his subjects. Any person who has a problem, big or small, can make an appointment to see him. It allows his people to feel like they can rely on the king to hear their needs. Otherwise, the council would try to block anything they deem unimportant."

Our footsteps echo through the long corridors, and I swear this place is like a maze.

"A wave of magic washed through the throne room, and when it dissipated, the crowns for the future queen and her mates were altered," the guard explains breathlessly. I'm almost certain it's not from exerting himself. Most shifters are fit, so I'm pretty sure it's the magic that freaked him out.

"Altered?" Lucas repeats.

"You're better off seeing it for yourself." The guard looks worried as he holds open the elaborate doors leading into the throne room.

I gape in amazement at the ostentatious room. The marble columns and floors are almost blinding in the light shining through gorgeous skylights inlaid in the roof. Massive, sparkling chandeliers hang from the ceiling, which must light the room like a Christmas tree when it's dark, but a startled gasp and a number of exclamations from my companions turn my attention to the problem at hand. I catch up with the others closer to the dais at the back of the room. Sitting on it is a large throne, for lack of a better word, and on either side of the throne are eight slightly smaller chairs. Above each chair floats a crown surrounded by a clear, sparkling, floating bubble.

"Eight crowns?" Gracelin murmurs as I try to make sense of what I'm seeing. "There were only six to start with."

"Can someone please explain what's going on?" I ask, completely bewildered by their reactions.

Lucas runs a frustrated hand through his hair, causing it to stick out in multiple directions, and paces back and forth in front of the dais, muttering to himself. Evie and Mia are having a quiet, intense conversation, and it's Layla who turns to me, her eyes troubled and confused.

"When a new king or queen is marked, the crowns we used to wear are taken by the goddess's magic and reformed for the new ruler and their mates. This happened on the night of our official retirement and the same night you got your marks." She points to the bands around my wrists. "This is how we know how many mates you will have to choose." She drops her voice and moves closer to me and the two girls, obviously not wanting the guards to overhear her next words. "With you having a mate bond, that's now changed, but it still doesn't explain this. Watch Team One still only has five members."

"Can you find Lady Sable please?" Lucas asks the same guard who got us. "She will either be in her clinic or the archives. Please tell her this is urgent."

The guard doesn't wait and tears off back the way we came.

"Leave us," Mia instructs the other guard, who salutes us and disappears in the same direction.

"Well, actually, Watch Team One has six members." I don't hesitate to explain now. "I saw their symbol on a man I met when I was staying with my grandparents for a couple of days when I was first marked."

This has everyone focusing on me, and I find their collective attention slightly intimidating.

"What do you mean?" Lucas asks and takes a seat on the steps leading up to the dais. The poor man looks overwhelmed.

"When I was first marked, I had a panic attack and thought that if I ran, no one would find me. I stayed with my grandparents and was walking along the beach when the goddess made it very clear that running wasn't an option."

"Did you say goddess?" Layla almost chokes on her words, her golden skin turning pale.

I explain my encounter with the deity and how I met Nox. I skip over the more intimate details, but I'm blushing, and it's not hard to guess why. While I appreciate their attempt at discretion, all five ladies' eyes sparkle in a knowing way.

"You say this human had a mark the same as our

boys?" Lucas asks, frowning. "That shouldn't be possible."

"Yeah, I don't think he was human. He was wearing a pendant exactly like mine. In fact, he gave this one to me. I now suspect he's a shifter, but as to why he's living in the human zone and not acknowledging the bond group marking, I have no clue."

"If he does have the same mark as the boys, then that means he is also your mate. We are going to have to go into the human zone and retrieve him." Gracelin crosses her arms stubbornly. "You can't be crowned without him."

"But what about the two new crowns? Does this mean I now have eight mates instead of six, and who are they? Will they be marked with the same mark? Did Watch Team One's bond group just grow by three?"

"Gryffin always insisted there were six of them. I guess it's within the realm of possibility that there are now eight. The goddess works in mysterious ways." The voice at the front of the room has us all looking at Sable as she walks toward us, her intelligent eyes assessing the display in front of us.

"Has this ever happened before?" Evie asks her. "Have new mates been added after the initial anointing?"

"No, but nothing about this new ruler has been the same as previous monarchs." She focuses her attention on me, and it's all I can do not to squirm under such intense scrutiny. "First, there were six mates, and then to have two more added later is unprecedented. Plus, Colbie is the first multi-shifter in years, not to mention she's a hydra, which hasn't been seen since the war. I have a feeling our lives are going to be very exciting."

She smiles at me now, and some of the intense pressure eases slightly.

Lucas stands up and brushes his pants, smoothing out some of the wrinkles. "Let's tackle this one problem at a time. Colbie, you need this Nox person. You should head into the human zone and convince him to come back with you. Once he realizes he's mated to the queen, I'm sure he will see reason. Take the boys with you. Normally shifters aren't allowed into the human zone, so this visit will have to be off the books to keep it quiet. If you get caught, we can use the excuse that you want to visit your grandparents before your life gets too hectic."

"Then I think we need to appeal to the equine shifters for some tracking help, because finding the shifter children is a priority. Maybe they can also help you track down the final two members of your bond group. That's *if* they haven't appeared while you are away. I don't doubt they are newly marked. It would be unusual for three members of a bond group not to present themselves to the bond placement team. They are probably as confused as you felt when you were first marked."

"Does this mean they will all be younger? Bond marks appear around seventeen," Violet points out, and I grimace at the idea of having two mates who are teenagers. I look at the king, queens, and Sable in horror.

"No, please tell me that's not going to be the case." I can already tell that none of them have a clue. Sable puts a hand on my arm and gives it a squeeze.

"Have faith in the goddess. She won't give you more than you can handle."

I scoff, the laughter that bubbles up after it bordering on hysterical.

"Seriously? She gave me eight mates. What am I supposed to do with eight mates?" I hear the desperation in my voice, but Gracelin just smirks at me and winks.

"Have a good time. A very good time."

EIGHT

Liam

I stare up at my bond mate as my bear thrashes inside my chest. He wants out so he can search for his mate. It took all of my stubborn strength to get him to run here when I shifted as opposed to running after the damn queen who smells like cupcakes and frosting, making my mouth water. He has a burning need for her. When Gianna put her hand on me at the breakfast table, he nearly pushed his way through and ripped her face off for touching him. He has done a complete one-eighty. He tolerated her before because she was pretty and let us fuck her, but now he just wants to eat her internal organs. I have no idea why. Every time I question him, all he can grunt is, "Mate." I'm worried that it's taken too long for the goddess to mark our mate and he's going insane.

"I need help," I repeat as Brodie just gapes at me. "My bear is getting too hard for me to control. He keeps insisting the queen is our mate, but she can't be. I don't know how long I'm going to be able to control him. I'm worried the next time I get close to her, he will force a mating bite on her."

He frowns, pursing his lips. "Shit, man. That's a death sentence, you know that."

I allow my head to hang so I can't see the look of disappointment in his eyes. "I know."

"Snap out of this. What the fuck is wrong with you? You're one of the strongest shifters I know. Get your shit together and don't let your animal rule you. Staying in bear form isn't going to make it any better. You'll become shift frozen." He shoves me with his foot, and I sprawl on the ground, the rough surface stinging my naked body.

My own anger flares, and I scramble to my feet and glare at him, fisting my hands like I'm going to slug him.

"Don't you fucking think I know that?" I shout at him, and his eyes glow with triumph.

"There he is, the Liam I know and love. None of this feeling sorry for himself crap." He sounds smug. I drop my fists and assess myself, and he's right. I do feel better. He got me out of my funk.

"Fuck, I don't know what's wrong with me." I run a hand through my hair before dusting the dirt off my naked body. Nudity isn't a big deal for shifters. Not everyone has clothes that are spelled to shift with them, so we learn to deal with it from a young age.

"I know how you feel. My wolf has been insisting the same thing. I wonder if we all feel naturally drawn to her because of her royal power," he suggests as we start to walk back to the entrance of the cave.

"I don't feel this way about Gryff's parents," I point out.

"No, but they still have that magnetic aura. I just don't want to hump their legs like I do the new queen." I chuckle at his admission and the thought of Brodie doing that to one of the queens. They would grab him by the ear and throw him into the palace pool.

"Come on, Bryson needs us. That will keep your mind off the pretty queen for at least a few hours." He grimaces. "Well, it might not because we're discussing her security, and we are helping her with shifting this afternoon. Are you going to be okay with that? Or do you want me to give your excuses? I'm sure I can come up with some plausible reason for you to disobey orders. It won't be the first time."

My bear roars inside me at the idea that we'll miss out on helping her shift. I argue with him internally, and he settles at the threat of me not going to the practice. He decides to behave, and I breathe out a huge sigh of relief. "No, I'll be fine. It seems we have come to an agreement," I assure my bond mate. He stops at the edge of the falls and studies me carefully before nodding.

"Okay, but be careful. If you start to lose control, promise me you will leave. I don't want to lose you because your bear made a stupid mistake."

"I promise. Hell, I don't even like the girl," I lie, and I can tell by the look he gives me that he doesn't believe me.

"Sure, buddy. Keep telling yourself that and someone might believe you." He pats me on the shoulder. "I think Bryson is going to have to send us away once her mates show up. I'm not sure I could stop my wolf from tearing into any of them if I saw her with them," he says quietly, like it's not something he really wants to admit to, but I appreciate him sharing with me. It makes me feel less alone.

"At least Gem, Gryff, and Hunter aren't going to be a problem," I mutter. "They are always the perfect little soldiers anyway."

I hear him scoff, and when I look at him, he's rolling his eyes. "If you believe they are unaffected by the new queen, you aren't looking closely enough. Didn't you see how devastated Gryff was when she walked away from him last night? They also have history. He even has an endearment for her—cookie."

I can't stop my lips from turning up in a small smirk. "It suits her." I frown. I don't want to think about the queen. The damn woman is giving me more problems than any woman ever has. "Enough about her. She's off-limits, and everyone should keep their distance. Bryson assigning our team to protect and help her with her shift is irresponsible. He should put someone else on it."

"Don't blame the man for your inability to control your animal. We are the top team for the job. The only other suitable team is Adam's, and they are all mated. I'm not sure their mates would be happy with them spending so much time with the queen."

"The fact that they are mated makes it better. None of them are going to be distracted or tempted by her."

"Yeah, but then we don't get to spend time with the pretty shifter, and I want to see what she can do with her animals. My wolf is dying for hers to come out and play." He grins and shifts, putting a stop to the conversation before throwing himself into the pool of water and paddling under the falls.

I'm not sure his wolf is actually any better than my bear. I will have to keep a close eye on him as well as my own bear. This is going to be a fucking disaster. My anger rises again, as does the resentment I feel toward the new queen. I'm pissed off that I want her but can't have her. I hate being denied the things I want, and I usually go out of my way to get them. This time, it just isn't going to work out in my favor.

I shift into my bear, and he roars his own disappointment before following Brodie into the water. He's a much better swimmer than Brodie's wolf, able to hold his breath and swim under the rush of water. By the time we come up for air, we've passed him and almost come to the side of the pool. We climb out and shake off the excess water before Brodie joins us. He does the same, and then we make our way back to the palace, our animals easily keeping pace with one another. By the time we get back to the edge of the forest, my heart rate is up, and I'm feeling less hopeless about everything. I certainly have better control of my bear.

"You know, I bet Colbie's hydra would love that pool. It's deep enough for her to swim around in. We should take her there to shift one of these days," he says as he pulls his clothes on.

I gather up the remains of my shredded clothes, knowing the queens will have my hide if I leave them behind, and the two of us walk toward the military barracks where we will find Bryson and the rest of our team.

"Stop, man. Let her mates do things like that for her. We are there for two reasons and two reasons only— protect her until they appear and help her get control of her shift. Romancing her is not one of those reasons."

He huffs, frowning at me. "I wasn't trying to

romance her. I just thought it would be good if she could learn to control her body in water as well."

I scoff. "You know that pool is a place where shifters go to fuck. That secluded area behind the falls always has aroused scents in it."

"Not since you claimed it and chased everyone off. The only aroused scents are from you and your flavor of the month. You're the only one fucking in that pool now, Liam," he argues, and I can't stop the smile from curving up my lips.

"You got that right. Chicks dig it. It's romantic, guaranteed to get them to drop their panties, and those sheets and blankets are self-cleaning. I have a handy witch charm that does it, so they are always scent free, and it doesn't piss off any of the women I take there. That's also how I know that we shouldn't be taking the queen there," I finish with a scowl as we enter the barracks, and I grab a pair of shorts from the bin off to the side for any shifter who needs to cover themselves. I can't really go into a meeting with the general with my cock hanging out, even if he has been like a father to me since I joined the same bond group as his son.

"About time," he snaps as Brodie and I join the rest of our team and Gretchin around the conference table. "We have to work out a schedule with the queen. I want you all working with her every afternoon on her shifts until she can shift on command and control whichever animal's body she is in. Brodie, you will be able to help her with her wolf, and I suggest you go to the archives and ask Sable for information on the hydra. As for the pegasus, we don't have any in our ranks due to the prejudice of the last few royals, so maybe she will have information on them too. It's not as good as learning from a shifter source, but I don't think they would willingly send one to assist us." Bryson looks and sounds tired. The shit show with the council this morning didn't help. I know he's under some pressure to keep the new queen safe, especially since no mates have appeared. It is their role to provide protection for the sitting ruler. Layla, Mia, and Evie look like refined ladies, but the three of them are fierce protectors. Their cats are savage in the defense of their mate.

Suddenly, before anyone else can say anything, a rush of breath stealing magic washes through the conference room. I shudder as it caresses my skin, and my hands change to paws before slowly switching back as the magic dissipates.

"Fuck, did you feel that?" Hunter grunts, smoke drifting out of his nose, and I see scales disappear on his arms much like my hands changed.

"That felt like the same magic that was in the throne room on blessing night." Gretchin's eyes are still feline as she shakes her head, trying to negate the magic's touch.

"Goddess magic," Gem agrees, his body awash in flames as he pushes back out of his chair and steps away from anyone to prevent anything else from catching on fire. His chair smolders on the ground behind him as he wrestles his flames under control.

Gryffin runs out of the room and returns with an extinguisher, quickly dealing with the still burning flames, and Gem winces.

"Shit, sorry. I couldn't control it all of a sudden."

Bryson gives him an absent wave and looks toward the door. "I have no idea what that was, but maybe we should head outside and check. The troops should still be at morning formations, so let's go and see if we have to put out any more fires. Hold on to that, some of our newer recruits may not have the same control all of you have," he tells Gryffin and gestures to the extinguisher.

We follow him out of the conference room and to the outside exercise area. Sure enough, the area is pure chaos. There are a few shifters running around in animal form, as well as a couple on their knees, struggling to control their animal. A dragon is still on the ground, but he's thrashing his head around, and flames are flying haphazardly across the yard.

Bryson marches up to him, puts his hands on his hips, and bellows at the recruit. "Shift before you kill someone." The change is instant. The shifter freezes, and his body convulses before he returns to a naked, huddled male on the ground, his training uniform shredded. The rest of us round up the other animals running around like they are in a panic and use our own alpha command to get them to shift back.

"What the fuck?" one of the shifters on the ground grumbles and flops onto his back, his chest heaving with exertion. He rubs a spot on his chest above his heart. I recognize him as one of Bryson's captains, a mer shifter who is a beast of a warrior. His long teal hair has fallen out of its tie and is spread out on the ground around him, moving like it's underwater. Scales flicker up and down his arms, and his body convulses, shredding his pants when his legs shift into a tail. Gills form on his neck, and he flops around like a fish out of water, gasping and clutching at his chest.

"Fuck, get Micah to the pool. He's drowning on land!" Gretchin screams. Gryff continues to battle the fires from the dragon as the other four of us hurry to follow Gretchin's instructions, lifting him and running toward the pool on the other side of the training grounds.

It takes a good couple of minutes to make our way through the barracks and to the pool, and when we get there, we slide him in. He disappears, sinking below the surface. His eyes were closed, and I'm not sure if he was breathing.

"Is he dead?" Brodie asks, not taking his eyes away from the surface of the pool.

"I don't think so. He felt like he still had a life force," Gem replies, his own gaze locked on the water.

"What the fuck was that?" Hunter asks and drops to his knees at the edge of the pool, breathing as heavily as I am. Micah wasn't light. He's a big, brawny dude in human form, but his mer form was even larger. "Why isn't Dad worried?"

"The goddess has never done wrong by us before," Gem murmurs thoughtfully as he turns and joins us at the side of the pool. I hear other people approaching our location, and despite the scent of smoke in the air, I can smell the general, Gretchin, and Gryff as well as Adam and another one I'm not familiar with.

"How is he?" Bryson asks, surveying the pool like he's looking for the shifter.

"We don't know. He hasn't surfaced yet." Brodie sounds worried, and I watch as the unfamiliar man who accompanied them peels off his clothes, dives into the water, and disappears.

"Elliot will check on him. He's one of the other mer shifters we have in our military and Micah's cousin," Adam explains.

"I can tell he's alive, but I'm not sure how long it will take him to heal or what was wrong with him. Micah is too old and too experienced to be shifting on land. The saltwater is the best place for him at the moment," Gem advises the general who nods.

"Okay, well, while we're waiting, let's help clean up the training ring. Once it's done, everyone can have the afternoon off to recover—except you guys of course. We need to go check on the royals and make sure they are unaffected."

"Shit, what if the queen shifted?" Hunter scrambles to his feet. "She has no control over her hydra yet."

"I think we would have noticed if she shifted anywhere in the palace that wasn't the safe room. We'd be hearing screams of terror." Gretchin chuckles but bites her lip with concern, looking in the direction of the castle.

"That's true," Bryson agrees and puts a hand on his son. Hunter visibly relaxes, the tension leaving his shoulders. Apart from the king and queens, Bryson is one of the strongest shifters, and his alpha energy has a way of soothing riled shifters, even us.

"Let's clean up, and then it will be time for lunch, and we can check on her then."

"Hopefully the rest of the council isn't joining us for that meal," Gryffin grumbles. "Breakfast sucked."

"That's just because you can't handle Gianna and Liana's flirting," his sister teases him, and he wrinkles his nose and moves closer to Gem, swinging an arm around him possessively. My eyebrows jump in surprise, but I can't stop the pleased smile that crosses my lips.

"Finally," I murmur to Brodie who moved closer to me.

"Yeah, I heard them return together from the ball last night. Thankfully Gryff managed to pull his head out of his ass. I hope he will drop the whole sixth member thing next."

"That's because I don't like their hands all over me. They make me feel dirty," Gryff replies to his sister, who is staring at Gem and Gryff with wide-eyed surprise before her face softens to joy, and Hunter shudders.

"None of us do except Liam." He glares at me. Obviously he hasn't forgiven me for my mistake.

I hold up my hands in surrender. "I swear I'm done with her. She was getting clingy, and you know I'm not into that. Plus, my bear wants to rip her face off now too."

Bryson narrows his eyes on me. "Hmm, well, that's good to know. That girl is as manipulative as her mother. You'd all do well to steer clear. I told Talon the same thing about Liana."

Hunter snorts. "Oh, I think Talon has set his eyes on a little something else." None of us have missed how much he's into the queen's new advisor, and I approve. The girl's cute and sweet, but he also has to be careful not to break her heart. His bond group has a destined mate too, and they need to be patient. I just hope he doesn't upset the queen by messing around with her friend.

"Go find some clothes, Liam, and we will see you at lunch. Elliot will let us know if Micah needs anything else." Bryson departs, the rest of us following behind. I leave them to help with cleanup and head back to the palace to find suitable clothes to wear for lunch and our task after it. I smile wickedly to myself as I make the decision not to put on shift friendly clothes. I want to see how the queen reacts to seeing at least one of us naked as we work on her shifts.

Colbie

I'm still stressing about my new extra mates when the royals insist we take a break for lunch. I agreed to tell Watch Team One about the bond mark and Nox this afternoon during my shift training with them. It doesn't seem fair to hide it from them. Lucas insisted they are just going to become more confused and their animals will be harder to handle when they are drawn to me and don't know why. It would be unfair to leave them perplexed.

Before we get to the dining room, though, I decide to head back to my room to change. I don't want to wear a dress to self-defense, so I separate and wind my way through to my wing of the palace.

I'm lost in my head and not really paying attention to my surroundings when someone steps into my path, and I literally bump into them. I put my hands up to steady myself and feel hard, hot, silky smooth skin beneath them.

"Look what we have here, a queen all on her own. Do you think it's such a good idea to wander around unprotected, little girl?" a voice growls at me as I look up and find Liam glaring down at me. "Especially with rogue magic just randomly flowing through the kingdom."

I'm instantly annoyed as well as incredibly turned on from feeling his bare skin on mine. Liam is the perfect outlet for my frustrations, because he doesn't even seem to like me, which just pisses me off. I'm his mate, there is supposed to be instant attraction, but he's been nothing but aggressive and downright rude since day one.

"Who the fuck are you to tell me what to do?" I snap at him and give him a shove, but he barely budges. In fact, he crowds me, and I step back, not wanting to be any closer to all the delicious naked skin in case I do something stupid, like stick my tongue out and lick it. He may be a dick, but he's a hot dick.

"I'm the person who has to keep your pretty ass safe until your useless mates get their heads out of their asses and present themselves to the castle, and you aren't making it any easier by being careless with your safety." He backs me up until I'm pressed between the wall and the solid surface of his body.

I almost scoff at him calling my mates useless. Man, he's going to kick himself when he finds out the truth. "I'm perfectly fine, as you can see. I've been walking since I was one and can manage to get around without falling on my face. We also know what that damn wave of magic was about," I argue, and he leans down, his lips a hairsbreadth from my own.

"You know what the magic was about? Tell me. What caused half of the kingdom's warriors to lose control over their animal. What put everyone in danger?" His eyes flash with anger as his body presses me to the wall. His delicious scent, frost and pine, whirls around me, and it's all I can do not to lean in and take a bigger breath. "Was it something you did?"

I put my hands up to push him away again, pissed that he's blaming me for the magic, but he cages them with his own, pressing them against the wall. "Tell me," he demands. "The barracks just about burned down because of that magic and a dragon shifter who wasn't able to hold out against the magic's call."

Fuck. I didn't even consider the magic affecting anyone else. I just thought it was localized to the palace. "It was the goddess's magic. She somehow decided she needed to fuck me over even further," I snarl at him, angry at both the deity who just made my life even harder and the asshole who decided I was to blame. "I had nothing to do with it, and if you think I'm happy with the outcome, you're fucking delusional."

His eyebrows jump, and I feel some of his anger seep away. "The goddess? What did she do now?"

A bit of my anger recedes, and my body slumps. I'm tired from the overload of emotions that have been bombarding my body for over a week now. I can't believe it's only been a little more than a week since my life changed beyond recognition.

"I have eight mates instead of six. There are now two more crowns in the throne room," I mutter, and I see him flinch, but he doesn't release me or move away.

"Eight mates? And none of them have bothered to show their faces?" he growls. "What the fuck is wrong with them? If I had been marked, nothing would have gotten in my way of getting here as quickly as I possibly could."

My heart skips a beat at his unexpected confession. Liam has been nothing but antagonistic toward me, but then I remember him jumping to my defense when my mother was here. He was protective and effectively ran interference, and I can't deny that we have some intense chemistry. Maybe having him as a mate won't be so bad.

I make a split-second decision, one that could backfire on me, but I'm sick of pretending. Need is riding me, insisting I tell him the truth.

"Well, that's kind of lucky then," I remark, and his brows furrow in a confused but adorable frown.

"What is?"

"That you would be honored to be my mate, because surprise, you are," I say lightly, bracing myself for his reaction, because I know it's going to be spectacular.

There's a moment of silence as he tries to process what I said. Before he can reply in any way, I push him, and when he steps back, I pull down the side of my dress so it's halfway down my arm and turn, showing him the mark on my back.

I hear his sharp intake of breath, and then his finger runs softly over the mark.

"That fucking explains everything," he mutters before turning me to face him. His mouth claims mine, and his body presses me back against the wall. I moan as his hands slide to my ass, and he lifts me. I wrap my legs around his waist, and he grinds his hard dick against my core. His kiss is punishing, his tongue licking and exploring like he can't get enough of me. I feel a ball of metal press against the roof of my mouth and shudder at the thought of it sliding across my clit in the same way. I thread my fingers into his short, spiky white hair and kiss him back with just as much enthusiasm. Sure, the guy's been a dick, but he can kiss like a demon.

When we finally break apart, we're both panting. He rests his forehead on mine and gazes at me with longing and fire. "Mate. But how?"

I shrug my shoulders as I drop my hands from his hair and clear my throat, feeling a little awkward and no small amount of turned on. "I guess the goddess decided the shifter realm needed some spice and blessed me with a bond group just to shake it up a little," I reply, trying to make light of the situation.

"But we only have five members," he argues, shaking his head and lowering me to the ground. He paces back and forth in front of me as I watch slightly bemused. He looks ruffled, and it's kind of cute. "We can't be your bond group. Let me look at that mark again." Without waiting for me to respond, he spins me and tugs my dress down. I shiver at the feeling of his hands on my bare skin and have to stifle a moan as he leans in to get a better look, his warm breath washing over my naked flesh. The creature inside me writhes and pushes for his attention, despite me wearing the pendant that should block me from feeling her. It's almost like being close to one of my mates is overriding the pendant's capabilities.

"It's not the same as ours. It has eight branches, and ours only has six. It's a different mark." My stomach lurches at the anger in his voice.

"What? No. How can that be? When I looked at it yesterday, it definitely only had six." I push away from him and hurry in the direction of my room, determined to look at the mark on my back. Did Gracelin get it wrong? My heart sinks, and I feel the possibilities of our future drifting out of reach.

I push through my bedroom door, not stopping until I get to the adjoined bathroom. I strip off my dress, leaving me in just my underwear, and turn to look at the mark on my back. I count the branches on the mark, and sure enough, Liam is right. There are definitely eight branches now, and it's bigger, no longer the size of a small apple. Now, it takes up a good portion of the upper half of my back. Not only have the branches grown, but there are also two new symbols at the end of both branches, and the roots look slightly longer as well. When did this happen? Something occurs to me. It must have been when the wave of magic washed through the palace and six crowns became eight. I sag, feeling disappointed, and I don't bother looking up or covering myself when Liam steps closer to me.

"It changed," I mutter flatly. "Yesterday, there were only six branches, which is why Gracelin suggested that you were my bond group."

He shakes his head. "I'm sorry, but she got it wrong." I see disappointment in his pitch-black eyes, and I tear my gaze away from his and look at the matching mark on his chest. As I catch sight of it and count its branches, much like I traced Nox's with my finger, my eyes widen in shock.

"Yours changed too." I point to the tree, and Liam steps closer to the mirror so he can see it unimpeded. His eyes widen in surprise.

Just like mine, his has sprouted two more branches. I step closer and run my finger over it. I never really got a good look at the one on Nox's chest, but up close, the tree is stunning. I can see the veins on the few scattered leaves and the knots and swirls on the trunk and branches. At the end of each branch is a symbol. I want to study them closer, but a flash of red draws my attention to the heart in the middle of the tree. That is new too. The heart was previously black, or the one on my back was, so I'm assuming his was as well.

"Fuck, I hadn't even noticed. We were so busy dealing with the fallout of magic, I don't think anyone noticed."

"Why are you half naked?" I ask him, and his lips twitch with amusement as I cross my arms over my own mostly naked form and scowl at him. "Were you off fucking Gianna?" I demand, my jealousy roaring to life at the thought of him giving any attention to that bitchy shifter, let alone his cock's attention.

"Shredded my clothes when I shifted and went for a run. I picked these up at the barracks so I didn't have to go into a meeting with the general with my dick out," he explains, stepping closer and running his hands up and down my arms in a soothing manner. "Don't worry. Ever since I met you, my bear has only had eyes for you. I thought we were going crazy."

One of his hands cups my cheek, and his other arm winds around my waist, pulling me into an embrace. I lean my head against his chest and breathe in his comforting scent, my nose tickling.

"I can't believe you're our mate, but what does this mean? We have three more members of our bond group out there?"

He sounds as confused as I am, and I drop my arms

and wrap them around him, snuggling into the warmth of his body. I take comfort in the fact that he's as bewildered as I am.

"I have no idea, but it's a good guess," I reply, not mentioning Nox just yet. "The goddess is obviously playing games, but why?" I feel him press a kiss to the top of my head, and I snuggle further into his body, enjoying how it feels to rub my mostly naked skin against his. My desire roars back to life, and I tilt my head back and push up on my tiptoes, catching his lips with mine once more. He groans as my tongue swipes across his lips for entrance, but before the kiss can turn even more heated, he wrenches himself away, clenches his fists, and squeezes his eyes shut as if he's trying to get control of himself. White fur rolls across his body like a gust of breeze across a wheat field. My stomach sinks in disappointment. He doesn't want me.

"Trust me, there is nothing I want more than to shred those dainty underthings and shove my cock as deep as possible into your tight channel, but I owe it to my bond mates to tell them what's happened," he says through gritted teeth and opens his eyes. His blazing need for me burns in his gaze, and I let go of the hurt.

I'm surprised. I expected Liam to be more selfish than that, and I'm pleased he is putting his bond group before his own pleasure. It bodes well for us.

"Get changed," he bites out and whirls around before stomping out of the bathroom. "I can't stay here, otherwise my bear is going to eat you up. I'll wait outside, and we'll go tell everyone the news. I won't let my brothers suffer any longer."

My eyes follow him as he leaves my room, shutting

the door behind him. I groan and lean against the cabinet, rubbing a hand over my tired eyes. That didn't go quite as I had hoped, but it could have been worse. I only hope that when we tell the others, things will go better.

CHAPTER

TEN

Hunter

When we get to the dining room, Gryff's parents, Gracelin, Violet, and my mother are already seated and talking animatedly as we sit. My father apologizes for our tardiness, explaining the magic situation to the king. King Lucas's eyes widen in shock, and he exchanges a glance with his wives.

"We thought only the palace was affected, but hearing that the grounds were as well is surprising. Is everyone okay? Were there any casualties?"

My father assures the king there weren't.

"Do you know what caused it?" Gryffin asks his dad, placing a kiss on each of his mothers' cheeks before finally taking a seat next to Gem. I'm pleased to see the two of them have finally worked out whatever the hell is going on between them, but Lucas's answer has my attention returning to him.

"Yes, it seems the goddess wasn't happy with the amount of mates Colbie has and decided to add two more," the king replies, his brow wrinkled in concern.

"Eight mates?" Brodie exclaims. "Then why haven't any of them shown themselves yet?" He sounds angry, and I can't blame him. I also want to wring their necks for leaving the new queen hanging. I'm wondering if someone interfered and stopped them from coming to the palace. If they wanted to interrupt the coronation, it would be a surefire way to achieve it.

Lucas shifts uncomfortably in his chair, and it's such a rare and unexpected reaction that I'm instantly suspicious.

I look around the table and take note of the fact that Gretchin, Violet, and Gracelin all seem just as uncomfortable. What do they know, and why are they reluctant to talk about it?

"Where is Queen Colbie? Liam is missing as well." Dad's eyes narrow. "What's going on?" he asks, and Mia clears her throat.

"Let's wait for the queen to arrive. She went to get changed for her shift training this afternoon." Her chin juts out stubbornly, and I smother a smirk. I know that look, and nothing else will be discussed until the queen reaches the dining room. Even my father, the powerful shifter general, knows when to back down, so he drops his head in a short nod of acquiescence.

"Where is Liam?" Layla asks, feigning casualness, but her body is tense.

"I sent him to get changed. He shredded his clothes during a shift and was only wearing a pair of shorts. I didn't think it was appropriate for him to come to lunch half naked," my dad explains gruffly. He's annoyed about not being in the know.

"Shredded his clothes?" Evie latches onto this information like a hawk, and Brodie chuckles. "He picked up every scrap of material, didn't he? I don't like it when you boys leave your bits lying around the grounds."

"Oh, I can assure you, Mother, none of us want to leave our bits lying around the grounds either," Gryff remarks dryly, and the rest of us chuckle, his comment loosening the tension at the table. My gaze goes to the man sitting next to Gryff. I can tell they are holding hands under the table, but Gem's eyes are slightly glazed, like he's lost in thought. My whole body tenses like we're on the edge of a cliff, and one wrong movement could send us tumbling down.

The doors to the dining room open with a bang, and Liam, fully dressed in a pair of jeans and a T-shirt with no shoes, strides through, followed by a frazzled queen. She's dressed in a tight pair of capris and a loose tank top, perfect for the light self-defense moves we are going to put her through today. I can't help but notice how well the material hugs her delicious figure, molding to the curves of her hips and breasts as well as accentuating the mound between her legs, which my dragon wants to lick.

My cock hardens with a rush of blood, and I shift uncomfortably when the scent of arousal hits my nostrils. Everyone must smell it at the same time, because their attention instantly turns to the two new arrivals, and now that I look a little closer, both of them appear disheveled. Liam's hair is in disarray, like he or someone else has been running their hands through it, and Colbie's cheeks are flushed pink, like she's been exerting herself.

"What the fuck did you do?" my father roars, jumping to his feet, his glare turning lethal as he looks at my bond mate, instantly suspecting the two of them have been up to no good.

Fuck, Liam has done it now. There is no helping him, because the general's ferocious wrath is focused on him. Liam stops in his tracks and looks at my dad with a flash of hurt before he continues walking, but Lucas gets to his feet and holds up a hand to stop the smoke puffing dragon at the same time as his wife puts a hand on his arm.

"Sit down, Bry, and hold your temper. Goddess, you're worse than a dragon with a thorn in its claw," my mother scolds him. My father struggles to gain control of his urge to shift and eat Liam as a snack. I jerk in surprise as Colbie reaches for Liam and whispers something in his ear that's too quiet for any of the shifters at the table to hear. Then, to my surprise, he leans in and presses a kiss to her forehead before joining us at the table while the new queen remains standing.

"What the fuck?" Brodie mutters next to me.

Gryff's eyes widen with shock, but Gem nods like he's finally worked something out inside his mind. My heart races as I smell Colbie and Liam's combined scent. Whatever they were doing, they were close enough to each other for their scents to mingle, but why were they that close together? Liam's bear is getting out of control, but he knows Colbie isn't the one for us. I feel my anger rise, and smoke drifts from my nose. He's such a manwhore, and I know his bear has been unruly, but putting his hands on the queen is going too far. She is off-limits.

Colbie takes a deep breath, her chest rising and falling with the action, and approaches her spot but stays standing. She laces her hands together nervously as all of us at the table focus our attention on her, but she ignores everyone else and instead addresses my team.

"Ah, so, um… Fuck, this is hard. Oh shit! Should I be saying fuck as a queen? That's probably not allowed, is it?" she rambles adorably, and some of my anger drifts away.

Gracelin giggles and gives her an encouraging nod. "You can say whatever you want, Colbie, you're the queen. Go on, tell them what they need to know."

Gracelin's words have the desired effect, and Colbie nods decisively, straightening her spine and looking at the five of us, her eyes sparkling with mischief.

"Could the five of you please remove your shirts and show me your chests please?"

Liam doesn't even flinch and quickly does as she asks. I think, like me, the other guys are stunned into inaction.

"You want us to remove our shirts?" I ask, trying to wrap my head around her request.

"Your queen gave you an order, boys, so I suggest you comply," Lucas growls at the four of us, and I slowly get to my feet and pull my shirt off, bewildered by the strange request. Gryff, Brodie, and Gem do the same thing. I toss my shirt onto the table in front of me and raise an eyebrow at our queen.

"Darling, if you wanted to get us naked, you only had to ask, but really, do you think the dinner table is the right place for this?" Gem smirks at the queen, his eyes sparkling.

She rolls her eyes and gestures at our naked chests. "If you would indulge me for a moment, please look at your bond mark. Is it different than it was when you woke up this morning?"

My frown deepens, and I exchange a look with Gryffin. Is the queen losing her mind? My eyes drift lower to his chest and widen in shock. The mark that is, or was, the exact match of mine has changed. It now has eight branches instead of six. I gasp and look down at my own, running a finger over the mark that has sat over my heart for ten years now.

"Holy fuck, it *has* changed. Did the magic do this?" I ask as the other three mutter something along the same lines as me, but Liam is not surprised. I narrow my eyes on him suspiciously. "What did you do?"

He throws his hands up in disgust. "Why does everyone automatically assume I did something?" he mutters, sounding pissed.

"We think the goddess made some changes when that wave of magic hit us today. Like we told you, there are now eight crowns in the throne room…" Lucas trails off as if he's expecting us to react, but for the life of me, I can't figure out why.

"Eight crowns and eight branches," Gem murmurs, his eyes going wide as his attention locks on the queen, and she nods her head.

"I guess it might make sense if I do this." She strips her tank top off, leaving her in a sports bra. Colbie turns around, and my jaw drops. In the middle of her back, sitting above the band of the sports bra, is a bond mark that is an exact match to the one above our hearts.

"Mate," I whisper reverently. Holy fuck, the queen is our mate. Brodie, Gryff, and Gem look as stunned as I feel, but Liam is smirking. He obviously knew about this already.

"When? How?" I stammer and lean forward to grip the edge of the table so I don't haul her over my shoulder and drag her back to our apartment to have my wicked way with her. My dragon is screaming to do just that, but we are a bond group of five, not eight, so we can't be a match.

"I knew there was another member of our bond group," Gryff shouts triumphantly before frowning. "Does this mean there are actually three more members of our group?"

"Put your shirts back on and sit down, then we can discuss our theories over a meal. Colbie needs all her energy if she's going to spend the afternoon shifting with you," Layla suggests, and I drop into my seat, quickly tugging my shirt over my head. There's an impatient silence as Lucas directs the staff to serve the meal. I can't tear my eyes away from my mate. I see her squirm under the intense scrutiny of all five of us, but she's smiling like she's happy.

"This explains so much, like why my tiger couldn't get enough of you in the stables and felt comfortable going to sleep on your lap." Gryffin stares at her with wonder. He reaches for Gem's hand again, but this time it's in plain sight, like it's automatic, and I sigh in relief when Gem doesn't push him away. Colbie will need to understand they come as a package, but I don't think she cares. She looks at their joined hands and smiles, squirming in her seat. A fresh waft of cookies and frosting hits my nostrils, and I almost groan out loud, not upset in the least.

Lucas instructs the staff to leave us and gestures for us to begin eating. Everyone else at the table does, but the six of us don't. It's kind of like nothing else exists around us and we're in our own little bubble, all of our attention focused on the queen and her on us.

Dad clears his throat. "Well, I'd say congratulations are in order and welcome to the family, Colbie." He beams at her and raises his glass to the six of us. "You couldn't find a better group of mates if you picked them yourself, but I don't envy you trying to keep them in line. It's taken the six of us all our strength since their group formed to keep them out of trouble."

Everyone at the table laughs, and the tension in the air breaks. "Eat, my queen," I rumble. "You are going to need all your strength," I tell her, not hiding the desire I feel for her anymore.

"For shifting?" she asks, picking up her fork.

"And other things." I wink at her, and it's like her brain short-circuits for a moment, her fork pausing on its way to her mouth. A pretty blush heats her cheeks, and I chuckle at her discomfort. God, she's adorable.

"Phew, the sexual tension at this table is off the charts." Gretchin wrinkles her nose. "Can we maybe discuss our theories about the magic and what happened?" she asks.

"So eight mates? Does this mean there are three more out there somewhere?" I drag my eyes away from the woman who just became the most important person in my life.

Gryff is frowning but is still holding Gem's hand

while he eats with the other one. "The witch only told me there are six of us."

"I told you she was a crackpot," Liam mutters.

"I think originally there may have only been six of you," Lucas says thoughtfully, "but something we did today must have changed it."

Violet gasps. "Colbie decided to invite the fairies and mers to have representation on the council."

My eyes widen in shock, and I look at our queen with surprise. I'm not the only one. Dad and my brothers are doing the same.

"You did?" Brodie asks her, and she nods and smiles, returning her attention to her meal.

"But she also invited the equine shifters as well, so why wasn't it nine mates instead of eight?" Mia argues, and Colbie puts her fork down.

"Actually, I think I have the answer to that." She looks like she's running some things around in her mind before she nods. "When I was first marked, I thought I could run away. I didn't want to be the shifter queen and thought that if I didn't appear, the magic would choose someone else." My heart sinks at the thought that our mate doesn't want to be here. "But the goddess quickly took care of that when she appeared on the beach and basically told me to suck it up. Shortly after that, I ran into a man who offered me shelter from a storm." She blushes again, and it doesn't take a genius to work out something happened between them.

My dragon roars inside me, and I bend the fork in my hand in my rage. Some other man had his hands on our mate. Growls and snarls echo from Brodie, Liam, and Gryff, while Gem's entire body lights on fire again. He swears and jumps back from the table again so he doesn't set anything alight. He stands there, staring at our mate with a look of betrayal.

Her eyes widen, and she stands as well, holding her hands up in a placating manner. "He had the same mark on his chest that the five of you do," she says in a hurry. "But at the time, I just assumed it was a tattoo. He told me it was from a former life, and I had the feeling he didn't want to talk about it, so I didn't push. He's the one who gave me this." Her hand goes to the pendant around her neck. "He had a matching one, and I'm assuming he was hiding the fact that he was a shifter. Before I got to the palace, I just assumed he was human, but too many things have happened for him not to be one and a part of your bond group."

"But why wouldn't he present himself to the bond center to find his group?" Gryff sounds bewildered, his snarling cutting off with her explanation. "I've been searching for him for years. I didn't look in the human zone because shifters aren't allowed to live there, so I thought there was no point." He sounds crushed.

Colbie shrugs helplessly. "I don't know, but I do know where to find him and will show you as soon as we can," she promises.

"He obviously doesn't want anything to do with us." Liam sits down and crosses his arms, a stubborn set to his jaw. Liam won't understand because being in a bond group was a blessing for him. His family members are assholes, and it gave him the means to get away from them. Most shifters see being part of a bond group as a blessing, and we are stronger as a group because of it, so why wouldn't this stranger feel the same way?

"Well, he's not going to have a choice. Colbie can't

be crowned without him," Dad points out, and Colbie winces.

"I don't want to force anyone to do anything they don't want to do. Nox has an underlying sense of sadness, but if I had to guess, I'd say he's been hurt by something or someone, and if we are going with the assumption that my other mate must be an equine shifter, it would explain why he's reluctant to join a bond group. You said they were treated as lesser because they aren't predators."

"That would also explain why you can shift into a pegasus. He must be one," Violet blurts with excitement.

My mother nods, a look of understanding crossing her face. "That actually makes sense. Equine shifters, even the mythical ones, have always been looked down on, and some of the shifter towns have made their equines feel very unwanted. Most of them have banded together in Zalfari to escape persecution."

Gryffin looks startled at this information, and his lips purse as he frowns. He's about to say something, but Mom looks at Colbie with intense scrutiny.

"If he is a pegasus, that means you can shift into two of your mates' forms." She nods at Brodie. "Brodie is a wolf, and Nox is a pegasus. I wonder if you can actually shift into all your mates' forms. When you practice this afternoon, you should try one of the others as well. If it doesn't work, it's not a big deal, but if it does, it would be incredible."

Lucas growls and slams his fist down on the table. "I tried to put a stop to the way the equines were treated, but the council wouldn't let me. They insisted that shifters are a hierarchical species and if the equines couldn't fight back, then they deserved what they got.

Even with the equine mythical species, most of their magic is passive—tracking, healing, illusions, and weather manipulation—so not much in the way of attack magic, and they were run out of towns."

Evie reaches over and grabs his hand, giving it a squeeze. "Don't beat yourself up. Colbie is going to fix everything that is wrong with our society, I just know it."

Colbie winces and looks unconvinced but gives Evie a small nod. "I'm certainly going to try my best," she promises.

"I was just at Zalfari, and I didn't see any sign of equine shifters. It was weird, actually, The village alpha was shifty as fuck and gave off distrustful vibes. He wouldn't let me question anyone except a few people selected specifically by him. He claimed that because they lived at the base of the Aramis Rift, a curfew was in place due to the ferals that occasionally wandered into town. It certainly wasn't the equine haven you make it sound like," he tells my mother, and she exchanges a worried glance with my father and the king.

"So where are the equines then? And if the feral problem in Zalfari is so bad, then why haven't they called in the armed forces?" Dad growls, and I know the alpha of Zalfari is going to get a visit he probably doesn't want.

ELEVEN

Colbie

"You need to take us to that shifter," Gryff blurts all of a sudden. "He shouldn't have to be alone anymore."

My heart melts. The prince is such a softie. I remember him being like that when we were small as well. He hated seeing me cry and would do anything to fix it. The throb inside me now that the bond has been acknowledged is constant. All I want to do is run my hands over their bodies and grind against them, but I need to focus on other things first, so I shake the fog of lust out of my mind and try to concentrate on what everyone is talking about.

"First, Colbie needs to get a handle on her shift. If she can't control it, then we can't allow her to go into the human only zone. We are going to reach out to the human authorities to get permission for her to visit her grandparents as a cover story, and then you can find that shifter," Lucas explains. "Gracelin already sent the message when you went to change." He turns his attention to me. "It might be a couple of days before we get a response, so you six can take the time you need to work on your shift."

"We can also tell the council about this so it will get them off your back." Layla sounds thrilled by this. "Man, are they going to be shocked. I can't wait to see Sophia's and Vallen's faces when they learn you are mated to the group they both wanted for their daughters."

"Pfft, if you thought Gianna was bad before, she's going to be livid that all of her dreams have gone up in smoke." Gracelin sounds gleeful as well. I would kind of feel sorry for the girl if I didn't know she's had her hands all over one of my mates. I can't control the glare I aim in Liam's direction.

"Hey, if you think they are the only two who are going to be disappointed, then you're sadly mistaken." He gestures to the rest of my mates. "None of us were angels in the past." He sounds defensive.

"You know what? I think we should give you some privacy," Sable announces, pushing her chair back from the table, and the other parents follow suit. "You all have a lot to work out. Shall we continue these plans at dinner?" She looks at the king and queens for approval.

"Yes indeed. Come on, girls," Lucas says to Gretchin, Gracelin, and Violet. "Let's leave them to bond." The king grabs onto Sable's suggestion like it's a life preserver and he's drowning in an endless sea. His wives laugh, and the girls grumble.

"But this was just starting to get good," Gracelin complains, but she does as Sable suggested, taking her plate of food with her.

"Violet and I are going to the shift room. She needs to shift and fly off some energy. We'll be there if you need us," Gretchin tells me, her eyes serious.

"I'll be fine. Go shake out those wings," I tell my friend, who is watching us with unrestrained interest.

"I'll see you later?" she asks, and I know she's going to grill me for every gory detail, but I nod my agreement. She takes her plate, then she and Gretchin follow the parents out.

"Ugh, we miss all the good stuff." Gracelin stomps her foot but hurries after everyone else, and then there are only the six of us left in the dining room.

The silence is slightly strained for the moment, but then Gem turns his attention back to Liam.

"We might have enjoyed our freedom, but you're the only one who fucked where you slept," Gem points out. "The rest of us were sensible enough to keep that shit out of the palace." He turns to me, his eyes pleading. "Shifters are highly sexual creatures, all supes are, but now that we're mates, none of us will look anywhere but at you." He side-eyes Gryffin, and I see the dismay in his eyes. I know I have to assure them that whatever they have going on is fine with me. I could see it the moment I approached the table, and thoughts of being the jelly in their sandwich make my panties damp.

"I'm not going to stop you and Gryff, if that's what you're worried about. Hell, there's only one of me, and there's going to be eight of you. I would say you are taking one for the team if you two are together." I wink at him, and they both relax. "In fact, I'm pretty sure Nox is bi as well. He kind of implied he was," I offer. "He's very pretty." I see intrigue in both of their eyes, but it's the only thing I'm going to say on the subject.

"What about the rest of you? Are you going to be fucking as well? I don't care, I'm just trying to work out the dynamic here."

They all stare at me with shock, and it's all I can do not to giggle.

"Ah, no, the rest of us are very much hetero, but that doesn't mean we don't like to share." Brodie recovers first and gives me a sly wink.

"Good to know." I give him my own wink back, and his mouth drops open in surprise. I think he was trying to shock me, but I assumed that's how things worked in a group dynamic. I'm kind of excited, to be honest. The thought of being shared by two or more of these men is exhilarating, albeit nerve-racking. I hope I'm enough for them. It doesn't seem fair that I get to have all of them, but they only have me. A frown creases my brows as I think about this.

"What are you worried about, pretty girl?" Hunter asks, and I turn my attention to the gorgeous dragon shifter. "The key to a healthy bond group is communication. You need to tell us how you are feeling, because despite our animal instincts, we are not mind readers."

"Not yet anyway." Liam smirks at me.

"What do you mean, not yet?" I ask him, and he shrugs.

"We can all mind speak, and once the bond is sealed, you will be able to as well."

"But that doesn't mean we can read your mind." Gem scowls at Liam. "You have to actively send your thoughts to us."

I breathe a sigh of relief. I don't want them to learn about all my insecurities, and being able to keep my thoughts private is essential to me.

"What about these two new bond mates? Do you really think they are going to be a mer and a fairy? That's what Violet implied earlier," Brodie asks and pushes back from the table, bringing his plate down to a chair closer to mine. It sets off a chain reaction, and the other four do the same thing, so we are all closer together. My head swims as their intoxicating scents hit my nose. I know Liam is the frost and pine aroma, but I can't distinguish the others yet. I'm assuming the smoky scent is from either Hunter or Gem, both of their animals having access to fire. I close my eyes and try to breathe shallower so I'm not overwhelmed by them.

"It makes sense," I agree, opening my eyes again to find them staring at me with adoration. It's a lot, but I'm going to have to get used to it. "So how are we going to work out who they are? Do you think they will go to the bond center and register? Should we put out some feelers so we know as soon as it happens?"

"Actually, I think I might know who one of them is." Gem rubs his chin thoughtfully, but before I can ask, Gryff jumps up.

"Micah!" he exclaims. "That's why he was rubbing his chest like that and suffered so badly from the wave of magic."

Gem nods his agreement.

"He will be a good addition to the team. He is one of my father's fiercest warriors," Hunter agrees. "And I like him. He's quiet and focused, but he's a good guy."

"That makes sense. Should I go find him?" Brodie also gets to his feet, bouncing up and down with excitement.

"No need." The deep voice has all six of us turning our attention to the dining room doors, and my mouth drops open in shock. The tallest dude I have ever seen stands there. He has to be close to seven feet tall, and he has broad shoulders and arms that look like they could crush a small car. His torso tapers into a thick waist, and his thighs look like they are one loose stitch from bursting out of his black cargo pants. I'm pretty sure this guy could bench press Hunter without breaking a sweat.

He has long, teal hair that is dark because it's wet, and his glowing eyes are the same color. He has a strong jaw, and his eyelashes and eyebrows are the same color as the hair on his head, which is a little startling. He's staring at me like I'm the answer to all his questions.

"Micah! Hey, man, come on over. I'm going to take a wild stab and assume you have a mark on your chest that matches ours now." Gem waves him over, and the man strides into the room, his attention not leaving me in the least. I scramble out of my chair so he isn't towering above me when he reaches the table, but it really doesn't do any good. He's just that much taller than me, and he has an intense aura that's almost suffocating when he reaches out and takes one of my hands.

"Your Majesty, I am Micah, and it's a pleasure to meet you," he purrs and bends, placing a kiss on my hand. I just about swoon with all of his focus on me. Phew, holy shit, this male is intense.

"Hi, call me Colbie. Do you want to join us for lunch?" I stammer slightly before pushing my shoulders back and trying to look confident.

"I take it you have a brand-new bond mark on your chest?" Liam says dryly as Micah releases my hand, pulls out a chair next to Hunter, and takes a seat. He gives the guys a nod before turning his attention to Liam.

"I do, and I happened to run into King Lucas and the general as they were heading back to the barracks to check on everyone. They explained the situation and sent me this way." He absently rubs a spot above his heart, which I'm assuming is where his new mark is. He shakes his head. "I can't believe I was marked. I'm forty years old, so I'd given up on being marked for a mate or bond group years ago and was focused on serving my kingdom, despite my community's reluctance to get involved in shifter affairs."

"Well, we can't really blame them." Gryff winces. "It isn't like the shifter nation has given you anything to fight for, but we think that's going to be different. Colbie is going to bridge the gap my parents were unable to." He beams at me with pride, and I shift uncomfortably. Everyone has so much faith in me, but I have my doubts. Until recently, I was happy with my lot in life and determined to find a small amount of joy in my career and make new friends. Everything has changed. I've made new friends, but that came with a life completely removed from what I planned.

"What are you?" I ask bluntly, giving up on all attempts to be subtle. So much is up in the air, I think the least I deserve is to know what each of my mates shift into. "Actually, can you all share with me what you are? I know that Gryff is a tiger and Hunter is a dragon, and you told me you're a phoenix, Gem, but what are you?" I look at Brodie and Liam before switching back to Micah. I know it's not polite to ask, but I figure since we're mates, I deserve to know.

Micah is still gazing at me, half bewildered and half amazed, like he can't believe what's happened, but then he frowns and his eyes take on a look of distrust.

"I'm a mer," he announces like he's bracing for a reaction.

"Like a mermaid?" I ask carefully, desperately trying to control the squeal inside me that wants to break free.

"Well, merperson or merpeople are the proper terms, but yeah. Is that a problem?" He crosses his arms defensively, and I bounce up and down on my chair in glee and clap my hands.

"Do you have a tail and everything?" I ask, unable to control my excitement anymore.

The distrust in his eyes fades, and he looks at me in wonder. "Uh, yeah, I do."

"And gills and you can breathe underwater?"

He starts to chuckle. "Yup, that's usually how it works. It would be pretty bad if we couldn't breathe underwater."

"Oh my god, that's amazing!" I turn to the others. "Do we have a pool so we can go swimming and he can show us?" I feel like a kid whose dreams have come true. I was obsessed with mermaid books when I was a tween.

"Huh?" Micah shakes his head with amazement. "She doesn't care," he mutters.

"Shit, man, neither do we. You'll find that none of us are like those assholes who made you feel worthless. King Lucas and his queens have been trying to stamp out that ridiculous prejudice against humanoid shifters for years," Hunter tells him. "No one in the service gives you a hard time, do they?"

"No, but General Bryson doesn't tolerate any of that crap. Anyone who did have issues was dishonorably discharged."

"That was due to my dad's orders," Gryff replies.

"The problem is the voices of the few with issues are

basically louder than anyone else's. Most of us animal shifters don't give a shit, and our new queen comes with an even blanker slate. Look at her, does she seem disappointed that you're a mer?" Brodie is laughing. "Hell, I don't want to tell her what I am now. I bet she'll be nowhere near as excited."

"What are you? Hang on, let me guess." I study Brodie, and if I had to guess, I would put him as a golden retriever. He has happy-go-lucky energy, but I know there are no domesticated animal shifters. "I bet you're a wolf. I can practically see your tail wagging," I tease him, and he beams at me, though I remember one of the queens something earlier.

"Yup, you guessed it. Aren't you a clever girl?" He winks at me, and I can't help but feel proud of myself and a little turned on by his words of praise, so I turn my attention to Liam in the hope nobody notices it.

"Well, darling, are you going to take a guess at what I am?" He smirks at me, and I smirk right back, deciding I'm going to give him shit.

"Hmm, I know monkeys are especially promiscuous, so I'm going to go with a chimpanzee or maybe a gorilla."

His mouth drops open in shock, and the rest of the guys burst into laughter at his reaction.

"You think I'm a fucking monkey?" He sounds hurt, and I shrug.

"Well, you all admitted to being manwhores, and they said you were the worst."

"Oh, so you're coming to us as a lily white virgin, are you?" He arches an eyebrow and folds his arms across his chest defensively. I feel a little guilty.

"No, but I haven't had many past relationships.

Being a baker is not very family friendly, and the ones I have been with all wanted me to change. I like who I am and don't feel like I have to change to fit someone else," I admit, and I see his anger soften. Liam is so bristly on the outside, but there's an inner softness that occasionally breaks through.

"To be honest, this scares the crap out of me. We're fated, but what if you don't actually like the person I am? What if we're mated, and we all end up completely miserable? I mean, you five have been together for years, but Micah and I are going to change that dynamic. What if it doesn't work and we end up fractured instead?"

All of my fears come writhing to the surface, and instead of bottling them up, I share them. Hunter did say communication was the key to a healthy and happy bond group.

Liam jumps up, comes around, and takes my hand, pulling me out of my chair. He turns me to face him and cups my cheek, his eyes locked on mine. "Trust in the goddess. Things may be a little rocky while we all adjust to this, but I have no doubt that it's going to be amazing." He presses a kiss to my forehead, and I hear someone sigh.

"Well, who the fuck knew he had it in him to be romantic?" Gem mutters to Gryffin.

"His bear has been pushing him for a mate for a long time. It's no wonder he's all in," the prince replies.

"I don't know about you guys, but I'm starving. How about we eat up so we can get to the shifting part of the program? I'm dying to see Colbie's creatures again," Brodie suggests, and Liam pulls away, but I grab his hand, and he faces me again.

"So what are you?" I ask, realizing I never got an answer to my question.

"Polar bear," he replies and growls at me, a deep rumble that comes from his chest. "And he's dying to meet you." I let him return to his seat and fan my face, trying to cool down. Holy crap, a polar bear. I'm pretty sure they eat people. Or are those grizzlies? I'm not sure, but sign me up for Liam eating me, I'm just not sure about his bear. My creature is waiting to be let out so she can play with her mates, but I know for sure that's not a good idea. She's so much bigger than all of them, except maybe Hunter's dragon. They are similar in size.

"What are you, if you don't mind me asking? It seems fair." Micah smirks at me, dragging my attention away from the bad boy shifter.

I return to my seat and wink at him. "How about I surprise you?"

"Let's go to the waterfall, and then Micah can be there to help Colbie in the water. Your creature might enjoy a swim," Hunter suggests, and I widen my eyes in surprise. Do hydras like water? Shit, I know nothing about the creature I house. Maybe I need to go to the archives and ask Sable for some help. Another thing to add to my to-do list.

"You're a water creature?" Micah sounds surprised. "There aren't many water shifters. There are a few krakens, sharks, and whales, so are you one of them?"

Brodie laughs and slaps a hand on the table. "Man, you have no idea. You are going to lose your shit, I can promise you that."

CHAPTER
TWELVE

Micah

I hadn't expected to fit in with this group of shifters. I'm almost double their age, and they are a well-known bunch due to the fact that the prince is in the group. I've worked with them before, but we've never been close, yet they welcomed me like I've always been part of the team. There's no posturing like there often is with a bunch of males, and I can't say I hate the dynamic. I'm still blown away by the fact that I now wear a bond mark.

I probably don't participate in the conversation while we're eating as much as I should, but I can't take my eyes off the queen, my mate. She's gorgeous. Watch Team One grills her for all of her favorite foods, colors, and things to do, and I'm surprised to learn she owns a bakery in the neutral zone. Although I haven't been there, it's a popular place where a lot of the military teams eat. They always rave about the delicious treats they can get there. This past week, they've been bringing back coffee with floating marshmallow animals, which have been a big hit.

Throughout the whole meal, she's open and bubbly and nothing like I expected a new royal to be like. I just hope and pray that doesn't change with all her responsibilities. The absolute delight on her face when she found out I was a mer left me speechless. It's gotten better, but for a long time, learning I was a mer was met with derision and scorn. She was actually excited, and to learn that she is an aquatic creature as well has me bristling with anticipation to swim with her this afternoon.

I'm not really sure what I have to offer her. I have no inner animal to shift into to defend her. My warrior skills are excellent, and in the water, not many can best me, but I still doubt what I can bring to the team. Mer are looked down on by a high percentage of the influential shifters, and me being Colbie's mate could be detrimental to her rule.

Watch Team One explained she's only shifted once, and that it's our job to get her used to it over the next few days. They also told me that I am not the only new member of their team. Apparently, they've always known there are six of them, but the final member had been missing. When the magic activated today and I almost drowned on dry land, two more were added to their group—me and another unknown.

General Bryson ordered for me to join Watch Team One, saying he will inform my old team of the switch. He assured me I will retain my title as captain, but that my responsibilities now lie in keeping the queen safe. That's not all it entails though. No, this woman is my mate, and not only do I want her to feel safe, but I also want her to feel the same kind of unconditional acceptance that she showed me. Unlike an animal shifter, there's nothing inside me pushing to be near her, but I feel it all the same—the pull to my mate and urge to hold her close and never let her go, amongst other more carnal desires, which will have to wait for now. We have a job to do, and making sure she has a handle on her new abilities is at the top of the list, as well as retrieving this other shifter.

It didn't surprise me when they explained the reasons they think he stayed away. More mer than I can put into words feel the same way, but my cousin Elliot and I could see that it was not productive to continue to shun the rest of shifter society. It builds animosity and hate, and a civil war between species won't do any of us any good, especially with the rise in feral shifters. We don't need to be fighting a war on two fronts. The two of us joined the shifter military in hopes that we could attempt to foster better relationships.

King Lucas has made every effort to reintegrate the mers, fairies, and equines into shifter society, but he has forever been rebuked. Hopefully with the new queen, we can usher in a change that is so desperately needed. When Colbie said she invited mer and fairy representation to the council, it renewed my hope in our cause. I can only pray that the mer council doesn't reject her offer, but I know my people are stubborn. Hopefully seeing her with a mer mate will be the chance we need, especially one whose father is head of the mer council. I will send my own missive to my father, asking for him to consider the offer. I just hope whoever he selects to interview aligns with the same ideals of fostering better relations.

"Come on. I don't know about you, but I'm dying to

get my eyes on Colbie's gorgeous creature again." Brodie, who is a bit of a clown, stands up and stretches before grinning at us. "Let's shift and run there." His grin drops, and he frowns at me. "Right, you can't shift on land."

"Neither can Colbie if she's a water creature," I point out a little slowly. Maybe he's taken one too many hits to the head.

"Colbie's animal is as comfortable on land as she is in the water," Hunter replies, also getting to his feet. "But I don't think she should shift so close to the palace. We're trying to keep her creature under wraps for now, so she has a card up her sleeve on challenge day, but I'll shift, and Micah and Colbie can fly with Gem and me to the waterfall."

What kind of animal is she that is at home both in the water and land? I rack my brain, trying to think of one, but come up with nothing.

"How about we make this interesting then? First one there gets to have the queen in their bed tonight." Liam stands up and is already walking toward the exit.

My eyes widen, and Colbie's mouth drops open in shock as Brodie and Gryffin jump to their feet and hurry after him, stripping off their shirts as they go. Gem huffs and rolls his eyes.

"Well, the palace staff are in for a treat with Watch Team One half naked in the halls. Rumors will be flying within minutes."

"Not going to join them?" Hunter asks with a gleam in his eye as he reaches out and tugs Colbie to her feet, dragging her along behind him.

"What the fuck?" she splutters, struggling to keep up with him as he all but drags her through the palace.

"One thing you need to know about us is that although we love each other fiercely and are loyal to one another beyond anything, we're competitive as fuck," Hunter explains as Gem and I hurry after them.

"Yes, and Hunter and I have a distinct advantage in that we can fly," Gem gloats. "They need all the head start they can get."

"Is my bed going to be a regular incentive?" Colbie asks, sounding exasperated. "I don't want you fighting with each other."

"Relax, darling," Gem coos. "When we come to your bed, there will be no fighting, only complete cooperation and focus on your pleasure, but anything else is fair game."

"I'm not a toy to be fought over." She sounds annoyed, and I feel the urge to soothe her, but before I can say anything, we arrive outside of the palace, and Hunter strips.

Colbie's expression becomes heated as she takes in all of him in his naked glory. I'm not into guys, but even I can admire his toned body. Like me, Watch Team One has honed their bodies to be lethal weapons, and you can see it in all the rippling muscles on display.

"We know, but there's nothing like a little incentive to get the blood flowing. Fancy a ride?" He smirks, and nobody misses the dragon's suggestive tone, but Colbie just huffs and waves a hand.

"Well, go on then. They already have a head start."

She and I watch as Gem also removes his clothes. The men, although similar in height, couldn't be more different. Hunter is large and brawny, his build similar to mine, but Gem is more streamlined, like a runner or a swimmer, but neither of them have an inch of fat. They are pure muscle. We watch as they shift. Unlike mine, which is only a slight change, both of them change completely.

Hunter's body twists and grows, morphing until he towers over both of us. His deep, eggplant purple dragon stretches his wings and shakes his body similarly to what I've seen a wolf do. He lowers his head, which is bigger than us, and smoke drifts out of his nostrils as he blinks large eyes with elongated pupils.

Gem's transformation is very different. He shrinks slightly, and flames cover his whole body as he turns from human to bird and hovers in the air. The phoenix shrieks loudly before pulsing his wings and shooting off into the sky like a flaming rocket. Hunter's dragon nudges Colbie, and she offers me a hand. "Come on, we don't want them to beat us."

She drags me over and tries to scramble up the side of the dragon, but she's just too small, so I wrap my hands around her waist and give her a boost before leaping up after her. We're barely seated before his wings expand, and with a leap and pulse of his wings, we're airborne. Colbie tips to the side, and I grasp her, hauling her up against me and holding her tightly while I grip one of his dragon's spikes.

"Whoa, thank you. I almost slipped," she shouts over the rush of wind as I tuck her in close, making sure she's secure. She wriggles back into me, and I feel her warmth seeping through the thin cotton of my shirt. Her rounded bottom presses against my groin, sending a wave of desire through my veins. Her scent of frosting and cake batter tickles my nose, and I can't stop the possessive rumble that leaves my mouth as I lean in to get a larger dose. Her hair whips around as I tuck my nose into her neck, unable to stop my tongue from darting out to see if her skin tastes as good as she smells.

"Did you just lick me?" she asks, turning to gawk at me incredulously.

My cheeks heat with intense embarrassment, but I shrug and smile. "You know what they say. I licked it, so it's mine." I don't wait for her response before I lean in and kiss her. I know she's new to this shifter dynamic, but as a whole, if we see something we want, we take it, and she's my mate, so there's even less of a reason to wait. Her lips are soft as she gasps, but her body melts into mine as she returns my kiss with enthusiasm.

Before it can get too out of control, the bastard dragon dives, and Colbie shrieks and grabs for his spikes to stop herself from falling. We plunge down, but as we rapidly approach the ground, he spreads his wings, and our descent slows before we touch down with a shaking thud. Colbie glances around, and there's no sign of the rest of the team.

She fist bumps the air. "Looks like we won. I guess that means I get you and Hunter in my bed tonight." She smacks another kiss on my lips and slides down off the dragon, leaving me speechless.

You should be saying, 'Thank you, Hunter. I'm so glad that I was able to share in this victory with you,' a voice rumbles in my brain, the tone amused. *Now would you please get down so I can shift?*

I jump in surprise and stare at the dragon in shock. His long neck is arched, and he's staring at me.

You're in the bond group now, so you get the added bonus of mind speak—not that it's much of a bonus when Liam is bitching or Brodie rambles about some ridiculous topic.

Can you hear me? I ask, projecting my thoughts at him, and his large head nods in acknowledgment.

Huh, that sure is handy. I slide off Hunter, and he shifts, leaving him completely naked. He looks down at himself and winces. "Whoops, probably should have thought about that."

Colbie stares at him unabashedly, but before either of us can reply, another scream signals the phoenix's approach. He arrives in a ball of flame and hovers in the air in front of Colbie. Distracted from the naked dragon, she studies the flaming bird with intense interest. I can practically see him preening at her attention as she circles him. He's large, probably twice the size of the biggest bird of prey.

She reaches out to touch him, but Hunter grabs her wrist, stopping her. "Wait, we don't know if his flames will burn you or not. Let's not test it out just yet." She drops her hand in disappointment, and the bird shimmers, morphing into his naked human form.

He picks up her hand and presses a kiss to the back of it. "I can't wait to feel your hands all over me, but Hunter is right. Until we know if you have your own phoenix form and are immune to my flames, we shouldn't tempt fate. Phoenix fire can do a lot of damage. Our bond group is immune, just like they are to Hunter's fire, but until the mating bond between us is sealed, let's not risk anything."

"Immune to your flames? And what did you mean about her having her own phoenix form? I thought you said she was an aquatic shifter," I ask, but my ears perk up as the sound of pounding paws reaches the clearing.

A white tiger, a black and gray wolf, and a large white polar bear barrel into the clearing, and all three of them crowd around the queen, snarling and snapping at one another as they try to scent mark her, rubbing their heads and bodies over every inch of her they can reach. She giggles and runs her fingers through their fur, cooing at them as each one vies for their mate's attention.

"What were you talking about?" I ask again, dragging their attention back to what Gem said.

"The queen is a multi shifter. We've seen three of her forms, but Sable, the general's mate and head archivist, suggested that maybe she would be able to shift into all six—sorry, I guess eight now, and once we get a handle on the ones we know of to push her to try," Gem explains as the big white tiger comes over and nudges him. His hands go into his fur as the tiger licks a wet stripe up his naked leg. Gem winces and pushes him away. "Jesus, your tongue can flay flesh, Gryff. I don't want it quite that close to my delicate bits. At least not in that form." He puts his hands over his dangling cock, protecting it, and I snort with amusement before focusing on what the phoenix just told me, a buzz of excitement filling my veins.

"She might be able to shift into a mer form?"

"That would be awesome!" Colbie exclaims as the other three shift. The two of us are now surrounded by naked shifters, and it's like she doesn't quite know where to look. I don't care. Being comfortable naked is a part of being a shifter, and we learn at a young age not to ogle one another when we are, but the poor girl looks like a deer in headlights, and the scent of her desire thickens and fills the clearing.

"See something you like?" Liam asks, winking at her, which seems to have the desired effect of distracting her.

She huffs and rolls her eyes. "Meh, you know I've probably seen better." We can all tell it's a lie.

"Pfft, we know that's not true. Humans only wish they could be as handsome and dashing as shifters." Brodie laughs. "But developing a poker face should be a priority. We can't have the queen ogling every naked person she comes upon," he teases.

"Stop teasing the woman," Gryff scolds his friends and heads over to a large tree not far from the edge of the pool. There, hidden amongst the gnarled roots, is a trunk. He pulls it open and drags out some fabric before tossing each of our bond mates a pair of shorts. "Cover up. We don't want Colbie's creature being tempted by all that dangling flesh."

Brodie blanches and quickly pulls on his shorts, and the other four follow suit. I return to the subject at hand.

"Multi shifting is quite uncommon. In fact, I don't think I know of another dual shifter."

"That's because our mate is special." Gem smiles gently at the girl and takes a step toward her, clasping his hands at his sides like he's restraining himself from reaching for her. "I can't believe you're our mate. We've waited so long for you."

She shifts uncomfortably and doesn't look like she knows how to respond.

"Easy, Gem. Give her time to adjust. Unlike us, who have known for almost ten years now, she's had this all dumped on her. We need to give her a little bit of patience and understanding," Hunter cautions, and Colbie smiles at him gratefully. Gem's smile dips for a moment, but Colbie doesn't miss his disappointment.

She reaches for his hand and gives it a squeeze. "I'm not saying I don't want this or you, just give me time.

Humans have dating rituals and a whole courting process before they decide to make things official. Maybe it would be easier if we all had destined mates. It would certainly save a lot of heart break. Just give me time to adjust. I'm not going to reject you, I promise. There's this ball of want in me that is screaming at me to throw myself at you, but my brain still has some catching up to do. We'll get there," she promises, looking at each one of us in turn.

Her words seem to ease some of his disappointment and settle them all slightly. My life just changed in an instant, and although I'm thrilled to have a mate, my mind is reeling at the change. It's nice to have some company, and maybe I can be the support she needs, since I'm experiencing some life-changing moments as well.

"How about you show me this mysterious creature? We can work on getting your shift to happen smoothly and help you feel comfortable in a different skin," I suggest, and she nods at me gratefully.

"Sounds good. So how does it work?"

I gesture to the other guys. "One of them will be able to explain it better. My change isn't as drastic as an animal's. Once I hit the water, it just kind of happens. I don't have to think about it at all."

"Hmm, really? I guess there's no time like the present to see if the queen has a mer form." Before anyone can react, Liam tosses Colbie over his shoulder and strides to the water.

"What the fuck? Put me down!" she yells and bangs on his back with her fists, but they seem to do nothing. He just gives her a sharp slap on the bottom, which has her gasping.

"Settle, Your Majesty. This won't hurt a bit," he promises before tossing her into the water. There's a moment of silence before she screams.

"You fucking bastard!" The rest of the words are lost as she plummets into the icy cold water.

"Aw, dude, you've fucked up now. Even if you had won the race, there's no way you're going near her bed anytime soon," Brodie says as we rush to the side and watch to see what happens.

THIRTEEN

Colbie

I only have enough time to take a deep breath before I plunge through the surface of the pool. The freezing cold water steals the air from my lungs, and my body seizes up. I struggle to move as my body temperature plummets, and I start to panic, trying to claw myself to the surface, but my limbs refuse to cooperate.

My chest heaves with the need for air, and I try to toe off my shoes, but my legs refuse to move. Glancing upwards, I see the cloudy sky through the surface and pray it won't be my last sight, but then warmth pulses deep inside me, and power rushes through my body, wiping away the numbness. My pants shred, and my shoes fall to the bottom, then I look down and watch on in awe as a change occurs. Pain ripples through me as my legs fuse together and form a tail covered in pretty, shimmery pink scales, then a blinding pain slashes across my neck, like someone took a knife to either side. The

agony is too much, and I can't stop myself from screaming. As I part my lips and surrender to the pain, water
rushes into my mouth, but instead of drowning, fresh air
infuses my lungs, and they expand in relief. I feel around
for a wound, because a pain that bad must mean I'm
about to bleed out, but instead of a gaping lesion, I feel
gill slits. Holy crap.

Trying to make sense of everything, I look around in
surprise. My eyesight has sharpened, and I've stopped
descending. Instead, I'm suspended, my tail waving back
and forth gracefully, and I can't help but gape in shock.
That sure was a dick move by Liam, but it seems it was
effective. Fuck him, though, I plan on making him panic
a little. The longer I stay down here, the more they are
going to worry that I actually drowned. I wonder how
long it will take before they send Micah in to rescue me.
Stupid shifters don't realize how fragile humans actually
are. If I were still human, there would have been no
hope for me whatsoever. I would have gone peacefully to
a watery grave, but that asshole was right, and launching
me into the pond triggered my shift.

The material of my tank top floats around me with
the gentle current, so I peel it over my head, leaving me
in just my sports bra. I release the tank and let it drift to
the bottom of the pool, relieving myself of the tangled
fabric. I give my tail a little flick and shoot forward. Holy
crap, that thing has some power. I giggle, bubbles rising
to the surface above me. I'm a freaking mermaid. The
cold water is no longer affecting me, and I might go as
far as to say it's energizing. I feel more alert and focused
than I have since I first stepped foot into the palace.
Maybe the water has rejuvenating properties. I will have
to ask Micah.

I decide to explore my new underwater environment, letting the guys sweat for a bit. It only seems fair. I don't want them to start this relationship thinking I'm a rational, logical woman. Nope, I hold grudges, and there is nothing more terrifying than a woman with a grudge—Liam is going to find this out the hard way. I want to explore this pool, so I swim toward the churning water at the base of the falls. Fish dart away as I approach, making themselves scarce at the sight of a much bigger creature. I guess I'm at the top of the food chain now. I wonder how merpeople fare against sharks, or if they are still an apex predator in the ocean.

I reach the tumultuous, swirling water at the base of the falls and swim through it. The water pounds over my back for a brief moment, but instead of being painful, it's almost like a massage, and when I exit on the other side, the water is serene but much darker. Light from the sky has been blocked out by a rock formation, so I swim to the surface to get a better look. Sure enough, the sky is obstructed by a cave carved out of the rock, but the ceiling is high above the pool. Turning in a circle, I notice the pool ends, and there is an opening—a small space with a dirt floor and not much else—but then I notice a tunnel that leads further into the mountain. I consider trying to get out and explore, but I'm not sure how to make the tail go away. The first time I shifted, I returned to human form because I was exhausted. I can't do the same here and be stuck, unable to swim back out.

Turning to face the thundering wall of water, I notice there's a weird glow, something that looks unnatural as opposed to the filtered daylight from outside. It starts off small and grows larger, spreading out and up, and just as I begin to become concerned, a familiar woman steps out of the glow and walks toward me across the water. My mouth drops open in shock as I take in the now familiar form of the goddess. Her long blonde hair and fitted red dress are completely dry despite her having just stepped out of a raging waterfall. She giggles with delight at my surprise and passes me, stepping up onto the dry land, wrinkling her nose with disgust before waving her hand. A surge of magic shimmers over the area, and a cozy couch appears right in the middle of the dank cavern. She takes a seat, crossing one shapely leg over the other, then tilts her head and looks down at me, smiling.

"Hi, Colbie, how are things?" she asks casually, and I continue to gape at the woman who got me into all of this in the first place.

"Aramis?" I stammer, looking down at my body and wondering how I'm supposed to bow or curtsy or show whatever sign of respect she requires in this form.

"Call me Ari, and I think we're past the whole groveling at my feet thing," she tells me, obviously able to read my mind or something. The smile drops, and she becomes serious, leaning forward in her seat. "We need to have a little chat."

"We do?" I ask, and my heart races. What have I done wrong that could warrant a visit from the shifter deity?

"You've done nothing wrong. In fact, you've completely met my expectations. I'm so proud of you. You're already doing exactly what I hoped you'd do."

I frown, annoyed that she's pulling my thoughts straight from my mind. "So why are you here?" I ask bluntly.

She sighs heavily, and I see the heavy weight of responsibility in her eyes. My tail slowly flicks back and forth, keeping me on the surface as I wait for her answer. I kind of wish I could get out, but I don't know how to shift back, and if I could work it out, I'd be naked from the waist down. That isn't really how I want to have a heavy conversation with a goddess.

"First, I have to give you a little bit of backstory. When my sister goddesses and I created humans and all the supernatural races, we didn't want to rule over you like tyrants. We were lonely and wanted to have purpose in our never-ending existence. You were our beloved children, and we were thrilled when we saw you not only survive, but thrive. We allowed our creations autonomy to grow, asking for nothing in return. We gave our creations the freedom of choice, of self-regulation, hoping against all odds that they would coexist peacefully, and for a while, you did, but jealousy is an insidious power, and it easily corrupts. Humans hated that the supernatural races were more powerful than them and had longer lives, but then we gave humans the ability to procreate easily, unlike supernatural races. We thought it would create balance, but I guess we were delusional. War came, and so many people died, but we were powerless to do anything because we had given the freedom of choice and never forced obedience. That's when we came up with the idea of selecting a human every forty years to rule over the supernatural races if the humans gave up their fighting. Eryx had her doubts, but it was surprisingly effective, and the kingdoms were at peace once more."

I scoff. "The chance for one human to rule every

forty years was enough to stop a war?" I always had my doubts about that being the whole truth.

She shrugs. "The humans were losing badly. Supernaturals were stronger and had abilities that even human weapons couldn't match. Eventually, they would have been wiped out, and their leadership knew this, but humans are stubborn as a whole and were willing to die on the hill for their cause. This gave them an excuse to back down without losing face."

Ah, okay, this makes a lot more sense, but it's been conveniently spun so that humans don't look bad. That is unsurprising.

"And for hundreds of years, it has worked fairly effectively, but once again, humans are no longer happy. Like you said, it's only one human in each of the kingdoms who gets a chance to become more, and they are no longer happy with the status quo. They have forgotten how decimated their population became after the great war because their ability to procreate repopulated their numbers very quickly, and so once again, there are rumblings of war—not to mention a small portion of the supernatural population resent that a human is gifted with powers to rule over them. Things are changing, Colbie, and I'm not sure if there is anything I or my sisters can do to stop it this time around."

"But what can I do? Hell, I've been queen for less than a week. I'm hardly qualified to stop a revolution. Surely it would have been better to leave Lucas in charge if war is coming." I didn't think my heart could beat any faster, but it does, and my body tightens with tension.

"Lucas was a kind and just king, but he wasn't able

to unite the shifters like I hoped. You can do this. You've already made decisions that align with my goals. Inviting the mer, fairies, and equine shifters to join the council is the first step in repairing the relationships that have troubled the shifters for years. It's also why I gifted you with two more mates—mer and fairy shifters. You have already found your mer mate, and your fairy one will appear soon."

"And Nox is an equine shifter?" I ask the question that has been on my mind since I realized he was one of my mates, and we assumed I am able to shift into the same form as him.

"Yes. You will need to find him as soon as possible. You have forces working against you from both the humans and the shifters, and I can't physically interfere. Both of them have their own agendas, but for now, they are united in their quest to see you remain uncrowned. It is why I gifted you a fully formed bond group instead of marking random people. They would have been picked off one at a time until none remained for you to choose from, thus causing you to be uncrowned. You won't have access to your full range of gifts until that crown is on your head. I can't change that. You are in danger, Colbie. The faction of unrest will do what they can to kill you before you can be crowned in the hopes that they can then control the magic. For now, it is in limbo. Lucas no longer wields it, and neither can you. That crown and the book in the vault are the keys to the rebels' goals."

"The magic to change humans to shifters?" I ask, and she nods.

"Yes. If they can change humans without them becoming feral, then they can create their own army to defeat the shifters. They can also fix the feral shifters they already have in their ranks," she admits, and my jaw drops as she confesses the truth about feral shifters.

"They can be fixed?" I ask, my tone hard, and she nods sadly.

"Yes. The crown magic can fix a feral shifter, but it was decided long ago not to allow it so shifters didn't go around biting unwilling humans, and humans didn't go looking to be bit for the chance of possessing magic. It was a harsh but necessary decision to make execution the punishment to discourage these actions."

My anger recedes as I acknowledge the truth of her words, even if I don't like it.

Her eyes soften in sympathy, and she leans forward, resting her forearms on her knees. "I know this is difficult for you to wrap your head around, but I need you to seal the mating bonds as soon as possible. I have gifted you the most powerful form I could and gave you exceptional mates and the ability to share their forms, because you are my final human queen. You will no longer rule for only forty years. From now on, the reign of shifters will be the responsibility of your bloodline. Your first born child will be the heir to the kingdom, and once you decide to step aside, they will take over. After the rebel faction has been dealt with, humans will be given the choice to receive a bite from a shifter if they so wish it. We were wrong in creating two species that differ so drastically, but any human wishing to remain will also be granted their wish."

"Is this only happening here in Aramis or everywhere?" I ask, a thought niggling at me that I can't quite grasp hold of.

Her expression turns cold. "What my sisters choose

to do with their kingdoms is up to them. All I can do is ensure peace here in Aramis, although I will tell you the other kingdoms have their own struggles. The rebels seem to have infiltrated all four kingdoms and stirred up a revolution. Only the King of the Chaos Kingdom has been successful in retaining complete control, but he doesn't have humans to contend with. Although we have allowed our creations autonomy, to outright flaunt our directives has done nothing to endear us toward their agenda. We have never asked for anything but peace between the races and given them everything, and now they will know what comes from flouting our wishes."

"Extermination of a species? Surely that isn't the answer!" I argue, and she shakes her head.

"No, not extermination. Any human who wishes to remain so will have their wishes adhered to, but how many do you think that will be? Maybe the older generations. Becoming a shifter will not make them younger, but how many young ones will remain as such? As the ruler, you will oversee everyone, humans and shifters alike. I'm pretty sure their leadership didn't see this coming, and they will pay for their envy in ways they never saw coming."

Fuck, the goddess is sneaky. I need to make sure I never get on her bad side.

She tilts her head to the side like she is listening, and the anger drifts away. She smiles then stands, smoothing her dress down. "Well, I have to be going. This won't be the last you see of me. I expect you and I will get to know each other well over the coming years, but for now, seal those mating bonds and find those children. Cut the rebels off at the knees. Without access to the crown and spell book, they are just creating a bigger problem for themselves."

"I won't execute any of the ferals," I warn her. "Especially if they have been changed against their will."

She nods, looking pleased. "Of course you won't, but your fairy mate will be able to help you discern who did or didn't volunteer to be changed. Those rebels will need to be punished, but I will leave it to you to decide what that punishment will be."

My fairy mate? Violet didn't mention fairies have the ability to read minds.

"How do I seal the mating bonds? In my hydra form? That seems like it could be difficult."

Her smile turns mischievous, and her eyes sparkle with mirth. "Well, I mean you could shift into hydra form—you'll find you have eight heads now—and bite them all at once. A hydra bite will transfer your regenerative properties to them. Do you fancy having a nine-way orgy."

I blink, speechless at her suggestion. Nine-way orgy? In hydra form? What the fuck?

She chuckles, slapping a dainty hand against her thigh in amusement. "Colbie, you should see your face. You have a dirty mind. God, it's priceless." I see her struggle to get her shit together as I glare at her.

"That's not fucking helpful, you know. You're the one who did this to me and didn't include a manual."

She collects herself. "Yes, you're right, sorry. Shifters usually give their partner a mating bite during sex, but it isn't required. A lot of shifters don't mate the same species, so all you need to do is a partial shift of your jaw then bite them. Sex makes the experience better, more intimate, but as long as they do the same, then your bond will be sealed. If you bite them in hydra form, your regenerative properties will transfer to them, giving them all the protection they could need, but any form will do to seal the bond."

I mull over what she's told me and tuck it away for now. We're not even close to being in the sex portion of our relationship yet, though I can't deny my body doesn't long to get up close and personal with those men, even Micah who I literally just met. The ache is real, but my mind is still fully in the human way of thinking, and I've never been a one-night stand kind of girl.

"Anything else you'd like to drop in my lap?" I ask dryly, and she shrugs.

"Probably, but where would the fun be in that? You're about to have a visitor, so I will see myself out. Remember, I'm always watching, and if you need me, just call." She disappears in a flash of light, leaving behind the couch she was sitting on. Oh well, I guess the cave could use a little sprucing up. Fuck, I hope she's not always watching. That would be creepy.

CHAPTER
FOURTEEN

Colbie

A splash behind me has me spinning in a circle, and I gasp in shock when I find Micah staring at me, his eyes wide with wonder. "Holy shit, Liam was right. We have a mer as the shifter queen. People are going to lose their shit."

I hold up a finger. "One, we never admit Liam was right. That would be unbearable for all of us. Two, I'm not just a mer shifter. I think my main form is the one I first shifted into. Three, I would like to avoid people losing their shit if possible. Apparently, I have a challenge day to get through, and I have no doubt if everything I have been told is correct, then being a mer will get me challenged up the wazoo."

His smile drops, and he frowns. "Yes, you would be at a disadvantage. Challenge day takes place on land, so you wouldn't be able to shift. You would have to fight in human form, whereas any challenger could shift. I assume you don't have a lot of fighting experience."

I shake my head as we bob in the water. "None. Hell, I don't even exercise. The most I do is walk to work in the morning."

"I would offer to be your champion, but that would only prove you need someone to protect you."

I see the worry in his eyes, so I decide to put him out of his misery. "Don't worry about me. I'm lucky enough to have more than one form, remember?"

"Yeah, but you don't have enough time to master any of them, which is a disadvantage."

"Micah, once shifters see what my original form is, no one will challenge me for anything," I assure him.

"What are you?" he asks again, and this time I decide to answer instead of leaving him hanging.

"I'm a hydra." His reaction is so comical, I can't help but burst into laughter when his eyes widen and his mouth drops open.

"A hydra? Fuck," he mutters, running all the possibilities through his mind. "No one will challenge you once they know that."

I nod. "Yes, that's what we're all counting on, and if they do, well, apparently the hydra has a few tricks up its sleeve—poisonous claws and acid spit or breath to start with, not to mention the ability to regenerate. I'm basically indestructible. I just need to learn how to stay on my feet, which hasn't been very successful." I feel my cheeks heat with a blush, and he chuckles.

"That's okay. I'm sure you will get the hang of it quickly. You did with this form." He waves a hand at me. "You scared the crap out of the others when you disappeared."

I scowl. "Maybe Liam shouldn't have tossed me into the pond. That was a dick move."

"Definitely a dick move," he agrees, "but effective. Let's relieve their panic though. They were freaking out, thinking they killed their mate, and the others were about to send Liam to his own watery grave."

To be honest, I kind of feel the same way about Liam right now, despite our rather hot interaction outside of my bedroom, but as a polar bear, he probably wouldn't drown. I guess he's as comfortable in the water as he is on land.

He offers me his hand, looking hopeful, and as I place mine in his, I feel a pulse of happiness. He looks around the cave, and his eyes twinkle. "I wouldn't mind coming back here when we have more time. I'd like to show you all the pleasures of having a mer form." He winks, and my eyes widen with curiosity.

"What do you mean?" The water flows around us, and he glides toward me, wrapping one of his hands around my waist before pulling me against his muscular torso. Our tails brush below the surface, and I moan as a rush of sensation courses through my limbs.

"Holy crap," I murmur as he brushes our tails together again with deliberate, powerful strokes.

"Unlike animal shifters, who don't often fuck in their animal form because they're mates are not always the same creature, mers can and do. I can show you the pleasures of what being a mer mate is about. Our scales are designed to send signals to the brain, warning us of dangers in the ocean, but they can also amplify pleasurable sensations as well. I can bring you to orgasm just by brushing my tail against yours."

My breath becomes shallow, and my nipples prickle beneath my sports bra, becoming hard points. Micah's smooth torso brushes against my exposed skin, and all I want to do is rub myself against him like a cat. Instead, I sigh, knowing I need to prioritize having full control of my shifts before any pursuit of pleasure.

Rain check?" I ask hopefully, and although I see the disappointment in his eyes, he gives me a nod.

"Anytime. Let's go put your other mates out of their misery and work on getting you to shift seamlessly between forms. If you can do that, even if there is some idiot who wants to challenge your hydra, then showing you have access to nine different forms will leave no one questioning your ability to lead."

He slowly sinks below the surface, dragging me with him, and I hold my breath, my body tense with the unnatural idea of breathing underwater. Soon, the need to inhale overrides my compulsion, and water flows through my gills, expanding my lungs once more. That's going to take time to get used to. "

Micah leads me under the churning waterfall, and light returns to the depths as the sun shines through from above. When we surface not far from where Liam threw me in, the remaining five are arguing with one another, but that quickly comes to a stop when they spot us.

"Oh thank God." Brodie sinks to his knees and gazes at me with relief. "I thought he killed you."

Liam scoffs, and I notice he has a split lip that dribbles blood. "She's a hydra shifter. Even if she didn't have a mer form, they are just as much at home in the water as on land, you fucking asshole."

He swipes the back of his hand across his chin and smears the blood across his face, yet it makes him look even hotter. I flip him off, and he smirks at me, looking pretty pleased with himself, and my gaze drops to his mostly naked body. He catches where I'm looking, and his eyes narrow in challenge. His hands go to the waistband of his shorts before he shoves them down.

"How's the water? I wouldn't mind a swim myself." He steps forward, and I can't stop my gaze from going to the weapon that swings between his legs. Holy shit, is that even legal? There is no way that's going to fit inside me.

He chuckles darkly, noticing that I'm looking exactly where he wanted me to. He fists his cock, and something glints in the sunlight—a piercing. Well, that might be fun. He strokes up and down, and my creature rolls around inside me in delight.

"See something you like?" he growls, his bear in his tone. I drag my eyes away from the mesmerizing sight of him handling his dick and arch an eyebrow.

"Meh, I've seen better." It's a lie, but he doesn't like it. He throws his head back and roars. It's a sound I've never heard come out of a human's mouth before. His body starts to contort, and within moments, a huge polar bear is standing on the side of the pool.

"Oh fuck, you're in trouble now," Gem mutters, grinning like an idiot.

The bear stalks toward the pool, his black eyes locked on me. I swim backwards, but he just keeps coming, launching himself into the water. A squeak leaves my mouth as a large figure brushes past my tail. He swims a circle around me, and I spin to keep him in sight.

"Stay still, Colbie. If you swim away, he's going to take it as a challenge and treat you like prey," Gryffin warns, crouching down and watching Liam's path. "Liam's bear has been on edge for months now. One wrong move, and it will take the mating choice out of your hands."

I don't take my eyes off the swimming bear who paddles circles around my body, brushing against my tail with every pass.

"There isn't really a choice though, is there?" I ask. "The goddess took that out of our hands when she marked us for each other."

"Yes, but we can work with your timeline. We know this is all very new for you and won't rush you," Brodie promises, and I think back to what the goddess said. I need to seal the mating bonds as soon as possible for everyone's sake. Without them, I can't be crowned, and the shifters are vulnerable to someone else usurping the crown and the powers it holds.

Coming to terms with being mated to eight men may take me a little time, but I want to be queen now. I want to protect the shifters, and if I have to be mated to eight men to do it, I can think of worse things to have to endure.

I concentrate on the shifting power inside me, reaching down and trying to get a feel for it. When I shifted before, it was kind of subconsciously, but this time, I want to choose which form to take. Imagining the figure of a polar bear, I nudge the power. I feel it swell inside me, and my body shudders. With a blinding flash of light, I change, shredding my sports bra that was still covering my breasts.

My body reforms, and my consciousness recedes slightly, taking a back seat to an overwhelming animalistic nature. I growl and paddle my front paws, then I hear a commotion from the side of the pool and turn my large head to look.

"Holy shit. She turned into a polar bear! Now she's fucked. Liam's bear is going to go nuts." I'm pretty sure that's Hunter, but my instincts zero in on the large white figure still swimming around me. I throw my head back and roar before diving. My body brushes against Liam's, and he stops, his black eyes widening in surprise. He shoots to the surface, and it's my turn to swim around him. My huge paws cut easily through the water as I paddle around him. Just as I'm passing him, my jaw opens, and I latch onto his rear, biting down. The taste of his salty blood hits my tongue, and a thrill of accomplishment flows through me. I release him and push to the surface, gulping for air and roaring loudly.

"Is that blood in the water? Did she bite him?" The four men on the side of the pool look at Micah, and I watch him pop below the surface before returning.

"Yup, she took a chunk out of his ass," he confirms, and Gem chuckles.

"Oh, she's fucked now." Gem looks at me. "Pretty lady, you better start swimming. You just baited the bear, and he won't stop until you wear a matching set of teeth marks."

A thrill of excitement goes through me, and my bear preens with pride. I turn my gaze to Liam's bear. He's gasping for air and looking slightly befuddled. I swim closer and lick a stripe across his muzzle before nudging him. His black eyes narrow, and he grabs for me with his huge paws. I manage to evade them and slip from his reach, paddling away from him, the thrill of being pursued flooding my body with endorphins.

Liam roars behind me, and I hear furious splashing as he takes chase. I take a breath and dive, the sound of the waterfall becoming silent as I plunge deep into the pool. I can feel Liam on my tail, but despite him being bigger, he doesn't catch up to me. My smaller body becomes more streamlined as I glide through the water and under the falls. I'm almost certain I know where this is going, and I don't really want to end up naked on my back, being fucked in front of everyone just yet. I know I have eight mates, but all of them deserve for their first time with me to be special. I don't doubt that group sex will eventually become a thing, and I'm looking forward to it, but I've had enough changes in such a short period of time. I can ease into orgies.

I surface inside the pool behind the waterfall. The noise becomes deafening, but I don't stop. I paddle for the edge and try to haul my large body out of the water, but I slip and scramble for purchase, and that's when he strikes. I roar out in pain as his teeth dig into my hip, and his paws wrap around me, pinning me to the rocky edge of the pool. I roar my displeasure, but it turns into a whimper when a sudden wave of rolling desire turns my limbs into putty.

He removes his teeth and licks over his mark before he releases me and surfaces. I can't hold onto my shift any longer as pulses of need flood my system, and I shift back, finding myself naked, my chest heaving and core throbbing. I moan and press my thighs together to stem some of the pulsing want.

Liam surfaces, also in his human form. He looks at me with wide-eyed wonder. "You bit me?" It's like he can't believe I had the audacity to make the first move.

"Ah, yeah. Was that not what you wanted?" I ask, desire receding as panic starts to flood my system. Fuck, I'm an idiot. In my desire to get the job done, I didn't think about asking. I'm as bad as those people who are turning the ferals.

"You do know this means we're mated, right? There's no switching it off or changing your mind." He reaches for me but fists his hands like he's trying to resist touching me.

"Yes, of course, but I'm sorry I didn't ask," I say quietly.

"You want me? You really want me?" he asks, sounding confused. "You didn't do it by accident or because your bear made you?"

"Of course I do. You're my mate," I assure him. "And while it isn't what I've known, it feels right."

"Thank God!" He lunges for me, and his lips press to mine. He drags my body against his and kisses me like I'm the air he needs to breathe. Our lips and tongues clash in a frenzy of desire, the ring in his lip cold despite his body heat. His hands caress every inch of my skin, like he can't get enough. I wrap my body around him and feel his dick press against my core. I grind into him and moan as I slide my clit up and down his thick length, feeling that hard bit of metal in the tip.

"I'm going to fucking ruin you," he mutters against my lips before pulling away and climbing out of the water. I whimper as the heat of his body leaves mine, but I don't have to wait long, because he bends down and tugs me out of the water. Holding my hand, he guides me through the first cabin then down a tunnel, our footsteps muffled against the rocky floor. Both of us are breathing like we ran a marathon, and the sound echoes off the tunnel walls, the noise of the thundering waterfall fading behind us.

It's dark, and it takes a bit for my eyes to adjust, but

when they do, I see better than I've ever been able to before. Liam is in front of me, and I don't stop my gaze from roving over his toned, muscular backside. I catch sight of a bite mark that's still oozing blood on his left butt cheek, and the bear inside me roars her delight. We did that. We marked our mate, and nobody is taking him away from us. Fuck that bitch Gianna. I should have marked him in a place for everyone to see. I will make sure I do that as well.

The tunnel opens up into another cavern, and this one actually looks cozy. There is a pile of cushions lying on the floor that have white fur all over them. I guess this must be Liam's bear's nest. Farther back, though, there are a few couches and a large bed.

"What is this place? How did you get this furniture here?" I look around, searching for another entrance, but behind the bed is a solid wall.

"I come here when I need to get away, and I paid a witch for a transporting rune," he replies, stopping in front of the big bed. He rummages around in a large wooden chest at the end of the bed and pulls out a glass ball. Liam gives it a shake and throws it into the air. The globe floats in the air and pulses a blue light, illuminating the cavern. I shiver as a cool breeze wafts over my dripping body, and he turns back to the chest, grabbing a towel out of it. It's big, white, and fluffy, and he uses it to dry me off. His hands are gentle, almost reverent, as he runs it over me, his eyes not leaving mine.

He tosses it to the side and steps closer, so our chests are brushing together, and he cups my cheek.

"You mated me?" Despite the dim light, I can see him perfectly, and he stares at me with wonder, like all of his dreams have come true. It makes me feel amazing.

"Well, yeah. I kind of thought that was what you wanted." I drop my gaze to my feet and shuffle on the spot, feeling all kinds of awkward. Did I already mess this up?

He lifts my chin so I'm looking at him. "You made all my dreams come true, and now I'm going to show you exactly how good being my mate can be."

He scoops me up in his arms and tosses me onto the big bed. A small screech escapes me before I can stop it, but when I land, it's soft, and I practically sink into the mattress. I scramble back as he crawls up the bed, feeling like I'm about to be devoured. He smirks as he grabs my leg and tugs me toward him, spreading my body out across the bed.

"Look who's sleeping in my bed." He chuckles as I roll my eyes at the nursery rhyme reference. "Luckily she's exactly where I want her to be." He spreads my legs and looks at my naked body. Liam runs a finger through my dripping folds, and I shudder as he brings the same finger to his mouth and sucks it. "And her honey makes this bear's mouth water."

FIFTEEN

Colbie

He grabs both my ankles and tugs me closer, pushing my thighs apart as he leans in and licks a path up my thigh until he gets to my throbbing core. His hands slide under my ass and haul me up as he leans down and feasts on my dripping pussy. He sucks, licks, and circles my clit. I squeeze my eyes shut and throw my head back, gripping the sheets as my body is flooded with incredible pleasure. The ring in Liam's tongue feels amazing as it slides over my clit, every wet flick driving my desire higher and higher.

"You taste like my best fantasy," Liam mutters as he drags his tongue down to my entrance and thrusts it in, groaning as he makes love to my cunt with his mouth. He slides two fingers deep into my channel, scissoring them back and forth. "So tight. I need to stretch you so this doesn't hurt." He thrusts his fingers in and out, and my core starts to tighten as my body tingles, hovering on the edge of ecstasy. He pulls out and slides in a third, the pinch of pain adding to the pleasure, driving my achy cunt closer to orgasm.

"Oh my god, I'm going to come," I tell him, thrashing my head back and forth, stunned at how quickly he could get me there. He pulls away and lowers my ass to the bed again, and I open my eyes, glaring at him for stopping. He chuckles and wipes his mouth against my thigh before pressing a kiss to the bite mark on my hip and prowling up my body.

"Why the hell did you stop?" I demand as he hovers over my body, his hands pressed into the bed on either side of my head. His black eyes glow with his emotions, and he looks down at me with intense want and need. Gone is the cocky asshole, and in his place is a vulnerable man I had no idea he could be.

"Because I want to look into your eyes the first time I make you scream my name." My mouth drops open as his lips turn up in a smirk. I thought he was going to say something deep and meaningful, but I couldn't have been more wrong.

He reaches down and grasps his cock. My gaze follows his movements, and I lick my lips as I watch him slide his hand up and down his thick length, the ring in the end of his dick catching my eye. I can't wait to feel that inside me. Leaning forward, he sweeps the tip through the wet mess he made of my pussy, and I whimper with anticipation. He continues to tease me, smirking at me the whole time, and my inner animal gets pissed off. I growl at him, baring my teeth, before hooking my legs around his hips and driving my heels into his ass. He shouts with surprise and grunts as his cock slides into my pussy.

Finally, he gets with the program and stops the torture, pulling out and driving forward again in long, rolling thrusts.

"God, you're so tight. You're everything I thought you'd be and more. My greatest pleasure," he mutters as I feel the ring in his dick slide against my G-spot, spinning my orgasm even tighter.

"Yes, more," I beg as my hands grip his biceps, my heels still digging into his ass. "Harder, faster," I plead, and he doesn't make me wait. He kicks up the pace, and a bead of sweat drips from his chin onto my chest. I release his arms and grab the back of his head, gripping that shock of white hair, then drag his mouth down to mine. We kiss, a clash of teeth and tongue, as he continues to pound his thick length into my rapidly tightening core.

"God, Liam," I wail as he slides his hand between us and flicks my clit.

"Come for me, my queen," he commands, and just like that, I shatter. Pleasure ignites my nerve endings, and my body caves to his demands. Like a lightning bolt to my soul, a hurricane of sensations washes through me. I arch my back and scream as he continues to pound into me. I feel his teeth on my neck as he bites down again, triggering another release.

Feels so fucking good. Can't hold on any longer, echoes in my mind, and my eyes snap open in shock. Before I can mention hearing him inside my head, my creature's energy forces its way forward, and I shout in pain as my mouth reshapes. Just as Liam groans, and I feel him fill my pussy with his cum, I bite down into the straining tendons of his neck, drawing blood. He shouts again and pulls back, thrusting two more times. More warm ropes of heat fill my core until I feel it drip down the inside of my leg. I lick at the wound on his neck, his blood salty and flavorsome against my tongue, feeling smug and satisfied before my jaw reforms into its normal shape. I focus on what I just did. There is now a large bite mark on his neck, allowing no one to mistake that this man is mated.

"My mate," he murmurs, pressing a kiss to each of my cheeks before resting his forehead against mine. "I didn't hurt you, did I?" He looks down at the mark on my neck, running a finger over it, and I shiver at the sensation.

"No, it felt good," I tell him, and he smirks before sliding off me and gathering me in his arms, pulling me closer.

"I like seeing my mark on your neck," he tells me, and I roll my eyes.

"I'm pretty happy with mine on yours too, but I'm not sure if there's going to be enough room for all eight of you to mark me."

He frowns. "I don't know how mer or fairies mate, but I don't think it's through a bite. They should be able to tell you. As for Gem, he will mate you by marking you with his fire, so really you only need to worry about five bite marks, and that will make a pretty little necklace for our queen to wear." He sounds smug as shit, and I guess I know how he feels. The mark on his neck is way bigger than I thought it would be, but we are possessive of him and will kill anyone who tries to touch our mates. It's actually a big fuck you to Gianna, and I'm adult enough to admit it.

I'm snuggled into Liam's side, my mind lazy with an amazing after sex glow. His finger runs up and down my spine as we talk for a while, getting to know one another.

"What's your favorite thing to make at the bakery?" he asks, his finger sliding down to trace the bite mark I have on my hip. It's all healed now, and I shiver with a wave of need as he touches it.

"I really like the new marshmallows I just added to the menu." I sigh, knowing I'll never go back to the bakery. I haven't told him what the goddess said to me about me being the last chosen human. I'm waiting until everyone is together to break that news to them.

"You feel disappointed and sad," he says as he lifts a hand to his chest and presses down, like he can feel my sadness.

"Can you feel that?" I ask, pulling out of his arms and sitting up. His gaze drops to my breasts. "Hey, eyes up here." I point to my own, and when he lifts his gaze, he's smirking, and his eyes twinkle with laughter.

"Babe, you can't blame a guy for being distracted by such a lovely sight." I roll my eyes, and his smirk falls away as he sits up, turning serious. "Yeah, I can feel your sadness. If you concentrate, you can probably tell how I'm feeling as well."

I turn my attention inward, and I feel my animal inside me. While I'm in human form, they all seem to feel the same, unlike when I was in my bear form and it stood out against the others. Next to the shifter magic is a feeling of complete and utter contentment and love. It's unlike anything I've ever felt before. Sure, I know Granny and Grampy love me, and they've always shown me how they feel, but this is something different. It's pure acceptance in its rawest form, and it feels amazing.

"Wow," I sigh, but then I frown. "Will I be able to feel all of you? That could become overwhelming."

"To start with, you might." He reaches out and rubs my thigh, his calluses scratching slightly. "But soon you won't even notice, and only extreme emotions will filter through."

"I'm not worried. It's nice," I tell him, grabbing his hand from my thigh and giving it a squeeze.

"Why do you feel so sad?" he asks, sounding worried. "I thought you wanted this." He gestures between the two of us with the hand I'm not holding.

"Oh, I do," I assure him quickly, "but I'm going to miss my bakery."

He gathers me in his arms and drags me down to the bed, and I feel his relief. "I'm sure once we get settled into our new roles, you will be able to go back there from time to time, and have you seen the kitchen in the palace? I swear it's a chef's dream."

"I don't want to step on any toes by asking if I can use it," I explain, and he scoffs, the breath of air lifting a strand of hair that tickles my face.

"You're the queen, they can't tell you no." His tone leaves no room for argument, so I'll accept it for now.

Liam suddenly grows tense, tightening his hold on me, and a rumble comes from his chest. "What do you want?" he asks loudly, and when I turn my head, my eyes widen, and my heartbeat increases at the sight of the dripping wet white tiger who is stalking into the room. He pauses when he sees the two of us wrapped around one another.

He shakes his body, and drops of water fill the air around him, then he starts running.

"No, not on the bed!" Liam shouts, releasing me and jolting upright. He holds his hands out to stop the tiger, but it's too late. He takes a running leap and flies through the air, landing on the end of the bed, and stares down at me.

"Fucking hell, Gryff. Now you've soaked the sheets and are getting cat hair all over them, you asshole," Liam grumbles with disgust as the cat sits down on his haunches and then lowers even further, still staring at me as he rests his head on his paws. He doesn't even blink as he stares at me with those deep, ocean blue eyes that stand out against his white fur.

"Hi." I tentatively reach out, remembering how cuddly this cat was when I was in the stables the other night. I should feel self-conscious, since I'm naked and have Liam's cum still dripping down my inner thigh, but I don't. His gaze is hot and heavy, and there isn't one glimmer of disgust or aggression in his eyes.

He must think I'm taking too long to touch him, because he shuffles forward and butts his head against my hand, chuffing when I scratch behind his ear.

"Fucking needy cat," Liam grumbles, but when I look at him, although he's frowning, his eyes are smiling like he's trying to stop himself from laughing. The cat's tongue darts out, and then he scoots even closer to me, his head just about in my naked lap, but before I can push him, his tongue darts out, and he catches our combined release, which he eagerly licks up before moving toward my pussy. My eyes widen with panic, and I push his head away, but a hand comes out and smacks him on the nose.

"Bad kitty. Your tongue will strip Colbie's pussy, and then no one will be playing with it," Liam scolds the tiger who snarls at him, but he sinks back onto his haunches.

There's a pulse of magic in the air, and the tiger's body contorts and shifts into a very naked Gryffin. He grins at me like a naughty child, but his eyes sparkle with heat and desire. He's still lying on his stomach, but my hand is now threaded through his black streaked silver hair. I go to pull my hand away, and he reaches out to stop me.

"Don't stop, it feels nice," he tells me, closing his eyes and leaning into my touch. I continue to run my hand through his wet hair, being careful not to catch it in any knots.

"What are you doing here?" Liam asks, leaning back, comfortable with his nudity.

"You've been gone for hours, and it's getting late. Although Colbie shifted into two new forms today, she needs to work on her primary form as well," he tells us without opening his eyes. I'm pretty sure if Liam invited him, he would climb into bed with us and remain here for the rest of the night, but unfortunately, too many people are relying on us at the moment. Maybe one day we can return to the cave and have some fun, when I don't have so many issues waiting for me to deal with.

I give him one more scratch behind the ear before stretching my arms and arching my body. I'm so comfortable and relaxed, I'm reluctant to leave, but duty calls. When I open my eyes again, both men are staring at my naked body.

"You guys have a little drool here," I tease, swinging my legs to the side and looking around, but then I remember I have no clothes. Well, fuck.

"How about we head back to the pool, and you can try shifting into your tiger form for the swim back to the other side?" Liam suggests, nodding at Gryffin who quickly bounces up off the bed. Holy shit. These men have incredible bodies. Gryff isn't as bulky as Brodie, Hunter, or Liam, but he still has a body made for sin, all sinewy muscles and silky smooth skin. My eyes drop lower, and holy shit, it must be a shifter thing to have a huge cock. It's at least nine inches and rapidly hardening. He looks down at it and shrugs unapologetically.

"You're my mate, and you're naked. I wouldn't expect any other result anytime soon," he tells me. "I can't wait to see your tiger, cookie. Do you need me to go first and show you?" He tilts his head to the side in a very feline movement, and I appreciate the fact that he ignored my blatant ogling of his body.

"Yeah, okay, show me your cat again and tell him to keep his tongue to himself." Gryffin's smile drops in disappointment, and I quickly add, "For now."

He smiles, and I watch as his body contorts once more, fur sprouting over his skin as his body elongates and shifts.

"Doesn't that hurt?" I ask Liam, and he shrugs.

"Not really. We've been doing it for as long as we can remember. The mythical shifters say it's agony the first few times they shift, but they adjust quickly and it becomes second nature. Yours doesn't hurt, does it?" he points out, and I wave a hand as Gryffin completes his shift, and his cat prowls around my legs, bumping into them. I'm almost knocked off balance. I grab for his back to steady myself, and he chuffs like he's laughing.

"No, but it doesn't feel like that looks. One moment, I'm me, and the next, I'm something else."

"Yes, your shift does look very different from ours. It's like the magic explodes out of you, reforming your body at the same time. I wonder why that is…"

"Probably because the goddess just had to add one more thing for me to worry about," I grumble, and there's a tinkling of laughter that echoes around the cavern. Liam looks around, fully alert for any danger, while Gryffin plants himself in front of me and doesn't move, a low growl coming from his chest.

"It's okay, the goddess is fucking with me, ignore her," I assure them, running my hands over his thick tiger fur. He really is gorgeous, white with black stripes and black tipped ears that are freaking adorable as he flicks them back and forth, searching for the source of the laughter.

"Not sure you should be talking about the goddess like that," Liam says as he approaches me and tugs me back into his arms, giving me a kiss. "I don't want to leave, but I know we have to. Promise me we'll come back again."

I melt into his arms, and Gryffin's tiger paws at my leg, missing my delicate skin with his claws.

"Of course we can come back. You'll sleep in my bed tonight?" I ask him, suddenly not so sure of what the protocol is, but I know I'm reluctant to let him out of my sight.

Liam beams at me. "You couldn't keep me away. I'm sure your bed is probably big enough for all of us, right?" I think about my room, and although the bed is big, I'm not sure it will fit me and eight mates, but it's definitely big enough for Liam, Hunter, and Micah, who won the earlier bet.

"Maybe not eight of us, but it's fine for tonight," I assure him before turning my attention to Gryffin, who is looking at me with round, pleading eyes.

I bend down and whisper in his ear. "You'll get your turn soon," I promise him, and it seems to do the trick. He spins and bounds off playfully, and Liam puts his hands on his hips and nods at me.

"Your turn."

I'm slightly distracted by his beautiful body, but I shake my head and turn my attention to the task at hand. I find the deep well of magic inside me and picture Gryffin's tiger in my mind. There's a flash, and I squeeze my eyes shut. When I open them again, I'm bigger and furry and on four paws. My tail twitches behind me as I take my first careful step. A roar echoes around the cavern, and a flash of white comes barreling toward me.

"Fuck!" Liam shouts and quickly moves out of the way as Gryffin pounces on me, taking me to the ground where he pins me with his giant front paws and starts grooming me with his tongue. Long licks sweep across my nose and ears as he rumbles his happiness.

My butt twitches, and my tail flicks as my tiger considers wrestling him, but after a couple of strokes of his tongue, she settles down, happily enjoying the care her mate is showing her. What a freaking pushover. Though it could be worse, she could take a chunk out of him, and then I'd be stuck fucking Gryffin for the next however many hours. I can't say I'm not tempted to give her a nudge, but I know we don't have time. Damn my morals.

"Oh, for fuck's sake," Liam grumbles and pushes Gryffin's tiger, but he doesn't move. "Jesus, dude, what the fuck have you been eating? You weigh a ton. Get off our mate. She needs to practice shifting."

Gryffin gives me one more lick and releases me, prowling back and forth and nudging me with his head impatiently. I gingerly get to my feet, unsure of myself, but it all comes naturally. Just like being a polar bear in the water, being a tiger on dry land feels right. I take a step, testing myself, and when I don't stumble, I take another. Gryffin stands next to me, his body brushing against mine like he's going to catch me if I stumble. The two of us follow Liam back down the tunnel to the waterfall. Liam shifts into his bear and gives us both an affectionate headbutt before flinging himself into the water and disappearing. We pause at the edge of the pool, but when Gryffin just leaps in and starts paddling, we follow him, trusting the two of them will keep us safe.

My tiger swims just as well as my bear did. The giant, saucer-sized paws move through the water, propelling us forward. We close our eyes and lay our ears flat as we go under the rushing wall of water, but when we come out the other side, we blink owlishly at the bright light, shake our head, and keep going.

"Finally," Brodie calls from the edge of the pool. Micah, Gem, Brodie, and Hunter are all seated under a tree, but at the sight of us, they stand up and come over.

"Nice, a tiger form too. That makes all but my dragon and Gem's phoenix, but we will have to try them another day. I don't think flying in the dark for the first time is the smartest idea, and we only have another hour of daylight." Hunter looks up at the sky, and when I follow his gaze, I see the sun has dipped below the tree line. "We probably have enough time for you to change to the hydra and get a feel for it."

I start to swim toward the edge, but Gem puts his hand up. "Why don't you change in the water? The hydra is amphibious, so it should be just as at home in there as on land. Probably more so because its body is so large."

Liam and Gryffin climb out and shift, and Brodie tosses them both a pair of shorts. My tiger licks her lips at the sight of their asses. She wouldn't mind giving Gryffin a matching mate mark to Liam's, but I manage to convince her to wait.

"Wow, you mated." Brodie points at the silvery healed mark just before Liam covers it with his shorts, then to the one on his neck, whistling with wide eyes. "She really marked you up. There's no mistaking that in the least. Congratulations, man, I'm so happy for you. How does your bear feel?" He grabs Liam and hugs him, and Liam beams at him with pride.

"My bear is the most settled he's been in years," he replies, rubbing his chest. "I feel... peaceful, and so fucking lucky." He looks at me with hearts in his eyes, and my tiger wants to preen at his attention, but instead, I think about becoming the hydra. I can't really picture it in my mind, but I pay attention to the biggest presence inside my well of magic and allow it to take over. Again, there's a flash of light, and I close my eyes, but when I open them, my vision is distorted and multi-focal, and it's disorienting. I look down on the guys despite still being in the pool, and they all stare up at me with awe. My hydra body is huge and towers over them.

"Holy shit, a hydra. That's incredible," Micah mutters as he steps closer.

"Didn't she only have six heads before?" Hunter asks, frowning at me, and Brodie nods.

"Yeah, she did. Now she has eight."

"Well, she has eight mates now too. I think maybe it correlates," Gem suggests, waving a hand at me. "Have a swim and then try to climb out. You need to get a feel for how that body moves. I'm not sure how helpful it will be in an enclosed environment. It would destroy most buildings, like Hunter's dragon."

I take his advice and swim around the pool. Thankfully it's deep and wide so I can get used to the feeling of using this form in the water, but it's still weird. All the heads seem to act independently of one another, and unlike my other forms, I am pushed right to the back of my consciousness, all eight minds taking over completely. I'm just along for the ride.

We finally emerge from the depths, lumbering up onto land to test our coordination. I find if I try to take over, there's a lot of stumbling, and it's kind of a disaster when we fall into a large tree, knocking it down, but if I let them do what they wish, it's a lot more successful.

"Holy shit, she's a fucking beautiful disaster," Micah says after I untangle myself from the destroyed tree.

"Colbie." Hunter approaches me, and one of my heads ducks down to nuzzle his chest. He startles and gapes at it for a moment before reaching up and scratching us between our eyebrow ridges. That head rumbles with pleasure, and all the other heads duck down to try and home in on the affection. "I can shift my dragon's size at will to allow for smaller spaces. Why don't you imagine yourself smaller? Hopefully you have the same kind of magic," he suggests, chuckling as he tries to give each head a scratch.

Obviously my hydra understands what he is suggesting, because I feel a tingle of magic, and I'm suddenly much closer to the ground and everything seems bigger. Hunter smiles at us.

"Good girl," he praises as the others approach.

"Huh, she's about the size of a horse now. That was a good idea, Hunter," Gryffin says as the others join us. Each of the heads turn their attention to one of the guys, all trying to grab some affection. They willingly give them the love they crave, and soon, all eight of them are purring weirdly.

"Come on, we have just enough time to get back to the palace before dark. Do you want to run back like this, Colbie? Or do you want Hunter to give you a lift again? You must be exhausted. Shifting takes a lot out of you when you aren't used to it," Micah asks. "There's a shirt in the box I can grab for you so you won't be naked if you want to shift back."

A trill of acceptance comes from one of the heads. Micah moves to the chest, pulling out the item of clothing as I feel another rush of magic, and I'm on two feet again. I stumble, but Liam jumps forward, wrapping his arm around my waist to steady me.

"Easy," he cautions. "It's disorienting the first couple of times." I'm suddenly aware I'm naked in front of all of them, but Micah is quick to hand Liam the shirt, and he helps me into it. It must belong to a male, because it's so long it just about sits at my knees.

"How are you feeling?" Gem asks, a frown of concern marring his brow.

I take stock of my body, and a wave of exhaustion washes over me.

"Tired and hungry," I tell him, and he nods.

"That's normal. Come on, let's get you something to eat, and hopefully there are no events planned for the night and we don't get ambushed by the council at dinner."

"She's the queen, so even if they are, she can tell everyone to fuck off," Brodie says, crossing his arms, and then a smile lights his face. "Double or nothing. First person back to the palace gets to spend the next two nights in Colbie's bed." He turns and starts running, and I watch in awe as he shifts on the fly. One moment he's a man, and the next, he's a black and gray wolf who quickly disappears into the forest. The guys exchange a glance, and Liam and Gryffin do the same thing, their tiger and bear following quickly after Brodie.

Gem rolls his eyes, but in a flash of fire, he shoots into the air.

"Cheating assholes," Hunter grumbles before stepping back and shifting. All of them have completely shredded the shorts they were wearing, and Micah and I gather the bits up, tossing them into the chest by the large tree. We scramble up Hunter's side and onto his back, and with a flap of his wings, we are airborne.

SIXTEEN

Earlier in the day

King Lucas

After lunch, my wives decide they need to make some changes to Colbie's suite. If she is going to have eight mates, then she's going to need more space, so they hurry off to make arrangements. Hopefully the magic took care of that too, but Colbie didn't mention anything earlier, so they want to check.

I don't want anything to do with that, so I head toward my office, or I guess Colbie's office, to clear out my personal items and transfer them to a new office. My family will move into the other wing of the castle once the councilors get their notice to vacate. I can't say I'm going to be sad to see them go. Most of them have been a thorn in my side since I first received the mark, constantly shooting down my ideas of making shifter society more inclusive.

I haven't been as successful as I would have liked,

and I'm hoping Colbie's suggestion to add a member of each race to the council will go far in bridging that gap. The equines made their home in a settlement on the far edges of the shifter kingdom in the hopes they would be left alone. I'm not sure how successful they were. It isn't right, they should be welcome wherever they want to live and not have to uproot their lives and make new ones because of some antiquated ideas about prey versus predator animals. The equines are just as fierce, even if they don't have claws or fangs.

My office smells like leather and ink as I take a seat in the large leather chair behind my desk. I sigh, rubbing a hand across my face. I'm tired, and I am not sad about stepping aside. There was so much I wanted to do during my rule, and the council blocked me at every turn. I'm happy to see the back of it, but I'm also happy to be able to support Colbie with her reign. Maybe with Mia, Sable, and me replacing the current council, we will be able to push for the initiatives I wanted, but was constantly blocked from doing. If only we had known how restrictive they would be when I first started my reign.

Standing up, I go over to a cabinet, pull out a crystal decanter, and pour myself a glass of whiskey, adding a couple of ice cubes from the machine next to it. Our staff keeps my office well stocked, knowing I regularly need a drink after dealing with the council, and I'm just taking a sip when my office door flies open.

"What is the meaning of this?" Vallen Tideman waves a piece of paper wildly in the air. His eyes blaze with fury, and I see fur ripple across his arms like he's trying to control his shift.

"Come in, Vallen," I invite dryly, gesturing to the

chair in front of me. "Would you like a drink?" I hold up my glass of whiskey, though I'd rather spit in it than offer him any, but I need to keep the peace for now.

"No, I don't want a drink," he snarls as he stalks farther into the room, still grasping the piece of paper in his hand like it's going to stab him. "I want to know what the fuck this is!"

He slams it down on the desk, and I sigh before moving over to look down at it, taking a sip of my whiskey as I do. The smoky warmth soothes my body slightly as I look over the information. My eyebrows jump when I read what's on it. It's a copy of the missive Gracelin sent out to the mer, equine, and fairy communities, inviting them to submit representatives for the council positions.

"How did you get your hands on this?" I ask him suspiciously. This information hasn't been made public yet, nor has the council been advised of the queen's decision. She was going to tell them at the same time she relieved them of their positions. We obviously have a loose-lipped employee, or he's paying someone to funnel him information—probably the latter, if I'm honest. I'm not surprised.

"It doesn't matter. I will not work on a council with inferior shifters on it," he declares righteously.

"I don't think that is really going to matter," I reply vaguely, moving around to my seat and sitting down. He doesn't know he's being replaced yet.

"The council has always had six members. Expanding it goes against tradition," he argues, slamming his hands down on the desk and staring down at me like he's trying to intimidate me. It doesn't work. I may have lost some of the magic that made me a ruler, but I am still more powerful than this slug of a man.

I raise an eyebrow and take another sip of my whiskey, refusing to be cowed. "There are no rules governing the number of council members. That is a decision for the crowned ruler."

He sneers. "The crowned ruler? Have the queen's mates shown up yet? She can't and will not be crowned until those mates appear. That is very clear in the rules."

I place my glass down on the desk, holding his gaze. "It doesn't matter if she has been crowned yet or not. She wears the marks, so she is the queen, and as such, she decides on the members of her council. If she wants to add new ones or replace current ones, that is completely up to her."

I didn't think his face could turn any redder, but it does, and again, a wave of fur ripples across his face before he locks it down. He really is very close to wolfing out. I bet the thought that he would shred his thousand dollar suit is the only thing keeping him contained.

"We'll see. She isn't crowned yet, and with the way it's going, she's never going to be. No mates have presented themselves. I wouldn't get too comfortable with her. She's weak and doesn't have mates to protect her, and the challenge day is still to come, so she could very well find herself in trouble."

He isn't subtle with the threat in the least, and I could summon one of Bryson's teams to have him arrested, but I'm much more interested in seeing this play out. I can't wait to see his face when he finds out my son and his bond group are her mates and that she now has eight of them, not to mention that she's a hydra shifter. I can't wait to see his face on challenge day. I pray to the goddess that he challenges her. I'd love to see his face when he finds out what creature she is.

"Careful, Tideman. You're walking a fine, treasonous line with those words. I have every right to call for your arrest." I stand up to my full height, which is slightly taller than him.

He scoffs but steps back. "Nonsense. Challenge day is for her to prove she can protect us against anything that may endanger the shifter race. If she's not up to the task, then it is a shifter's right to challenge her."

"Yes, it is, but if something were to happen to her between now and challenge day, then you will be the first person I look at," I warn him, and he snatches the piece of paper off my desk.

"This isn't over. I'll be informing the rest of the council of her choices. She might not like what the consequences of her actions are," he threatens before storming out of my office, slamming the door behind him as he goes.

"Fuck!" I run my fingers through my hair before dropping down into my comfy leather seat. "He's going to be a problem," I mutter.

"Yes, he is." The voice comes from the corner of the room, and I startle, spilling my drink I had just picked up.

A man steps out of the shadows, and my eyes widen. "Holy fuck, Titus, you scared the shit out of me," I snap at the Chaos king's assassin and spy, who wears a smirk on his face. "How long have you been there?" I ask him, knowing I hadn't seen him when I first entered the room.

He shrugs. "Since you arrived," he admits. "So your new queen is going to replace your current council?" he asks, pulling a book out of the bookcase and slowly flipping through it.

I watch him closely. Titus has been my contact with the Chaos king for the last few years since his predecessor decided to retire. The Chaos king has a league of assassins who spy for him, and he has one assigned to each kingdom. Titus is mine and chose to make himself known to me so we can share information with one another at the blessing of the Chaos king. Titus is a half fairy shifter, half fae, which is why he was assigned the shifter kingdom. His mother is a fairy shifter who fell in love with a fae and chose to leave for the Chaos Kingdom so they could be together. He's tall and slender and has pointy ears like a fae with long pale green hair, which I assume is from his father. I haven't seen him in his fairy form, but the man is a living, breathing weapon with knives strapped all over his protective black leathers.

He puts the book back on the shelf and helps himself to my bar, pulling out his favorite fae wine, which I keep specifically for his visits.

"Yes, she is," I confirm when he doesn't ask anything else. "Queen Colbie may be just what this kingdom needs—a breath of fresh air," I tell him. "She sent missives to the mer, fairy, and equine shifters, inviting them to submit candidates for council representation.

"And how does she feel about the Chaos Kingdom?" he asks, taking a sip of his pale purple wine while holding my gaze.

"We briefed her on it this morning, and she seemed agreeable to the concept. I didn't mention our relationship yet. She has enough to contend with without knowing that a fairy assassin is her contact with the Chaos Kingdom."

He studies me carefully, and I watch him consider what information he will choose to impart to me today. While it took a period of time, I have come to trust that Titus has both the shifter and Chaos kingdoms best interest in mind.

"There is word on the breeze that a hit has been put on the queen. The assassin's guild was offered a significant sum to take care of the problem," he tells me, and my heart starts to race in panic. The assassin's guild very rarely fails to complete their tasks. My hand tightens on the glass I'm holding, and he doesn't miss the movement.

"And what did the Chaos king decide?" I ask, trying to come up with a plan to keep Colbie alive. Her hydra has regenerative properties and is nearly immortal, but I doubt it carries over into her human form, otherwise the humans would not have been able to kill them off during the previous war.

He takes another slow sip of his drink. "The king chose to decline the offer. He doesn't want any trouble with the monarchs of any of the kingdoms. In fact, he issued a warning to anyone who may try to assassinate the queen that retribution would be swift and final."

I can't control my reaction, and my eyebrows jump in surprise. "He did?"

He nods, slowly putting his feet up on my desk. I scowl at them, but his boots aren't muddy, so I let it slide this time. "Yes, you could say our king has a vested interest in your queen's well-being. In fact, he would like to meet her. He has issued an invitation for her to dine in the Chaos Kingdom, and it would be in her best interest to do so." I can hear the threat behind his words, and I don't like it.

I jump to my feet, spilling my drink on my hand, and slam the glass down on the table. "For Aramis's sake, Titus. The queen has enough to worry about without receiving an invite from your king. We have the fact that she's missing mates and can't be crowned, missing shifter children that need to be found, and a damn problem with someone creating ferals, and you heard that cretin. The council will be gunning for her now too." I pace back and forth behind my desk, and he watches me with curious eyes.

"Lucas, it isn't like you to overshare. You usually keep everything close to the chest."

I scoff and throw my hands up. "Like you assholes don't know all of that already." I face him, putting my hands on my hips. "Do you deny it?"

He purses his lips and hums. "No," he answers slowly. "You are right, we are aware of all your internal issues." He stands up, throwing back the last of his wine and placing the glass on my desk. "The queen is still missing mates? I was under the impression that she found them."

Again, I'm surprised, but this time, I manage to keep my reaction to myself and think about what I should share regarding the recent wave of magic. I consider keeping it to myself, but I don't doubt the whole damn kingdom will know soon. "The goddess felt it necessary to award Colbie two more mates earlier this morning. One has made itself known to us, and the other remains a mystery. Until that shifter comes forward, Colbie can't be crowned. We are also searching for the whereabouts of one other. Although we know who he is, he has yet to be notified."

He waves his hand and pulls a long, black hooded cape out of the air, swinging it around his shoulders. "I must go, but make sure the queen visits my king. He may have an answer to your feral problem."

"Does the Chaos Kingdom have something to do with our missing children and feral issue?" I have to ask, even though I am fairly certain they have nothing to do with this.

He gives me a look that would make a lesser man piss his pants. "I will forget you ever asked that in the name of continuing good relations between our kingdoms. I can assure you that our king detests abuse toward children as much as, if not more than, all of the other kingdoms combined. Do not forget how our kingdom came to be. We are the outcasts and rejects your kingdoms deemed unworthy."

I wince at his accusations. He isn't wrong. I'm not sure which generation of kings and queens declared cross matings illegal, but it's another thing I have been trying to change the laws on. I'm sure Colbie will continue my fight once she is crowned, and seeing the good people of the Chaos Kingdom would be a step in the right direction.

I incline my head in apology. "I will see to it that she makes time to visit King Loki."

"Sooner rather than later," he warns before he disappears in a flash. Titus obviously got his ability to teleport from his father. Usually, children from cross pairings favor one parent or the other. On a rare occasion, like him, they take on characteristics of both parents and are a force to be reckoned with. I believe this is probably why cross mating was prohibited. The children of such matings can be very powerful.

I grab my glass and pour another generous amount of whiskey into it before flopping back in my chair again. "Fuck, I haven't drunk this much since my own coronation," I mutter, taking a large sip and closing my eyes. Poor Colbie. Her reign is going to be anything but easy. I should stock the office bar for her. It seems like she's going to need it.

SEVENTEEN

Titus

Sifting out of Lucas's office, I decide to follow the irate councilor and see if I can catch him scheming. I spend a lot of time hiding in the shadows of the shifter castle. I arrived earlier in the day once news of the new queen's arrival reached Chaos Kingdom. King Loki dispatched me at once with an order to gather information. Concealed in the shadows—an ability gifted to me by my fae father—I listened in on the luncheon conversation. Learning that the queen was gifted a bond group instead of having to choose from a group of individuals was enlightening to say the least. The information about her knowing who the missing member of Watch Group One was interesting, and something I tucked into the back of my mind to address later. With the appearance of her mer mate, the final member of her bond group was revealed to me, but they still have no clue who the missing member is.

I rub the spot on my sternum where my new marking throbs beneath my skin. It takes a lot to shock me, but when that mark appeared on my chest after the wave of magic, even the clumsiest of assailants could have caught me unaware. I never expected to be gifted a mate, and I'm not really sure what to do with the revelation now. I'm one of five assassins and spies who work directly with the Chaos king.

Loki handpicked me and my brothers from the academy all Chaos children attend. A lot of half-breeds will inherit the traits of only one parent, but about thirty percent of us end up with dual powers, and learning to get a handle on them requires discipline and training. My brothers and I were five of the strongest, and Loki decided we were meant for more. He assigned four of us to each kingdom and kept one to be his internal spy master.

I've been Aramis's liaison for five years. Loki has a special interest in each of the kingdoms—a task set for him by the four kingdoms' goddesses. They knew a time of upheaval was coming and set wheels in motion to combat the unrest many years ago. Although they are supposed to give their creations free will, it hasn't stopped them from meddling and manipulating to get the outcomes they desire, and Loki was the key to achieving their outcomes. I just hope he can be forgiven for his actions when the time comes.

I follow the agitated wolf, but when he stops to speak to the young prince, I leave, wanting to spy on the queen and her mates. I don't know what kind of shifter she is, and I would like to give that information to my king when I return to the Chaos Kingdom to report.

I sift from the palace to the forest close by the waterfall where they were taking the queen to shift. I stay down wind so their sensitive shifter noses can't scent me and lean against a tree, listening to their conversation. Four of Colbie's mates are sitting under a tree not far from me, talking about heading into the human zone to find the other shifter mate. I sneak a little closer and learn that he lives in the same village as the new queen's grandparents in a secluded cottage. A quick phone call to the king will tell me which village that is, and from there, it will be a piece of cake to find him. That's where I'm going to head next. I want to scope out this other mate. From what they are saying, it sounds like he's probably not going to be too happy he is the queen's mate, even though it sounds like they have a prior relationship. I feel a little guilty not revealing myself as her final mate. The ache inside me keeps nudging me to do just that, but I owe the king my report and an explanation. I'm pretty sure he didn't expect to lose one of his prized assassins permanently to another kingdom, but I won't split my loyalty between her and him. I'm not sure how he's going to take it. Hopefully he won't decide to get rid of me, because then there will be no chance for her to become queen.

King Loki's grandfather was a ruthless asshole who was as judgmental and biased as the former kings and queens who originally outlawed mixed races. He refused to be open to the idea of trading with the other kingdoms. Ten years ago, when Loki took the crown from him, life in the Chaos Kingdom got better. Loki negotiated trade treaties with all four kingdoms and opened our borders, allowing for other kingdoms to travel to ours to enjoy all the pleasures it has to offer, and our kingdom finally started to flourish. We're still a dirty little secret as far as the humans knowing about us, but we like it that way. There is no place for the humans in our kingdom. If a human were to overindulge and end up on the wrong side of a supernatural, it would end in war.

Movement in the pond draws my eyes, and I find a polar bear swimming toward the bank, followed by a white tiger. That's the white-haired pierced asshole of the group and the prince. I've always kept an eye on Watch Team One since all of them live in the palace. They don't know about me, but I know everything there is to know about them, and I can admit they are perfect mates for the queen. They are a powerful bond group with their mixture of animals. Even the new addition of the merman is a benefit. He is a fierce fighter and well respected in General Bryson's army, despite his usually sneered at designation.

Another white tiger follows them out, and I watch as it moves closer. "Finally," the wolf shifter calls, sounding exasperated. I wonder how long they've been in the cave and what they were doing back there. The queen's a tiger? Huh, I hadn't expected that she would be the same as the previous king, though there is no denying that a tiger is a strong predator and a good animal for a royal to have.

The dragon says something, but a gust of wind blows the words away from me. I consider trying to creep closer to hear better, but I don't want them to catch sight of me. The bear and tiger shift and climb out, and I get my answer as to what they were doing behind the waterfall. Liam's neck has a shiny new scar on it from a mating bite. It looks like he was mauled, and so does one of his butt cheeks, which I see when he pulls on the shorts one of the others tosses at him. My gaze drifts to the prince, but he doesn't have any mating marks on him yet. That's interesting.

There's a sudden flash of purple magic, and I blink, stunned speechless, when Colbie emerges from the wave of magic as a huge, eight-headed fucking beast that towers above her mates, her blue body still in the water. Holy shit. My heart races as I take in the sight before me. The queen is a multi-shifter, and one of her forms is the legendary, hard to kill hydra. I bet Lucas would laugh his head off if he could see me now. He kept that one close to his chest. I wonder if he was going to tell me or let me find out when it became common knowledge to the kingdom.

She swims around the pool, and I'm amazed at her elegance in the water, which is nothing short of spectacular. Finally, she lumbers out of the pond, and it turns into a beautiful fucking disaster. She stumbles and falls, crashing down into a tree not far from where I'm hiding, sending branches flying. I stifle a yelp and duck deeper in the trees as her mates hurry to help her, the dragon suggesting she attempt to change size. I don't wait around to find out if she can or not. I don't want anyone to find me spying on them. I will meet them when they visit the Chaos Kingdom as requested. I'm sure Lucas will see to it that the king's demand is passed onto them. By then, I will be ready to take my place by her side.

I sift to the neutral zone. I want to check out the cafe the queen used to run before she was marked. It's late in the afternoon, and there aren't a lot of customers in it when I enter. I overheard her mates talking about her grandparents being here to run it, and they are worried that her mother, who is a real piece of work, will cause trouble for them and the queen, so I'll do my thing and pretend to be a nosy shifter to gather more information. I allow an illusion to wash over me, hiding my black assassin leathers and cape, showing an image of a casual tourist in a pair of jeans and a cozy sweater. There is plenty of snow close to the rift, but it isn't quite cold enough here yet, although it won't be long.

I pull open the door to the bakery and head in. A couple sits in one of the booths, and a small family sits at another table, but the rest of the bakery is quiet. There's an older human gentleman behind the counter drying a couple of mugs, and he looks up as I walk in and smiles.

"Are you here to dine in or take away?" he asks pleasantly.

"I could eat," I tell him, and he nods to the seating area. "Grab a table, and I'll bring you a menu. You're just in time, we're about to close up the kitchen."

I follow his instructions, and before long, he is standing at the table with a menu in hand. "Can I get you something to drink?" he asks, placing the menu on the table.

"How about a coffee with a couple of those cute marshmallows floating in it?" I ask, having heard all about the cute gimmick the queen has going on in here.

"Sure thing. Any particular critter?" the man asks.

"Surprise me," I tell him, and he gives me a wink and heads back to the counter. I hear the coffee machine grind beans and the hiss of the steam as he heats the milk. I look over the menu and decide on a grilled cheese sandwich and soup. The family gets up to leave, and the gentleman calls something . A few moments later, an older human woman bustles out to clear the table. She stops when she sees me and smiles.

"Hello there, sorry about the wait. We let the other staff go home early today. Are you ready to order?"

"What's the soup of the day?" I ask her.

"Tomato and basil, and I have to say it's delicious, even if it's my own recipe." She chuckles, and I place my order. "Won't be too long," she promises and hurries to clear the plates off the table the family left behind before returning to the kitchen.

The couple gets up and leaves as the gentleman returns to the table. "I don't think I've seen you in here before," I comment casually to the man. "Are you new to the neutral zone?"

He places my coffee in front of me, and my eyes widen a little when I see a cute dragon floating in it.

He nods, his eyes sparkling with excitement. "Yes, we are. This is our granddaughter's place, but she was marked as the new shifter queen," he tells me with pride. "We offered to help her out until she can make permanent arrangements."

I round my eyes, feigning shock. "Wow, the shifter queen! That has to be…" I pause as I think about what it must be like for a human to be marked. "Terrifying," I finish, and he nods.

"Yeah, I think our girl had a small meltdown and tried to run away, but she came to her senses, and the shifters couldn't get a better human to be their queen. She will be amazing." I can hear the love this man has for his granddaughter in his voice, and I decide to probe a little more.

"So you aren't from around here?" I ask, taking a sip

of my coffee, smiling as the dragon slides around inside. It really is adorable.

"No, we're from the human zone, a village called Ocean Reef, but this was a way to help out our girl and reduce her stress, so to speak. It's one less worry for her to have."

"That's kind of you. What about other family members? They must also be proud of your grand-daughter." I'm not very subtle, but thankfully this man doesn't notice.

"Oh no, it's just Jenny and me. Colbie doesn't have anyone else except for her mother, and she can be a little difficult," he says with a grimace.

"Joseph Karridge, stop boring this young man with our family drama," Jenny, his wife, scolds as she appears with my soup and grilled cheese. She slides it onto the table and shoos her husband away, pointing to the empty booth that needs to be cleared.

"Now there's no rush, but I'm going to put up the closed sign, otherwise Joe and I will never get out of here. Let us know if you want anything else while we finish tidying for the day, okay?" Jenny puts a stop to my questioning, but I learned enough to know where to look for this other mate of Colbie's, so I nod politely and eat my food.

They leave me to enjoy the delicious meal. I groan with delight at the flavors and hope that my mate has inherited her grandmother's talent for cooking, because I truly suck at it—not that a queen will be doing her own cooking regularly, but I hope she knows how to make this soup, because I could happily live off this and grilled cheese.

Once finished, I pay my bill, thank them, and take

my leave. I'm bound to meet them again, and they will probably recognize me because I didn't glamour my features, but I will deal with that when the time comes. I decide to poke around Malina Karridge's business, but when I get there, the shop is closed, so I leave it for now. I can investigate her later. Joseph made it sound like Colbie and her mother aren't close. King Loki said as much, but I didn't push for details at the time because it didn't matter. It does now, and I want to know everything he does.

I sift to the seaside village of Ocean Reef, and it doesn't take me long to find out about the loner who lives in the forest near the lighthouse. I decide to wait until dark and kill some time wandering the boardwalk of the cute seaside village. The whole time, my mind obsesses over the woman who is my mate and the men I have been linked to for the rest of my life. I have a good bond with the four other men handpicked by Loki to be his spies, and my relationship with the king is solid. He is my parents' friend. In fact, he introduced them to each other, and he's like a favorite uncle who is always getting you into trouble. I've killed for the man, but I've never been good at the friend thing with others. I'm abrasive, and because of what I do, I am secretive and insular. I have no idea what it's going to be like to be a part of a bond group. Am I going to be able to open up to these people, and will they accept me for who I am, or am I destined to live on the outside, always looking in?

My thoughts take on a toxic loop of doubt that is very unfamiliar and throws me off-balance. I'm unsettled and restless when the sun finally goes down, and I make my way through the forest surrounding Nox's cabin on foot, but when I get there, I instantly know he isn't in residence. I sift inside the building. He doesn't have any wards up that would prevent me from doing so, but then he probably didn't think he had to worry about a half fae shifter getting into his place. I can tell that it's alarmed against human intruders, but my fae magic allows me to be imperceptible to them.

I poke around his things, trying to get a handle on Queen Colbie's missing mate. There is a cat tree sitting in one corner of the room, but no sign of a cat, and despite the lingering scent of cinnamon and sugar, which I'm pretty sure belongs to this male, the place shows signs of him being gone. It has the slightly musty scent of a room that hasn't seen fresh air for a few days. There are dishes on the drying rack near the sink, but they are bone dry, as is the sink. The bed is made in the bedroom, but there is a lingering scent of cupcakes and frosting that makes my cock twitch. Damn it, what is that smell? If I had to guess, I would say it's the queen. I haven't been close enough to scent her yet, and the water was masking it earlier. I would say this shifter and the queen know each other intimately. So why did he run?

I'm even more curious now, and after shuffling through some correspondence he left on his desk in the office, I learn this male is from Zalfari. He's an equine, another one of those disregarded shifter races, much like the fairies that sent my mother running from any possible match in this kingdom and straight into the arms of my fae father. Her life was difficult, and that was without her having to worry about human wing hunters and collectors who make being a fairy shifter dangerous. They still exist in hidden, underground markets, but I've made it my mission to search them out in my free time and explain why hunting fairy shifters and the fae is a bad idea.

Knowing there is nothing else for me to learn here, I decide to return to the Chaos Kingdom and tell Loki everything I have uncovered. I also have to inform him of my new bond mark. That's certainly going to be an interesting conversation.

CHAPTER

EIGHTEEN

Colbie

Thankfully there are no parties, and dinner is a family affair with Gryffin's and Hunter's families, as well as Violet in attendance. My friend looks radiant, her skin glowing with health, and I mention it to her.

"Gretchin took me to the warded room, and I was able to shift, then Layla showed me the queen's secret garden, and I was able to spend time playing with the plants." She giggles happily, and I give the queen in question a grateful smile.

"Thank you," I tell her, and she waves a hand.

"Our garden has never looked so incredible. I knew fairies were good with plants and animals, but I had no idea they were that good. Despite winter being on its way, the flowers are blooming again, and she rejuvenated the vegetables and herbs so they will continue to produce during the cold weather. She's very talented," Layla praises, and Violet blushes prettily.

219

"You're a fairy?" Talon asks, and Violet blanches, biting her lip in worry before nodding.

"Yes. Is that a problem?" she asks, and I glare at Hunter's brother, daring him to say it is. I'll shift and bite his head off, future brother-in-law or not.

He shakes his head, and the sudden tension at the table eases. "No, not at all. I'd love to see your shifted form sometime. I've never met a fairy shifter before."

I breathe a sigh of relief as Violet releases her poor lip and smiles shyly at him. "I'd like that."

"You mated Liam!" Gracelin shouts, suddenly pointing at the matching bite marks on our necks. I was hoping nobody would notice—not because I'm embarrassed or ashamed, I just kind of wanted to enjoy it without the added pressure of sealing the bond with the others. Of course I can't get anything past these shifters, and my beast really didn't go for subtle.

Everyone's attention switches to us, and it's my turn for my cheeks to heat. "Yes, I did." I glare at her for drawing attention to us, and she smirks at me.

"That's wonderful, Colbie." Evie claps her hands as everyone congratulates us.

"One step closer to being crowned!" Lucas beams. "Now you just need to mate the rest of them." Layla nudges him in the side, and he coughs. "Uh, I mean no pressure or anything," he mutters, and Layla rolls her eyes, but it makes me smile. I hope we end up with an amazing relationship like theirs.

"No!" The cry has me turning my attention to Archie, who is seated between his parents. He scrambles in his chair, standing up on it, and waves a hand at me. I frown when I see it's bandaged, but before I can say anything, he shouts, "You are going to be my sidepiece, remember? I got you a ring and everything!"

My mouth drops open in shock as he digs around in the pockets of the robe he's wearing over his pajamas. He frowns and pulls out a box. "Ha! Here it is."

He scrambles out of his chair and, avoiding both his mom's and dad's arms, he rushes toward me. I push my chair back and crouch down as he approaches me, worried about how upset he is. Tears stream down his face.

"Please, Colbie, please be my sidepiece. I love you more than he will." He holds out the box, and I gasp in shock when I find it contains a huge ass ring, one with a diamond big enough to feed a small nation. Archie glares at Liam, his eyes shining brightly, and he bares his teeth and growls.

Liam smothers a grin, but my attention returns to the ring in his hand. "Wow, Archie, that's…" I trail off, not sure how to even describe it.

"Archie, baby, where did you get that from?" Mia asks, staring at the ring in confusion. "I'm almost certain it's from the royal vault." She looks at Lucas and the other two queens for confirmation.

"You know, I think you might be right," Lucas says, frowning, but then he shakes his head. "But no, that can't be."

"Say yes, Colbie," Archie pleads, ignoring his grandparents, and I take the box from him and put it on the table before pulling him into my arms, hugging him tightly. He sags against me and inhales deeply.

"You smell so nice," he mutters, and I rub a hand over his back, trying to calm him down.

"Archie, you will always be my first friend here in the castle, but Liam is my mate, and so are Gryff, Brodie, Hunter, Gem, and our new friend, Micah." Archie pulls away and glares at the men around the table before his gaze stops on Micah, and his eyes widen.

"I know you. You're on Dad's team. You're a fish man, and you have a big weapon." He pushes away from me, hurries around to Micah's chair, and climbs up into his lap. "You're going to be my new best friend. Can I see your weapon? Is it really sharp?" Archie mimes stabbing things while I gape in surprise. Archie has completely forgotten me in his awe of his new friend.

"Wow, how does it feel to be replaced by Micah's big weapon?" Gracelin sidles up to me, and we watch with amusement as Archie, completely distracted now, talks to Micah who just blinks, a little shell-shocked.

"Can't say I wouldn't mind seeing Micah's big weapon either," I mutter to her, and she giggles while Liam, who must have heard what I said, snorts with amusement.

"Getting greedy, are we?" he asks, pulling me down to sit next to him again.

"Archie, where did you get this ring?" Mia holds it in her hand, looking perplexed, unable to let go of the issue.

"Oh, Mr. Vallen told me I could have it if I helped him with a special task," Archie tells us, and the table falls into a loaded silence. "There were lots of rings in the big room, and he let me pick which one I wanted. That one was so big and shiny."

"What task did you help him with?" Lucas asks,

standing up, his body tight with tension. Everyone else in the room instantly becomes on edge, and goosebumps erupt across my arms as my creature reacts in kind.

"Oh, he said if I was a very brave boy and let him cut my hand and put it on the lock and say the special words, the door would open, and we could see the treasure. He was right! It was just like magic, and I said the special words, and the door opened for me. Mr. Vallen says I'm very special, and not everyone can do what I did." Archie's chest puffs up with pride, but Lucas growls.

"That fucking bastard. How dare he use Archie to do his dirty work?"

"What's going on?" I hear Violet whisper to Talon, who shrugs.

"I have no idea."

"You think he got into the royal vault?" Bryson is also on his feet now, his hands clenched into fists. Gracelin hurries around to Archie and grabs his hand, pulling the bandage off it.

"I thought it was from playing pretend with Lucy," she tells us, but when she holds up his hand, we see a large, slightly healed cut across his hand.

"It hurt, but I was brave and didn't cry," Archie says, tugging his hand away from his mother and crossing his arms defensively. "I was a hero. Mr. Vallen said so."

Gracelin scoops Archie up, tears in her eyes. "Of course you were."

"The royal vault is keyed to our bloodline. Only someone with our blood would have been able to get in," Evie explains, looking sadly at Archie. "How dare he con a child into helping him break into the vault?"

"But Colbie is queen now. Surely it changed to her bloodline," Gryffin argues.

"Not until she has been crowned." Sable shakes her head. "But what could he have wanted from the vault? Unless he was helping himself to a bonus for years of service. It's filled with highly valuable items, but all of them are recognizable as belonging to the crown."

Something occurs to me, and I jump to my feet. "Didn't you say the spell book that contains the spell for humans becoming shifters is in there?" I look at Lucas, and he pales and rushes from the dining room. I hurry after him, and I hear a lot of the others following as well.

I trail him through the palace and down a flight of stairs to a room I haven't been to before. It contains a huge, barn-like door that has a locking mechanism with a control panel. Lucas shifts a finger, and a claw forms. He slices across his palm and slaps it against the biometric scanner. The light on the panel turns green, and there's a loud click. Lucas grabs the handle and pulls. The door is large and heavy, and even with his strength, it takes a moment to open, but when it's ajar enough, he slips through, and I follow him.

I stop just inside the door and gape at what I see.

This is like a pirate's treasure trove or a dragon's hoard. There are piles of gold coins and bars, jewels, paintings, and sculptures just to name a few things, but toward the back of the vault is a glass-covered display case, and that's what Lucas makes a beeline for. When he gets there, he looks down, and I see his body sag for a moment.

"It's gone. That bastard took the book. Bryson, bring me Vallen Tideman and his family now!" Lucas roars.

Turning back toward the entrance, I find everyone there except for Violet and Hunter's siblings.

"Right away, sire." Bryson salutes the king before snapping his fingers.

"Boys, care to join me in tracking down a traitor?" I watch as my mates and Adam all stalk after the general and shudder. I wouldn't want to be Councilman Tideman right now. The menace and air of violence coming off those men is enough to send the bravest man running and screaming.

"So is Tideman behind the ferals? Did he kidnap the children?" Gracelin has Archie on her hip, and she jiggles him slightly when he tries to climb down and touch all the pretty items.

"He could be, or someone could have paid him to get the book. I can't believe he thought about using Archie to get it. It never occurred to me that it would be a possibility. I'm so sorry." Lucas scrubs a hand through his hair. I still haven't told them about my meeting with the goddess and that the book can fix the ferals.

"Let's return to dinner. Tideman and his family can wallow in the cells for a few hours. There's nothing like knowing you're going to be interrogated to make a person sweat," Mia suggests, and the rest of us return to the dining room. The atmosphere is subdued as we continue our meal, but I want to wait for the others to return before I tell them everything I learned.

It's Evie who breaks the silence. "Why would he want the book? He can't use it. It's less than useless for him without the royal power and he can't open it. Unlike the vault which opens to anyone in the royal family, the book will only open with a drop of Lucas' blood,,"

"I might have an answer for that," I tell them, putting down my fork, but before I can share my conversation with the goddess, the general, my mates, and Adam return, and none of them look happy.

"We searched the entire castle for him, but he's gone, as are his wife and children. It looks like they left in a hurry though. They didn't take many of their personal belongings," Bryson grumbles as the rest of them retake their seats. "I'm going to send a team to track him."

He turns to leave, but I jump to my feet.

"Wait, I have some information to share with everyone. You should hear it," I tell him, and he looks at Lucas, which annoys me, so I glare at him. "Bryson, I know you have been serving Lucas for a long time, but I am queen now."

I see Sable smother a grin and look down at her hands, and I get a nod of approval from Layla. Bryson frowns and nods, taking a seat. "You're right, forgive me, my queen. It will take a little adjustment for me," he says ruefully.

"It's okay. It's going to take a little adjustment for all of us, I'm sure. A few more minutes aren't going to make a big difference. To be honest, I have no doubt Tideman is long gone. The cut on Archie's hand is almost completely healed," I point out.

"Shifters heal a lot quicker than humans," Gem says and holds out his hands to take Archie from Gracelin. "But I can make it so it's completely healed." He tickles the boy, and Archie squirms, giggling with delight as Gem sits down with him on his lap and cups his injured hand with his own large ones. "This might be a bit warm," he warns as his hands start to flame. Archie squawks with surprise but holds still.

"Archie, when did you and Mr. Vallen go into the vault and get my pretty ring?" I ask him, drawing his attention away from the healing flames.

"Miss Lucy was going to take me to see the kittens in the stables before I had a nap, but she was taking too long talking with Miss Isla, and I didn't want to wait, so while they weren't looking, I snuck off. Mr. Vallen stopped me when I got to the abominable fountain."

"The what?" I ask, completely confused, and there are a couple of chuckles around the table. Gracelin pulls out her phone and sends a message, glaring at the screen.

"There's a fountain in the middle of the front entrance of the castle. You didn't come that way when you first arrived, so you probably haven't seen it. It was commissioned by Queen Rowena. It's supposed to be in her likeness, but it's the most gaudy, horrific thing I've ever seen. I wanted to have it removed, but apparently it would damage the foundation of the palace, so it has to stay," Lucas explains, and Evie laughs.

"He calls it the abomination, but Archie can't say it."

"Abominable is actually fitting," Mia admits, but Gracelin is glaring at Archie.

"Are you telling me you were going to leave the castle again without anyone? Archer Lucas Frankland, you have pushed your luck one last time. You are banned from having dessert for the next week." Her calculating gaze slides to me. "And I forbid you from having Queen Colbie as your sidepiece."

There's a small, loaded silence, and I see Adam

wince. Archie bursts into tears, wailing loudly, but Gracelin just picks him up once Gem finishes healing his hand and passes him to another female shifter who ran into the room. Unlike the palace staff who all wear a uniform, she's wearing a smart pair of pants and a fitted shirt with sneakers on her feet, which actually makes sense if this is Archie's nanny.

"I am not happy, Lucy. You were derelict in your duties, allowing Isla Tideman to distract you. This is not the first time Archie has gotten away from you. Consider yourself on notice. If this happens again, I will have to replace you."

"Yes, ma'am. I'm so sorry. Isla and I went to school together, and she was just asking about some mutual friends. I swear I turned my back on Archie for mere seconds," Lucy explains, her cheeks pink with embarrassment.

"Take him to our apartment. He's grounded until further notice."

Lucy retreats with a wailing Archie, and everyone breathes out a sigh of relief once the door closes behind them.

"You are vicious," Gretchin compliments her sister.

"Pfft, it won't last. That child could get into trouble in his sleep."

"So the Tidemans have at least a five hour start on us. Hell, they could be in another kingdom by now." Hunter brings the conversation back on track.

"But why take the book? It doesn't make sense," Evie says, and I know it's time to share what the goddess told me.

"Because if they can stop me from being crowned and get the power to accept someone else, then they can make as many shifters as they like and fix all the ferals they've already created."

"What do you mean, fix the ferals?" Lucas snaps, and I sigh.

"I had another enlightening conversation with the goddess," I reply, then I proceed to tell them everything she said.

CHAPTER
NINETEEN

Colbie

"Are you telling me we could have been healing the ferals all along instead of killing them?" Evie's eyes brim with tears, and she sounds heartbroken.

"Yes, but to be honest, I understand why they chose to punish anyone flaunting their rules. The shifter population would have been overrun, humans definitely would have been outnumbered, and there would have been no stop to the war," I point out.

"But they are going to give all humans the option to change now," she argues. "Why not before?"

I shrug. "I don't know what their reasoning is, but I have a feeling the humans are being punished. They will all be under the rule of the shifters from what I understand. They will not have their own government, the neutral zone will be dissolved, and all citizens of Aramis will cohabitate. I think they are hoping the majority of them will change, and the ones who don't will eventually die out."

"And you are going to be the queen of everyone?" Gryffin asks, and I grimace.

"Yes, until I either choose to step down or die, and any heir I have takes over, but if I am queen of them all, then that will make you kings of them all."

"No wonder the goddess gave you eight mates. I can't imagine this is going to go smoothly with shifters or humans," Lucas says dryly.

"Doubtful. I'm sure there will be some pushback. First, though, I need to be crowned, or all of this will be for nothing. We have two factions gunning for us at this stage, and I would like to make sure we put a kink in their plans by finding my final mates and getting those crowns on our heads. At least that way, I'll control the power," I tell them, even though I'm plagued with doubts. This is what the goddess wanted, though, and who am I to go against divine authority?

"How are you going to make so many humans into shifters? You can't bite all of them," Brodie growls possessively.

"The book is the key, so we need to get that back. I don't need to bite them if we have it. We will allow anyone who wishes to be a certain animal to petition a shifter of that species and be bitten if they want. I will not force anyone to bite. If not, they can take their chances with the royal magic and get what they are given."

"I'll make sure our armies are ready for any fallout," Bryson assures me.

"And I will start work on an updated manual for all new shifters," Sable suggests. "We will probably need to have mandatory shifting classes so the new shifters can learn our culture. Otherwise, we may have more problems than we care to deal with if dominance fights become an issue because a new shifter doesn't know the rules."

"Yes, we always make any human mates we change learn all of those things. This can be an extension of that. I'll help you with the program," Layla offers, and Sable quickly accepts.

"Then you need to focus on getting to your other mates. Head into the human zone tonight. We haven't had a chance to reach out to the humans yet, but their government would want a meeting with the new queen, and we don't have time to waste. In fact, we don't know if you would be safe. This conspiracy could go as far as the ones who are in charge. It's better to sneak in and ask forgiveness than ask permission and end up dead," Lucas advises.

"And you need to seal those other mating bonds as soon as you can." Gracelin smirks at me, and Adam snickers like a tween boy.

"Enough," Gryffin snaps at his sister. "Leave Colbie alone. Teasing her isn't going to make it any easier."

"No, but challenge day is in less than two weeks, and those matings need to be sealed. If they aren't, they will question her dedication to being queen. Even with her kickass animal, she will get challenged, because being unmated makes her weaker," Mia says, giving me a sympathetic look.

"I'm working on that," I mutter, feeling my cheeks heat, and when I glance around the table, I find my mates looking at me with feral intensity.

"And you six need to be on full alert. Colbie doesn't

have the fighting skills you all have. Even though this is a covert mission, we have to assume the Tidemans are not the only shifters who want change. I'm going to have the other councilors watched as well just in case," Bryson orders my guys.

"Should we leave tonight?" Hunter asks his dad.

Before he can reply, I jump in. "I'm exhausted from shifting. I'm already going to be a liability, so would it be alright if we go tomorrow night? I wouldn't mind checking on my bakery tomorrow morning, and if we go early, no one will be around to see us go. We could hide in my apartment until nightfall, and once curfew comes, we can go into the human zone then. We just have to avoid my mother at all costs."

"That would also give us a chance to speak to Brock Tideman and see if he knows his parents' plans," Gem suggests.

I'd forgotten about Brock. I'm not sure how helpful he will be since my mother got them banned from the shifter zone for the time being.

"That's a good idea," Lucas confirms.

"And instead of staying at your apartment, we can use ours at the watch headquarters. If you are seen, we can spin a tale about you learning about your new responsibilities," Brodie offers.

"It seems like we have a plan then. Eat up, because you are all going to need your energy," Evie says, and we're quick to do as she suggests. During dinner, the guys and I tell them about my shift training in the afternoon, minus my fuck fest with Liam for obvious reasons.

The following morning, I wake up early, my internal clock still working on baker time. Through a crack in the curtains, I can see that it's still dark outside. A warm body is wrapped around me, and the sound of soft snoring is loud in the quiet room. Each breath tickles my ear, and I clamp my lips shut so I don't giggle at how bear-like Liam sounds. I stay still and simply bask in the feeling of having his body pressed against me, resisting the urge to push back against that delicious naked skin pressed against me.

Liam proceeded to show me how amazing being mated to a shifter with no refractory time can be. To say my body aches deliciously this morning would be an understatement. For someone who was so aggressive and surly, he really is just a snuggly, cuddly sweetheart now that we are mated and his bear is content.

I invited Hunter and Micah to join us as well last night—after all, they won fair and square—but both declined, letting Liam and me spend the night together on our own. Micah needed to return to the barracks, get his personal items, and move them into one of the king's rooms that now flank my suite. The goddess magic rearranged this section of the palace to correlate with the fact that I now have eight mates. There are eight separate suites for each of the guys, and my bedroom is now enormous with a bed that is large enough to accommodate all of us if we were so inclined. I'm not sure how this will work, and if they'll want to share my bed or sleep in their own rooms, but I guess we have time to figure it out.

"Little girl, if you keep wiggling like that, my bear is going to have you for breakfast." The growly voice has me freezing. I hadn't realized I started squirming at the thought of all eight of my mates and what our sleeping arrangements may be.

His hand drifts up my naked thigh and slides up the front of my tank. He cups my breast and scrapes his teeth over the bite mark on my neck, sending a thrill of excitement through my body. My nipples pebble, and I groan as I rub my ass against his rapidly hardening dick.

Before he can do anything else, though, the door to my room slams open, and Brodie appears in the doorway.

"Uh-uh, none of that. We need to get going if we don't want to be seen moving through the neutral zone."

I turn my head to glare at him. He smirks, crosses his arms, and leans against the doorframe as Liam mumbles, "Cockblock," in my ear.

I smile as my grumbly bear snarls at his bond mate, and then I throw back the covers and slide out of his hold. I stand and stretch, pushing out my tits, and Brodie pushes off the doorframe and stalks over to me. He's patient and waits until I finish my stretch before he slides his hands to my hips and tugs my body against his.

"That was mean," he says, resting his forehead against mine and looking into my eyes.

"What you did was mean too," I retort, pressing a soft kiss against his lips. He flinches, his eyes widening with surprise before he swoops in and takes my mouth in a blistering kiss. I melt into him, unsurprised by his boldness, and enjoy an intense kiss from the normally playful wolf. He tastes like sunshine and happiness, and when he pulls away abruptly, I whimper at the loss.

Liam tugged him away from me and is pushing him out of the room. "Nope. If I can't get my morning sugar, then neither can you," he argues, and my door bangs closed behind them, leaving me needy and sad.

Sighing, I head for the shower to wash away the remnants of our fun from last night. My body aches in delicious ways as I run the loofah over my skin, and I smile as I remember all the things Liam and I did to each other while we satisfied the mating need.

When I finally emerge and dress, Violet, Gretchin, and Gracelin are waiting for me.

"There you are. Have a good night?" Gracelin teases, and I roll my eyes at her.

"You're all up early." I ignore her as I brush my hair and braid it so it's out of my way. I'm dressed in some of my old clothes today—leggings and a shirt in case I need to help out in the bakery when we stop in. I also have a backpack of clothes I packed for our trip before Liam and I got busy last night. He told me they will give me a watch uniform when we go there today. I'll wear that during our trip, because I can shift in it without worrying about being naked if I have to shift unexpectedly.

"We just wanted to wish you luck. I hope you find Nox quickly, and then we can focus on that last mate of yours. He will be a fairy, so I've sent a message to my parents, asking if any of the males in our village have received a new mark," Violet tells me.

"After you speak to the equines about tracking the shifter children, then you can head to her village and see for yourself." Gretchin watches me with worried eyes. "I wanted to come with you, but Bryson and Dad vetoed the idea. I hate that you'll be going without me. I'm supposed to be your bodyguard."

"Yes, but she also has six mates keeping an eye on her ass. They won't let anything happen to her," her sister reminds her, and Gretchin rolls her eyes.

"Please, they will all be distracted by the mating need. She needs me because I'm not going to be focused on getting into her pants," Gretchin argues, and I feel my cheeks heat a little.

"You only wish you were getting a piece of this." I wave a hand at myself, teasing her, and she grins.

"You wish. I have mad skills that would rock your world," she tells me, and I feel a sense of relief as I see her lighten up a bit. These girls have quickly become family to me, and I don't like it when they worry.

"Come on. The guys are already waiting for you near the stables. You're going through the forest and then straight to the bakery. At this time of day, no one should be about in the neutral zone." Violet hands me my phone, which I tuck into my pocket, and then I throw my backpack over my shoulder.

I pick up the ring box that Archie gave me and pass it to Gracelin. "Can you see that this gets returned to the vault?"

She winces but nods. "I won't let Archie see me do it. He's going to make my life miserable when he learns his sidepiece is no longer in the palace."

I have an idea, so I hurry back into my closet and dig around in my jewelry box, which the guys brought from my apartment. I find a ring I've had since my childhood. It's one of those mood rings that changes color depending on the temperature of your body. It's too small for me now, but for some reason, I couldn't ever part with it. A flash of a memory comes to me, and I smile. Gryffin gave it to me during one of our games where he was the prince who saved me from the villain witch sisters, promising to make me his princess.

"Here, give this to him and tell him that I would love to be his sidepiece." I shove my hand out to Gracelin, and her eyes widen in surprise.

"I remember this. Gryffin won it at one of the shifter festivals and gave it to you. I can't believe you kept it."

I shrug. "I guess past me must have had some inkling that he would be important to me in the future."

"Doesn't this seem like maybe someone has been manipulating you for a long time?" Violet asks hesitantly, voicing some of my own inner thoughts. "The fact that you have a prior relationship with the royals and you found Archie outside of your bakery..."

"It really wouldn't surprise me," I tell her.

The other two don't comment, but their expressions indicate that they have the same suspicions. "Alright. Don't come with me. We don't want any of the palace staff questioning why the four of us are up so early and moving around. I'll message you when we have any news," I promise them, and they wish me luck and return to their rooms.

I move quietly through the palace, not coming across any of the staff. When I make it to the stables, the guys are standing around, talking softly. They are wearing their watch uniforms, and Micah is in his armed forces fatigues. I'm guessing they are all wearing them for the same reason they are going to give me a uniform. I can't say I'm not a little sad that I won't be able to see all that delicious male shifter flesh, but on the other hand, these guys are my mates. I have a lifetime to appreciate them. I say a small little prayer of thanks to Aramis, and a slight breeze wafts around me like she's saying, *You're welcome*.

"Good, you're here. Let's get moving. I'd like to make it in and out of the bakery and to watch headquarters before the sun comes up, and we only have about three hours," Gryffin says as I approach them. He seems to be all business now, and I appreciate it. Although we have personal stuff we need to work out, focusing on the task at hand will keep me from becoming overwhelmed.

"Colbie, you and Micah will fly with me and Gem again, and the others will shift and meet us at the bakery. I'm too heavy to land at the bakery, but I'll land at the watch building, because it's closer to your shop than the edge of the forest, and we will go on foot from there," Hunter tells me as the others shift and take off through the forest.

CHAPTER

TWENTY

Colbie

Like me, Micah has a pack, but the rest don't. I guess they have what they need at their apartment. They haven't moved everything to the palace yet, because we haven't exactly told anyone but their families that they are my mates. It will be common knowledge soon enough, but for now, we want the people who are after me to think they still have a chance at the crown. They might get sloppy and reveal themselves, or that is at least what we hope. Essentially, I'm bait, which isn't exactly comforting, but I'd prefer they make a play for me and fail than for this to drag out too long. I'd hate to be constantly looking over my shoulder for my entire reign.

Hunter shifts, and Micah and I climb onto his back. Micah wraps his big arms around me and drags me back against him as Hunter takes off into the sky. The temperature drops rapidly as he picks up speed, and I shiver, my shifter body heat not doing a lot against the frigid temperatures. The clouds are thick, and the smell of snow is in the air. Hopefully it won't actually happen, or it will make our mission uncomfortable.

"Are you okay?" Micah murmurs into my ear.

I tuck my chin in, making myself smaller, and mumble, "Yes, but I think I'm going to need some warmer clothes."

Hunter must hear me, because his body warms beneath us, making my stiff legs relax.

"You will be fine when we're on the ground again. Gryffin says they have a vehicle for us to use in the human zone. It wouldn't be very stealthy for the humans to see a group of shifters running through the streets or flying overhead."

A flash of light out of the corner of my eye catches my attention, and I turn my head to find Gem's phoenix keeping pace with us.

"I bet he isn't cold," I grumble, watching his flames with envy. "He also isn't very stealthy," I point out. Despite being huge, Hunter's dragon's dark purple scales blend in with the night, but Gem's phoenix is like a beacon, but just as the words leave my mouth, Gem disappears from sight. I cry out and lurch forward, looking around the sky for him, but he's gone.

"What happened? Where did he go?" I shout to both Hunter and Micah, and Micah tightens his grip so I don't slide off in my panic.

"Hunter says Gem has the ability to go invisible. He must have heard you comment about lacking stealth. He's still there, we just can't see him—something about a phoenix being able to bend light."

I sag with relief but turn my head to look at the merman. "Hunter said?"

"Yeah, it's pretty cool. We have telepathy now that I have the bond mark. Hunter says that you should be able to do the same with Liam. Just concentrate on that feeling inside you that you gained when your mating bond snapped into place and push your thoughts to him."

I do as he says and find that ball of warmth that I know is Liam inside me. *Liam?*

Colbie, are you okay? I hear his voice in my mind, and I feel his concern. That is so cool!

Everything's okay. I just found out about the telepathy with bonds and was trying it out, I assure him, and his worry recedes before I feel his amusement.

Yeah, it's pretty handy. It means I can do this. His amusement fades, and I'm gripped with an intense rush of desire that causes me to gasp while my core throbs with need.

"Colbie, are you okay?" It's Micah's turn to sound worried, but I just wave a hand at him, signaling I'm fine because I'm doing everything I can not to moan and beg him to touch me to ease the ache.

"Colbie, why do you smell like you want to fuck?" he rumbles in my ear, then he pulls me tighter against him, his cock pushing against my backside as one of his hands slides from my waist up to my breast where he cups it firmly.

"Liam is showing me the fun things he can do with the bond," I rasp, and Micah groans.

The desire eases away, and I hear Liam in my head again as the lights of the neutral zone come into view. *Your mer mate is no fun,* he grumbles, but his presence recedes. I guess Micah must have used their bond to tell him to cut it out. I appreciate it, but I'm also kind of intrigued about what it would feel like to fuck Micah on Hunter's back while we're thousands of feet in the air. Jesus, maybe the high altitude is getting to me.

Micah gives me a little squeeze but stays silent as Hunter coasts over the neutral zone, descending slowly until we get to the tall building that I recognize as night watch headquarters. He touches down gently on the roof of the building, and Micah and I climb down before he shifts. A guard pokes his head out of the security building, and Micah steps in front of me, blocking his view.

"Commander Hunter, you're here early," he says, and Hunter also moves to block me from his view.

"Not an early start, but a late evening, if you get my drift," Hunter replies suggestively. "My friends and I are just heading to our apartment." He makes it sound like we're having a late night booty call, and it seems to work.

"Have fun," the guard calls with a laugh and returns to the building. Hunter wastes no time ushering us to the stairwell and down into the structure. No one else seems to be around, but I keep my head down so I can't be recognized on any security cameras the building may have.

We don't talk as we make our way down in an elevator then out into the street. Thankfully there weren't any teams around. Hunter quietly explained that they should all either still be out on patrol or in their apartments sleeping.

The weather has gotten worse. It isn't quite cold enough to snow, but there is a steady drizzle, and I wrinkle my nose. Ugh, although it isn't raining heavily, we are still going to be wet by the time we make it to the bakery, so we don't waste any time. The three of us move swiftly, but not too hastily to attract any attention if we happen to come across a watch team. They should know Micah and Hunter have permission to be out after curfew, and hopefully they won't stop to question us. I also have permission, but we don't want it to be common knowledge that the queen has left the shifter zone. The girls, the king, and queens will cover for us for a few days, even if they have to share that I found a mate and I am busy sealing the bond. That will buy us time if the rest of the council starts poking around. I'm supposed to have a meeting with them in a few days, but Lucas told me he can delay it if we tell them I'm in the mating frenzy.

We use the back alley to the bakery when we arrive, and I call out so I don't give my grandparents a fright when I surprise them with my visit.

"Granny, Grampy, it's just me," I call as I push the door open. The heat of the kitchen rushes out, and I sigh with relief as I enter, clothes completely soaked from the drizzle. Both the guys seem to be in better condition, and I wonder if their uniforms are water repellent.

"Colbie, what a lovely surprise." Grampy has a piping bag in his hand, and there is a smudge of white powder on his nose, which makes me grin.

"Goodness, child, you are soaked," Granny scolds me and hurries to the cupboard, pulling out some towels and passing them around.

"Micah, these are my grandparents, Jenny and Joseph. This is Micah. He is one of my mates," I tell them. "And so is Hunter." My grandparents both greet them warmly.

"You found your mates!" My granny looks at me with sparkling eyes. "And such handsome ones too. You're a lucky girl." She gives me a wink, and the guys chuckle while I blush.

"We aren't the only ones. She has a few more," Hunter tells her, and Grampy frowns.

"How many?"

"Ah… Um… Six more," I tell him awkwardly, and his mouth drops open in shock, but Granny's grin just gets wider, if that's even possible.

"Very lucky girl," she says as Grampy grumbles under his breath. "And what kind of shifter are you?" she asks, and this brings a look of excitement and anticipation to Grampy's face, distracting him from the other news. She's such a clever woman.

"I'm a hydra," I tell them, and they both gape in shock.

"A hydra? Oh my, that is certainly a surprise." Grampy sounds proud and relieved despite his shock. "Nothing will stop you now."

"No, but we need to keep that on the down-low. We haven't been making it common knowledge," Hunter explains as he towels off his hair. Micah is doing the same, and I take a moment to look around my kitchen, feeling a pang of longing. I miss being normal so much, but I can't deny that my life is certainly a lot more exciting now, and wasn't that what I secretly wanted?

I take stock of what they have already made, and it seems like all the muffins and cupcakes are baked but need to be iced. Granny has something bubbling on the stove, which I'm assuming is the marshmallow that Grampy has been piping into animals. He has half a table full of them. I see dragons and wolves so far. He sees me eyeing the creations and winks at me. "I'll have to come up with a hydra design for your coronation."

My eyes prickle with tears, and I concentrate on drying myself off so no one sees them.

A commotion at the door has everyone turning to look at it again, and Gem, Brodie, Gryffin, and Liam all walk in. Liam strides straight to me and tugs me to him, giving me a quick kiss before stepping away and inhaling deeply.

"God, I missed you," he mutters quietly. "That was rough. I don't want you out of my sight again, if possible, for a little while. The mating bond is making me needy."

"Pfft, you're always needy," Gem scoffs, grabbing my granny by the waist and spinning her around before kissing her on the cheek. She squeals with surprise but smiles at him when he says, "Jenny, you are looking gorgeous, as always."

"Get your damn hands off my wife," Grampy grumbles, but I see his eyes sparkle with amusement, and I'm a little shocked by how comfortable they are with one another.

"What is going on?" I ask, and my granny pats Gem's cheek.

"These boys have come by every day to make sure your mother isn't here causing us problems," she tells me, and I gape at the guys in surprise.

"Well, we couldn't have her stirring up any more trouble for our queen, who is also our mate," Gem says, and Granny claps her hands.

"All of you?" she asks, looking at them as Brodie snatches a muffin from the cooling rack.

"Yup, isn't she lucky?" He winks, breaking it in half and shoving one piece into his mouth.

"More like you're the lucky ones, and the damn menaces have been conning your grandmother out of our wares. Been cutting into our profits," Grampy mutters and starts piping again so the marshmallow doesn't set before it can be formed into creatures.

Jesus, how did I get so lucky? They didn't even know we were mates before yesterday, but they were still making sure my grandparents were okay. I fall in love a little more with all of them.

"Now how about you all get out of my kitchen? It's too crowded with all of you assholes in here." Grampy shoos them away with the piping bag. "Going to get stray hairs in my little critters. Go make yourselves a coffee or something."

I give my mates a nod of reassurance, and thankfully, they don't argue. They all march through the kitchen door and into the café, and Grampy sighs heavily with relief.

"Have your hands full there," Granny comments as she returns her attention to the pot bubbling on the stove.

"You have no idea," I reply, smiling. Her eyes go to the bite mark on my neck, and she sighs happily.

"It's such a relief to know you have mates who will look after you like you're the most precious thing in the world."

"And so they should," Grampy mutters, "though I don't know why she needed so damn many of them."

I grab the sieve of corn flour he uses to set the marshmallows and start shaking it over the animals as he pipes, and then I fill my grandparents in on everything that has happened, knowing I can trust them. They listen intently, only interrupting for clarification here or there, and we have a neat row of tigers and bears by the time I've finished telling them everything.

"Phew, Colbie girl. Seems like you are in a right pickle," Grampy says while washing and drying his hands before leaning against the sink. "Well, don't you worry about a thing here. Jenny and I are loving it here, so at least that's one worry off your shoulders."

I give him a big hug, and he hugs me back. I sag against him, feeling no small amount of relief at his words.

"Thank you. Both of you have made this transition so much easier. I know I'll probably never be able to return, but I would have hated closing down my dream. Once I'm crowned, I'll put out feelers for a full-time baker, I promise." I tell them, but they quickly assure me there is no rush. I feel no small amount of relief that at least one thing in my life is going right.

TWENTY-ONE

Colbic

"Why don't you make sure the boys haven't broken the coffee machine? I'm assuming you won't be staying?" Granny asks, and I shake my head.

"No, we're just waiting to speak to Brock, and then we'll head out," I explain, and Granny frowns.

"Oh dear. The bookstore has been closed for the last three days. We haven't seen Brock or Niles since they burst in here screaming about being kicked out of the shifter zone for helping your mother."

"Haven't seen your mother either," Grampy says, exchanging a worried look with Granny. "We expected her to come and rant about being prevented from seeing you, but we haven't heard anything. We were going to call and tell you today if she didn't appear. You know Malina, she's likely sulking with some man, having her ego stroked."

They aren't wrong about my mother, but I'm surprised about Brock and Niles. Apart from the day of the parade, the store never closes. They are normally open seven days a week.

"That's strange, but we'll wait until after normal opening time, and if they don't open, then I guess we'll try to figure out where they ended up. I know they were banned from the shifter zone, but I think they have a place here as well. Maybe I'll ask one of the guys if they know."

I head out into the cafe and find my guys with Olivia and Justin. I hear them grilling my mates for information, but the guys are doing a good job of being vague. They all have coffees in front of them, and the coffee machine still seems to be in working order, so that's a relief.

"Colbie!" Olivia jumps to her feet and starts to move toward me, but she stops and frowns. "Am I supposed to curtsy or something now?" she asks, looking from me to the guys and back again.

"No, don't be silly," I say, waving her to me for a hug.

"Not yet anyway," Gryffin mutters quietly so Olivia and Justin don't hear. I guess he's right. If they decide to become shifters once this is all over, then they may end up having to curtsy to me after all, but that's a future Colbie problem.

"How are things going?" I ask, looking between them when I pull away from Olivia.

"Great. Your grandparents have been amazing. Olivia and I are learning so much from them," Justin says enthusiastically, and I blink in surprise. He hasn't ever been particularly excited about working at the bakery. I always thought he was only killing time until he moved on to the next thing, but it seems I was wrong. Maybe he just needed a challenge. This is good. Maybe I won't have to look for a baker, and they can take over those duties, and we can hire two new servers.

"Joe even taught me how to pipe some of the animals." Olivia grins, and I feel a small amount of sadness, but mostly relief that my life's work is going to be in the hands of someone who loves it as much as I do.

"That's awesome. Learn as much as you can, and the two of you can take over in the back when they decide they've had enough, and we will hire two new servers," I say, and they both kind of puff up with pride and assure me they will.

I turn my attention to the windows and notice it's still overcast and drizzling. "I'm going to duck out the back and see if Brock and Niles are next door, then we can get going," I tell my guys.

"I'll come with you." Gryffin drains the rest of his coffee and stands up. I wait for the others to insist on coming, but none of them move. Maybe they already discussed it. If too many of them accompany me, they might overwhelm the two male shifters. Gryffin is a good choice because of who his dad is. Even if they don't view me as the queen, but as the girl who worked next door, they will recognize his authority as prince of the shifters.

"Drink up, boys. We need to open in ten minutes," Justin warns the others as Gryffin and I make our way through the kitchen.

"I'll come back and say goodbye before we leave," I tell my grandparents as they exchange a worried glance.

Out in the alley, Gryffin follows me as I walk to their back door. It's closed, but that's not unusual given the weather. I knock and then rub my hands together to warm them, the cold quickly seeping into my skin.

"I can't believe how cold it is compared to yesterday," I murmur as we wait. Gryffin grabs my hands and rubs some warmth into them. I instinctively move closer, seeking the heat his body is putting off. My beast twirls with excitement at his proximity, and when I look up at him, he's smirking at me.

"You okay?" he asks, knowing full well the effect he has on my body. "Is the mating call giving you a hard time?"

I arch an eyebrow and look down at the bulge in his tight pants, and my lips lift in a smirk.

"Not as hard a time as it's giving you."

He shrugs unapologetically, but I turn my attention back to the door. It's taking too long for them to answer.

"Come on, we'll go around to the front. They might be inside the store and not hear us banging on the door." I reluctantly pull my hands from his and lead the way to the storefront, but when we get there, the closed sign is still on the door and the lights are off.

"Doesn't look like anyone is around," Gryffin says, peering through the window. "There aren't even any lights or movement farther back."

"That's really weird, and if what Granny said is true, then this is the fourth day in a row that they haven't opened."

He turns back around, and he's frowning. "Do we think that Niles and Brock were in on it with his family?"

I shake my head. "I doubt it. They shunned him

when he mated with Niles, and then Tideman got him banned for giving him permission to bring my mother into the shifter zone. Also, Tideman only stole the book two nights ago."

"Well, maybe they are just licking their wounds from being banished by my father."

I sigh and pull my phone out of my pocket. "I'll call my mother and ask her if she knows what happened when they were left at the border and if she knows where they went."

Before Gryffin can stop me, because I can see he wants to, I press the screen and put my phone to my ear. It rings a couple of times and then cuts off. I look at the phone in surprise before trying again. This time it goes straight to messages.

I roll my eyes and shove my phone into my pocket.

"I think she declined my call and then turned her phone off. That's weird. Then again, she's probably pissed at me. I bet she blames me for the consequences of her own actions. It wouldn't surprise me if she found someone to lick her wounds for her—metaphorically and physically."

Gryffin grimaces.

"Come on, let's go. There's no point in wasting our time. I wouldn't even know where to start looking for Brock and Niles, since I don't know where they live."

"The watch teams should have changed over now, and it should be easy enough for us to get back to our apartment, then we can sneak you in so no one asks any questions. Bryson was going to make sure that all on duty teams were out patrolling in areas that aren't close by."

When we return to the bakery, I give my grandparents hugs and promise to keep in touch. Granny packs us a bag of things to eat for breakfast, and with a goodbye to Olivia and Justin, we walk from the bakery to watch headquarters. Thanks to the rain, we only come across a couple of people who don't pay attention to us because they are too busy trying to get out of the weather.

We make our way through headquarters without being accosted, and then we eat breakfast in the guys' living area. We talk about the mission and all the possible scenarios, but eventually, we decide to go to sleep since we will be getting up at midnight to travel into the human zone.

I share Liam's bed, but I can't help noticing that Gryffin and Gem go into the same room. Gem gives me a wink before he closes the door, and I imagine what the two of them might get up to.

"Does it bother you?" Liam asks, sounding concerned as I close the door behind me. I find him sitting on his bed, already stripped down to his briefs, a small frown between his eyebrows.

"What? Gem and Gryffin?"

He nods.

"No, not at all."

He loses the frown as I toe off my shoes, remove my pants, and undo my bra, pulling it out from underneath my shirt. He watches with amusement as I toss them off to the side and climb into bed with him. He inhales deeply and arches an eyebrow. "No indeed. I would even go so far as to say you might enjoy it very much. Am I right?"

I shrug and snuggle down as he pulls me into his arms. "Sure, we will get there eventually. As much as everyone is encouraging me to rush this, it will happen as it needs to happen. I won't deny that I like the idea of having multiple men in my bed. It isn't what I'm used to, but I'm intrigued, and I'm not going to feel ashamed of it."

"You're perfect for us," he murmurs and places a kiss on my forehead. "Now how about we get some sleep? We didn't get much last night." He sounds smug, and he has good reason to, but he's right. We'll be on the go for the next few days, and sleep might be hard to come by. I don't know how long it will take to get from the human zone to the equine village after we find Nox —if he's even there. I don't even want to think about where we would need to start looking for him if he isn't. We may get lucky, and he might be from the same village we need to go to, but I won't count on that. Even if he is, the likelihood he returned is slim. He made it seem like he never went home, which makes total sense now that I know the context, but he did mention his sister and her family, so he must still be in contact, and maybe that will be a lead.

"You're not so bad yourself," I mumble as I snuggle into his warm chest, and he pulls the covers up over us. It's the first time I've felt warm today, and it feels amazing. "Did you set the alarm?" I ask him.

"Yeah, baby. I have. Don't worry, I'll get us where we need to go and find this elusive mate of yours. He's going to kick himself when he realizes what he's been missing."

"I'm not so sure about that. He definitely doesn't want to be part of shifter society. He knew I was the queen, and he could have said something. Sure, he helped me with the pendant, but he drove away without a backward glance and didn't say anything about being a shifter to me. There's also the issue of the last one. We have no idea who he is or where to find him."

He tugs me against him, pressing my head to his chest, and I breathe in his frosty scent and relax even further, my creature purring with happiness.

"Hopefully by the time we return to the shifter zone, someone will have come to the bond office with a new mark," he says.

"Somehow, I don't think it's going to be that simple," I mutter, closing my eyes and trying to clear my mind of everything so I can get some sleep.

"No, but we still have a little over a week until challenge day. If the equines can help us find the kids, then maybe they can track down your final mate for us too," he suggests, and I feel an inkling of hope.

"That's a good idea," I reply, and he cups my butt cheek and gives it a squeeze.

"I'm not just a pretty face." His chest rumbles with laughter, and I drift off to sleep with a smile on my lips.

TWENTY-TWO

Gem

The sheets are cold against the backs of my thighs as I slide into them and wait while Gryffin uses the bathroom. My heart races, and I feel twitchy for any number of reasons, but mostly because I'm spending the night in his bed. It will be the first time since we admitted our feelings to one another, and I'm nervous as fuck. We've been dancing around each other for so long, and if Colbie hadn't revealed herself as our mate, I would probably pounce on him the minute he climbed in next to me, but I kind of like the idea of waiting so we can share our first time with her.

He walks out of the bathroom, wearing nothing but a black pair of boxer briefs, and my mouth goes dry. Sure, I've seen Gryffin like this before, but I've always tried to keep it friendly. Now I can look at him like he's the last drop of water in the desert, and I'm thirsty. He's all hard, sculpted muscle, and I can't wait to feel him wrapped around me. I drag my gaze down his body, past his brown nipples and rippling eight pack, to the large bulge behind the thin cotton of his underwear. I know how he tastes and how he feels, having explored him with my mouth, but there are so many more things I want to do to him and for him to do to me. I want Colbie to be involved in it all.

I fist the sheets, nervous for the first time in a long while. Is Gryff going to change his mind? I've wanted him for so long, the idea that he might reject me now is terrifying. When we messed around at the ball, we didn't know about Colbie, so does knowing she's our mate change things for him? He hasn't tried to hide anything from her, and he's been open, if a little reserved, with his affection in front of her and our family, so he isn't trying to hide me like a dirty little secret, but I can't help worrying.

He strides toward the bed, turning off the overhead light and leaving the bedside lamp on before sliding into the sheets next to me. He tugs me down and wraps his delicious arms around me before placing a kiss on my lips. I melt into him, his stubble scraping deliciously against my skin as his tongue explores my mouth. I groan and rub my cock against his, allowing my hands to wander over his mostly naked body. Both of us are breathing heavily when he finally pulls away.

"As much as I would love to keep exploring your delectable body," he says, one of his hands cupping my ass and grinding me into him, "we need to get some sleep. It might be in short supply over the next few days, and I'd really like our mate to be with us for the first time." I can see he's worried and bracing himself for my reaction, but I just smile and sigh with happiness before snuggling into his chest, his naked legs tangling with mine.

"I couldn't have put it better myself," I tell him, and I feel the tension in his body seep away. "I've dreamed of this for so long that a few more hours or days won't hurt. I'm just happy to have you in my bed."

"I wouldn't want to be anywhere else," he murmurs, pressing a kiss against my head.

I chuckle. "Liar. I know both of us would like to be a couple of rooms over, but we'll let Liam have his time. He's waited for so long, and thankfully his bear seems to have settled down since they sealed the mating bond."

"Hell, I saw the guy smile at least a dozen times today. I can't remember the last time that happened," Gryff says as my eyelids grow heavy. I'm warm and comfortable and in the arms of the man I've wanted forever and never thought I could have. All is right with the world, and when we finally get our mate between us, things are going to be explosive.

"Probably never," I agree. "Can you believe the queen is our mate? I can't believe how lucky we are. She's powerful, compassionate, and not concerned one bit about appearances or who we are. It's such a relief. I know fated mates are supposed to be the perfect complement for each partner, but it seems the goddess doesn't always get it right. Look at Councilor Mason. He cheats on his wife every opportunity he gets. That's not supposed to be how gifted mates work."

"Unfortunately gifted mates doesn't always mean happiness. Some people are just rotten to the core, but I agree, Colbie is amazing, and I'm so happy to be fated to her. Hell, I was seriously worried we'd end up with Gianna or Isla Tideman."

"Agreed. I'd rather have no mate than either of them, but we need to watch Colbie's back. They'll both be gunning for her once they find out. Even if they can't harm her physically, they can do a lot of damage with their poisonous tongues, especially once they find out their parents aren't going to be on the council anymore."

"Council? The Tideman family will be lucky if they aren't sentenced to death for treason," Gryffin snarls. "But yes, I'll make sure my sisters are watching out for Gianna. She's terrified of Gretchin, and Gracelin is no slouch with cutting comments and disdainful looks either."

I scoff. "You don't have to tell me, I've been on the wrong end of their tempers over the years, but they seem to be happy about you and me," I say softly, and he gives me a squeeze.

"Of course. They have both been telling me to pull my head out of my ass for a long time. I just wish I would have listened sooner, because then I would have had you in my arms for much longer."

My heart skips a beat at his confession, and I melt like a damn ice cream in the sun. I was so angry that he wouldn't give in to the very obvious thing between us, but I now realize everything happens for a reason.

"Sleep well, Gem. When we wake up, we'll be that much closer to sealing our bond with our mate," Gryffin murmurs and rolls his hips, brushing his cock against mine again.

I groan with frustration, and he chuckles. I pull away

and roll over so I don't end up groping him in his sleep, but he just snuggles in, spooning me.

"That's not helping," I grumble as his hand strokes my abdomen, and I feel his rock-hard cock against my ass. My own cock jumps, and my balls tighten, but I grit my teeth and ignore the temptation. Once Colbie is between us, I can show both of them how amazing this will be.

Gryffin's breathing evens out, and his arm gets heavier across my waist, but my mind continues to race as I try to figure out how we can find Colbie's last mate. Putting out a kingdom wide announcement would be dangerous. If Colbie's unknown final mate gets killed before they can seal their bond, then her chance of wearing the crown will disappear. The sooner we can find Nox, the better. Even if they don't seal the bond straight away, we are safer as a unit, but judging by Colbie's blushes when she told us about him, I doubt there will be any delay. Hell, he might seal it before all of us. Then again, she was annoyed and hurt that he didn't tell her he was a shifter. If he rejects her, it's going to be difficult to stop my phoenix from turning him to ash on the spot. Hopefully the mating bond, which has now been triggered, will override his aversion to other shifters and help him see how being a part of our family is going to be the best thing for him.

I also wonder if he has a contact with the unicorn shifters, so that we don't have to beg one of them to help us track the children. Shifter children are sacred, so it should override any animosity they have.

"Stop thinking so hard, I'm trying to sleep," Gryffin grumbles behind me. "Or do I need to distract you from everything that's running through your mind?" I stiffen as his hand drifts down my abdomen and slides into the top of my boxer briefs. I thought he'd fallen asleep. Was I projecting all of my thoughts into his mind by accident? Gryff wraps his hand around my cock, and all my troubled thoughts float out of my brain as I focus on how amazing his tight grip feels as he strokes my rigid length.

He nibbles my neck as he alternates between stroking my length and rubbing his thumb along the underside of my tip, using the fluid that is now steadily leaking from it to lubricate his caresses. I groan and push my ass back against his hard dick.

"Hold still or I'll stop," he commands, and I freeze.

"Please let me touch you too," I implore, and for a moment, I think he's going to reject me, but instead, he allows me to reach back and slide my hand into his underwear. We stroke each other in tandem, my mind struggling to keep up a smooth motion when all the sensations of him finally touching me make my body tremble as my orgasm builds to a fiery peak.

His own breathing gets harsher, and his strokes falter a bit as I swirl my hand up and down his length, his precum hot against my palm.

"Your hand feels so good around my dick, and all I can think about is how you looked kneeling before me with my cock in your mouth. Such a good boy, pleasing me like that. I loved fucking your throat and seeing your eyes water. The only thing that would have been better was having Colbie at my feet as well, taking turns having me fuck her throat. If she was, I would have made you hold my cum in your mouth and feed it to her when I was spent."

Gryffin is dirty as fuck, and his words and the images

now planted in my brain have me moaning, my balls tightening. I can't hold back my orgasm any longer. I gasp, and cum erupts from the tip as Gryffin pumps my cock through my release. I feel my own hand get coated in his sticky, hot fluid as he growls in my ear. "Such a perfect fucking boy."

He pulls his hand from my boxer briefs and grabs my chin, his cum-covered grip like steel as he turns my head and kisses my mouth.

"Now hopefully we can both get some sleep," he says as he releases my chin and brings his hand to his mouth, licking my cum from his fingers. My cock kicks again as I groan at the filthy sight. He grins, rolls off the bed, and disappears into the bathroom. I hear the sink running, and I contemplate getting up and washing off my hand, but he returns with a washcloth and tosses it to me. He then goes to the drawers and pulls out two pairs of underwear, stripping off his own before replacing them. He brings the other pair over to me, and I do the same. He takes both pairs and the wash-cloth back to the bathroom to throw them in the laundry basket.

When he returns to the bed, he switches off the lamp and plunges us into darkness. Our rooms have black out blinds because we often work night shift, and no light gets through. I feel him climb into the bed, and he rolls me over and scoots me back into him again, the little spoon to his big spoon. The room is silent except for my and Gryffin's breathing, and it doesn't take long for my eyelids to grow heavy as he gently strokes my stomach in a soothing pattern. "Sleep, my pretty firestorm," he whispers as I drift off to sleep, comfort-able and sated.

The alarm on my phone rings, and I reach out to turn it off, but I realize I can't move because my body is trapped beneath a giant, hairy white tiger. Gryffin must have shifted in his sleep. Sometimes our animals take over when our subconscious is asleep, and he rumbles with annoyance when I try to extract myself from his grip. He places a large paw on my chest, pinning me on my back, as he licks my face, and I grimace as he leaves slobber behind.

"Not cool, dude," I complain, trying to push him off me, but I can't budge him. He moves his grooming to my neck, and I feel a tooth scrape the skin and freeze. The tiger's actions are very territorial and mimic how he would treat his mate. Does his tiger want to claim me as well as Colbie? My phoenix screams inside me with part defiance, part want. It's all we've ever dreamed of, Gryff's teeth marks beside our mate's. Hopefully one day, it will become a reality, but right now, I need the big hairy fur ball to get off me so we can get ready for the mission. Instead of fighting him, I use my brain to manipulate him into wanting to get off.

"Hey, fluffy kitty, how about you get off me so we can get our mate some food? She's going to need to keep her strength up for the mission," I coax him, and he freezes and tips his head to the side. The same ocean blue eyes he has in his human form stare at me, his elongated pupils shifting as I see him think over my words. I guess he likes what I have to say, because with one more lick across my face, he leaps off the bed, heading for the bathroom. Gryffin must grab control, because I hear the shower turn on not five minutes later as I drag myself out of bed and look at the time. It's midnight, and the neutral zone curfew goes into effect in an hour. We have just enough time to order some food before we need to be on our way. I place a large order with a food app and contemplate joining Gryffin in the shower, but that would probably be a bad decision. I wouldn't be able to keep my hands or mouth off him, and that would make us late, so instead, I grab my clothes and head back to my own room to shower.

When I emerge dressed in a clean watch uniform that will shift with me if I need it and a pack of essentials, I find everyone in the living area passing around boxes of Chinese. I placed a huge order, so there's enough for everyone, and I feel happy when I see Colbie has a big plate of food in front of her.

"Good call on the food." Hunter lifts the box he has in his hand in thanks. "I was just going to place an order when the front desk called and said there was a delivery for us."

"I figured we want to keep a low profile in the human zone, and going through a drive-through probably isn't the way to do that," I reply as I grab a plate from the kitchen counter and start serving myself. "I'm sorry, I probably should have asked what you two like, but I was trying to be efficient," I say to Micah and Colbie.

Colbie shakes her head, but her mouth is full, so she can't say anything, but Micah just waves a hand.

"I'm not fussy. Hell, I eat raw fish and sea life when I'm in the ocean. Honestly, one thing I love most about being in the military is the variety of food. Although we don't live in the ocean, we source most of our food from it, and it becomes boring after a while. There are only so many ways you can cook fish or shellfish."

Colbie finishes her mouthful and looks at Micah. "You don't live in the ocean?"

He shrugs. "We have a couple of underwater colonies, and the majority of the mer live there. My family has two residences, one underwater and one on the coastal village that is the mers' life blood. We survive on supplying seafood to the rest of the kingdoms. Although the fae, witches, and vampires all have their own coastal villages, none of them are as efficient with sea life as we are." He stops for a moment. "Actually, some of the fae are, but they tend to keep all their produce for their own people, so despite the indifference from shifters, we're the reason they get seafood."

"I just don't understand the prejudice. Who cares what you shift into? It's stupid," Colbie mutters aggressively, and I smile. She's exactly what the shifters need. Lucas tried to integrate the three shunned breeds, but he wasn't successful. I'm sure our queen will have more success, especially since she has three mates of those exact species, and she won't stand for them being treated badly.

"Come on, eat up," Hunter announces, standing and putting his plate in the dishwasher. "We need to get going soon. Curfew came into effect ten minutes ago, and the streets should be clear. I want to get to the human zone and the pegasus's house while it's still dark. The less humans who see us around, the better."

"The human zone will probably still be busy, since they don't have a curfew," Brodie points out.

"My grandparents' village is out of the city a ways. I

wouldn't worry too much. Nox's place is secluded, and there are no houses around. We should be able to get in without being detected."

"Okay, good. We'll leave in half an hour," Hunter warns us, and the rest of us finish eating as he disappears, probably to brief his dad on our departure.

Colbie

We move quickly through the neutral zone, keeping to the back alleys and arriving at the checkpoint without too many hassles. A human man is waiting for us there. He hands us the keys to a car and an access pass to open the gate to the parking structure. He nods his head at me and wishes us a safe trip to visit my grandparents, though I can see by the speculation in his gaze that he knows we are doing something completely different.

Of course he does. There would be a record of my grandparents entering the neutral zone and staying, but it seems like General Bryson's counterpart is going to look the other way. Hopefully that means he isn't in on the plan to take me out before I can accept the crown. He disappears into the checkpoint office as we climb into a large black car that fits all seven of us. Hunter takes the wheel, and Micah is in the passenger seat.

Brodie, Gem, and Gryffin are in the middle row, then Liam and I are in the back. Liam looks a little squashed, and I wrinkle my nose.

"Maybe we should take two cars. Nox isn't going to be able to fit in here with us if we find him," I reason as Hunter pulls the car out of the parking structure and onto the road. It's clear, with no other traffic coming and going from the neutral zone.

"Hunter or I can fly if we find him, but probably me because I can cloak myself from human view."

"Gem's right. I'd rather us all stick together than worry about being separated if we are attacked," Gryffin says, and the car falls silent. Only the quiet sound of music playing over the radio can be heard above the sound of the tires on the road as we make our way to the city. The roads stay relatively empty, and it takes a lot less time to get to my grandparents' village than it did on the bus. There's no constant stopping and starting to let people on and off.

When we get to the village, I give him directions to Nox's off-road track to get to his cottage. When Hunter pulls in behind it, there are no lights shining through any of the windows, but then again, he wouldn't expect company at almost three in the morning. We pile out of the car, but I hold up my hand as the others head toward the house.

"Whoa," I hiss at them. "The last thing Nox needs is to be ambushed by a group of you. He's obviously hiding for a reason, and seeing all of you on his front porch is a good way to send him running out the back door. Hold back and let me speak to him first," I order them, and Gryffin goes to argue, but Brodie doesn't let him.

"Gryff, the queen gave an order, and your mate is asking nicely." He turns to me and smiles.

"Call out if you need us. We'll be there in seconds."

"Actually, I'll be there quicker." Gem fades out of view, and I sigh. I guess one of them is coming with me after all, but it seems to make the other guys less anxious. Gryff nods and leans against the front bumper of the car, crossing his arms over his chest.

"Be careful." Liam kisses me on the temple, and I start toward the front steps. The salty smell of the ocean reaches my nose as I get farther away from my mates, but I can still smell Gem's ashy whiskey scent, even though I can't see him. The sound of the waves crashing against the shore muffles the sound of our feet. I mount the steps, and in the moonlight that shines through the thick cloud cover, I notice the chairs that used to be there are gone, as are the surfboards and surfing paraphernalia. The deck is completely empty, and my heart sinks. I have a feeling when I knock on the door, I'm not going to get an answer.

Taking a deep breath, I do just that, but like I assumed, Nox doesn't come stumbling to the door, sleepy and sexy like I imagined. There's nothing but silence and the sound of the crashing waves. Gem fades into view and puts his hand on my shoulder.

"I'm sorry, sweetheart."

I sigh. "I should have known that once he saw I was the shifter queen, he wasn't going to stick around for me to find him. Now what? He could be anywhere in the kingdom. Hell, he could have fled to another kingdom. That's what I would do. That's what I contemplated when I was first marked with these." I shove my wrists out, showing the marks on them.

He frowns. "Yeah, but you realized there was no running away and stepped up to accept your responsibilities. This dude just keeps running. Being marked as part of a bond is supposed to be a privilege. It's an instant family."

I scowl. "I only stopped running after being given a stern talking to by the goddess who told me there was nowhere I could escape to. Don't be angry with him, we don't know what Nox has been through. There must be a reason he felt like he couldn't be a part of something like that. Maybe he thought he didn't deserve it." I think about something he said to me. "But I have a feeling it wasn't his family that made him that way. He mentioned his sister visiting."

"Well, if he has a sister, then the equine village should be our next stop," Gem says as we walk back to the car. "He's not here," he tells the others when we get there.

"We guessed he might not be, and I heard what you guys were saying. The equine village will be the best place for us to look next. Zalfari is quite a distance. It sits at the base of the Aramis Rift."

"Can we take the car?" I look at it with hope, not relishing the idea of flying all the way there on Hunter's back. It's probably going to be pretty damn cold.

Hunter nods. "Yes. The neutral zone doesn't actually separate the two zones completely. We can drive around it and go through one of the other checkpoints along the divide closer to the village."

"We will have to stop when the snow gets too thick, since the roads aren't plowed that far out, and go on foot. It's already quite thick at that elevation, or it was when I was there last," Gryffin tells me, and I frown.

"When were you there?" I ask. I remember him mentioning something when I told them about being their mate, but I had so many other things running through my head, I didn't really pay attention.

"That night when I saw you in the stables, I had just returned from there. I was looking for our sixth, but it was weird. The alpha of the village was cagey, and you said it is supposed to be an equine village, but he's a lion shifter, and I didn't scent any equines close by."

A rumble comes out of Liam's chest. "I don't like the sound of that."

"He said there was a curfew because of feral shifters hiding out in the Aramis Rift, but something just seemed to feel wrong about it. There is something off about that village. It was like they were just trying to get rid of me, and I had to get back so I didn't really question it."

"So we need to go in expecting trouble then? We didn't bring any weapons with us." Brodie shifts uncomfortably. "Should we return to watch headquarters and grab some?"

Micah shakes his head. "If we go through the checkpoint on the way there, then there is a military base where we can grab what we need."

"We don't really need weapons with the combination of shifters we have, and with Micah's experience, we're kind of a formidable team," Liam points out, unable to keep his hands to himself any longer and tugging me against him. I smother the smile that wants to cross my lips at the fact that he can't seem to keep his hands off me. I can't even begin to imagine what it's going to be like when I'm bonded to all of them.

"Let's go. It's going to take a couple of hours to get where we need to, and I'd like to approach the town in daylight so we aren't at a disadvantage due to the dark. Gem, you should probably do a fly over in stealth mode and see if you can spot any problems before we go in just to be sure," Hunter says.

I thought Gryffin was the head alpha of this bond group, but it seems he and Hunter share the role. Perhaps being the general's son gives him more tactical experience, and Gryffin acknowledges that. I don't know, but none of them seem to take issue with Hunter's orders.

We head to the car, and I look back at Nox's cabin as we drive away, sighing.

"Don't be sad, angel." Liam tugs me against his side and puts his arm around my shoulders. "We will find your wayward mate, and all will be right with the world. Soon, all of this will be behind us, and you will wish for excitement in your days of dealing with petty shifter squabbles."

"With eight mates, I don't think my days are ever going to be boring," I mumble, closing my eyes as the car lulls me into a dozy state.

He chuckles, and his whole body vibrates beneath me as he presses a kiss to the top of my head. "No, you may be right," he says as my eyelids drift closed, and I get more much needed sleep.

"Don't wake her. I'll just grab a few things, and then we can be on our way again," Micah says, but it's too late. Something disturbed my slumber. I'm not sure if it's my stiff body from sleeping upright or the fact that the car stopped, but I yawn and stretch my back, getting off of Liam's lap where my head somehow ended up.

"It's okay. I would like to stretch my legs," I mumble, wiping my mouth to make sure I haven't been drooling on his crotch.

The car doors open, and the guys in the middle row get out, allowing Liam and I to follow them. After the heat of the car, the cold air makes me shiver as I look around. We are at some kind of military outpost with a huge wall that seems to stretch as far as the eye can see in either direction.

"Wow, I knew the human and shifter zones were divided, but I had no idea that was literal."

"Shifters are very territorial, and while they generally don't have a beef with humans, it is best not to test them. The wall runs the length of Aramis, and only the section with the neutral zone doesn't have it. The goddess herself erected it at the end of the war when tensions were still high." A voice I don't recognize has me spinning to see a male shifter in military fatigues approaching us.

"Major Payne." Micah salutes the man, and Hunter does as well, which surprises me.

"At ease, captains," he says, and my eyebrows jump. I hadn't realized Hunter had a rank. I thought he was just a part of Watch Team One. Maybe that's why Gryffin deferred to him. "Prince Gryffin." The man bows his head slightly, and it's Gryffin's turn to acknowledge him. "What are you all doing here? I had no reports from the general or the king saying you were coming through." His tone is neutral, but there is suspicion in his eyes, and his gaze lingers on me too long.

"Queen Colbie is on a diplomatic mission to Zalfari. She is extending an invitation to the equine shifters to nominate a member of their ranks for a council position." Gryffin gestures to me, and the major snaps to attention, kneeling and bowing his head with respect.

"My queen, it is an honor to meet you," he says and waits for me to give him the command to rise. I don't know if I like all this genuflecting, but I guess it must be a shifter custom, because most of them have done it when meeting me.

"Please rise, and it's a pleasure to meet you too, Major Payne," I say, and he gets to his feet.

"Zalfari you say? What do you need from us? An armed escort?" he asks, but Micah shakes his head.

"No, that won't be necessary. I just wanted to grab a few weapons as backup."

"But you can conjure yours out of thin air," the major says. "Why would you need more? Are you expecting trouble? If so, we could accompany you."

"You can conjure your weapon?" Liam looks impressed, and Brodie looks like he's dying to ask Micah to show him his sword. Micah rolls his eyes and holds out his hand.

In a burst of magic, a three pronged trident appears in his hand. It's silver with markings on it, and there is a gorgeous, large, white pearl in the center of it. "I can, but it's not very practical. A gun is quicker and cleaner than me stabbing everyone with this," he explains as it disappears again.

"That's so cool!" Brodie is giving off that golden retriever vibe, and I bet if he was in wolf form, his tail would be wagging.

"Yes, but slightly impractical. I'll head to the armory and get what I need, if that's okay with you, Major?" Micah asks, and the major gives his approval.

"We aren't expecting any trouble, but I like to be prepared for any occasion. I won't take risks with the queen and prince's safety," Hunter explains, and the major seems to accept his reasoning.

"Do you have a restroom I can use please?" I ask the major, my bladder becoming very insistent all of a sudden.

"Of course, follow me." He starts back toward the large building that Micah disappeared into, and I follow him, flanked by Brodie and Liam, with Hunter bringing up the rear.

"Are you coming?" I ask Gem and Gryffin, but the phoenix shakes his head, gesturing between himself and the prince.

"We're going to take the car and fill it up at the gas station, then grab us some food for the rest of the journey. We will have to shift in about an hour, and we are going to need all the energy we can get."

"Okay." I wave and follow the others inside, happy to be out of the cold.

"Have there been any problems in Zalfari recently? Any reports on an increase in feral numbers?" Hunter asks the major as he leads us through the command post. I look around, trying to take everything in, but it's mostly just cubicles with a few uniformed men and women sitting in them.

The major frowns. "Not that I know of. I haven't

had any reports come across my desk, but why don't we ask Staff Sergeant Jamison. He mans the switchboard that takes reports of any feral sightings, and he has family in the village, from what I understand." We stop by a desk that has a large blond shifter sitting at it. He looks up with surprise, but his eyes narrow ever so slightly as he takes in the major.

"Can I help you, sir?" he asks politely, his gaze shifting to the rest of us before resting back on his commanding officer.

"Yes. Have there been any reports of feral shifters coming out of the Aramis Rift recently? Specifically in Zalfari?" the major asks, and although he tries to hide his reaction, I see him stiffen at the question.

He shakes his head. "No, sir, not recently."

"See?" The major turns his attention to Hunter who frowns.

"That's strange. Prince Gryffin was there recently and said they had a curfew in place due to the rise in ferals."

The major's eyes widen with surprise. "A curfew? Really? I mean, it makes sense if there has been a rise in sightings. The residents of that village are mainly equines, which would make a tasty snack for the ferals, so a curfew is a sensible thing to put into place. We know they are more active at night. I'm surprised they haven't reported it though." He turns back to the sergeant who is listening closely to the conversation. "You have family in the village, don't you?"

The sergeant nods. "Yes. My uncle is the alpha shifter there. He takes the safety of his village seriously."

"What is the main livelihood of the village of Zalfari? I know they guard the pass through the rift, but they must have some other form of income," Liam asks conversationally, but his jaw is tight with tension. He suspects there is more going on. I can't say I don't blame him. My stomach is also tight with tension. Something just feels off, even to me.

"Well, equine shifters aren't really useful for anything, and they are too prideful to be used for transportation or to pull carts, and the pegasus and unicorns refuse to use their magic to aid anyone else," the sergeant sneers.

"What the fuck?" I mutter, disgusted by his comment. "Of course they are. They aren't pack mules."

"So how do they make any money to survive?" Brodie asks.

The sergeant scoffs. "They sell their magical abilities to other kingdoms. Fucking traitors, if you ask me. They refuse to help shifters, but happily pimp themselves out to anyone who needs them."

I see the major's eyes widen in surprise at the venom in the sergeant's tone, and I can tell all of this is news to him. Before anyone else can say anything, Micah appears, carrying a duffel bag with two guns strapped to his thighs.

"Okay, I'm good to go," he tells us, gesturing to the bag.

"Oh, Your Majesty, I was going to show you the bathroom. Right this way, if you don't mind." The major shows me to the ladies' restroom.

When I return, we head back out through the base, but I feel eyes on me, and when I turn around, the sergeant is watching me closely. I ignore him and put it down to the fact that he overheard the major call me by my title. So much for keeping a low profile.

TWENTY-FOUR

Colbie

W e're back on the road within half an hour, tucking into the food Gem and Gryff picked up.

"Did that sergeant give anyone else bad vibes?" Brodie asks around a mouthful of sandwich before taking a sip of his soda. "I bet he picked up the phone and called his uncle to tell him we were heading his way the minute we left the building."

Hunter tells the others who weren't there what we talked about with the major.

Gryffin groans. "I have no doubt you're right," he says, agreeing with Brodie.

"Doesn't matter. We'll go in alert, ready for anything. We're loaded for a fight now. I grabbed some-thing for everyone." Micah sounds confident, and Hunter grunts an agreement.

"I doubt they would try anything. They would be

stupid to take us on. I'll just shift into my dragon form and set them all on fire."

"I didn't like the sergeant's attitude. That village is supposed to be a haven for the equines. How did a lion shifter end up as the alpha?" Liam grumbles next to me.

"No, there was no love lost for the equines with the sergeant," I point out. "He sounded downright aggressive toward them. Do you think they are holding them hostage or something?"

"It wouldn't surprise me. It makes me rethink this visit. It sounds like we are going into a hostile environment, and I'm not sure we can guarantee Colbie's safety," Hunter says, and I can see from here that his hands are tight with tension, his knuckles white from how hard he's gripping the steering wheel. "Maybe we should turn around and come back with a couple more teams."

"No!" I shout and lean forward in my seat. "What if Nox is one of those shifters? What if they'll kill them now that they know we're coming? We need to stop them." My heart races with panic. "Please, we can't stop now. I promise to listen and do everything you tell me to." I have a sense of urgency flooding my system. We're running out of time, and I need to be crowned sooner rather than later. "Not to mention the missing children."

"The sergeant made it sound like the equines won't help us find the children. We need to be prepared for that," Liam warns me gently.

A growl of anger barrels out of my chest, and he flinches with surprise.

"Their poor families must be so worried. We need to at least appeal to the equines for their help."

"And if they won't?" Gem turns to look at me. "Are you prepared to throw your weight around as queen and use the power the goddess gifted you? You may further damage the already shaky relationship they have with the rest of the shifter kingdom."

My stomach rolls at the idea of forcing the equines to help us, but I will do anything to bring those kids home. "If they won't help us, then we need to focus on finding my final mate and getting the crown on my head. Then, they won't have any choice but to help us," I tell him, and he gives me a nod of approval.

"Good girl. Sometimes you have to make unpopular choices that benefit others."

"I hate the idea of children being out there, scared and unable to shift back. I don't want to make them wait longer, and I certainly don't want to have to force the equines to help us, but I will if it means they will bring those children home to their parents. You said that shifter children are sacred, though, so I'm hoping it won't come down to forcing the equines."

"You may be right. Finding the children should override any feelings of being rejected." Micah nods. "The mers would help out if it involved children despite despising a good portion of the shifter population."

My stomach sinks at his words. How did the relationship between the general shifter population and those three outlining breeds get so bad? And how has it been allowed to fester? Lucas told me he tried to do something about it, but was blocked by the majority of the council at every turn. I won't be sad to see the backs of the ones I'm replacing. I'm going to have to work extra hard if I'm going to create harmony amongst the shifters, but that's going to have to take a back seat for the moment.

After about an hour, Hunter pulls the car into a

clearing in the forest. There are a couple of other vehicles in the lot, so I'm assuming it's used by other people from Zalfari as well. My eyes land on a familiar vehicle, and excitement thrums through my body.

"That's Nox's truck." I point to it, practically vibrating with enthusiasm at the sight of it.

"Well, that's a positive sign." Brodie offers me his hand to help me out of the car, and Micah goes around to the trunk to grab the duffel bag, then he starts handing out weapons. I look around the clearing, shivering slightly, but it's not as cold as I thought it would be. I guess the watch uniform has layers of protection from the weather. I don't see any sign of Nox, though, not even footprints. When I turn my attention back to the guys, they all have guns and knives strapped to various parts of their bodies.

Micah looks at me. "Do you have any experience with weapons?"

I shake my head. "Hell no, unless you count a carving knife. I'd probably shoot myself in the foot."

He chuckles. "That's okay, just stay close."

"So we aren't going to shift?" I ask, pointing to all the weapons. Wouldn't they all fall off if they shift?

"These all have witch runes on them. They will shift with us, much like the uniforms we're wearing," he explains.

"Huh, that's cool." I can't help sounding impressed.

"Gem and I are going to take to the air. Gem is going to fly ahead to the village and scope it out, and I'm going to clear the snow in front of you to make an easy trail and keep watch from overhead," Hunter says. "I think you should shift into your tiger form for the trip through the forest. It thins out the closer we get to the rift, but the tiger will manage the terrain just fine. Stay close to Gryffin. The shadow the mountains cast makes it harder for the trees to grow. The village sits on the other side."

I could see the huge mountain range the closer we drove, and it doesn't surprise me that it casts a large shadow over the village.

"What about Micah?" I ask, worried about my mer mate. He doesn't have an animal to shift into. I bet the merman probably doesn't have much snow experience either. Would he even be able to keep up with us in our shifted form? Is this why the other shifters look down on the mers?

"Don't worry about me. Mer are fast on our feet, even if we aren't in our shifted form," he assures me, but Hunter shakes his head.

"He can ride with me again. It won't hurt to have two sets of eyes watching over you." He looks at Micah, who quickly agrees to the suggestion. Micah reaches into the trunk and straps a crossbow and a quiver of arrows to his back as well. He also grabs our backpacks, tossing them on the ground.

I frown. "You look like you're expecting trouble." I nibble my lip in concern. "Maybe I should stay in the car. I'm just going to get in the way if we do get attacked."

"No, you need to be with us to speak to the equines about the children. They will have a harder time refusing you than any of us," Gryffin tells me. "And you aren't necessarily safe in the car either."

"Don't worry, we will protect you. Nothing is going to happen to you with all of us here." Brodie grins and changes into his wolf. I watch with amazement as his clothes and weapons morph, disappearing beneath his fur. I have no idea what the mechanics or science is… or maybe we should go with magic. It has to be, because nothing else makes sense.

He bounds over to me, wagging his tail, and bumps his body against my legs in greeting. He's so large, his head is level with my breasts, and he sniffs around my boobs before licking one of them. I yelp in surprise, and he gives me a naughty wolf grin, his tongue hanging out. I run a hand through the fur on his head. He is predominantly black but has patches of gray and white on his underside.

"Away with you," Liam growls, shifts into his bear, and tackles Brodie. I gasp in shock and step forward to break up the fight. They are roaring and barking and rolling around on the ground with fur flying everywhere, but Gryffin stops me before I can get too close.

"Ignore them, they are always like this," he grumbles, eyeing them with annoyance.

"They have always been. The two of them can't help themselves. Stick with Gryff, and I'll see you in the village." Gem gives me a wink, shifts, and shoots into the sky, leaving a trail of fire behind him before disappearing from sight.

"Invisibility is so cool." I try to find him in the sky, but there isn't a single sign of him.

"Yeah, until he uses it to perv on you in the shower," Gryffin grumbles, but he doesn't sound particularly perturbed.

"Keep your senses on high alert," Hunter growls at Gryffin before stalking away to give himself room to shift. I watch and wince as his body morphs, growing and changing until the deep dark purple dragon spreads his wings and stretches like a house cat. Micah loads the backpacks onto Hunter's back, securing them to one of his spikes with a strap. When he's finished, Micah turns to me, lifts my hand, and presses a kiss to it.

"Be safe, Colbie," he says, narrowing his eyes on Gryffin before he runs and leaps onto Hunter's back, and the dragon launches into the air. I gasp at the magnificent sight as he soars away from us, spiraling upwards.

"Show-offs," Gryffin says, but he doesn't sound upset. "Come on, shift into your tiger form, and we will race those two idiots to the village."

Before he can shift, I grab his arm, my nerves erupting now that it's my turn to change forms. "What if I can't keep up?" I ask him, and he smiles, his ocean blue eyes warm and encouraging.

"Trust me, I'll make sure you won't fall. It will feel like you've been running on four paws all your life."

The other two idiots have given up their fight, and they amble over to us. Brodie sits on his haunches and releases a reassuring yip, while Liam nudges his huge, polar bear head against my chest in reassurance, and I just about tip over. Gryffin grabs me, stopping me from falling backwards into the snow-covered parking lot. A shadow overhead has me looking up to see Hunter breathe a steam of fire, melting the snow in a line toward the thick forest we need to travel through.

"Won't he burn the forest down?" I ask as Gryffin helps me stand.

"He won't be able to melt the snow under the trees. We will have to plow through that ourselves, but don't worry, our animals will move across it like it isn't even there. It's just the expanse of flat plain before the village that he will help with. To be honest, it isn't that bad. I did it with no problems. He's just trying to make it easier for you. Mostly, he is our eyes in the sky."

"But the thick tree coverage will make it hard for him to see," I argue.

He winces. "He has great eyesight, but it's not like he could be on the ground with us anyway. A dragon would knock the forest down, not move through it stealthily."

He has a point, and I hadn't thought about that. I just don't like the idea of splitting up.

"Okay, but promise you won't leave me?" I ask him, and he pulls me into a hug.

"Never. I promise." He pulls back and looks like he's going to kiss me. I hold my breath and wait, but Liam shoves his head between us and grunts.

"Cockblock," Gryffin mutters, but he pulls away and shifts into his tiger. I take a deep breath and picture myself turning into a tiger like the huge creature that yawns lazily in front of me. My magic explodes, and I shift, the bite of pain familiar now.

My senses expand, and my whiskers twitch as my tiger scans our surroundings. I take a back seat as she leaps forward toward the forest, following the bear and the wolf as they take the lead. Gryffin's tiger, who is bigger and more muscular than mine, sticks to my side like glue, and when we stumble, he uses his body to support us so we don't fall on our head. After a few yards, we seem to get control over our body, and she leaps forward with more speed. Gryffin matches our pace and chuffs his approval as we reach the forest and move through the crowded trees with ease. I have no idea where we are going, but I am comfortable with allowing the guys to lead. My tiger's eyesight can see a lot farther than I can, and her sense of smell is so much stronger than mine. She can even feel the vibrations of small critters taking cover from the predators that now grace the forest.

I lose track of time and allow my mind to wander, confident that my tiger is in control. What are we going to find when we get to the village? Where are the equines? Has something sinister happened to them or are they under curfew for their protection? They are considered prey animals and would probably be fairly vulnerable to any feral shifters who hide in the Aramis Rift. Apparently, there is a tunnel that leads through the rift, which allows access to the vampire kingdom of Eryx, but the actual mountain range is wild and untamed and a perfect place for the ferals to hide from their punishment. Despite being feral, their animals still long for packs, and they occasionally leave the rift in search of something they've mostly forgotten in their feral state.

We've been running for at least an hour, and my tiger is starting to puff from exertion when a strange scent hits my nose. The others must smell it too, because they slow down, their bodies tense with antici-pation. Before we can figure out what has put us on high alert, though, a twang echoes through the trees, and an arrow hits Liam directly. I slide to a stop and watch in horror as his snow white chest bleeds to red, and he tumbles over, an arrow sticking out of his torso.

I lose my shift, and my human form explodes out of me. I find myself on all fours, the snow cold against my human skin as I scream in horror.

"Liam, no!" I scramble toward him as blood seeps

across his white fur before dripping into the snow, creating red craters where it lands.

Figures jump down from the trees and circle us. My wolf and tiger growl in warning as they flank Liam and me to protect us, but we are outmanned.

I hear a man chuckle evilly. "Well, well, well, what do we have here? A queen and her useless protectors."

"I call it a pay day, Alpha. Did you see the way I took out the polar bear? His pelt will make a nice rug for my floor. I want to fuck the queen on it," a raspy, low voice says as I get to Liam and drag his polar bear head into my lap. His eyes stare blankly up at the sky, and I know instantly from the aching hole inside me that he is gone. I sob, completely heartbroken at the loss of my mate.

"Kill the wolf and tiger and bring me the queen. We will have some fun with her before we get rid of her as well."

I lift my head and glare at the dirty blond male who is in charge. He's stocky but not very tall, and his face has a scar across one eye.

My gaze slides around to the other men with him. All of them have weapons aimed at us, some holding bows and others guns. We are completely outgunned, even with Gryffin and Brodie to defend us.

"Why?" I snarl. "What do you gain from all this?" If we're going to die, I want to know why.

"Like Brant said. We're going to be rich for taking out the queen and freeing up the royal power for someone else to claim. Hell, maybe I'll be king now—a lion king. It's only right that the king of the jungle is king of the shifters." This must be the head alpha of

Zalfari. We knew they were suspicious, but this is beyond bold. This is war.

They don't know that they don't need to kill me. The power is up for grabs now that one of my mates is dead, but they don't know Liam is my mate, and I'm not going to enlighten them.

Before I can reply to his ridiculous claim, a thunderous roar echoes through the forest, and the shifters surrounding us bristle with agitation. I glance up and smile sadly. Hunter is about to descend on us, but it's too late to save Liam.

"What the fuck is that?" one of them asks, looking skyward, and I feel a deadly smile cross my lips.

"That is your worst nightmare," I tell them as Hunter crashes through the trees, splintering wood and sending branches flying. He lands and sprays a burst of fire at the fleeing shifters. Two of them disintegrate on the spot as Micah leaps from Hunter and aims his crossbow at another, shooting him through the back. He grunts and falls to the snow, spread eagle and very dead, an arrow piercing his heart just like my mate.

Three down, eleven more to go. Those eleven have found cover behind trees, though, and they start to fire back. Hunter ambles forward and puts himself between me and the line of fire, bullets pinging harmlessly off his dragon scales. My wolf and tiger leap forward and attack, dodging bullets and arrows. The two shifters they target abandon their weapons and shift. Two wolves take their place as Brodie and Gryffin lunge at them, their teeth and claws digging into fur. I hear another gunshot and then a grunt, and I look over to find Micah has been hit. A bullet hole in his arm causes blood to run down his bicep, and he drops the crossbow before snatching a gun out of his hip holster with his left hand and firing.

Seeing his blood triggers something feral inside me. My magic explodes out of me, and I shift into my hydra form. All eight heads roar with anger as I push past Hunter, who is chomping down on a screaming man. Brodie and Gryffin have both taken care of the shifters they were fighting, leaving eight alive, including the man who killed Liam and their lion leader.

Their mouths drop open in shock as they stare up at me. "What the fuck is that?" the one who killed Liam asks, and the lion starts to back up.

"A fucking hydra. Run," he replies and starts to turn, but my hydra isn't letting them get away. After making sure our mates are out of range, each head focuses on one of the remaining combatants. We inhale and breathe out, a plume of green vapor encasing the assholes who dared to attack us. They start to scream and claw at their faces and chests as they inhale the acidic haze. I watch, horrified and slightly awed, as their skin starts to melt, exposing bone and tissue until the remaining eight shifters are nothing but bloody mounds of goo staining the snow. The silence in the clearing is deafening, the only sound from Hunter's dragon's heavy breathing.

"Holy fuck," Brodie, who must have shifted back into his human form, mutters with a small amount of fear, but I also hear the pride as well. "Our mate is spectacular." I turn my back on the gruesome sight, and one of my heads ducks down to nudge Brodie. He absently scratches it between the eyebrow ridges, unable to drag his attention from the carnage, but to my relief, there's no fear, he's just distracted.

Another one of my heads nudges Liam, a mournful wail escaping its mouth. It grabs hold of the arrow shaft in Liam's chest and yanks it out, tossing it to the side before licking the wound. All of my guys have shifted now, and they gather around their fallen bond mate. Hunter's eyes are haunted, and his hand is shaking.

"We didn't see them," he murmurs. "They were hidden in the treetops."

Gryffin clamps a hand on his shoulder and gives it a squeeze. "We didn't even scent them until it was too late. They must have been using a charm to conceal themselves." He tries to reassure the dragon, but it isn't working.

I hate seeing them like this, but a feeling of inner peace washes over me, and I know everything will be okay. My hydra makes me see the truth. It concedes control to me, and I shift back into my human form. I rush over to them as Liam suddenly changes and gasps for breath.

"Holy fuck, he's alive!" Micah shouts as I stumble over to Liam's side and throw myself at him.

"Their mate bond... Her hydra bite gave him the ability to regenerate from death." Gem appears from the trees, looking haggard and broken. "Thank fuck, because I couldn't make it here to save him. I felt him die, and I couldn't do anything."

My lips press against Liam's, and despite him looking a little disoriented, he kisses me back. The rest of the guys fall to their knees and surround us in a group hug, laughing and crying at the fact that their bond mate is still with us.

I pull back and check him over, poking my finger through the hole in his uniform that should have protected him from the projectile. The wound is gone, and there is nothing but smooth skin.

"Fuck, that hurt," he mutters as Hunter gets up and nudges one of the shifters Gryffin or Brodie killed. He squats down and digs through his pockets, pulling out a small rock then holding it out for us to see, a look of distaste on his face.

"Runes are etched into it. It must be why we couldn't hear or sense them and why it penetrated your uniform, which should have protected you from projectiles. I'm not sure if they are witch or fae runes, but this is no longer just an internal shifter problem. They are getting assistance from other kingdoms."

Brodie helps Liam to his feet as Gryffin does the same thing to me.

"Thank goodness it was Liam who was hit. If it had been Gryffin or Brodie, then they would be *dead*, dead," Micah says, looking around the clearing at all the dead shifters. "I'm going to guess this was a welcome party from Zalfari. It's the only option. No one else knew we were coming here." He looks at Gem for confirmation.

"Yes. When I did a fly over of the village, it was basically deserted. I saw a couple of people moving between dwellings, but not as many as there should be for the middle of the day."

My mind is stuck on Micah's comment. He's right. If it was one of the others, then there would be no resurrection or regeneration. They would be cold corpses lying in the snow. My hydra screams inside me, and my body explodes into that form once more. The guys stumble backwards out of the way so they aren't crushed underfoot.

"Hey, Colbie, easy. Liam's alive, He's fine. You need

to calm down." Brodie talks to me like I'm an injured creature about to lash out, and he isn't wrong. Five of my heads duck down and strike, biting into the shoulders and necks of the five men who don't have my mating bite yet. They shout out in surprise and pain as my hydra mate bonds them. Even if it isn't reciprocated yet, they will be safe from any future attacks. The rush of blood explodes across my taste buds, each of them a distinctive flavor as my side of the mate bond locks into place. A wave of heat rushes through me as my heads release their prey, and I shift back into my human form. I shake with need as I sink to my hands and knees and gasp for air, the cold snow melting beneath my overheated hands.

"Oh shit, Colbie." Liam gapes at his bond mates, who all look at me like I'm prey they want to devour. "You've initiated the bonding heat with all of them."

TWENTY-FIVE

Colbie

Before I can say anything or apologize, Brodie leaps toward me and scoops me up in his arms, running away from the carnage and deeper into the forest.

I hear shouts behind us, but they die away the farther Brodie runs.

"I'm sorry. This isn't how I wanted to do this, but my wolf is feral," he says as he comes to a stop and slides me down his body before pushing me back against a tree. Brodie kisses me like I'm the air he needs to breathe. His chest heaves as he strips my confining clothes from my body, tossing my boots to the side. My core aches, and I have no complaints as I find myself suddenly naked, the tree bark scratching my back and ass as Brodie drops to his knees and runs his tongue through my soaked slit.

"You taste like heaven," he murmurs before lashing his tongue across my clit. I moan with delight and grab his hair as he tongue fucks me to a quick, intense orgasm. My hydra wasn't thinking clearly, her need to protect her mates outweighing any logic. I should stop him, but truthfully, I ache with the one-sided bond, and I want this as much as he does.

The sound of an argument somewhere behind us echoes through the trees. Poor Liam is having to deal with the fallout of my rash actions when he only just recovered from dying. I lift my head to look in that direction. I can't see the others, but they aren't far behind me. The mating heat is going to ride each of them hard, but I hope they can control themselves long enough for Brodie and me to have a moment alone.

Brodie drags my attention back to him, shoving two fingers deep into my pussy and sucking hard on my clit. Another orgasm rushes through me, and I scream as my body convulses around his fingers.

"Such a good girl, coming all over my hand," he praises before sucking on his fingers and standing up. He unzips his pants and shoves them down around his knees, palming his cock and giving it a stroke, then he lifts me, and I wrap my legs around his waist as he kisses me. I taste myself on his lips, and I shudder with anticipation as he lines his cock up with my entrance. "I promise I'll make this up to you later," he says, keeping his eyes locked on mine as he pushes me against the tree and drives his cock home, bottoming out in one thrust. I scream again, the intrusion slightly painful. He's big, and my pussy is tight from the first two orgasm, but his groan of pleasure has me relaxing, and the pain eases as the fullness becomes pleasurable.

"God, you feel so good—all tight and hot and mine," he growls before pulling out and rolling his hips in a way that lights my body up. Instead of the furious fuck I thought I would get, his pace is measured and controlled, and he works my body like a master, using his cock in a way that sets my nerve endings on fire again as I desperately beg for more.

"God, more… harder," I beg, grabbing his shoulders for purchase. I dig my heels into his ass, trying to urge him on, but he continues the maddening pace.

He chuckles wickedly and takes one of my nipples in his mouth, scraping his teeth across it before sucking it hard. My head falls back against the tree, exposing my throat to him, and he growls and presses a kiss to my pulse point.

"I'm going to bite you now and seal us together forever. You will never escape me." His words come out all growly and gruff. His wolf is on the surface, his eyes glowing with his inner shifter.

"Do it," I beg, wanting everything from this male.

He reaches between us and pinches my clit as he starts to pound into me, giving me exactly what I need to push me over the edge. My muscles seize, and my core ripples around him as an orgasm blasts through me. I scream again as his jaw shifts, and he bites down. The pain and pleasure are so exquisite, another orgasm barrels through me as he howls before licking the wound, and then I feel him fill me with his cum. He groans loudly, and his breathing is ragged as he thrusts through our orgasms before finally slowing. Still buried inside me, he tends to his bite mark, mumbling words of praise as the bond between us solidifies. I can feel his essence sitting next to Liam's, and it feels right. My eyelids drift closed as I enjoy all the sensations of his tongue on my neck, his hard cock in my pussy, and the wave of love that seems to loop between us.

"My perfect mate, my queen," he says reverently as he pulls back and kisses me. He tastes like copper, and my blood stains his lips, but I don't care. All I care about is that he is now forever linked to me and safe.

I'm not sure how long we stay locked in place, but eventually, I become aware of the bark scratching my back, and I wriggle to avoid the discomfort. Brodie swears and pulls me away from the tree, then he gently lowers me to the ground, pulling his cock free. I feel his hot cum slide down my leg and the cold snow on my feet. I shiver, and he swears and picks me back up, cradling me in his arms.

"Shit, I'm sorry. My wolf took over," he apologizes, looking around for my clothes. He helps me dress, since I'm still wobbly on my feet, then he takes me into his arms and gently cups my cheek, his bright blue eyes shining with love. "But I'm also glad I can feel you inside my chest. My wolf is content and slumbering, pleased you are now joined to us forever. I love you, Colbie," he tells me before placing a tender kiss on my lips, and I melt into him. I can feel that he means it, and it makes me breathless with joy. "When I get you to a bed, I'll worship you like the queen you are."

I giggle, giddy with the mate bond buzzing inside me. "I'm not sure I can handle much more worship."

Brodie opens his mouth to answer, but a shout behind us has him instantly tensing before he grimaces. "Well, I'm not really sure you have a choice. Your hydra messed up. There are four other shifters who will want to worship you like a goddess, and it will get harder and harder for them to resist it now that you've marked them. The one-sided bond will become painful for all of you." He winces. "Thankfully they seem to have more self-control than I did."

He takes my hand and leads me back to the destroyed clearing. There's a fire burning, and the smell of burnt flesh makes me wrinkle my nose. Hunter is in his dragon form, and his eyes glow as he turns his head to watch us approach. Liam and Micah stand next to him, and Gem and Gryffin are sprawled on the ground at their feet.

I shout and pull my hand out of Brodie's, rushing toward them, but Hunter's tail slides in front of me, stopping my forward momentum.

"Are they hurt?" I shout, pushing at his tail, which is kind of like shoving a large boulder—impossible.

Liam grimaces and shakes his head. "No, just unconscious. We had to knock them out to stop them from coming after you."

"Why aren't you affected?" Brodie asks Micah before gesturing to Hunter's dragon. "Or him? I would have thought Hunter would snatch her up and fly away to hoard her."

"Mer aren't driven by an inner animal like you are, so it's easier for us to control our instincts. We also don't bite to seal the bond."

"You don't?" I ask as panic makes my heart beat faster. "Did I do something wrong?" I ask him, but he shakes his head.

"No, you claim with your bite, but I need to shift, pluck one of my scales, and insert it under your skin to finish my part of the claim. I can't do that unless I am in the water. I will be alright until we can find a body of water for me to shift," he assures me, and my heartbeat settles.

"And you're right about Hunter's dragon. He wants to seal their bond in his hoard, but he knows that Colbie can't fly away at the moment. He agreed to go to the equine village and see what is going on there before he snatches her away," Liam says, smirking at my ruffled appearance. "Sounds like you had fun, mate." He winks, and there's no sign of any jealousy. "Congrats, my friend. I'm so happy for both of you," he tells Brodie, who tugs me against him and wraps his arm around me. It seems like he's going to be as touchy-feely as Liam was, which I absolutely love. My mother wasn't big on affection, and I've been slightly touch starved in the last few years, unable to visit with my grandparents as much as I would have liked while setting up my business.

"What are we going to do about those two?" Brodie nods at my two unconscious mates.

"There is a small hunting cabin a little farther in that direction." Micah points. "It didn't seem occupied. I think maybe we should take them there and let them seal their bond with Colbie. We can't have half the group distracted by the mating bond if we are going to protect her. I don't think that will be the last attack we'll see. Whoever wants Colbie dead seems set on succeeding."

"While they do that, the rest of us can continue on to the equine village and see if we can figure out what happened to all the damn equines," Liam says, and Hunter's dragon rumbles his agreement. It seems like they made some plans while Brodie and I were otherwise occupied.

I blush at their suggestion, but my inner creature

trills with excitement. She's all for having these bonds reciprocated as quickly as possible, and I've certainly come around to the idea. Seeing Liam dead was the kick in the ass I needed to understand that I can't survive without these men. They have quickly become the most important part of my life, and I want to make sure they are permanently by my side.

"Fine, I guess Liam and I will carry their heavy asses there, and you and Hunter can go onto the village. A bit of distance might make things easier for the two of you. We will meet you there," Brodie grumbles, and Micah gives him a quick nod.

"Thank you. We will see you soon, our sweet mate," he says as he leaps up onto Hunter's back, and Brodie and I back away from his tail, which is still blocking us.

"Wait. What if you are ambushed there?" I call out before Hunter can jump into the air, putting my hands out as if I could stop the dragon from leaving if he wanted to.

"Don't worry. Even with the one-sided mating bite, they should have developed your regenerative powers. Sable said you could bite anyone and give them the power—not that I recommend you go around biting people so they won't die." Brodie tries to tug me closer, but I'm literally plastered to his side, so it's more of a comforting squeeze. "I'm not sure we could handle our mate putting her mouth on anyone else." That last bit is said with a growl, and I feel his claws burst through the tips of his fingers and dig into my side. I squeak, and he loosens his grip a little. Thankfully they didn't break through the material of my watch uniform.

Hunter takes off into the air, and my stomach leaps

into my throat as I watch them fly away. I feel a tear trickle down my face, and my heart aches.

"Shit, baby, it's okay." Liam hurries over to me, and the two of them sandwich me between their huge bodies, surrounding me with their warmth. "It's not forever. We just need to get those two idiots locked down, and then we can meet up with them. Maybe the village has a pond you and Micah can take a swim in, and I know Hunter keeps his hoard somewhere in the rift. A lot of the dragons do. He can whisk you away and take care of his bond too." Liam strokes a hand over my head, lifting my chin for me to look at him, while Brodie's heat seeps into me from behind. "Don't cry. It makes my bear want to break things."

"I'm okay," I sob. "It just hurts in here." I slide my hand between us and push against my chest in the hope it will ease the ache.

"That's the unfulfilled bond. Come on. Micah pointed in the direction of the hut. Let's not wait any longer." Liam pulls away from me and moves back to the two unconscious shifters. He picks up Gem and slings him over his shoulder fireman style.

"Great, that leaves me with lard ass," Brodie grumbles, giving me a kiss on the cheek and moving to do the same with Gryffin. "Damn tiger weighs a ton."

Liam starts moving, avoiding the mess of remains that weren't able to be burnt, and walks deep into the forest on an angle to the way we were heading previously. I follow him, and Brodie brings up the rear. The trees get thicker again, and I hear him curse. When I look back, I notice he stumbled slightly. When I raise an eyebrow in question, he blushes.

"Whoops, Gryff might have a bit of a headache

when he wakes up. I'd appreciate it if you didn't tell him I bashed it into a tree."

I mime zipping my lips, and he looks relieved.

"Come on, we're burning daylight. At this rate, we will have to spend the night in the cabin. It's still at least another two hours on foot to the village, and I would like to do that before the sun dips below the rift. It isn't safe at night with the ferals and all the natural animals that live in it. We will be vulnerable on the plain." Liam is huffing, and despite their strength, the two limp males they carry are dead weight.

I hurry to catch up to him. Trudging through the snow in human form is nowhere near as easy as it was in my tiger body. It would have taken us twice as long if we had originally been moving like that. Finally, after about fifteen minutes, when I'm breathing like a fucking race-horse and sweat is pooling between my breasts, the trees thin out, and I can see the hunter's cabin. It's made of dark wood that has faded with the elements, and the roof is covered in snow. I'm not sure how Hunter even saw it, but I heave out a sigh of relief. I am not fit enough to traipse around in deep snow in my human form.

I look around the clearing, but there is no sign of an inhabitant and no smoke coming from the chimney, so I hurry past Liam and up two steps and knock on the door. I only wait a very small period of time before I try the handle, and when I find it unlocked, I shove the door open. A rush of stale air drifts out as I step into the dark cabin. It looks like it's only one room, and it's sparsely furnished. There's a camp cot on one side, and a small rudimentary kitchen. There is another door on the other side, I wonder if there is a bathroom in here. I would like to wash the sweat and Brodie's cum off me. I move farther in to allow room for the other two. Liam dumps Gem on the camp cot, and Brodie slides Gryffin into the armchair that is positioned in front of the fireplace.

"Well, it isn't the Aramis Arms, that's for sure," Liam comments, looking around with a sneer.

"You really did luck out with having us as mates. First a cave, then a tree, and now a dingy abandoned cabin. Hopefully your other mates can make up for the lack of luxuries and romance." Brodie winces and runs a hand through his hair, looking embarrassed.

Before I can answer, Gem groans and rolls onto his side. I hurry over to him and brush his unruly burgundy curls off his face. I feel a lump on the back of his head and scowl at Liam. "What did you hit him with?" I ask, and he shrugs.

"A branch. Don't worry, they are fine. They will heal quickly, and neither of them will even notice once you distract them with your luscious body." He grins lasciviously and winks. I roll my eyes.

Brodie heads into the small kitchen and digs around in the cupboards. "There are a couple of cans of beans in here. If we get the fire started, you can eat those when you get hungry. We don't have time to hunt down something to cook."

I wrinkle my nose at the thought of eating a rabbit or whatever else is available in the forest, and they both chuckle.

"Don't knock it until you try it, though my bear is partial to fresh fish." Liam turns on the tap at the sink, but the pipes groan, and nothing comes out. "Frozen solid."

I get up when Gem doesn't wake and peer into the other door. There is a small bathroom with a wooden tub for washing. Liam looks over my shoulder, slides past me, and grabs a wooden bucket that's next to the tub.

"I'll go get a couple of buckets of snow, and when Gem wakes, he can heat the water for you," he tells me, smiling when I squeal with excitement. "Brodie, why don't you grab some firewood? I noticed some stacked next to the cabin. Gem can also light that, so you'll be warm."

The guys head outside to do their jobs, and I go into the kitchen and check out the food Brodie was talking about. I grimace when I see it's a couple of very old cans of beans, but then I remember our backpacks. Micah handed me one before he left on Hunter's back. I hurry to where I dropped it when I came in and dig around inside, finding a couple canteens of water and some jerky. I sigh with relief and pull out a piece, chewing on it before taking a sip of cold water.

A rumbling sound has me spinning, and I find Gryffin is awake, his eyes glowing as he stares at me with animalistic hunger.

TWENTY-SIX

Colbie

Liam walks through the door carrying a bucket full of snow. Gryffin snarls, and Liam drops the bucket and holds his hands up.

"Easy, Gryff. We're just going to make our mate comfortable, and then she's all yours." He slowly picks up the bucket and moves toward the bathroom, not taking his eyes off the aggressive shifter. Gryffin tracks him, a rumbling sound vibrating through the air as I hear Brodie come up the steps.

"Here we go, plenty of wood to keep you nice and warm. Luckily they had a tarp over it so it's mostly dry." He doesn't even notice the angry shifter sitting in the chair because the pile of wood is blocking his view. He moves over to the fireplace and drops it into the wood box next to it. Gryffin snarls at him, and he squeals in surprise and jumps backward, falling on his butt.

"Gryffin, you asshole!" he shouts as he scrambles backward out of the way.

"His tiger is fully in the driver's seat." The voice has us all turning to find Gem sitting up on the bed, rubbing the bump on the back of his head. "Did you have to hit me so hard?" he grumbles to Liam when he returns for another bucket of snow.

"Dude, you were burning us when we restrained you," Liam argues. "We're just lucky the suits are fireproof."

"Sorry. My phoenix is unruly, and Brodie didn't help by taking our mate away from us."

Brodie has the grace to look ashamed, and he apologizes quietly, but Gem is staring at me with hunger in his eyes. He gets up and walks over to me, pulling me into his arms. He sniffs then tips my head to the side and stares at Brodie's and Liam's marks.

"I can't wait to see my flames alongside those," he murmurs, and my eyes widen in surprise.

"You have to burn me?" I ask, starting to feel a little nervous. Biting is one thing, but being burnt is a whole other issue.

"Sort of, but I promise you will feel nothing but pleasure," he replies before releasing me when Gryffin snarls again as Liam walks inside with another bucket of snow.

"Stop that," Gem snaps. "They are looking after our mate. If you can't be nice, then get out until you calm down." The verbal beatdown seems to work. Gryffin shakes his head and takes a deep breath, and we watch as his body relaxes.

"Here, maybe you're hungry." I hold out the bag of jerky that's still in my hand, and the others laugh. Gryffin stands up and comes over to me, taking the bag from me.

"I'm hungry alright, but not for this." He tosses the

bag onto the chair he just got out of and picks me up, throwing me over his shoulder. I yelp in surprise and feel slightly nauseous as he moves to the bathroom.

"Come on, Gem, our mate wants a bath, and I refuse to let her freeze." I hear footsteps on the floor behind us but can't lift my head high enough to look, so I'm assuming Gem is following us.

"We'll leave you to it," Brodie calls cheerfully. "Just light the fire when you're ready. I set it up for you. Liam and I will shift and keep an eye on the perimeter."

"Yell if you need us," Gem tells him as Gryffin stops and slides me down his body. I don't hear Brodie's or Liam's response, because I'm captivated by a flowing pair of ocean blue eyes.

"I need Brodie's scent off you the first time. My tiger is livid that he took you away from us. Once the bond settles, I promise he will get on board with the others, but for now, he wants you all to himself and covered in our scent," he explains as Gem steps up next to me. "Both of ours." He nods at Gem who sticks a flaming hand into the tub of snow, and I watch with wide-eyed wonder as it melts and becomes a bubbling, steaming tub of water.

I don't wait for an invitation before I strip off my uniform and climb in. It's just big enough for me to sit in with my knees against my chest, and I groan as the hot water caresses my cold, naked skin. It's almost painfully hot, but I love it.

Gem and Gryffin gape at me in surprise. "That should be too hot for you. I was going to get another bucket of snow to cool it," Gem explains.

I shrug. "I've always liked hot baths, and even though I haven't shifted into dragon or phoenix yet, I guess they are protecting me. This feels amazing." I lean my head back on the rim of the tub, and they move closer. There are a couple of bottles of bath product on the small vanity counter. Gem picks one up and squirts it onto a folded washcloth, while Gryffin urges me to lean forward.

I do as they request, resting my head on my knees, and Gem washes my back and arms before encouraging me to lean back. He pauses as he takes in my breasts, which are sitting slightly above the water. He slowly moves the cloth toward them, almost like he's waiting for me to give him permission. I give him a small nod, and he swoops in, brushing over both efficiently. He then hands it to me and steps back, his nostrils flaring.

"I'm going to light the fire," he announces and leaves the bathroom. I raise an eyebrow at Gryffin, who was watching us both. He shrugs.

"No clue, but he was probably worried his phoenix would take over and mark you before we even got to the good part." He holds out a hand, and I take it. Gryffin helps me stand up then takes the washcloth from my hand and runs it over my stomach and between my legs, paying close attention to my core. I know he's just trying to rid me of Brodie's scent, but it feels good, and I squirm, clamping my thighs together. He grins and drops the cloth into the tub before grabbing a towel and wrapping it around my body, then he lifts me out of the tub and carries me back into the main room.

Gem has the fire going, and he has pulled the blankets and mattress off the cot and set them just in front of the flames. He pushed the chair back and pulled the few cushions off it, creating a little nest. Gryffin sets me down in the middle of the pile before standing upright.

He and Gem exchange a wordless glance, and then both of them tear their clothes off. I giggle at their frenzied movements, but it soon dies away as they reveal their amazing bodies. They both prowl up the bed, their focus completely on me. Gryffin stops at my ankle and places a kiss on it, and I shiver at finally having his mouth on me. Gem keeps going all the way to my mouth, and I learn he tastes like smoke and whiskey, and I almost feel drunk on him.

I slide my hands into his gorgeous burgundy curls as his tongue dances with mine. My skin burns where his hands touch me, heightening everything I'm feeling. The contrast to Gryffin's cold lips against my legs as he moves his way slowly up my body is a tease to my senses. My brain doesn't know where to focus, so I'm kept in a state of constant change. Gem pulls back, and the small flame that usually flickers in his bourbon brown eyes is blazing, almost consuming the whole pupil. He smirks before taking one of my pebbled nipples into his mouth and rolling his tongue around the tight peak. I moan and squirm, needing to close my legs to ease the ache that's burning deep inside, but Gryffin's large hands push against my thighs, stopping me from moving.

"So perfect," Gem mutters, turning his attention to my other nipple. I move to touch him, but he catches my wrists, circling them and placing them above my head. "Keep them there," he orders, and I pout.

"But I want to touch you," I grumble, and he grins.

"Oh, there will be plenty of touching, but let us have this. We've waited so long for you, and now we need to stamp our claim all over you," he murmurs, kissing me again before moving his mouth to my neck. I feel him suck on the junction between my neck and shoulder, exactly where Brodie's and Liam's bites are, and I groan at the exquisite pleasure it brings me—it's almost a mini orgasm in itself.

"Fuck!" I cry out and grip his hair like my life depends on it.

"Mating bites are sensitive. I could make you orgasm just by sucking on this spot. I can make Brodie and Liam orgasm, too, if I really wanted to," he tells me, his eyes alight with wicked glee.

"Stop messing with our bond mates," Gryffin grumbles, almost jealous at the idea of Gem giving the other men pleasure.

Gryffin finally gets to where I need him, having spent an unpleasant amount of time teasing every bit of flesh down there apart from where I want him. I bet my thighs are covered in hickeys from his work. Thankfully my shifter healing will have them fading quickly instead of making me look like an abuse victim. He swipes his tongue over my folds, and I arch my back off the bed. His tongue is rougher than a normal tongue, and I wonder if his tiger is getting in on the action.

"Did that feel good?" Gem whispers in my ear, tweaking one of my nipples and rolling it between two fingers, the bite of pain a sharp contrast to the feeling of Gryffin between my legs.

Gryffin laps at my clit and slides a finger into my aching core, his hair brushing across my thighs. Each and every movement drives me closer to my impending orgasm. I'm desperate to touch him, my fingers clenching involuntarily.

"Keep them above your head," Gem growls, noticing the action. "Grip the sheets if you have to, but don't move them." My eyes roll back as I grab hold of the sheets as Gem moves down my body, pressing kisses to all my exposed skin. The lick of heat that follows his lips borders on painful.

I open my eyes when he reaches Gryffin and grabs his hair roughly, turning his head and licking his lips, tasting me.

"Holy shit!" I gasp as the two of them kiss, my core throbbing around Gryffin's finger.

"She likes that," he murmurs against Gem's lips, and they turn to look at me, their eyes filled with wicked intent.

"Are you going to take both of us?" Gem asks as he slides a finger in next to Gryffin's, leaning down to take his own taste of me. His tongue lashes a fiery stripe across my clit, and I groan as the two of them lazily slide their fingers in and out.

"Are you going to take both of us and allow us to mate you at exactly the same moment?" Gem asks as he slips his finger out of my pussy and drags it down to circle the tight ring of my asshole. I flinch slightly. I haven't done that before, but I'm not opposed to the idea. Gryffin drops his head and continues to lap at my clit as he presses another finger in next to his, while Gem pushes against my asshole.

"Relax for me," he purrs as he slides his finger inside. It's too much with both of their fingers in me and Gryff's tongue on my clit. The pleasure is intense, and I can't stop the orgasm as it barrels through my body, lighting me on fire.

I scream, trying to clamp my legs together, but they force me to ride the wave, my eyes clenched tightly shut against the onslaught, my hands gripping the sheets like my life depends on it .

"Good girl, but we need to stretch you a little more if you're going to take Gryffin. He's a big boy," Gem murmurs, and just as my orgasm starts to ebb, they increase their ministrations again. "Spit on my fingers, Gryff," he asks before sliding another finger in next to the first. He scissors them, and I stiffen again at the intrusion, but Gryffin renews his attention to my clit, and I find myself relaxing into the pressure.

"Such a good girl," Gryffin mutters as he lifts his head and stares at me with those ocean blue eyes. They blaze with need, and I don't think I've seen a sexier picture than the two of them between my legs, but then they kiss again, and I groan at how right it looks.

Gem pulls away, and I can tell by the way they look at each other that they are talking telepathically. Griffin nods his head in agreement of whatever Gem says to him. I'm tense with anticipation as Gem climbs up the bed and lies down next to me. He pulls me over his body as he kisses me, and I feel Gryff's hands stroke my back as he places a line of kisses up my spine. I shiver at his touch and lean into him as his mouth reaches my neck, and he sucks lightly on the bite marks from the others.

"Can't wait to add mine to these," he murmurs in my ear, pulling me away from Gem's lips and turning my head so he can kiss me. He kisses differently than Gem. Gem is forceful and aggressive, while Gryffin is lazy and languid as he rolls his tongue against mine, nipping and sucking my lips. I taste myself on him, but I don't hate it. He sits me up without taking his mouth away from mine. I feel Gem's thick cock throb underneath me, so I slide my wet core along his length, and he groans. It makes me feel powerful, and I can't help but smile against Gryffin's lips.

"Ready to make him come undone?" he asks after pulling away. I nod, and he helps me lift, moving Gem's cock into position before I slide down onto it, wet and ready to feel him inside me. The moan that leaves Gem's mouth as I take him to the hilt is intoxicating.

"Fuck, you feel amazing." He looks at me with reverence. His cock is thick and long, and I feel full. I'm not sure if I'm going to be able to take Gryffin at the same time, but I'm going to try. I want these two to mark me together—it just seems right.

He rolls his hips, and the moan that leaves my mouth is loud and guttural. I lean forward, placing my hands on his chest as he thrusts up and down.

"God, that feels good," I murmur, and he smirks.

"Just wait. Gryff, get up here so we can get your dick wet for her." My eyes widen with delight as Gryffin shuffles up to Gem's head. I watch with wide eyed interest as he takes Gryff's cock into his mouth. My pussy spasms, and Gem winks at me. I lean down so I can help lube him up. Gem and I lick and suck Gryff's thick length together, making sure he's wet enough for something that really should need lube.

Gryff's hands are in our hair, and I feel his body shudder just before he pulls away. His chest is heaving as he growls, "Stop, or I'll come before I can even get into her." He maneuvers around behind me and puts a hand on my back, pinning me to Gem's chest. I feel him slide two fingers into my pussy next to Gem's dick, and I grunt at the intrusion. He swirls his fingers around before he pulls them up and slides them into my tight ring, scissoring them again before removing them and placing the head of his cock against it.

"Breathe, Colbie." Gem slides a hand between us

and starts circling my clit with one finger. "And bear down against him," he encourages, and Gryffin slowly starts to push forward. I freeze, and my breathing hitches, but Gem's finger on my tight bundle of nerves does a good job of distracting me. Gryffin pulls out before pushing in again, this time going further, and both Gem and I groan, and Gem's hand tightens on my hip.

"Fuck, babe, I can feel you," he mutters, squeezing his eyes closed. "It feels amazing."

"Imagine both of us inside her pussy at the same time," Gryffin growls as he slides farther in, and I feel Gem's cock pulse inside me.

"God, we should have done that," Gem agrees.

"Next time," Gryff promises, and I shake my head.

"No, next time one of you gets to be the double adapter. I want to watch one of you fuck the other while they are inside me," I purr.

Gryffin freezes in his tracks as Gem's eyes pop open in shock, and he stares at me with no small amount of amazement. "You would want that? You would allow us to be together too?"

I can't believe they didn't trust me when I said that before. "Hell yes. I don't want to deny you two anything. Heck, if the others were into men, I would insist on the same thing. There's only one of me and eight of you, and I worry I'm not going to be enough," I explain, looking away from his intense gaze. He grabs my chin and turns me back to face him.

"You are everything to us, a perfect gift from the goddess, and you are enough, I promise," he assures me, distracting me enough for Gryffin to slide home. All three of us forget our conversation in light of the intense pleasure that holds us in its grip.

"So fucking good," Gryffin mumbles, and I breathe heavily, trying to adjust to feeling so full. They both murmur whispers of praise, their hands roaming my body and touching me all over. Gryffin nibbles on my neck and licks over the bite marks, and my body shudders.

"Move now," I demand, and Gem's hands slide to my ass while Gryffin's circle my hips. He starts to thrust, and his movements push me up and down on Gem's cock. It's fucking intense, and I shout, but Gem smothers the noise with his mouth, kissing me with a passion that matches the blazing sensations flowing through my system. They light my body on fire, igniting it like a stick of dynamite on the cusp of explosion.

"So fucking tight." Gryffin gives my ass a slap, and that sends me shooting over the edge. My pussy clamps down on Gem's cock as my muscles shake with an orgasm that floods my body. He shouts, and I feel his cock erupt with his own orgasm as he presses a hand over my chest, burning my skin. Gryff thrusts twice more before he stills deep inside me, flooding my ass with his release as he clamps down on my shoulder next to Liam's and Brodie's marks. His teeth sink in, drawing blood, but the pain in my chest and shoulder soon turns into intense bliss, driving me over the edge one more time, the three of us groaning through it.

The intense pleasure finally drifts away, leaving the three of us a sweaty, panting mess. Gem looks wiped, and I feel smug that I did that to him.

"Holy shit, I can feel you," Gryffin mumbles against my back before sighing and heaving himself off me. The delicious, smothered feeling leaves, and I feel a pang of loss as he disappears into the bathroom. Gem snuggles into me and chuckles.

"He hasn't gone far, just getting something to clean you up with." He rolls me to the side and wraps his arms around me before looking down at where he placed his hand during my orgasm. He smiles at whatever he sees and traces his fingers over it.

"Now you'll always have a part of me inside you, even if you can't always have this." He rolls his hips again, and I groan, feeling all kinds of aches as well as no small amount of need. He chuckles again, and I roll my eyes as he pulls out. I feel the evidence of both their releases leaking between my legs, and I wrinkle my nose, but all he does is slide a hand down and use two fingers to shove it back in. I flinch at the invasion, my pussy protesting the intrusion. I'm glad for quick shifter healing, because otherwise, I'm not sure if I could get off the bed, let alone make it to Zalfari. Gryffin returns with a wet cloth and hands it to Gem.

"Heat it before you use it. It's freezing," he cautions the phoenix, who cups it in his hands before his flames gently rise around it. Once he's happy with the temperature, he uses it to clean me up.

"One day we won't waste it. Once we're ready to have babies, we'll fill you with our cum every time we can," he tells me, and I hear a rumble of approval from Gryffin.

"We have a lot to get through before we can even consider kids," I warn him. "And remember, shifters are notoriously bad breeders. It might take a while."

He scoffs. "Please, you have eight mates. All that baby batter will make the process quicker."

I wrinkle my nose again, and the two of them laugh, breaking the tension.

Gem tosses the cloth to one side, and Gryffin climbs up the bed again, and the two of them surround me. Gryff licks over his bite mark as Gem snuggles into my breasts and sighs with contentment. I thread my hands into their hair and enjoy this small break in the chaos.

TWENTY-SEVEN

Colbie

I grumble when Liam bangs on the door and tells us we need to get moving. All I want to do is lie in front of the fire and enjoy snuggling with my two new mates, but that isn't going to happen.

"Come on, we're losing daylight. Let's go," he shouts, but he doesn't come in. Brodie would have just let himself inside, so I appreciate Liam's restraint. I groan and stretch and untangle myself from our pile. Gem mutters something and snuggles closer to Gryffin who just lifts his arm and pulls him closer. I giggle at the sight. Both of them are lightly dozing and don't look like they have any intention to move.

"Fucking cockblock," Gryffin grumbles as Liam bangs on the door again, but he kisses Gem. "Come on, we need to move. Colbie is in danger until we cross the plain and get to the village."

Gem grumbles again and pushes a rogue curl back off his face. "Fine, but I vote we spend a couple of days doing nothing but fucking and snuggling when we get back."

"Sure," Gryffin agrees, stretching before getting to his feet. "After she's crowned and challenge day is over."

Gem grimaces and does the same thing, and the three of us get dressed. My clothes are in the bathroom where I left them, and when I return, the guys have covered up all their delicious, mouthwatering flesh, and I pout.

Gem winks. "Don't worry, mate. You get all this for the rest of your life now," he tells me, brushing a finger over the living flame beneath my skin on my chest, which is exposed by the small V-neck of my shirt. I shiver at the touch, and he grins.

"Right, let's go. It's still a bit of a distance, and Liam is right, we want to get to the village by dusk." He waves a hand, and the fire in the hearth extinguishes with a puff of smoke. I blink in surprise.

"That's handy," I remark as we walk out the door.

"I'm not just a pretty face and a sexy body," he retorts.

"No, but they help," Gryffin teases as he follows us out. Gem scowls at him, but I know they are being playful. Before I can say anything, Brodie tackles me, sweeping me into his arms and swinging me around while planting little kisses all over my face.

"I missed you," he says breathlessly when he finally puts me back on my feet. He rests his forehead on mine and sighs. "So much. My wolf has been howling, insisting we join the three of you in front of the fire, but I told him he had to wait. There is plenty of time for group activities." My eyes widen at his suggestion, and his lips turn up in a grin.

"Group activities?"

"Yes, baby. When all your mates worship you together. Imagine eight cocks and tongues seeing to your every want and desire."

My sated creature perks up and cracks open an eye, tempted by the suggestion, but then she closes it again. She knows we have two more mate bonds to seal soon, and she's resting in preparation.

"No time for that now," Liam growls, snatching me out of Brodie's arms and giving me a quick kiss. "Did they take care of you properly, mate?" he asks, his black eyes serious.

"Yes, they definitely did," I promise him, and he releases me, looking pleased.

"Good, then let's go. Hunter and Micah will be getting antsy, and I want to know if they found the equines."

He shifts, as does Brodie and Gem. Gem takes off into the air, a loud screech echoing through the small clearing. I see him fly through the trees, his flames contained against his body so he doesn't set them on fire, but he circles around before he is out of sight, waiting for us. I guess we're not taking any chances again.

Gryffin shifts, but I hold up the backpack. "Are we taking this with us?"

He shakes his big tiger head, but I hear Liam's voice in my head.

No, Brodie and I polished off the jerky and water, and we won't need it once we get to the village. I don't want you getting tangled in it. We need to run fast if we are going to get to the village before dark.

I toss the bag back inside the cabin and pull the door closed before stepping down into the snow and shifting into tiger form. It's a little smoother now, but there's still a bite of pain. As soon as I stretch, Liam and Brodie move out, and Gryffin flanks me again. We move fast, almost in a full-on sprint, Gem keeping pace above. There is cloud cover now, and the forest seems darker and even quieter than before. All of us are on high alert, but nothing jumps out at us again, and we finally breach the edge of the forest. I pause, staring in awe at the mountainous Aramis Rift that seems to stretch forever, looming above the plain we need to cross. My tiger eyesight can see the village in the distance, and there's nothing between us and it that I can spot.

The four of us start across the plain. Gem flies low in front of us, skimming the surface of the snow, and his body explodes. The snow melts, creating a path for the four of us to run along, unencumbered. We move a lot faster, mud flying up behind us as our paws thunder across the plain. We're still on high alert, but we can see for miles on either side. Unless the enemy is buried beneath the snow, there is no sneaking up on us.

We make good time, and just as the sun sinks below the rift, we approach the outskirts of the village. We shift into human form and look around the quiet, eerie community.

There is no sign of Hunter or Micah anywhere, but there are a couple of piles of ash, and some of it swirls around our feet with a gust of wind.

"That's not good," Gem mutters after he lands and shifts, crouching down to study one of the piles. "Yup, this is the work of Hunter's dragon, and they used to be shifters." He wrinkles his nose and stands up, brushing his hands off on his pants.

"So where are Hunter and Micah now? I don't see

any blood, so I doubt they are hurt." Liam scans the surrounding area, and my own gaze follows, looking for a hint of my two remaining mates.

"Do you think something happened to them?" My heart races, and it isn't just from exertion. I'm worried they were attacked when they arrived, but there doesn't seem to be any sign of a fight. Nothing is on fire, so Hunter's dragon didn't lose his shit.

"This way. We'll check out the town council building, and if they aren't there, then we'll go door to door and see if anyone else has seen anything. If there is a curfew in place, then everyone is behind closed doors this close to dusk." Gryffin takes the lead, the rest of us following behind him.

Brodie grabs my hand and gives it a squeeze. "It will be alright. Neither Hunter nor Micah have said anything telepathically to us."

"Can't you ask them where they are?"

"Neither of them is responding," Liam replies, and that makes me even more worried. "But they may just be distracted. Sometimes it's hard to concentrate on two things at once, even for shifters like us, who have been doing it for a long time. Micah's new to the connection, so it's even harder for him."

That sounds reasonable, but it doesn't lessen my concern. Streetlights come on, and I take in the quaint little village. It's picture perfect, with snowy streets and cute, old-fashioned lamp style lighting. The houses are adorable but spacious, with large yards giving everyone their privacy while still maintaining that village ambiance.

We reach what looks like a town square. The houses give way to shop fronts, and in the middle is a large building with a fountain out front. The fountain is stunning, with gorgeous colored lights lighting up the water and a gorgeous pegasus statue that has streams of water coming from its outstretched wings. Behind it is a large, three-story building with arched windows in the second and third floors. I can see lights on through some of the windows, but there is still no sign of anyone.

"Come on, hopefully someone will be in there. It's the alpha's house." Gryffin turns back to us, and my mouth drops open. I thought it was a council building, but it's a residence. He must see my surprise, because he chuckles. "The bottom levels are all public space, but the top two are personal living quarters for the alpha. I wonder if the alpha had a family. I didn't see one when I was here before, but he may have kept them hidden from me."

He doesn't hesitate to approach and open the door, and when he does, there are finally signs of habitation. Voices can be heard from inside, some are shouting, and I hear the sound of crying as well. Brodie and I exchange a worried look and follow Liam, Gem, and Gryffin inside the building.

The foyer is empty of people, but we follow the direction of the noise and find two large doors thrown open. When we stop in the doorway, we find an enormous meeting space full of males and females of all ages as well as children. I blink in surprise. There must be at least three hundred people in this space. All of them look dirty, unkempt, and tired, and some of the children are whining about being hungry.

None of them notice us. I see Micah and Hunter in the middle of the group, talking to a woman flanked by three men. She has Hunter's hands in hers, and tears are streaming down her face.

"What is going on?" I mutter to Gryffin, who looks as bewildered as I do.

"Your guess is as good as mine," he says and moves into the room. People part, allowing him through, all of them eyeing him with no small amount of suspicion or fear. Silence falls as more people notice our presence. The rest of us follow behind him, and I hate the wide-eyed terror that starts to appear on the faces watching us.

Micah notices us and gestures us over. "Gryffin, Colbie, good, you're here."

"What's going on? Why are all these people here? Where did they come from? I don't recognize any of them from when I was last here." Gryffin sounds bewildered and frustrated.

Micah scoffs. "You wouldn't. When we arrived, there were a few guards left behind by the alpha. They attacked us as soon as Hunter landed and didn't last very long. We found all of these people locked in the extensive cell system below the building."

Gryffin's mouth drops open in shock before his brow furrows and his eyes narrow in anger.

"How did they end up there?" he demands as Hunter turns his attention to us, bringing the four people with him.

"Lena, may I introduce to you the new shifter queen, Colbie Karridge. Colbie, this is the true alpha of the village, Lena Stormfront and her mates, Johan, Christos, and Santos."

I turn my attention to the woman, and I'm surprised to find she's actually slightly shorter than me and delicate. Most shifters are taller and muscular, but Lena is the opposite. She is also glaring at me like I'm responsible for whatever happened to them. She has long blonde hair, with gorgeous pink and purple streaks through it, and pale skin that seems to shimmer, even in the dull light of the assembly room.

"Well, let's hope she's going to do a better job at it than the last king," she sneers, and I frown, surprised by her outright aggression. I'm not sure that Lucas or I deserve the animosity she's projecting. "None of our complaints in the past have been acknowledged, so I have my suspicions that it won't change."

The three men with her look slightly uncomfortable, but they don't disagree with her.

"Whoa, hang on a minute. My father wouldn't have ignored you. Why don't you tell us what happened, and we can see if we can get to the bottom of this?" Gryffin jumps in before I can say anything, but I've had enough of being talked around. I clear my throat and raise an eyebrow at the woman.

"Shall we allow all of these people to return to their homes so they can recover from their ordeal? I don't believe they need to be here for this," I suggest flatly, not bowing down to her dominance. I can feel it battering at me, but she isn't even close to my hydra's level.

"So you can sweep all of this under the rug? I don't think so. I want witnesses to whatever we discuss here." She crosses her arms stubbornly.

"Lena, love, she's right. They all need good meals and warm beds, especially the children. Our people trust us to have their best interests in mind, and the queen is here now. She can't claim she doesn't know what has happened when she hears it directly from us."

She huffs but gives him a short nod, and the three men disperse to usher the rest of the villagers out of the meeting room. There's a huge sense of relief that seems to emanate off them as they depart, murmuring amongst themselves. I get quite a few side-eye looks, but nobody else seems to be outwardly aggressive toward us.

"I take it you didn't get my invitation for an equine representative for the new council I'm assembling?" I turn my attention back to the woman, and I think my words shock her, but she recovers quickly.

"Being imprisoned by a self-entitled asshole kind of puts a brake on any mail one might receive," she snaps.

"I take it the male lion claiming to be the alpha of this village did this to you?" I ask as Lena's mates return and close the double doors behind them.

"Let's all take a seat. There is a smaller conference room through those doors," Christos, the dark-haired, blue-eyed mate suggests and points to another set of doors at the far end of the assembly space.

"That would be great. I must admit it's taking me a while to get used to this shifter thing, and I'm not as fit as everyone else, so the run wore me out," I reply pleasantly, not afraid to admit my weaknesses. Lena sneers at me like she wouldn't spit on me if I were on fire, but the three men seem sympathetic.

"I've never envied the human who was selected to be our ruler. It almost doesn't seem fair that they have to have a crash course in everything shifter and face a challenge before they have even hit the ground running, so to speak," Santos, the tallest of Lena's mates, murmurs gently. He's an umber-skinned man with pitch-black hair and equally dark eyes that I'm sure don't miss anything.

"What did you mean by invitation?" Johan, the last

man, asks. He is pale, with long, chocolate brown hair that I'm sure would glow with vitality if he hadn't been locked up.

We all take a seat at the table in the conference room. Lena chooses the largest chair at the head of the table, and her mates flank her, leaving me and my mates to take places across from them.

"I have dismissed most of the previous council." I pause, trying to think of how I can word this diplomatically, but I decide that maybe the pure truth might score me some points. "I found them distasteful, to say the least. I have only retained the council of the Coldicotts, who seem more than willing to listen to my suggestions and work with the changes I wish to make." I mean, I haven't really spoken to them about it yet, but I plan to before I'm crowned. Once that crown is on my head, I'm stuck with the council.

Actually, that law may have to change if my heirs and I are going to be the permanent ruling family. We need to allow for flexibility. I'll have to speak to the others about drafting new rules.

"And? Which sycophant have you chosen to replace them? Probably another egotistical speciesist asshole who thinks they are better than everyone else."

Fuck me, Lena is getting on my last nerve. Yes, I can forgive her anger, since the equines have been unjustly treated, but blaming me, a recent human, for all of their past betrayals seems unfair—not to mention Lucas tried, but was circumvented by the majority of the council at every turn.

"I have asked Lucas and Mia to join the council—" I start, but she cuts me off with a scoff, looking at her mates.

"See? I called it."

"Enough." Micah slams his hands down on the table and stands up, leaning forward and glaring at the woman. "You may not like it, but you are speaking to your queen. Show a little respect," he growls menacingly, and I shiver with delight. I'm turning a little feral myself around these males.

The men blanch, but Lena continues to scowl. My hope that they will help us track the children is dwindling.

"We understand you may harbor ill will because of your treatment, but I can assure you my parents tried to advocate for you, as well as the fairies and mers, but the council majority was always against them," Gryffin says calmly, reining in his temper now that Micah has put them in their place.

"I have also asked Lady Sable to join the council. As chief archivist, her knowledge will be invaluable to me. Lastly, I extended invitations to the fairies, mer, and equine conclaves to put forward a couple of potential applicants. Of course, I get final say because I need to be able to work with them, but I hope that having representation on the council will go a long way to break the barrier between the various shifter factions."

"You really think offering us a seat on the council will erase hundreds of years of poor treatment?" Lena snarls. "You have no idea what we have suffered and what our children have had to deal with growing up. They were ridiculed and considered outcasts because they are perceived as lesser since they aren't a predator animal. My own son denied his shifter side and retreated to live in the human zone, shamed because when his animal presented, he was a pegasus and, because of my unicorn genes, he was pink. Teenagers are cruel, and rejection for a young man is heart and soul breaking." My heart skips a beat at her words, and Brodie isn't quick enough to stifle the gasp that escapes his lips. Luckily, Lena misses it, so caught up in her tirade.

Fuck me, this is Nox's mother. My stomach rolls, and I groan internally. Oh well, I guess I couldn't have been lucky with all my in-laws. I'm going to be eternally grateful that both Gryffin's and Hunter's parents seem to be happy that I am mated to their sons.

"The only thing that King Lucas ever did right was declare Zalfari an equine only zone, and even that wasn't observed. That lion waltzed in here six months ago and has been making our life hell, and every time we sent a communication to our closest military barracks, asking for help, it was denied. On the day of the retirement party, they rounded us all up and shoved us into the cells where we've been since. We couldn't even fight back. He had a runed staff that made us compliant." She is furious, and I can't even blame her.

I exchange a glance with Hunter. It looks like that staff sergeant will need to be replaced and imprisoned, and an inquest will need to be launched into rogue agents inside the military ranks.

"Yes, it seems like there are a couple of factions actively trying to undermine the goddess and her decisions." I make the snap decision to confide in them, and between the seven of us, we fill her in on everything we know, from the missing children and the feral problem, to the fact that I will be the final human queen, as well as the plans to offer all humans the chance to change to shifters. The only thing I don't share at the moment is that we are looking for Nox. If I'm right and these are his parents, then I'm concerned with how they are going to react to him being my mate, considering how openly hostile she is.

Her and her mates' expressions run the gamut of emotions during our tale, but by the end of it, she seems to have calmed a little. She still has a stubborn set to her jaw, but I think it's probably born out of the need to protect her people rather than sheer hatred toward me.

"Wow, it seems like you have walked into a veritable storm. There has definitely been an increase in feral activity. The curfew the lion told you about is one that has been in place for a while. It wasn't him who enforced that," Johan tells us.

"No, another thing we asked the outpost for help with that got ignored. They've started running in packs, terrorizing the village. Thankfully it's been confined to nighttime, and as soon as the sun starts to appear, they melt back into the mountains. They are typical ferals with no reasoning, so they act more like rabid animals than cool and calculating shifters—lots of snarling and fighting and marking their territory. If they saw a shifter, they would attack, but if we stayed inside and out of view, they just ran around the village, slightly confused. It's like they could smell us and recognized we were shifters, but didn't know what to do about it. They are drawn here, the need to be around pack guiding them, but they can't recognize that." Christos sounds forlorn. "It is sad, really. So many lives wasted."

One thing I didn't share was that I have the ability to fix them. With the book missing, I'm not sure I'm going to be able to, but I guess if we can track the children, we can also have them track the whereabouts of the Tidemans and the spell book.

"Is there a unicorn who will be willing to help us track the children?" I ask, not wanting to beat around the bush any longer. "I just want to bring them home to their families."

Lena's eyes soften, and she exchanges a glance with her mates who all give her nods of encouragement. She sighs. "Do you promise that you will accept an equine onto the council?" she asks me, and I decide to be honest.

"As long as they are willing to work with me and not be outwardly petty because of their previous treatment. I won't work with someone who is going to hold your past against me. That was out of my control, and I need someone open to the changes I wish to make," I warn her.

"Yes, I have a person in mind—someone who suffered greatly in the town they were born in before we all moved to Zalfari. They would work hard to make sure the equines have fair representation and to ensure none of the newer generations have to suffer the same kind of bullying."

I have a feeling she's talking about Nox, and I know it's time to come clean about him, but I hold my tongue a little longer. Tomorrow is soon enough to ask for his whereabouts. I'm worried because I didn't see him amongst the crowd earlier. If he isn't here, then where is he?

"I'm sure we can come to an agreeable arrangement for everyone," I say vaguely, knowing Nox will not be able to take a council position because he is my mate, but I need the children and the book found.

"Then yes, I will track the children. I will start first thing tomorrow morning. I need to go home and eat some decent food and get a real night's sleep in a comfortable bed. If you have something belonging to the children, it will help immensely. I will do a locator spell, and my mates and I will find the missing children for you," she says.

Thankfully the guys thought to bring an item from each of the children that Bryson had on hand. It's protected by plastic, so the scents remain.

"It's getting late, and we need to get home before the ferals start flooding into the village. The seven of you can use the upstairs living quarters. Make sure you stay inside though. I don't want to be held responsible for the queen getting hurt in our village." She stands up, and I know I should talk to her about Nox, but I'm going to wait until the morning when she's not still enraged about what happened here.

"We can't thank you enough for getting rid of the alpha," Christos tells us. "We tried, since his power levels weren't all that strong, but he threatened the children of the village, and none of us were willing to take a chance that he'd hurt one of them."

"And we understand that completely. He made a mistake coming after the queen and didn't live to regret it. Trust me, he suffered in the end." Liam grins evilly, and I roll my eyes, but Lena and her mates seem just as pleased to hear of his demise.

"Isn't the alpha space upstairs yours?" Brodie asks. "You are the alpha of this village, right?"

"I am. The top level is our space, and I will be glad to get it back and clear out his stench, but the second story, which he took over for his men, was always guest quarters for any visiting shifters. There is plenty of space for all of you, though I am afraid we don't have a swimming pool for you." She turns her attention to Micah. "We haven't had the need to accommodate a mer before."

"That's fine. I don't have the need to slumber beneath the waves like a lot of our people do. I will be just fine in a bed," he tells her appreciatively.

"Then we will see you in the morning." Her aggression seems to have receded, but she still has her reservations, which is understandable. With a polite good night, they leave the room.

We seem to pause as we listen to their footsteps fade away, then we wait a little longer until we are sure they are completely out of hearing range. Finally, Gem can't wait any longer, and he explodes.

"Fucking hell. She is going to lose her shit when she finds out her son is the queen's mate." He grimaces, and I wince.

"You aren't wrong," I grumble, not exactly thrilled to have her as my mother-in-law, but where is Nox?

TWENTY-EIGHT

Colbie

"I need to speak to my dad and tell him what happened here and let General Bryson know that he needs to investigate that sergeant. We can't wait. He's going to figure out his uncle is dead when he doesn't hear from him soon," Gryffin says and stands up, stretching.

"Your phone is in one of the backpacks, which are by the door of the assembly room," Micah tells him.

"I should speak to them too," Hunter says, but he's staring at me. His eyes are glowing, and smoke drifts from his nose. My core clenches, and I gasp at the pain mixing with heat and need now that there is nothing to distract me. "But my dragon is insisting on finishing the mating bond. He's scratching at my brain and clawing at my insides." He grits his teeth and clenches his fists like he wants to reach for me but is restraining himself from leaping over the table.

Brodie claps him on the shoulder, and Hunter snaps at him with his teeth. Brodie snatches his hand back and grins. "Go, we've got this. Take our queen and show her all your pretties, and I'm not just talking about your cock."

Liam rolls his eyes at his bond mate, and Gem chuckles. Micah looks as confused as I do. "Hunter's dragon hoard is somewhere in the mountains here. Dragons like to hoard pretty things. I have no idea where he gets them all from. Thankfully there aren't thousands of dragons, because all the kingdoms would be poor."

"Dragons bequeath their hoards to family members when they pass on. My family can trace our ancestry back thousands of years," Hunter mutters, not taking his eyes off me.

Something inside me opens its eyes and stretches languidly. There's a flash of scales and the taste of ash in my mouth. This must be my own dragon form, whom I haven't met yet. She stares back at Hunter with no small amount of interest. My throat tickles, and I can't stop the cough that comes from nowhere. Smoke drifts out of my mouth and nose as my eyes water.

"I can see you, my pretty. I can't wait to meet you." Hunter's voice is rough and growly, and it makes goosebumps erupt across my flesh and my panties get even damper.

"Gryffin and I will deal with your dads," Gem assures him. "Take good care of our mate."

"I also think before we leave, it would be a good idea for Colbie to shift into her dragon and phoenix forms. There's enough snow around, so we wouldn't have to worry about her setting anything alight if she loses control. There is also that large expanse of plain so if she's going to crash, she won't damage anything but herself." Liam approaches and gives me a kiss before leaning in and whispering, "Have fun. My bear is having a tantrum that we're not going to share your bed again tonight, but he can play nicely for his bond mate's sake. When this is all settled, we're going to lock ourselves away in our room for at least a week and show you what having eight mates is all about."

A shiver runs down my spine as his breath caresses my ear, and my mind conjures images of being worshiped by eight of them, one who is still just a blank space. Hopefully it won't be too long before I have an image to fill it.

Hunter has lost his patience. He pushes his chair back and stands before moving around to me. He looks like a panther stalking its prey, and I giggle, slightly over-whelmed by the intense attention.

He scoops me up bridal style, and I wrap my arms around his neck. "Ready?" he asks me, and I nod, words failing me with the intense wave of attraction and need battering my insides.

Without another word, he hurries out of the confer-ence room and through the assembly area to the large double doors. I hear the guys yell something behind us, but whatever they say doesn't register, my focus completely on the tall blond god who has my attention.

The night air is frigid, and when I drag my attention away from Hunter's glowing green eyes and look around, I notice that the clouds have cleared and the half-moon illuminates the snow around us, making it easy to see. There's an eerie howl that has Hunter's arms tightening around me as he steps away from the building. The square in front of the alpha's residence is large enough for him to shift, so I wiggle to be let down, but he tightens his grip. Before I can argue with him, wings erupt from his back and stretch high and wide before settling behind him. I stare in awe at his partial shift, the shiny purple scales glistening in the moonlight. I reach up to run a finger over one, but before I make contact, he bends his knees and takes off into the air.

It gets even colder as we climb, and my teeth start to chatter, but then Hunter's arms and chest heat like a radiator, and I snuggle into him. There's a purring sound coming from his chest, and it makes me slightly sleepy as he soars into the mountains, through rugged peaks, and past sheer cliffs. I peer around through sleepy eyes to see if I can spot any of the ferals, but we're too high up, and the valleys are covered in snow and vegetation.

Hunter swoops down to one of the craggy cliff faces, and I squeak as he shoots through a large opening in the rock, landing just inside in an area large enough for his dragon to stand. He puts me on my feet, and I take a couple of tentative steps and peer out the gap. There is no landing in front of the cave, just a steep drop down that would probably kill me if I happened to fall over the edge.

"Come," Hunter rumbles, grabbing my hand and leading me into the cavern. He has a torch in his other hand, which he must have grabbed while I was distracted by the drop.

The torch crackles and smokes, hazing the air as we

move farther back into the cave. It's a huge tunnel, big enough for Hunter to move comfortably in dragon form. "How do you protect your hoard from other dragons or flying creatures?" I ask, keeping my eyes on the ground so I don't inadvertently trip or stumble into an uneven divot.

"No other dragon would dare steal another's hoard without opening themselves up to retaliation from the rest of dragon kind. As for other flying creatures or anyone who may try to steal my hoard, the cave is spelled to look like the rock face. They would have to be unlucky to stumble over it."

"But I could see it," I argue, and he grunts as the floor starts to slope down slightly, but instead of getting colder as we descend into the mountain, it grows warmer and humid.

"That's because you're my mate. My bond group can see it too, but the illusion cast on it would make anyone else look away. I paid a pretty penny for that spell. There is a witch who regularly works with dragons for such things, and she is loyal to us. She knows we wouldn't hesitate to turn her to ash if she betrayed us."

Hunter slows down as the tunnel opens into a huge chamber, and I stumble to a stop, my mouth dropping open as I gape at the sight before me. It's a massive, cavernous room with mountains of gold and precious gems. Some of them are in settings, and some of them are loose. Paintings and furnishings and various other items are scattered haphazardly through the room. There is even a corner full of formal dresses and suits and bolts of luxurious fabrics. There is no order to anything, and right in the middle is a dragon-sized nest full of cushions.

"Holy shit," I mutter, not knowing where to look. When I eventually settle my gaze on the male beside me, he's running a hand through his hair, and there is a slight tint of pink in his cheeks.

He shrugs. "My dragon likes pretty things." His eyes heat, and he turns and puts his hands on my hips, dragging me against his body. "Which is why he hasn't been able to take his eyes off you since the day we met."

"But you didn't know we were mates then," I remind him, and he shakes his head.

"No, and I felt like an asshole who was betraying the woman who would be my mate by being obsessed with a human," he admits, and I can't help but feel pleased at his confession.

He slides his hand into my hair and pulls the elastic out, letting it fall around my face, then he cups the back of my head and slowly brings his lips to mine. One of his thumbs sweeps across the healed bite mark from Gryffin as he kisses me. He starts tentatively, but when I sink into him and open my mouth, he takes control, kissing like a storm smashing the shore—relentless and unforgiving. When he pulls away, I touch my lips, which are swollen from his attention, and then I growl, and smoke drifts out of my nose as my body gears up for a fight. Adrenaline pumps through my veins, and my inner creature snarls at the man before me. A smile creeps across his lips as he meets my eyes.

"There she is. Your dragon is making herself known. Dragon matings are full of violence. The female will want to fight so the male can prove he is strong enough to force her to submit. Don't let it frighten you," he cautions me, but the dragon inside me has taken over. I ball my hand into a fist and sock him in the nose before I can even consciously stop myself.

His head snaps back, and a trickle of blood runs from his nose. His pupils change, and he growls, smoke drifting out of his nostrils.

I gasp and step back, but the dragon inside me trills with glee. He grabs for me, but I duck and move out of the way, spinning and running farther into his hoard. A loud roar echoes through the cavern, and when I glance back, Hunter's wings have snapped up as he leaps into the air.

Well, that's not fucking fair. The dragon inside me screams, and I feel a searing pain down my back. I stumble to my knees as wings explode out of my skin, tearing through my uniform. I gasp and shudder from the intense pain, but a whoosh of air lets me know that Hunter is closing in. I feel the ground shudder as he lands next to me, and I turn, instinctively throwing out a foot and kicking his knee. My dragon is a mean bitch who preens as he falls onto his ass, but she doesn't let me hang around to make sure he's okay. She forces me to my feet, and I feel an inner knowledge wash through my mind as my wings flap and I take to the air. I squeal with surprise when I'm suddenly flying—not well, but enough that I make it across the pile of hoarded items before Hunter catches up to me. He wraps his arms around me and takes me to the ground, the soft nest cushioning our fall. My wings fold in instinctively as he pins me on my back, growling loudly, his teeth sharp inside his mouth.

"Dragons are the only shifters who have an alternative form. All the others have their human form and an animal one. We have one that is somewhat in between," he tells me, and I see him shudder, trying to control the inner beast as his claws dig into my shoulders.

I can tell he's trying to do his best to explain what is happening to me, and I appreciate his restraint. "In this form, I also have a knot. Do you know what that is?" he asks, and my inner dragon screams with want as I slowly nod my head. I read about knots and other special things that bears, tigers, and wolves have, but I thought it wasn't anything I would have to worry about in human form. Nothing I read suggested that dragons had a third form.

"Kind of," I admit, "but I thought only animal forms had them."

He nods. "Yes, all other shifters only have them in their animal form. Dragons are the exception. It means the base of my cock swells, and when it enters you, it locks into place, ensuring my cum can't escape. It's to allow me to fertilize any eggs you may have. Dragons are the only species who don't need everyone in the mating group to breed. It's why my parents have three children close in age."

"I can lay eggs in this form?" I can't help how horrified I sound. He chuckles and shakes his head.

"No, you would shift and lay them in your dragon form. We would then take turns keeping them warm until they hatch. Any children from you and me will be dragons. Children from mating with the others will be anyone's guess."

My mind is reeling at everything I just learned.

"But what about other dragons who are mated to non-dragon shifters? How does that work?" I ask despite the impatient dragon who growls inside my head.

"Their children would be whatever the mother is.

Only dragon females can have dragon babies. If a male dragon is mated to a non-dragon, they won't ever have dragon children. The children will still be theirs, just not a dragon shifter."

I roll all the information around in my head, but my dragon is done waiting. She bucks her hips, unseating Hunter who relaxed slightly during our conversation. He tumbles to the side, and I scramble to get up again, but I'm too slow, and the new wings make it awkward. Hunter circles my ankle with his fingers. I try to kick him away, but he is too strong. He looms over me, his chest to my back, and I feel a claw slice down the back of my pants, shredding them as cool air brushes across my skin. My shirt, which is in pieces due to my wings, slides down my arms, and I toss it off to the side. Hunter's hands slip around my front and cup my breasts as he leans in and bites the shoulder that has no marks on it yet.

"This is where I'm going to put my mark on you for everyone to see that I'm your mate, but first I'm going to fuck you, knot you, and then claim you, and you are going to take it like the good little she dragon you are." I feel his hard, pants-covered cock rub against my ass, and I buck my hips, trying to escape. My dragon isn't ready to submit yet, so I snarl and try to twist out of his embrace, but he has me well and truly pinned.

He chuckles wickedly, and one of his hands leaves my breasts. I hear him unzip his pants, the sound loud in the silence of the cavern.

Hunter shoves them down his thighs, then his hand cups my pussy. "Mmm, so wet. Your pussy knows whom it belongs to, all dripping and ready to take my cock." His fingers circle my clit before he roughly shoves them into my core, stretching me wide. I pant and groan at the intrusion, but it feels incredible, so instead of fighting him, I let my head hang and squeeze my eyes shut as he finger fucks me, whispering dirty words of encouragement.

"Such a pretty, perfect pussy. I bet you taste amazing too." He removes his fingers, and then I hear the sound of him licking them. I turn my head, my eyes widening when I see the forked tongue that flicks out of his mouth. Holy fuck.

He smirks and gives me a wink. "I promise you'll get a chance to feel it before we leave this cave, but I can't wait any longer. I need to make you mine." With those words, he slams home, and I scream, the sound echoing through the cavern. His huge cock is almost too big despite him having done some prep work.

"Fuck, you're so tight," he growls as he retreats and thrusts in again. This time, it feels incredible, and I moan and brace my arms in front of me, pushing back in time with his movements. Hunter strokes my wings, which are kind of just hanging since I don't have a clue what to do with them, but it feels amazing. My pussy spasms around his cock, and he grunts with pleasure.

"Your cunt grips me so tightly, so hot and wet. I bet your mouth feels the same. I want to fuck your throat while I tongue fuck your pretty pussy." Oh my god. Straitlaced Hunter is kind of dirty. "And if your pussy is this tight, I can't wait to feel what your ass is like."

His words are straight porn, and I am here for it. My body tingles in all the right places, and he surrounds me, one hand gripping my breast while the other circles my clit, and my impending release climbs. I claw at the cushions in front of me, desperate to cum, but it's just out of reach.

"Please," I beg. "I need more, give me more." He starts to thrust even faster, and the base of his cock swells, slamming against my entrance, which seems to give a little with each pass.

"Good girl, that's it. My knot is almost inside you, and then we'll fly together."

Huh? Does he mean literally or figuratively? Fuck it, who cares. I just want to come.

He growls, his mouth on my shoulder, and just as it slips in and sends me shooting into the stars, he bites down. Pain and pleasure collide, and I almost black out. I lose all strength in my arms and collapse with him on top of me. Electricity ignites my nerves, and my pussy pulses as wave after wave of pleasure flows through me. Hunter releases me and roars, the sound bouncing off the cavern walls as I sob and cry out.

Tears stream down my cheeks, and I'm pretty sure I'm drooling, but I don't care. It feels incredible. He rocks his hips, and another mini orgasm pulses through my body, smaller but no less intense than the first one. I'm boneless, and all I can do is enjoy the ride. He brushes a big hand over my hair and croons words of praise.

"Such a good mate, taking my knot and letting me fill you with my cum. You're going to be so full, it's going to drip out." He slides a hand under me and cups my belly, and my eyes widen as he starts to come again. I can feel it squirting out of him. It seems to go on and on. Holy crap, I'm going to be a walking cum bucket. My dragon is preening and crooning inside, happy about how strong and virile her mate is. Fucking animal souls are crazy as fuck. He rolls off me and onto his side, taking me with him, wrapping his arms around me as he licks the mark on my neck and caresses me like I'm as precious as everything he has in his hoard.

"My greatest treasure," he mumbles as I relax and my eyes drift closed. "Rest, my sweet. We are going to be here a while." Those are the last words I hear before I drift off to sleep.

CHAPTER

TWENTY-NINE

Nox

The mark above my chest aches incessantly as I toss back another shot of whiskey. It hasn't hurt this much since I was originally marked. I'm assuming it means one thing—that my bond group has found the mate that was meant for us. It's why there is a line of shot glasses in front of me, but nothing seems to dull the need to head back toward the shifter kingdom and find the woman meant specifically for me. I turned my back on all that when I decided I would deny the bond rather than risk rejection from the group of males I was destined to spend the rest of my life with.

The pleasure den I find myself in is deep in the capital of the Chaos Kingdom, and it offers any kind of temptation a person may require—women and men to fuck, games to gamble on, and drugs to indulge in. I wave my hand at the bartender, indicating I want another drink, before I amble over to a recently vacated booth that has gauzy curtains surrounding it, giving the occupants the illusion of privacy. When the sexy little waitress brings me my drink, I ask her to bring me a smoking pipe. It's been a long time since I indulged, but I really just need to get out of my head, and hopefully by numbing myself, it will numb the ache deep inside me.

I people watch as the waitress sets up the pipe before handing me the mouthpiece. "Is there anything else I can do for you?" she asks suggestively and leans forward, giving me a good look at her breasts, which are almost spilling out of her skimpy uniform. I shake my head, and she looks disappointed for a moment, but then she disappears behind the curtains in search of someone else to take her up on her offer.

I put the mouthpiece to my lips and take a deep drag. The intoxicating smoke is harsh and burns its way into my lungs before I breathe it out again. It only takes a couple of inhales before my body starts to relax and become languid, and all of my worries and concerns drift away on the breeze much like the smoke. The scent of sex and the sounds of passion become clearer, and my cock hardens beneath my leather pants. I wince and palm myself, trying to ease the ache. I had forgotten the side effect of this particular drug. Although it relaxes you and drives all your worries away, it also makes you horny as fuck.

I consider calling the waitress back to take care of my raging hard-on, but a shadow appears behind the gauzy curtains, and then a stunning, lithe man lets himself into my secluded booth. I slide my eyes up and down his figure. This establishment really has stunning whores for hire, and I decide to indulge. It's been a long time since I've been with a man, and this one is the very essence of temptation. Part fae, part something else, his gossamer wings are a sparkling kaleidoscope of greens and silvers that shimmer with his elegant movements. His plump lips are turned up in a seductive smile as he flicks a lock of pale green hair over his shoulder and takes a step toward my table. All he's wearing is a pair of black leather hot pants, and his skin looks to be covered in glitter, sparkling where it catches the light.

"Hello, handsome. Do you want some company?" Surprisingly, his voice is husky and has a slight menace to it that is exciting and tugs at my balls. He runs a wet tongue over his pink lips, and I imagine it circling the head of my cock. He doesn't wait for me to respond before he slides into the booth and tugs the mouthpiece from my hand before wrapping his lips around it. I can't tear my gaze away as he inhales deeply before blowing out, creating rings, his mouth a perfect circle as he blows.

"Fuck," I mutter, my cock throbbing at the sight. He passes the pipe back to me and then straddles my lap, and I feel his hard cock press against mine. He's not shy as he grinds down into it, and I drop the pipe and grasp his hips, holding him in place. This man may be just what I need to erase any thoughts of my bond group and bond mate. I chose to walk away, and I am not going to regret it.

His fingers fiddle with the buttons on my shirt, undoing them slowly one by one, like he's giving me a chance to say no, but instead, I slide my hands around to cup his ass and drag him against my cock. His eyes are heavy-lidded, and I see a shudder of desire course through his body, making the wings at his back shimmer as well. I reach up to caress one of the gossamer limbs, and as my finger runs over the edge, he groans and pushes my shirt back before leaning in and nipping my nipple.

He pulls back, his pupils blown, and he can't stop squirming on top of me. "What's this?" he asks me, running a finger over the bond mark on my chest. It seems to heat at his touch, and I push his finger away.

"Nothing you need to concern yourself with," I tell him before snaking one hand through his long hair and yanking him toward me, taking his mouth with a vicious kiss. He doesn't shy away and meets my tongue stroke for stroke, his hands flat against my chest, the stupid bond mark throbbing beneath his right palm.

I want to fuck this half-breed with a need that is vicious and fierce. If the bond between me and my mate had been sealed, then they'd be able to feel it, but because it remains unsealed, I won't cause them any pain.

I run my hands up and down his spine, caressing the base of his wings, and he moans into my mouth before pulling away, his chest heaving. He has a small frown between his eyebrows, but it quickly fades as he slides off my lap and onto his knees, where he makes quick work of the buttons on my pants. I lift my hips to allow him to drag them down my legs, my cock springing free.

He licks his lips and smiles like all his dreams have come true. "Whoa, you're big. What kind of shifter are you?" he asks as he runs his tongue around the head of my cock.

I ignore his question and groan, dropping my head back against the booth. He slides one hand between my legs and fondles my balls, while the other one grips the base of my dick as he engulfs the head with his mouth. He pays special attention to that spot under the head that's so fucking sensitive, and my toes curl. I slide my hands into his hair, holding him in place to ensure he doesn't move. His mouth is warm and wet and feels sublime, and I groan as he slides farther down, taking my cock into the back of his throat. I feel it constrict around my length, and I groan, threading my fingers through his hair and fucking his face. He takes it like the pro he is and swirls his tongue and uses suction, and I feel my orgasm tingle in my balls. I clench my butt cheeks to hold off a little longer, but he slides one finger into my asshole and presses that trigger deep inside.

"Fuck!" I shout and hold myself deep as I unload my cum down his throat. He swallows like a champion, breathing through his nose with every spurt. I finally sink back in the chair, my cock falling from his mouth, my body lax in the aftermath of my release.

He looks up at me, and his face is a mess. Tears drip down his cheeks, and there's a dribble of my cum at the corner of his mouth, but he looks fucking stunning. I did that to him. I made a mess of him, and now I want to bend him over the couch and make him moan just like he made me. I pull him to his feet, tug him onto my lap, and kiss him. I taste myself on his lips as I run my hands over his chest, feeling all his muscles beneath his sleek skin. He may be a whore, but he has the well-honed body of a warrior. While I enjoy the softness of a woman, I also enjoy making a strong man come apart beneath me. I pull back, noting his swollen lips, but when I meet his gaze, his eyes are cold and calculating. He sighs and pushes against me. I allow him to get up, and he adjusts his cock under his black shorts then pushes his hair back behind his shoulders.

"That was fun, but I have to run."

"Wait," I call as he goes to slip out of the gauzy curtains. "What about your payment?" I ask, and he shakes his head.

"I got everything I needed for now," he says cryptically, and without a backward glance, he disappears into the crowd.

What the fuck did that mean? I think about our whole interaction, and I stiffen in shock. He knew I was a shifter. He specifically asked what kind I was, not what kind of supe. I grasp the pendant around my neck. It should have made me seem human to him. How exactly did he know? I jump to my feet, tucking myself back into my pants, but I frown at the smear of something on my black pants from my hands. I look a little closer, bringing my hand up so I can see it better in the dim light. Is that makeup? I run a finger over it before rubbing the greasy, skin-colored substance between two fingers. It is. Why on earth was he wearing makeup on his body? I guess he could have been covering scars, but I didn't feel any. Maybe it hid a tattoo he doesn't want seen. I shrug my shirt on and do up the buttons before going in the direction he went. I want to know who he is, but when I push my way through the crowded pleasure palace, he's nowhere in sight.

I walk to the bar. "The male fae you have working here, with the silver and green wings… Where is he?" I ask the bartender who gives me a quizzical look and shakes his head.

"We don't have a male fae with silver and green wings working here."

I frown at his response. Fuck, who was he then, and what did he gain from our interaction?

I thank the bartender and head out. I need to return and get some sleep. I have an interview with the Chaos king tomorrow. It's why I'm here in this kingdom, and it gave me a good excuse to leave Aramis. As much as I longed to see Colbie again, she would insist I integrate back into shifter society—it isn't legal for shifters to live in the human zone—so I left. I may return eventually, but when King Loki contacted me regarding my security services, I decided it was too good an opportunity to turn down.

Unlike Aramis, Chaos rarely gets cold, and it's a hot, stuffy night as I walk back to my accommodations. The streets are loud and crowded, with people parting and seeking their vices in every manner. Random shouts of glee or disappointment come from the gambling establishments, and the balconies of the whorehouses are filled with stunning, scantily clad males and females flaunting their wares. Music pumps out of the bars and clubs, and if you want your vices a little on the dark side, then the fighting ring is a hot spot and drugs are easily found on every corner.

There is no segregation here. Half breeds, shifter, fae, witches, and vampires all intermingle, mostly without trouble. The only race not accepted in the Chaos Kingdom are humans. They don't even know this kingdom or half-breeds exist, and that's how we want to keep it. They see only a great desert on their maps, which is inhospitable and dangerous to venture into. That's not to say they don't attempt it, but the witches warded the borders with a spell that turns them around, and all they remember is a barren wasteland with nothing of any value.

I reach the central square of the city. There's a huge park surrounded by hotels. Mine is on the other side, so I walk through the park. It's well lit so people are wandering about, making use of seating areas and the licensed food trucks to grab a late-night snack or soak up some of their indulgences. In a particular thick copse of trees, I can hear the sounds of people fucking. I guess they couldn't wait to get to a bed. Good for them.

In the center of the park is a pond, and in the middle of the pond is a fountain dedicated to the four realm goddesses. Chaos doesn't have a patron god, so instead they worship all four, giving thanks for their lives and the acceptance found for all four races in the Chaos Kingdom. Personally, I think Chaos has the right idea. We don't need to be segregated to maintain pure species. Like will always be attracted to like, and mixed breeds are not going to weaken the species.

A group of giggling teenagers on the verge of adulthood pass me. They all have that swaying, stumbling motion like they've had a few too many beverages. One groans and puts her hand over her mouth then sprints for the nearby trash bin, but she doesn't make it and instead throws up at my feet.

I grimace, my shifter nose way too sensitive for something like that, and she looks at me with pink cheeks and eyes filled with tears. "I'm sorry," she slurs as one of her friends, one who doesn't look quite so drunk, wraps her arms around her and leads her away.

Fuck, maybe living in a kingdom of excess isn't going to be so fun. I look down at my splattered sneakers and make a note to send them out for cleaning when I get back to the hotel.

I pick up my pace, ready to be back in my room. A hot shower, a late supper, and bed sounds perfect. The shouts and sounds of the party district disappear as I approach lodgings. I splurged on a five-star hotel, wanting to enjoy a few days of luxury, but it isn't as fun as I imagined on my own. It would be nicer to share it with someone. A dark-haired, fresh-faced beauty comes to mind. I bet Colbie would love the dessert menu the hotel has to offer. I feel a pang of longing for the potential that will never be.

The doorman of the hotel I'm staying in nods his greeting as he holds open the door for me. The receptionist flutters her eyelashes at me and gives me a flirty wave as I pass her. She informed me she gets off at midnight when I left earlier, but I have no intention of taking her up on her offer. The temporary reprieve from the pain in my chest I got from the drugs and the unexpected company lifts, and it throbs with renewed vigor.

Fuck, I'm going to have to find a witch or a fae and see if they can help me with it. I had gotten used to the dull ache from the bond group pull, so I learned to live with it, but this new ache is different. It burns, an incessant throbbing that doesn't seem to let up. Either I need to find something to mask it and become reliant on the drug to ease it or give into the pull and go in search of my bond group and our mate. The latter option is what I want the most, but the thought of rejection when they find out what kind of shifter I am is too much to risk. Here in the Chaos Kingdom, nobody cares that I am an equine. If I go back to the shifter kingdom, I risk running into my bond group. Being in close proximity to the other males marked with the same mark on my chest is enough for the telepathic link to activate, and then there will be no escaping them. I'll constantly have to feel how they feel about having an equine in their bond group, and I refuse to let myself be belittled and ridiculed like I was when I first shifted. We didn't live in Zalfari then. We had a home in another village, and we were tolerated. Only my mother and one father are equines, and the village was a little more tolerant because one of my fathers is a dragon, and the other is a panther, and both of them served under General Bryson for years.

Everything was okay. My older sister is a panther, but when I was born and didn't shift immediately, they knew I was going to be an equine. Dragons only happen when the female is a dragon, so my father knew I wouldn't be one, which left me as a pegasus or a unicorn. At first the children at my school didn't care. I don't think any of them realized I was a mythical shifter who would change when I was a teenager, but then we learned shifter lore in school, and they put two and two together, and many of the kids who were my friends rejected me once they learned I would be an equine shifter. I still had a few friends, ones whose parents weren't assholes and taught their kids that being an equine didn't make us less. Technically, we're prey animals, and our magic is mostly passive, but everyone is equal in human form, and my pegasus has a mean streak. You don't want to get too close to either end if he decides he doesn't like you.

The elevator ride to my room is over quickly, and I toe off my shoes as I enter the suite, leaving them by the door to be picked up by housekeeping. I order some food and strip, jumping into the shower. My meeting tomorrow with the king is a dinner, and I want to do some sightseeing beforehand, maybe some shopping as well. My sister's kids would love presents. I don't get to see them enough, and when I do, I like to spoil them, but a good night's sleep is definitely on the cards first.

Colbie

I groan and stretch. My body feels like it's been beaten to a pulp. I have aches and pains every-where. Last night with Hunter was the most active I've been in ages. I really need to work on my physical fitness, but I have a feeling life with my guys is never going to be boring. I roll over on the mountain of cush-ions and come face-to-face with a giant dragon head. His head is on the ground, and he looks relaxed, but his eyes are focused completely on me.

"Uh, hi," I murmur as I lift a hand to wave at him, and he chuffs, a puff of smoke drifting out of his nose. He shuffles his head closer, and I reach out and give him a little scratch between the eyes. His eyelids drift closed, and he makes an adorable purring sound.

"I guess we should be getting back." I sigh, and his eyes open, and he rumbles a displeased sound. "I know. I wish we could ignore everything and stay here too," I tell him, understanding his disappointment, "but we have responsibilities we can't ignore. I promise we will get a chance to return. You have so many pretties I'd like to get a look at."

He preens before lumbering to his feet. I watch with awe as he shrinks and contorts until a naked Hunter stands before me. I sit up and wipe a hand across my mouth, making sure I didn't drool in my sleep—or right now at the sight of his incredible body.

He grins at me and offers me a hand. I look down at the blanket covering my own naked form, feeling a little self-conscious. Despite our mating and feeling his emotions inside my chest, I'm still that girl whose mother never made her feel good enough, and my body was a large part of that. Although Hunter spent hours worshiping me with his talented tongue and dick, there was only dim light for him to see by. Now, though, the cavern is lit up like a chandelier. I glance around the room, noting torches built into the room all burning brightly, making his gold and gems sparkle beautifully. It's as if the dragon wanted to show off his treasures.

"Don't be shy, my precious. I know every inch of your body intimately, and I could see it all perfectly with my enhanced eyesight. You have nothing to hide or be ashamed of. You are perfection, the jewel of my collection," he says roughly, unable or unwilling to hide the desire in his tone.

Despite being secretly thrilled at his words, I take his hand, and he drags me to my feet, causing the blanket to fall to the ground. He pulls me into his arms and kisses me, caressing my naked back and ass. When he pulls away, I look around for my discarded clothes and grimace when I remember they are completely destroyed.

"I don't have anything to wear," I tell him, and he smiles and gestures to the pile of fabric in one corner.

"My dragon has prepared for everything. Help yourself. I was thinking maybe we could let your dragon out and we could fly back together. Mine is dying to see what she looks like."

A rush of excitement flows through me, and I can't deny that I want the same thing. "But what about Zalfari? I can't exactly wander around naked," I point out, and his eyes sparkle.

"I'll pack a bag. My dragon will happily carry it if he gets to see you dressed in one of the outfits he procured," he promises and leads me over to the corner with all the garments. He digs through a chest, pulling out a backpack and what looks like a spare watch uniform like the one I was wearing. He shoves it into the bag and then gestures for me to pick something from the garments.

"Everything is spelled so when you put it on, it will fit you perfectly. Take whatever you want, they are yours."

I step forward, and I hear a rumbling sound of approval come from his dragon. He stares at me with his dragon's eyes, like he's sharing the same space with the creature. I flick through the hangers and pull out a seafoam green dress that is fairly plain compared to the rest of them. It has a heart-shaped neckline and three-quarter sleeves, and it's long and flowy but without too much material that would make it a hindrance. It also looks like it would roll up without wrinkling, which is a big plus.

I pass it to him, and he stuffs it into the backpack, along with a pair of black slip-ons that I select. Hopefully the shoes have the same kind of magic, because they look slightly too big for my feet, but I can make them work.

Once that's done, he returns to the nest and dons his own watch uniform, which managed to survive our lusty encounter. "I'm sorry I don't have any food for us, but breakfast should be available when we return to Zalfari. I wasn't prepared to come here on this trip. I will make sure the place is fully stocked next time we come."

I look around but don't see a fridge or any place for food to be stored. He must understand what I'm looking for, because he points across the cavern. In the wall of the cave is a door that is well hidden in the rock face.

"Through there are some living quarters—a kitchen, bathroom, and a comfortable lounge as well as a couple of bedrooms for the team. I haven't brought them here before, but my dragon insisted that we would need them one day," he explains. He must have known we would need a place to escape to one day when everything becomes too much for us, which I'm sure will happen eventually.

"That's very thoughtful of him. Will he be alright with the others being around your treasures?"

"You are his greatest treasure, and he already shares you with them. Having them here will be no issue, I assure you."

He holds out his hand, and I take it, then he leads me down the large tunnel toward the exit. The flames in the sconces extinguish behind us, leaving us in the dark, but my eyes quickly adjust as I feel my dragon rise to the surface. Her excitement is palpable, and it makes my skin tingle with anticipation. She's going to be let out to fly, and I think she's almost as excited about that as she was about him proving his dominance last night.

I hear him breathe deeply and chuckle. "I can smell your excitement," he growls. "I'm tempted to turn around and take you back to the nest, but I know we have important things to do. Next time, I won't be as understanding," he warns, and I shrug.

"I'm okay with that," I admit, and he squeezes my hand.

The tunnel starts to brighten as we approach the exit, the early morning light shining inside. There's no ledge, just a sheer cliff face when we reach the end. There's enough space for one of us to shift, but not both, and my nerves rise to the surfacc.

"How are we going to do this?" I ask him, and he drops my hand and steps to the side.

"I'll shift first and wait outside for you."

I grimace. "But how do I fly? What do I do?" I ask him, panic welling inside me, and he grips my shoulders and stares at me, his expression reassuring.

"It should all be instinctual. Let her take over, and don't fight for control. She will know what to do, just enjoy the ride. I will be here if she goes off track and guide her to where she needs to be." His voice is soft and encouraging, and I can't help but trust him. None of these guys have done wrong by me, even before they knew I was their mate. Sure, Liam was an ass, but I have a feeling that behavior wasn't reserved just for me and that's how he was with everyone except his family— maybe even them at times.

"Okay, but if I die, I'm going to haunt this hoard. Your dragon will know no peace," I threaten jokingly, but he nods seriously.

"If you die, he will know no peace anyway, but it isn't going to happen. When I shift, strap that bag around one of my forelegs, okay?" he instructs and steps back, and I watch with a wince as he shifts. It always looks so painful, but they assure me it isn't anymore.

His dragon huffs and nudges me with his giant head, almost knocking me over. I give him a scratch between the eye ridges before dealing with the backpack. He ambles over to the edge, spreads his wings, and pushes off into the air. I watch, wide-eyed, as he circles around before returning and hovering like a massive humming-bird, his wings flapping madly just outside the entrance like he is waiting for me.

"Here goes nothing," I mutter and let my dragon rise. There's a blinding flash of light and magic, and suddenly, my perspective changes as my soul recedes, allowing my dragon to take control. I watch through her eyes, and when she lowers her head, I catch a glimpse of her legs. She is a paler shade of purple, almost lavender in color, compared to Hunter's shimmery eggplant hue. She spreads her wings and arches her back in a cat-like motion, stretching like she's been asleep for a long time, which, I guess, she has been. She finally steps forward and off the ledge without a care in the world, and we begin to plummet. I scream, but of course the sound goes nowhere. I struggle to take over, but she has a tight hold on the reins. I hear a bellow of fear behind us, but as the ground rushes up, she snaps her wings out, and we glide to safety. She roars triumphantly as we take to the sky, our wings flapping slowly as if she didn't just come close to splattering us on the ground. She circles her way up, the air whipping past us as she gains speed and altitude. Out of the corner of my eye, I see

Hunter's dragon come level with us before slightly taking the lead, directing us toward the village.

The view from up here is glorious, and I feel her pleasure as the wind rushes over our scales and the sun shines on us, doing little to ease the cold, but her body starts to heat, warding off the chill as we fly through a cloud bank and then head below it, breaking through to reveal the village of Zalfari in the distance. The return journey is a lot quicker than the one we took last night, our dragons' speeds far superior to Hunter's in half form. Before long, we are landing just outside the village. There are people out and about, unlike the last time we arrived, and the children cheer and clap as both dragons land, though they refrain from coming any closer.

Hunter lands between me and the gawking villagers, allowing me privacy to shift and clothe myself despite nudity being commonplace amongst shifters. It is still a long way off for me to feel comfortable being naked in front of people, if that will ever even happen.

I wear the dress I selected to return to the council home. I have a meeting with Nox's parents to get through before we decide our next move, and I want them to take me seriously, so if that means I have to look like a queen, then I will. Hunter reaches into the bag and pulls out something shiny. When he lifts it, I see it's a small tiara. He settles it on my head, pushing a lock of my hair back over my shoulder.

"My dragon insisted you needed this. It's obviously not your official crown, but he was adamant you needed this today," he tells me, shrugging sheepishly when I raise an eyebrow.

I reach up and cup his jaw. "Thank you," I tell him, pressing a kiss to his cheek.

Before he can reply, the sound of hooves has us turning our attention to an approaching animal. It's a small horse, a child, I think, if I'm guessing correctly. It has long, gangly legs, and it slides to a stop just in front of us. It's a pretty white thing with a mane that sticks up at all angles. It snorts, its attention going from me to Hunter, then it squeals and turns and takes off in the direction it came from, bucking and kicking its back legs.

Hunter chuckles. "I guess it caught scent of my dragon," he explains when I frown at the reaction. "It will be able to smell that we're predators, but I bet it couldn't stop its curiosity."

We walk hand and hand through the village, the residents watching us with wary eyes. A few give us nods of respect, but most of them remain neutral, if not a little suspicious and leery. I'm not upset, since I would be cautious as well if I had been through what they just experienced. I just smile at them and focus on the tasks ahead. Mending bridges is going to take time, and I don't have it right now.

THIRTY-ONE

Colbie

We let ourselves into the council building and climb the stairs to the second floor. The familiar scents of my mates reach my nose, and we track them to a closed door. Hunter doesn't bother to knock, instead pushing it open and letting us in. We find my other mates sitting around, drinking coffee, and they turn their attention to us. Each of them is in a state of undress, wearing only a pair of sweatpants they must have had in their backpacks. I swallow deeply at seeing all their delicious shifter flesh on display. Liam smirks and gives me a wink when I wipe the corner of my mouth to make sure I'm not drooling.

"You're finally here!" Brodie jumps to his feet and comes over, pulling me to his chest. I drop Hunter's hand, who growls, but Brodie just shushes him before giving me a scorching kiss.

"Easy, you big lizard. We're all going to feel a little

needy until the mating drive settles. You know it can take a while," he scolds the dragon when he pulls away. Suddenly, we are surrounded by the others, and I'm passed from Brodie to Liam, then Gryffin and Gem. They smother me with affection, telling me how much they missed me before I finally end up in Micah's arms.

I'm a little unsure about us. I barely know the guy, but my creatures don't care. They know our mate, and they pulse with the unsealed bond, pushing me to take care of what nature intended. I grit my teeth and squeeze my hands into fists to stop myself from mauling the mer. I can see by the lines around his lips and eyes and the tension in his body that he is also having trouble restraining himself.

"Hi," I murmur, and I hear him take a deep breath and blow it out again before he grimaces.

"Wow, fighting the need is a lot harder than I thought it would be," he admits, "but unless we want to run the bath and have a very awkward mating, it's going to have to wait," he explains, knowing exactly what I'm feeling.

"Okay, but as soon as we find a body of water big enough, we are taking care of this unbearable need," I tell him, and he nods.

"Even if it's frozen solid, we will get fire starters to melt it for us," he agrees before leaning in and pressing a gentle kiss to my lips, then he pulls away and stalks to the other side of the room.

I clear my throat and take a couple of breaths, centering myself so I don't chase him. "Okay, we need to speak to Lena and her mates. We have to ask her about Nox. I didn't see him anywhere yesterday, and I'm worried about what that means. His truck was definitely in that parking lot, and if he isn't here, then where is he?" My worry returns with a vengeance, my mind conjuring all kinds of scenarios. Did the lion kill him like he attempted to do to us? Did they already succeed in blocking me from the crown? Or is Nox out there somewhere in the world, doing his darn best to avoid me?

"Yes, let's get them working on the location of the children, and then we can focus on finding your last two mates. Maybe they know where Nox might have gone since he isn't here." Gem tips his coffee mug back, finishing it before going to the kitchen and placing it in the dishwasher.

He grabs the pot of coffee and two cups and pours both Hunter and me a mug before adding milk and sugar to mine and leaving his black. Gem passes them to us, giving me a kiss on the cheek before walking in what I assume is the direction of the bedrooms. The rest of them follow suit.

"There's cereal in the cupboard and milk and fruit in the fridge if you're hungry," Gryffin tells me before following the others.

I sink down on one of the chairs and take a sip of my coffee, sighing with relief as it hits my taste buds while Hunter pulls out a couple of bowls and holds up a box of cereal.

"Yeah, I guess I should eat, though my stomach is in knots at the thought of this meeting. I assumed unicorns were supposed to be all gentle and serene, but Lena is more like a freaking dragon," I grumble as he pours us bowls and adds milk before bringing them over to the table.

He chuckles. "Yeah, she certainly doesn't fit the stereotype, but years of needing to put your walls up to avoid being hurt probably did that to her, not to mention resentment at how her children had to suffer is enough to make any parent defensive."

He slides the bowl over, and I waste no time inhaling it. We certainly worked up an appetite last night, but I still wasn't tempted when Hunter suggested we shift and go find a deer or something for our dragons to snack on. Gross.

It doesn't take long for the others to return dressed in their watch outfits with backpacks over their shoulders. Mine was left behind at the cabin, so it's lucky that Hunter had this dress and a spare uniform for me.

We finish our breakfast and clean up, leaving the suite as neat as it must have been prior to the guys' visit. There are a few personal items lying around, and I assume they belong to one of the dudes we killed, but they won't be needing them now.

"Let's go. I'd like to knock on the door of their house. I'm hoping having us in their home might keep them a little off-balance." Hunter opens the door and leads the way outside, and we cross a clearing, heading in the direction they told us they lived before they left last night.

"Good thinking. She might not be so aggressive in her own space," Gem suggests, and Liam scoffs.

"Or even more aggressive."

We knock on their door. It doesn't take long before a bleary-eyed Johan opens the door and does a double take when he sees us.

"Sorry to wake you," I say, realizing just how early it is, or maybe they are still recovering from the last couple of weeks. "We need to get moving, and I wanted to iron out a few things with you."

He rubs his eyes but gestures for us to enter. "I apologize. We planned to meet with you this morning, but I guess we were more tired than we realized."

He shows us into a comfortable but stylish living area and gestures for us to take a seat. "Just give us a moment, and we will be right with you," he tells us before hurrying to retrieve the rest of his family and get dressed. I can't stop myself from eyeing his muscular back as he leaves. Nox's dads are hot, but then so are Hunter's and Gryffin's dads. The slow aging of a shifter makes them look like they are only in their late thirties.

"Are you creeping on your mates' dads?" Brodie laughs as I wince, feeling my cheeks heat.

"Not really, I was just marveling at how good shifter genes are. I wonder how old they are. Hell, Gryff's moms and dad are in their sixties but barely look old enough to have kids, let alone ones as old as him and the girls," I point out, scowling at them when they continue to find amusement in my observations.

Before anyone can make another comment, a gray and white streak of fur flies at me from somewhere. "Agh!" I scream, holding my arms up as it launches itself at me, its claws catching me across the back of one hand.

It doesn't get any farther, because Liam snatches it out of the air and holds it in front of him with two hands. It instantly relaxes and starts purring, so he tucks it under his arm and strokes its head. I glare at them, not hiding my feelings for the insufferable animal.

"Damn, love, that cat really doesn't like you," Gem comments with wide eyes.

I glare at Stormheart with loathing. "The feeling is fucking mutual. Stormheart is a fucking menace to society," I mutter when a clearing throat has us turning our attention to the newcomers in the room.

Nox's dads look bemused, but Lena narrows her eyes on me much like the stupid animal. "How do you know my son's cat?"

"Stormheart and I are familiar with one another," I reply vaguely.

"And it doesn't like you? Why is that?" Before I can answer her, Santos chuckles.

"Don't be like that, Lena. You know that cat doesn't like any female around Nox. It's just as aggressive toward you."

She scowls at her mate before reluctantly nodding her head. "Despite me giving him to Nox, he has an aversion to me. Nox must have stopped in some time recently, and when he didn't find us, he left a note asking us to watch the damn thing for him while he went to Chaos Kingdom for a job interview. Would you care to explain just how you know my son?"

I decide to give her a half-truth, not quite ready to reveal everything. "Nox and I are recent acquaintances. He lives in the same town my grandparents are from, and we ran into each other one day when I was out walking on the beach."

"How didn't he notice something was wrong in this village?" Hunter asks, sounding suspicious. I can't blame him. Even if his parents weren't here, he should have noticed things weren't quite right with everything else.

"I'm guessing he dropped by at night. He would have assumed we were asleep, and he knew that everyone would be inside due to the curfew," Christos replies.

"And he wouldn't have had to use the pass to get to

the kingdom if he shifted and flew, so he wouldn't have needed to worry about ferals," Santos reasons.

I guess that all makes sense.

There's an awkward pause and I guess it probably time to approach the subject of Nox

Lena hasn't torn her gaze away from me, and I can see her eyeing my new mate mark on my neck. I don't think there is much this woman misses, and I really don't want to be an enemy to her.

"Do you recognize this mark?" I ask her, waving a hand at the guys, and Gem lifts his shirt, showing Nox's parents their bond group mark.

The three males let out noises of surprise, but Lena hisses at me. "You stupid girl. What have you done? Nox doesn't want anything to do with a bond group."

"Lena, enough," Johan snaps. "We have been telling him he's wrong since day one. His bond group would not reject him, just like ours didn't reject you or me." I guess that means Johan is the pegasus in the family.

Tears well in her eyes. "You don't know that. He's suffered enough," she argues, but Gryff shakes his head. Before he can open his mouth and say something, though, Christos gestures to the furniture.

"Take a seat. Let's be comfortable for this discussion."

We do as he suggests, and Gryffin continues. "We don't care what he is, only that he is missing. We were told by a seer a few years ago that we would have another bond mate. I have been searching for him ever since. In fact, I was here, in this village, a few days ago, looking for him. The alpha I saw denied knowing a shifter with the same mark, but I now know he wasn't the rightful alpha."

"He wouldn't have known anyway. Even though equines are welcome here—or were—Nox is gun-shy from his treatment in the village we lived in previously, so he kept it to himself. Not all of them were bad, but a good portion of his friends turned on him once they realized he was going to be a pegasus or a unicorn," Santos explains.

"Yes, they hadn't understood there wasn't a chance he would be a dragon until they learned about dragon mating in high school shifter biology, and then it all went downhill from there," Johan adds.

I nod, remembering my brief lesson on dragon matings.

"And then not only was he a pegasus, but when he first shifted, he was pink because of my genetics. They never let him hear the end of their torment," Lena admits, tears streaking freely down her face.

"He's a pink pegasus?" I ask carefully, grabbing Gem's hand while trying to control my excitement. He gives me a small squeeze.

"Yes," Christos confirms warily, a frown between his eyebrows.

"What color was my pegasus?" I ask the guys with excitement. I don't think anyone mentioned it, and I can't remember.

"She was a beautiful white with a gorgeous pink mane and tail," Brodie says cheerfully, and Nox's parents gape at me.

"You're a pegasus too?" Johan asks carefully.

"Amongst other things," I confirm, and they look confused. I sigh. It's probably time to come clean, and maybe they will trust me a little more. "I have multiple forms. In fact, I have one for each of my mates as well as a hydra," I explain.

Santos stammers, "A hydra? Holy crap. And a multi shifter as well? You really are impressive, Queen Colbie."

My cheeks heat with embarrassment.

"How many mates do you have?" Lena asks, her eyes calculating as they move from me to each of the guys.

"Eight in total, and Nox is one of them," I tell her, and she shakes her head adamantly.

"No, bond groups are never eligible to be mated to the queen."

"Well, this time I can tell you that isn't the case. I have their mate mark on my back, otherwise I would show you," I state firmly.

"We can confirm she's telling the truth. We would never have gone against the goddess and mated her if it wasn't there," Liam growls, sounding just as annoyed with her as I'm starting to feel.

"Eight mates," Johan murmurs. "I don't think there has ever been a royal with quite so many."

"And there won't be again." Gem puts an arm around my shoulders and tucks me in next to him. "The goddess told Colbie that she will be the last chosen human, and that the title will be hereditary now." Gem takes the time to remind them of the long conversation we had the night before.

"So essentially you need to finish gathering your mates so you can be crowned and take on the human and shifter factions that are plotting against you?" Johan crosses his arms and slumps in his chair. "And you need our son to do that."

"Yes. Challenge day is coming soon, and although she's powerful, she can't be crowned if they kill one of her mates before they are mated, and then the power will be free to grab," Micah replies, and Lena looks at him.

"How many mates does she have left to bond with?"

"Me and two others," he answers. "We need a body of water for us to use, otherwise I would have already sealed the deal," he says boldly, and I feel my cheeks heat at his declaration. His confidence is sexy, and he isn't wrong. I want to go swimming with him so badly.

"So Nox and one other…" Christos looks at me. "Do you know who it is?"

"We assume it's a fairy because of some choices the queen made, mainly to include the three outcast breeds on the council," Gryffin replies, "but we were hoping once you track down who has the children, you could track her final mate."

"You don't want us to track the mate first?" Lena raises an eyebrow in surprise, and I shake my head vehemently.

"No. Those children and their parents need your attention first." I think I surprise her, but she looks pleased.

"But some might say the future of the shifter race lies with you, so it's important that you find your final mate," Santos counters, playing devil's advocate, and I grimace.

"Yes, you may be right, but I can't stand the thought of those children being scared and alone and forced to bite others."

The four of them seem to have a silent conversation

between them. They are probably using bond telepathy, but they don't leave us hanging long.

"Very well. We will start the search for the children while you go to Chaos Kingdom and find my son. You can use the rift access point easily enough," Lena announces, standing up and plucking Stormheart from Liam's arms. He yowls and tries to scratch her, and she screws up her nose and thrusts him at Johan who takes him. The cat settles down once again, and I can't help the burst of laughter that barrels out of my chest.

"I'm sorry," I say when they all look at me, "but it's a relief to know I'm not the only one he hates."

She grins wryly. "Yes, it really is."

"What did you mean about rift access? I thought we would have to cross the desert," Gem asks, and she winces.

"Zalfari isn't just the access point to the vampire nation through the rift. There is a secret underground passage that leads directly to Chaos Kingdom." She looks at her mates and nods like she's decided. "Actually, all the kingdoms, if I'm honest. It makes it easier than traveling through the desert for days. It's at the midway point between here and Eryx, and it allows you to pass through to any of them without going through official routes."

Hunter grunts and tilts his head to the side. "That's how you make your money, isn't it? Smuggling things back and forth?"

She has the grace to look sheepish. "We do what we have to for our people," she says unapologetically.

"How?" Gryffin asks, and it's Santos who answers.

"The Chaos king commissioned it when he took the throne from his grandfather and approached us."

"The Chaos Kingdom comes up in every conversation. For an unofficial kingdom, they seem to have their fingers in every pie," I point out, and I can tell by the looks on my mates' faces that they are as suspicious as I am.

"You need to be cautious when you go there. King Loki isn't above manipulating people to get what he wants, and having one of the ruling royals in his kingdom may be too much for him to pass up," Johan cautions.

"You think he's a danger to us?" Gem sits up, letting his arm drop from my shoulders, on full alert.

"I don't know, just be careful. Get in, find our son, and get out. You don't have time to spend catering to the man's every whim. He's kind of batshit crazy. You need to find your last mate and get that crown on your head. Then, we can focus on who is causing all the trouble." Lena is adamant, and it appears she's dropped the rest of her hostility and is going to work with us for now. "Once we find the children, we will contact you and let you know what we find, then we can work on that final mate for you."

"Thank you, I appreciate your help," I tell her, and she stands up and strides over to me, taking my hands in hers.

"Just look after my son. He needs all the love you can give him. I wasn't able to protect him from the abuse he suffered, and I'm hoping you can fix all that." She moves her gaze to the rest of my mates who all murmur solemn promises.

"He will have so much love, he won't know what to do with it," I promise her, and her eyes shine with unshed tears as she gives me a nod of gratitude.

A yowl breaks the tension, and Johan curses, dropping the cat to the floor. Stormheart streaks away and up a cat tree situated in the corner of the room.

"That cat may be another story though," I grumble, and Lena chuckles but gives me a knowing look.

"You will just have to learn to avoid him like I do, because Nox won't leave Stormheart behind," she warns, and my stomach sinks. How did I know she was going to say that?

THIRTY-TWO

Colbie

We decide we need to get moving as soon as possible. We still need to cross a small portion of the rift to get to the tunnel, and although the ferals are usually active at night, the rift is shrouded in shade, so they may be just as active during the day.

The guys and I gear up for war. All of them strap on weapons, and I change out of my dress and into my spare watch uniform Hunter's dragon provided.

"Keep an eye out for the Chaos Kingdom's symbol on the wall of the tunnel. When you press a hand against it, a secret passage will open and lead you directly to it. It will still take a few hours, but nowhere near as long as it would if you were going the normal route," Christos explains when they come to see us off.

Hunter hands over the bag of children's items we got from their parents. There are DNA samples, items of clothing wrapped in their scent, favorite toys, and photos of each of the children. We weren't sure what a unicorn needed to track, but Lena assures us she has everything she needs when she glances at the items.

"Keep an eye out for the Tideman family," Gryffin tells Nox's parents. "They are wrapped up in this somehow, and they stole a book from the royal vault that we need to get back."

"We will add it to the list," Santos assures us.

"I can't stand that asshole and his stuck-up wife. They were tolerable until they banished their son for mating a man, which is inexcusable. We should love our children no matter what," Lena growls. "It will be our pleasure to see him punished."

A sense of relief washes over me as we walk toward the rift and the tunnel. That is one less task we have to concentrate on, which lifts a weight off my shoulders, and I feel like I can focus on finding Nox now.

"Colbie, stay in the middle of the group so we can protect you if the ferals find us," Micah instructs as the guys surround me.

"If anything happens, let us deal with the ferals. Only shift as a last resort. You don't have the experience to fight in your animal form, even though they will instinctively protect you like it did when we were attacked yesterday," Hunter adds.

"She seemed to do alright yesterday," I point out, feeling a little annoyed, but I also know they are right. I need to focus on getting better in all my forms as well as learn some self-defense in human form. I love that they want to protect me, but I want to be proactive in the same thing. I also acknowledge I don't have those skills yet.

"She did, but shifters are different than the ferals. Shifters have reason and logic and are calculating. Ferals run on pure animalistic instinct. They will act first without pausing to think," Gem explains gently. I can feel how conflicted he is about harming the ferals.

"Do we have to kill them? Can't we just incapacitate them until I get the book to fix them?"

"All of the guns are loaded with tranquilizers today. I took care of it while you were getting changed," Micah tells me, and I smile at him, grateful for his forethought.

"But we won't hesitate to use the other weapons if it comes down to you or them," Liam warns, and I feel nauseous. I'm just going to pray we don't run across any of them.

It's a half hour walk across the open plain to the base of the rift, then another half hour through a craggy canyon with dense vegetation before we get to the tunnel entrance. There is a guard station, but it is currently unmanned. Lena said the faux alpha had his people stationed there since he invaded the village, and she needs to reassign her own people to operate it, but it might take a few days.

The hour journey is spent in silence, the seven of us not wanting to draw any attention to us, but I can't help feeling like we are being watched the whole way. Just as we pass the guard station and prepare to enter the dimly lit tunnel that leads to Eryx, the vampire kingdom, a snarl echoes around the canyon. I stiffen and feel the guys, who were already on full alert, turn in the direction the noise came from. They fan out in a semicircle in front of me, their weapons up.

I watch in horror as a creature barrels out of the trees, my mouth dropping open in shock and surprise. I assumed ferals would be in their animal form, but this one looks like it's stuck mid-shift. It is upright but hunched over like its spine is twisted, and its hands are clawed. Its clothes are shredded, and I can see fur sprouted all over its body. The feral's face is twisted, like it got stuck, and it has a snout, but the eyes are still human, and that's what makes me feel sick. The sheer agony in its gaze almost brings me to my knees. I also can't tell if they are male or female.

They don't seem to comprehend they are in danger, continuing to rush at us while snarling and spitting as Micah raises his gun and fires. The tranq dart lands in its chest, and the feral stumbles but keeps coming. Two more darts hit its torso from Liam's and Brodie's weapons, and it finally stumbles before it goes down hard.

We wait to make sure it's definitely out before Gryffin approaches and flips it over. It's unconscious, but I can see from the rise and fall of its chest that it's still alive.

"What are we going to do with it?" I ask, feeling incredibly sorry for the creature. They can't help that they have become this.

"I think we will just leave it to nap. We will be long gone by the time it wakes, and it will just get aggressive and agitated if we take it back and put it in the cells under Zalfari," Hunter replies as he scans the area for more trouble.

"We will round them all up once we have the book and you have full access to your powers, then we can fix them all in one go," Gem assures me, running a comforting hand up and down my spine. I'm pretty sure he needs as much comfort as I do, so I turn into him and wrap my arms around his waist. He and I both sigh as we soak in the reassurance.

"How can anyone be so cruel?" I ask him, and he shakes his head.

"I don't know, but it's definitely not limited to a specific species. Cruelty is found throughout the kingdoms, and we just have to do our best to punish those responsible," he mumbles into my hair.

"Come on, let's get going. I want to be in the secret passage when that thing wakes in case it tries to track us, and I don't know how long it will be down," Micah urges, and we start moving toward the tunnel.

Unlike the huge entrance to Hunter's hoard, which can fit a dragon, this one is much smaller and only big enough for a large pickup or SUV to get through.

"It's to limit traffic so neither nation can flood into the other in case either decide to go to war," Liam explains behind me. He and Brodie are bringing up the rear with Gem and Gryffin at my side, and Hunter and Micah take point in front.

Despite my enhanced eyesight, I struggle to see more than a few feet in front of us. A ball of flame bursts to life in Gem's hand, and he tosses it into the air where it hovers, keeping pace with us.

"That's handy," I tell him, admiring his magic.

"It sure is. I just have to concentrate to keep it where I want it so I don't accidentally set anything on fire."

Gryffin chuckles. "Like you did at that party in college. Remember that? Burnt down half the frat houses. The parentals were livid because they had to pay for it to be rebuilt."

The other members of the bond group, apart from Micah, hoot with laughter.

"I thought Evie was going to have a coronary when they were called into the neutral zone by the dean," Hunter agrees.

"Why was that again? What caused you to lose control?" Liam asks in a teasing manner, and Gem turns and glares at him.

"You know how hard it was for me to gain control of my fire when I first shifted. I'd only been doing it for six months by then."

"Funny thing, Colbie. When mythicals first shift, they are warned that heightened emotions are a trigger for their new magic and that they should avoid situations that could cause them to lose control." Brodie has a teasing tone, and when I turn to look at him, his eyes are twinkling with undisguised glee.

"That makes sense. So did you get into a fight or something?" I ask, returning my gaze to Gem, who winces.

"Ah, no, the opposite actually," he says cagily, and I think about what the opposite of fighting would be, and then it clicks.

"Oh…" A wave of jealousy floods me, but I push back at my creatures. These guys had a life before me just like I had one before them. I can't get stabby over past actions. It's the future ones that count.

"It was my first threesome, and the Sanderson twins were kinky as fuck," he argues. "They liked fucking the same person. You try holding in your powers when you're being railed from behind while someone is trying to suck your soul out of your cock."

My eyebrows jump in surprise. I automatically assumed he had been with two girls, not two guys.

"Didn't you burn all of Bella's hair off her head? It

took her ages to grow it all back." Hunter snickers in front of us.

"And Blade had third-degree burns on his chest. Dad had to pay their family compensation." Gryffin sounds as jealous as my animals feel.

"The twins were male and female?" I ask, and Gem winks at me.

"Told you they were kinky. I'm pretty sure Blade got off on watching his sister. It was kind of uncomfortable when I realized what was going on, but by then, it was too late. I didn't get laid for a good six months after that. No one would come near me, too worried that I would lose control again," he grumbles.

The bond group bursts into laughter, and this time, Micah and I join in. We spend the next hour getting to know each other better. I find out that all of them attended college before joining the watch or the military like Micah. They all have degrees, and I am blown away to find out Liam is actually a qualified elementary school teacher but has never used his qualifications, moving straight to the watch with the other guys instead.

My heart is full and my mind is distracted from the interaction with the feral when Micah and Hunter stop abruptly in front of us. Micah pulls out a flashlight from one of the backpacks and shines it on the wall to the left. "I thought I saw something. It glows slightly, kind of like some of the phosphorus corals near my family's sea home."

The spotlight illuminates a symbol that isn't familiar to me. It's eight arrows in a circular pattern kind of like a sun. When Hunter puts his hand against it, there's a grinding sound, and then the wall slides back, revealing another tunnel. This one is slightly smaller than the one we've been traveling in, but still wide enough to walk three abreast. Unlike the previous one, though, that seemed to cut straight through the mountain and was cold and clammy, this one appears to slope downward, and the farther we go, the more it warms up.

Sweat starts to pool between my breasts, and my hair begins to stick to my face. "Is it me or is it getting hotter in here?" I ask, fanning my face. Gem and Hunter don't seem to be affected, but the others have a sheen of sweat on their faces as well.

"The tunnel must be connected to the thermal pools and underground springs that run under and through this mountain range, or at least adjacent to them. It's too warm for it not to be," Hunter says, pulling out a canteen of water and passing it back to me. The others follow his lead and pull theirs from their backpacks.

"I think I can see light a little further up." Brodie squints down the tunnel, beyond Gem's flame, which has kept us out of the dark yet again. "Do you think we are almost there?"

Micah frowns. "No, we've only been walking for about two hours. Lena said it would take at least four."

"This walking crap is bullshit," Liam grumbles.

"Apparently they have an ATV and electric carts they use, but because this trip was unexpected, they couldn't arrange for anyone to have them waiting in the tunnel," Hunter tells his teammate who perks up.

"So we can use them on the return journey?"

Hunter rolls his eyes but nods. "Yes, Liam, you lazy fucker."

Liam flips him off, and we continue on our way, but Brodie was right, and the tunnel does get lighter the farther we go. I'm excited, although I feel a little claustrophobic knowing there's a massive mountain range on top of us, but instead of an exit, the tunnel opens into a huge cavern with a shimmery pool of water and a small waterfall trickling prettily over rocks. The light comes from a weird moss-like plant that glows brightly.

"Oh, wow, this is amazing." Gryffin sighs as we look around. There is more than one tunnel leading away on the other side of the grotto.

"Which one do we take?" I ask, pointing at the exits.

Hunter hurries over to them, studying the edges of each tunnel. He runs his hand over something on the one on the left. "This is the Chaos Kingdom's symbol again, so this one. The others have the other kingdoms' symbols. We will be fine. Shall we keep moving?"

Micah is distracted by the shimmering pool of water, though, and the throbbing desire inside my body has kicked into overdrive. It's always been there, but the walk and the conversation were enough to keep it contained. Now that there is a body of water nearby, however, the need to finish the mating bond with Micah is screaming at me.

He squats down and runs a hand through the liquid before lifting it to his mouth to taste it.

Gem cries out, "Wait! What are you doing? You don't know if it's drinkable."

Micah rises to his feet and turns and smiles. "It is. It's fresh with some minerals, but it's fine. I knew you could heal me if it wasn't, plus Colbie's hydra bit me, so I would be okay," he replies, and Gem sags with relief.

"Oh yeah, it's going to take a while to get used to that."

Brodie throws himself on one of the thick bits of moss covering the ground, puts his hands beneath his head, and closes his eyes. "I'm just going to take a nap while you two go do your thing," he mutters, and the rest of the guys spread out, pulling out canteens, granola bars, and jerky. I ignore all that and focus on the shifter in front of me who is slowly removing his clothes, his eyes bright with desire as he gestures to the water.

THIRTY-THREE

Colbie

"Want to go for a swim with me?" He sounds a little unsure, so I start to strip off my own uniform, no longer concerned about nudity in front of my guys. They've seen and worshiped every possible part of my body by now and seem fond of it.

I shiver when I'm completely naked, but it isn't from being cold—it's from anticipation for what's about to happen.

"Have fun," Gryffin calls as Micah takes my hand. Without another word, we both step into the pool. A squeal leaves my mouth as we plummet. I expected it to be a gentle slope downward, but instead, I'm completely submerged in an instant, the water covering my head. It isn't cold, so it doesn't take my breath away, and by contrast, it's warm and comforting.

I start to panic slightly and begin to swim to the

surface, but Micah wraps his arms around me as I watch him shift. His isn't as aggressive and painful looking as the other guys'. It's like a wave of magic flows over him, and his legs fuse and scales appear, as do gill slits in his neck. I feel the same thing happen to me, and I wonder if that is always going to occur whenever I'm in water… though it didn't when I was in the tub in the cabin.

Micah shakes his head. *The change is automatic, but it requires you to be fully submerged for longer than a minute*, he says inside my head. *Come on, let's check out this pool to make sure there isn't anything living in here we need to worry about.*

I gape at him with dread before spinning around and eyeing the depths. The water is crystal clear, but it obviously glows because of the moss above. There are only shadows down here and the absence of light.

I can't see anything, I tell him, and he flicks his tail and takes the lead.

Use your other senses as well. You'll find your tail is sensitive to movement in the water, and you will have a kind of echolocation sense now as well. It helps us navigate the depths, but your eyes will adjust, just give it a moment.

I flick my own tail, not wanting to let him get too far in front of me. There is a flash of light that has me squinting as his trident appears in his hand, and my heart starts to race.

Holy shit, did you see something? I ask, spinning around in search of danger, but he shakes his head and holds out his free hand for me. I take it, and we swim side by side.

No, but it doesn't hurt to be prepared. I will defend you with my life, he vows, and my body feels all warm and tingly at his declaration.

We leisurely explore the bottom of the pool, taking

our time and talking about everything and nothing. Micah tells me he is an only child and that his upbringing was very regimented but didn't lack in love. His mother is a very affectionate person, although his father is slightly more reserved. He thinks it's because of his position on the mer council, which takes up a lot of his time. Neither of them were thrilled when he decided to join the shifter military, especially with the strained relations between the mer and the rest of the shifter population, but they eventually accepted his choice.

He teaches me how to maneuver quickly through the water, showing me how to use my tail to my advantage, and eventually, it feels like I've had one my entire life.

What are those? I ask, pointing to a rock formation that sparkles with veins of bright green gems that look like they have an inner glow.

They are called aqualibrite. They are highly prized in both the witch and fae kingdoms because they can store and amplify fae or witch power. The stones can be drawn on when they are drained from overuse. They are rare and highly regulated, though, and are supposed to be tricky to mine.

They are pretty. I run my finger over one of them, and I feel a pulse of power explode from them, the shock wave washing over us and pushing us backward, sending me tumbling head over tail.

Whoa, I groan as Micah snags me, pulling me against this chest. *That was unexpected.*

He chuckles. *I have a feeling that's why they are hard to mine. They have their own inbuilt defense system.*

It's certainly effective. I rest my head against his chest, enjoying the feeling of having his arms around me. I'm not sure where his trident went—probably back where it came from—but as his tail brushes against mine, sending a wave of desire washing over me, I don't really care.

I lift my head and find him looking at me with a wealth of love and desire. *Colbie, you're beautiful. I never dared to hope to be blessed with a mate mark. I'm a little bit older than the rest of your mates, and I thought I wasn't worthy, but if you'll let me, I will try my hardest to make sure you are loved and loved well for the rest of your life.* His tone is sweet but seductive, and I press my mouth against his in response.

Kissing underwater is weird. Our gills make it so we can fuse our mouths together without the need to breathe, but water constantly flows in and out of them. His tongue tangles with mine as he pulls my body tightly against his, and the bottoms of our tails kind of weave together until I don't know where I end and he starts.

He slides a hand between us and cups my breast, squeezing it gently before leaning down and taking my nipple into his mouth. I arch my back, giving him better access, and he switches between both, giving each nipple plenty of attention.

Lower down, a hard ridge rubs against where my pelvis would be in human form, and I moan at the delicious sensation it causes. Air bubbles dance elegantly to the surface as Micah releases the nipple in his mouth.

Are you ready to become my mate? he asks, pressing his forehead against mine and staring deep into my soul.

I'm still unsure of the exact logistics of that, but I'm eager to find out, so I nod in agreement. *Yes, teach me how to mate in mer form.*

He releases me and untangles his tail from mine before moving backward, and I frown with disappointment.

He smiles at my reaction. *We just need to pluck our heart scales first, so we can insert them under each other's skin. Then, we'll make love, and at the moment of climax, the skin will heal over the scales, mating us forever,* he explains, curving his body so his tail sort of bends up in front of him. He's way more flexible than I thought he would be.

I focus on the scales at the base of his tail and spot the very one he's talking about—a perfect heart-shaped scale that sits in the center of his caudal fin. He slides a fingernail under it and tugs sharply. He winces, and I feel his pain through our bond, but he beams happily when he holds it up for me to see.

Your turn, he encourages.

I contort my tail in the same way, and even though I just saw him do it, I'm surprised at how flexible I am. It curves up in front of me, and I reach out and repeat his motions, plucking out my own heart scale. There is a bite of pain that sends a line of fire through the middle of my tail, up my torso, and into my chest. Fuck, that isn't pleasant, but the pulse of approval through our bond quickly makes the pain recede.

Now what? I ask him, and his eyes smolder as he swims slowly forward so our bodies align, our tails twining together once more.

Now I'll insert this under your skin. Sorry, there is no way to make this pleasant, he cautions as a long claw extends out of the tip of one finger. My eyes widen in surprise as he brings it to my chest and runs it over the top of my right breast.

I grit my teeth against the pain, but the nail is razor sharp, and the incision is almost medical grade, straight and precise with no ragged edges. Blood clouds the water, and I pray that there are no predators in this pool. Micah slides the pretty teal scale deep into the wound, and I can't stop the scream that barrels out of my lungs. A boiling cloud of bubbles shoots to the surface of the pool, and I hope none of my other mates panic. I send them waves of assurance when I feel a spike along the bond, then I look down as he pulls his hand away. The wound is slightly large now with the scale lodged inside it, and it throbs painfully. I reach up to poke at it, but Micah gently pushes my hand away.

Trust me, he implores. *Now it's your turn. Do the same thing. Will your nail to extend and draw it across my chest.* He points to where I need to place it.

I concentrate on turning a nail on my free hand into a claw. It happens easily, but then I hesitate. I don't like the idea of causing him pain, even if I know it won't last.

Go on. I can hear his excitement, even if I can't feel it yet. Taking a deep breath, I slide my nail across his skin. The claw cuts his skin like butter, a tiny trickle of blood flowing into the water, but apparently, it's not good enough.

Deeper. He groans in my head, and it's not a groan of pleasure.

I'm sorry, I sob, but he shakes his head and brings his own hand up to grip mine, pushing down. This time, blood spills into the water, creating a thick red cloud around us, and when he releases my hand, there is a large enough wound for me to slide the heart-shaped scale into. I quickly jam my scale inside. His whole body shudders with pain, and his gills work like they are breathing heavily, his chest heaving with exertion.

When it's firmly lodged deep inside, I drop my hand and bring my gaze back to his face. *Now what?*

His eyes hood, and he wraps an arm around my waist and tugs me closer, our bodies pressing firmly against one another. *Now I'll make you my mate.*

But how? I look down at our tails, wondering about the logistics of everything.

Don't overthink this, he tells me before taking my mouth with his.

His tongue plunges into my mouth as one hand slips into my hair and he gets a good grip so he can angle my face to his liking as he pours his desperation, longing, and need into the kiss. I feel his stomach muscles ripple against my own, and his tail starts to beat back and forth, taking mine, which is tangled with his, with it. Every brush slides our sensitive scales together, and I feel my arousal quicken and the tails glide more freely. I look down and notice that they are both coated in a clear secretion that seems to be coming from the gaps between the scales.

He tugs my hair, bringing my head back to the angle he wants. *Don't look, just feel,* he commands as a pins and needles feeling starts to tingle in my pelvis area. The sensation gets stronger, and I feel something else happen down there, but I can't look because Micah is controlling my head.

His tail starts to beat a little faster, and all I can do is go along for the ride. The pins and needles feeling recedes and is replaced by a pulsing, throbbing need.

Oh God, I murmur as the need builds, and I feel something push against my tail right in that spot. I'm assuming his cock has emerged from wherever it is hidden in this form. With a quick thrust, it slides into my sexual slit, and I groan, clutching his arms to hold myself upright as my body becomes boneless with pleasure.

I close my eyes, and my head drops back as he moves his lips down to my throat, pressing kisses against the other mate marks, and I feel my other mates' interest pulse inside the bond, which drives my desire even higher. His tail starts to pulse faster now, thrusting his cock in and out as the walls of my pussy flutter and the tension in my body grows.

Feels so fucking good, he murmurs, taking one of my nipples with his mouth and scraping his teeth against it. My eyes widen at the sharp prick, and when I look down, he's grinning at me with a mouthful of very sharp teeth. His eyes have changed as well, becoming dark wells of blackness that I can see my reflection in.

My lips round in surprise at the sight of this deadly predator whose arms I'm currently trapped in. His taloned fingers scrape against my scalp and hip where he has a tight grip on me so I can't escape.

A sharp pulse of fright races through me, and I struggle, trying to pull away, but he just holds me tighter, and I hear him say, *Let go, Colbie. Give me your inner beast.*

I can't stop what happens next. It's like I'm suddenly in the back seat and a more primal, animalistic version of me rises to take control. I feel my fingertips turn into talons, and my jaw aches as my teeth become so sharp I pierce my own lip when I gasp with surprise. My eyesight changes, and my hearing tunes into the pulsing beat of his heart and the flow of blood through his veins. I lean in and lick the mark my hydra left on his neck, crowing with joy at the sight of it, before digging my teeth into it as my nails pierce his back, trapping him in place.

He shouts and pulses his tail harder as I suckle the blood that wells on the wound, feeling an almost visceral need to mark him again.

His cock pistons into me, and I feel ridges rub against the sensitive inner walls of my core, my orgasm teetering on the crest of a wave.

Come with me, mate. Join us forever, he growls, and the ridges on his cock expand and begin to vibrate, pushing me off the precipice. I open my mouth and scream as a shockwave of energy explodes outward from us, sending a pulse of power radiating out from our joined bodies. I shudder as pleasure rolls over me and through every part of my body, and I feel the wound in my chest scal over as I watch the same thing happen to his. The wave of pleasure rolls over me again and again, slowly getting weaker before finally disappearing, leaving us both limp and exhausted as we sink deeper into the depths of the pool, our bodies fused together in mutual satisfaction.

· ‹ ‹ ● ● ● › › ·

When Micah and I emerge, we find the others all napping, but Gem hears us and scrambles to his feet, coming over and holding out his hand. He helps me climb out of the pool, water streaming down my body, and then ignites flames in his hands and quickly dries me off so I can put my clothes on.

"Thanks," Micah tells him as Gem gives him the

same treatment. "Putting on clothes when you're wet is a pain in the ass. I didn't think to bring towels."

"No prob." Gem winks. "It's no hardship to look at either of you naked."

I giggle and elbow him as I zip up my pants before pulling my top on. "You're just a pervert," I tease him, and he shrugs good-naturedly.

"Guilty as charged."

By this time, the others have roused, and Brodie offers us a canteen and some food while the rest pack their bags again.

I take the proffered food. "Thanks, I'm starving."

"I bet. I need all the details on fucking underwater. Like, where does he stick his—" Before he can finish his sentence, Liam smacks him on the back of the head.

"Shut up, you idiot," he growls before giving me a kiss on the cheek and clapping Micah on the back. "Congrats, guys, we're so happy for both of you."

My mouth drops open. Who is this man and what happened to the grumpy asshole he used to be? He and Micah do that bro hug thing, and Hunter steps up next to me, puts a finger under my chin, and pushes my mouth closed.

"What is happening here?" I ask, and he shrugs.

"It's the bond. There's no jealousy, only happiness that everyone is where they need to be. Now let's get going and find the last two wayward members so we can get that crown on your head, and you can take your rightful place."

He gives me a quick kiss on the lips, and I shove the granola bar into my mouth, chewing furiously to finish before we leave, then I wash it down with a sip of water.

We head for the tunnel with Gryffin and Gem

leading us, another ball of flames guiding the way. Micah throws his backpack over one shoulder and grabs my hand as he and Hunter flank me for this leg of the journey.

I hear Brodie grumble something about having to take the rear again, but Liam's reply has me smiling.

"Yeah, but this way we get to watch that fine ass for the trip."

"That's true," Brodie replies, and this time, he sounds a lot happier.

THIRTY-FOUR

Colbie

I'm not wearing a watch, and my phone is in a backpack because it's useless underground, so I lose track of time, but it feels like we've been down here for days. When we finally see light at the end of the tunnel, I'm not the only one who picks up the pace, but the six of them do shove me to the back of the group and pull out their weapons, preparing for anything that may be waiting for us.

Good thing they do, because when we emerge from the tunnel, I discover we are surrounded by armed and masked guards bearing the symbol of the Chaos Kingdom.

"Drop your weapons, and no one will be hurt," one of the masked men orders. "The king requests your presence for dinner this evening, and I would prefer that you come willingly than have to drag you there, chained and cuffed."

The man's voice makes me shiver with unease. The only thing visible on him are his eyes, which are a stunning pale green very unlike Hunter's beautiful emerald green ones. The rest of him is covered by a formfitting leather uniform with a hood and cowl covering his head and face. A long sword is strapped to his back, and he is covered in knives and guns in various holsters.

I slide my gaze to the side, sizing up the men and women accompanying him. Some of them are wearing the same hooded uniform as him, but the rest are just wearing normal military garb with no head coverings. They are, however, all armed to the teeth. We are definitely outgunned, and I'm not sure any of us could shift quickly enough without getting injured. This is also the Chaos Kingdom, which means all of these armed assailants are a mix of species and, as such, unpredictable.

The guys must realize the same thing, because they drop their weapons. "Fine, but if anyone so much as looks at the queen strangely, then all bets are off," Hunter growls, smoke drifting from his nose.

"Of course, dragon. We want her safety as much as you do," the original man says as his team separates. He leads the way, the rest of them surrounding us. No one makes an aggressive move as we follow him to a cavalcade of cars awaiting us.

I glance around at the desert surrounding us on all sides, apart from the sealed road that leads away from the area. The first man opens a door to one of the middle cars, a luxurious limo large enough for all of us. He gestures for us to climb in as the rest of his team enters the remaining four cars. Hunter and Micah climb in first, and Gem gestures for me to follow them when he hears Hunter call, "Clear."

The leader of the guards holds out a gloved hand and helps me into the vehicle with a polite head nod. I perch on one of the bench seats, and I'm surprised to see him follow directly after me, taking the vacant spot beside me. The others enter after him and spread out on the remaining seats, Gryffin on my other side, all of them focused on the armed man next to me.

"Who are you?" Liam asks as the door closes and the vehicle starts moving.

I peer out the window and see two cars are in front of us and two guard the rear. All of the vehicles are flying little flags on their hoods bearing the symbol of the Chaos Kingdom.

"I am the king's head assassin," the man replies as he sprawls in his seat, relaxed and calm like he has no concern about being surrounded by seven powerful shifters. "And his liaison between the Chaos and shifter kingdoms."

Gryffin tilts his head to the side. "You're Titus?" he asks, and I hear the curiosity in his voice.

The assassin's eyebrows jump in the first sign of emotion he's shown so far. "You have heard of me? Did your father share secrets with you?"

Gryff shakes his head. "No, I overheard him talking to one of my mothers about you a few years ago—something about being grateful the new king wasn't as big of an asshole as the previous one, but he wasn't sure if his new liaison wasn't going to be one."

I feel Titus shake with what I think is amusement if the twinkle in his eye is anything to go on.

"Yes, I'm sure he still feels that way."

"What does the Chaos king want with us?" I ask him, and he turns those stunning pale green eyes my way. He seems to be looking directly into my soul, but without seeing the rest of his face, I can't even begin to guess what he's thinking.

He shrugs elegantly. "That isn't for me to say, but I can assure you he means no harm. A ruling royal from one of the other nations hasn't set foot in Chaos Kingdom before." He slides his gaze to Gryffin. "Though that isn't the case for you, is it, princeling? You and your bond mates have made use of our delights a few times." Gryffin scowls but doesn't deny it. Titus returns his attention to me. "My king is a curious male with many secrets. I'm sure he is just extending the hand of hospitality. He will put you up at the castle, you can speak to him, and then you can continue on your way, but it could be you find exactly what you are looking for when you speak to him," he says vaguely before turning his attention to the window, like being in our presence doesn't concern him one bit.

The tension in the vehicle is stifling. My mates are on high alert, and my creatures are bristling with agitation, but it's not aggressive agitation—it's curiosity and no small amount of lust. They are attracted to this male and curious about how he can be so relaxed surrounded by all of us. I squirm in my seat, unable to keep still, and try to distract myself by watching the scenery go by. I know I'm not fooling anyone. I bet my mates can smell exactly how I'm feeling. Brodie smirks at me with knowing eyes, and Liam alternates between glaring at me and the male beside me. I bet I'm going to get an earful when we're finally alone. I do appreciate his restraint though. When I catch Gem's gaze, his face is pensive as he glances back and forth between the two of us. Hunter, Gryffin, and Micah all watch Titus closely, but I think the three of them are having a telepathic conversation as well. I'm sure they will fill me in if it's anything I need to know.

"The Chaos king's assassins always wear those cowls and hoods when out in public so no one can ever identify them," Gryffin whispers quietly in my ear, but I don't doubt that Titus can hear him. I don't know what crossbreed he is, but all supes have good hearing.

"So what kind of half-breed are you?" Brodie asks bluntly, and although I was just thinking something similar, I scowl at his lack of tact.

"Brodie," I hiss, "that isn't polite. You shifters hate it when people ask you the same thing."

"Aren't you a shifter as well, Your Majesty?" Titus drawls calmly, ignoring the tactless wolf.

I startle at his question but feel my cheeks heat with embarrassment. "Yeah, but it's new for me, so I don't care if someone asks me what I am."

"So what are you?" He leans forward slightly with anticipation, but before I can answer, Hunter growls.

"That information is need to know only at the moment, and you don't need to know."

Titus waves a hand, casually dismissing the dragon. "Oh, I already know. Quite the special little cupcake, aren't you?"

My mouth drops open in surprise, and my mates' animals all respond with aggression, the limo filling with growls and rumbles.

"How do you know?" Micah asks, reaching for a knife sheathed on his thigh.

"Uh-uh, I allowed you to keep your weapons in a show of good faith. Stabbing me now would go badly for everyone." Titus's tone is deadly, and I reach over and place a hand on Micah's, halting his movement.

"It's fine. He's an assassin and spy, and for all we know, Lucas told him." I narrow my eyes on the assassin who gives me a slow wink. I'm almost certain he's grinning beneath his face shield.

The tension in the vehicle is still high, and the silence we've drifted into is stifling as the desert soon gives way to a lush tropical oasis. I lean forward in my seat to get a better look out the window. Exotic palms and bushes dotted with a flower I don't recognize line the streets and gardens of the residences we pass. Cute little cottages and family homes spaced far apart to give everyone a sense of privacy soon give way to a denser area. Apartment buildings, shops, and entertainment venues are in abundance, and the streets are full of people socializing and having a good time.

"What time is it?" I ask Titus. I know we left Zalfari around eight, and we walked for at least six hours to get here, as well as the stop we made at the hot springs, plus we've been driving for half an hour.

"It's almost five in the evening, just in time to have dinner with the king," he replies, pulling a cell phone out of one of the numerous pockets in his uniform. He sends a short text message as the buildings give way to more lush tropical land, and we pull up to a large set of closed gates. Guards exit a nearby gate box, both armed and wearing severe expressions on their faces. Titus merely lowers the window, and once they catch sight of him, they melt away, and the gates open.

"They can't even see you beneath that getup. You could be anyone," Gryffin points out, and Titus chuckles.

"I can assure you they know who I am, and no one would dare try to impersonate me or my four brothers. They would find themselves on our bad side, and that is never good."

"You're that confident?" I ask.

"The Chaos king's assassins get whispered about in all corners of the kingdoms. He probably has the right to be that confident," Micah says flatly.

Before anyone else can say anything, the vehicle pulls up in front of a lavish palace, and it's at least the size of the one I now reside in. Steps lead up to double doors with guards standing on either side who are also fully armed. Neither of them move a muscle as the vehicle comes to a stop and the driver jumps out and opens the door for us. We climb out, and once again, we find ourselves surrounded by the rest of Titus's team, who have piled out of the other vehicles.

"Is this all really necessary?" I ask, waving my hand at them. "We came along peacefully." I narrow my eyes on the assassin. "And if you know what creature I am, you know I could have shifted and killed every one of you within seconds."

"But could you have? You are still new to all this, and I'm sure you haven't had a lot of opportunities to practice shifting. We could have put bullets through all of you in the time it would have taken you to change." He stares at me, his gaze calculating, and I have the urge to rip that fucking mask off his face so I can see it.

"Maybe, but I guess we will never know," I taunt him. "Unless you're scared that you don't actually have a chance against us, which is why you need all of this backup. The great Chaos assassin is scared of a bunch of shifters and their new, inexperienced queen." I smile widely, and his body stiffens as he clenches his fists. Typical male. Have a go at their skills, and their pride overshadows any common sense.

He waves a hand, and his team stops in their tracks. "But, sir," one of the females starts to argue. His head swings toward her, tearing his gaze from me, and she blanches at whatever she sees. Nobody says another word, and they make themselves scarce. I'm sure there is a barracks around here somewhere just like at the palace in Aramis.

"Come," he snaps, and the two guards open the double doors as he approaches, giving him a head nod as he passes. Titus doesn't even wait to see if we follow, and the seven of us exchange a glance.

"We could make a run for it now. I could shift and fly us out of here," Hunter suggests, but I shake my head.

"No, let's just get this over with so we can find Nox. The last thing we need is to have to avoid the Chaos king's assassins and guards while we look for him, and I don't doubt he'd send them after us if we ran. He obviously knew we were coming, and it won't hurt for me to meet him," I reply quietly.

"I agree," Gryffin says, his eyes staying on the assassin's back. "My father trusts him, so I say we do too. Dad is rarely wrong."

"How does he explain his council then?" Liam says dryly.

"Inexperienced and the shock of being the shifter king," Gryffin growls at his teammate.

"Fair," Brodie agrees as we follow the assassin into the palace. Unlike the shifter palace, there are people everywhere in this one. We pass many parlors filled with beautiful people who are talking and laughing, drinks in hand. None of them pay any attention to us. Staff members dressed in uniforms stop and move aside whenever they see the assassin approaching, their eyes wary and postures tense.

"Not winning any friends here, are you?" I call out, trying to get a rise out of him, annoyed at how blasé this man is. He doesn't consider us a threat at all, and that has my creatures gnashing their teeth, wanting to bite him just to prove they can.

We pass a fountain that makes me pause.

"Now that is much nicer than the abomination in the front of the Aramis castle," Gem says, stopping with me.

It's of four ladies, all with their backs to each other in a circle. Each one is slightly different. One has fangs, talons for nails, and almond-shaped eyes, while another has wings coming from her back. A third has a book and a potion bottle in her hand, and I recognize the final one, except she has clawed fingers, her eyes have elongated pupils, and she has the tail of a wolf.

"That's Aramis." I point her out to Gem. "Or I think it is. She didn't have those animal features when I saw her."

"The others are Eryx, Shayla, and Tanith." He points to each of them. "The four goddesses of the realms. It seems the Chaos Kingdom reveres all four. It's not surprising, since they don't have one of their own and they allow all manner of people to reside here. It makes sense, to be honest."

We move on, winding through a myriad of corridors. There are so many that I feel completely turned around, but Micah hums his approval.

"This setup is genius," he mutters to us.

"What do you mean?" Gem asks just as quietly.

"This is designed to cause confusion for any intruders who may try to breach the palace walls. They would end up turned around and lost on their way to what I'm assuming is the throne room in the middle of the building."

"Very good, Captain," Titus calls back with approval in his tone.

"I bet they have secret passageways with a more direct route for anyone in the king's trusted circle," Hunter murmurs under his breath barely loud enough for us to hear, let alone Titus, but he does.

"It is a good theory," he says flippantly as we approach another set of double doors with guards standing on either side. They push them open without a word from the male, and he doesn't even slow in his pace.

What I thought was going to be an extravagant throne or ballroom actually looks more like cozy, comfortable, yet spacious living quarters. There are sumptuous couches scattered around the room in bright jewel colors. A large bookcase with a fireplace built into it lines one wall, and a huge skylight overhead shows the rapidly darkening night sky, the stars beginning to appear.

A blond man reclines on the couch, looking up as we enter, and a huge smile crosses his face when his lavender eyes meet mine. I can't stop the gasp that leaves my mouth at the sight of him. Apart from his blond hair, it's like looking at a slightly older, more masculine version of me.

"Holy shit, do you have a twin?" Brodie exclaims as the man and I stare at each other, his expression full of hope.

THIRTY-FIVE

Colbie

"Your Majesty, may I present Colbie Karridge, the Queen of Aramis, and six of her mates." Titus names and points to each in turn, but the king can't tear his gaze away from me. "I present King Loki Asmina."

He seems to jolt out of his fascination with me when Titus mentions his name. "Please, come in and sit down. I'm delighted to meet all of you." He waves a hand at the sofas, and my mates, though confused, take a seat, but I remain standing as the king approaches me, holding out both hands.

"Colbie, I have waited for this day for years." He takes both of my hands in his. "I have so much to explain."

"Who are you?" I ask bluntly, feeling my stomach roll as I ponder the implications.

"Colbie, I'm your father," Loki tells me gently, but I shake my head, yanking my hands from his.

"No, you can't be. My father was a human who left my mother for another woman," I splutter, stunned beyond belief at his claim as my guys all make exclamations of surprise.

"Impossible." Liam shakes his head. "Colbie's mother is most definitely human, and supes can't procreate with humans unless they have been changed."

"Why don't we let the king explain?" Titus interrupts. This is obviously not the first time he's hearing this information, because he doesn't sound surprised in the least.

"Thank you, Titus," the king says fondly before frowning at his assassin. "Why are you still covering yourself? You don't need to hide yourself from these people here."

Titus rolls his eyes and strips off the hooded cowl and cloak, tossing it over the back of a chair. He shakes his shoulders slightly, and large green and silver wings appear against his back, and I stare in surprise. He's beautiful, with long pale green hair, sharp, elegant features, and plump lips, but he also radiates a cool, lethal aura.

"You're fae?" I ask, and he gives a casual shrug.

"Part of me is," he says before heading over to a drink cart and pouring a glass of wine before taking a seat.

"So polite," King Loki mutters with annoyance. "Would anyone else like a drink?" he asks, and I turn my attention back to him, focusing once more on what he just announced.

"No, you can't just drop a comment like that and not elaborate," I hiss at him, and he sighs before nodding and gesturing to a sofa.

"Why don't you take a seat? I will explain everything," he encourages, but I cross my arms and stubbornly shake my head.

"I'll stand," I snap, my body vibrating with emotion. Who does this man think he is, telling me lies like that?

Again, he sighs like I'm a troublesome toddler having a tantrum, and I grit my teeth so I don't say anything to the Chaos Kingdom king that I can't come back from.

He opens his mouth to start talking, but there is a flash of light, and a woman appears in the center of the room—a very familiar, albeit slightly annoying woman.

"Aramis!" I exclaim as the gorgeous blonde woman gives me a wink and a wave before looking around the room and frowning.

"Hmm, I see you are still missing a mate or two," she says absently.

Loki doesn't even blink, like he's used to deities dropping in for visits, and neither does Titus, but my guys all gape at the goddess with wide-mouthed awe.

"Close your mouths, boys, that's how you swallow flies," she says with a giggle before taking a seat and patting the space next to her. "Come on, Colbie, give Loki a chance to explain."

"Why are you here?" I ask.

She shrugs. "I thought maybe I could help with this conversation."

"Oh thank God," Loki mutters before he collapses on one of the sofas.

"It's goddess, actually, but that doesn't mean I'm going to tell the whole thing." She arches an eyebrow at him, and he nods his acceptance.

"Almost thirty years ago, my sisters and I came to Loki and gave him a task," she starts.

"Some freaking task. More like a fucking journey from hell," he mutters, and she glares at him, and he mimes zipping his lips. I smother the grin that wants to cross my lips. He is sassy, even if he is a liar.

"We knew a change was needed, and because we decreed that we wouldn't interfere, we had to circumnavigate the rules."

"Circumnavigate? I would say you blasted them to smithereens." I guess the man can't take a hint, but she just ignores him.

"We had to put a plan of action into place, and we had been watching Loki for years. We knew we needed him to implement the change. Unlike his grandfather, he had no prejudice against any species, including humans. He was open-minded and basically a good person."

"Grandfather was an asshole, he held a grudge against the shifters who rejected him in the first place for falling in love with my grandmother a vampire. Which is why they appealed to both of their goddesses to help them create the Chaos Kingdom," Loki explains joining the narrative.

"Your grandfather was the first king of the Chaos Kingdom?" Gem asks and Loki nods his head.

"Yes and unlike the rest of the kingdoms he wanted this monarchy to be for life and hereditary. He and my grandmother had my father who is half shifter half vampire. He married my mother who was a half fae witch. They were estranged from my grandfather but agreed for him to name me as his heir because my father did not want the position. They live in the city and I still have dinner with them weekly."

"And you and Eryx approved this?" Gryffin asks the goddess who inclines her head.

"All four of us did. We saw the mistakes we made and wanted to give star-crossed lovers a place where they could be happy and accepted. All of us had people who found love and mates in other races. It was an unexpected evolution we did not see coming, which really shows a lack of foresight and that even deities are fallible." She stops talking, and her eyes grow distant for a moment before she lets out a heavy sigh.

"We did so many things wrong, and hindsight is twenty-twenty. There was no putting the cat back in the bag, so to speak, so we made a deal with the former king. In exchange for creating the Chaos Kingdom, he would owe us a future favor for either him or one of his descendants to fulfill."

"And I was the lucky soul who was tasked with repaying the favor," Loki says dryly, but her focus is fully on telling us her tale.

"What was the favor?" Brodie asks, unable to hide his curiosity.

"Thirty years ago, the first time since the great war between humans and supernaturals, rumblings of discontent reached us," the goddess starts.

"Surely it wasn't the first hint of that?" Liam scoffs, and she shakes her head.

"No, you're right, there has always been an uneasy truce between the two factions, but the humans knew if they were to start something again, they would be easily outgunned by the supernaturals. Then it came to our attention that the humans were messing with magic. Somehow, they had convinced a few individual supernaturals to assist their cause. It didn't really go anywhere, but we realized it was only a matter of time before someone would attempt this again, so we put a plan in place. We selected four human women to bear the final humans that would be leaders for the four supernatural races. As I have explained to Colbie, it will be her family line that will rule the shifters, and all humans in Aramis will be given the opportunity to be changed if they wish to. Taking the human factor out of the equation should bring balance to the kingdoms."

"And this is going to happen in the other kingdoms as well?" Hunter asks, catching on.

"Yes, in fact, it is already in motion. The fae and witch royals are all due to retire within the coming months. The vampire royals are not supposed to retire for another year, but they are going to find that timeline is accelerated. They are my sisters' concerns, however, and you are mine."

"But what does he have to do with all of this and his claim that he is Colbie's father?" Micah jabs a finger in Loki's direction, his anger almost as obvious as mine. He doesn't like that Loki dropped that announcement on me any more than I do.

"That was the favor we called in. We decided that it would be better for supernatural relations if they had a common link. We are hoping to avoid future wars between our creations," the goddess explains, looking at the king.

"But that tells us nothing," Hunter argues, but Gryffin is staring at the man with calculating eyes, like he figured something out. "You claim you are Colbie's father. Does that mean you are the father of all four children?"

My mouth drops open as Loki nods his head. "Yes.

The task I was given was to impregnate the four chosen human women." He looks at me with pained eyes. "Then let them raise their children without any interference from me. I was bound to this by the agreement my father made with them."

Tears well in my eyes at the revelation, and I shake my head, speechless and devastated, unable to process this fantastical information.

"But how? Supernaturals can't procreate with humans," Gem argues, and the goddess shrugs.

"Actually, crossbreeds can, but the children are always born human. It takes magic to trigger the change in them. Again, another little quirk of evolution. There are probably more humans out there with supernatural genes who will never know because they aren't subjected to the magic that activates them."

Everyone stares at the goddess with various displays of shock and surprise, but then something occurs to me —something triggered by what Loki said.

"I have sisters?" I look between him and the goddess, and both of them smile warily like they are scared of how I'm going to react.

"Yes, the future queens of Shayla, Eryx, and Tanith are all your half-sisters," the goddess says. I don't know how I feel about this. On one hand, I'm giddy with excitement since I always wanted brothers or sisters, and that longing was even stronger after Gryffin and the two girls visited. On the other hand, will they want anything to do with me? After everything that has happened, are we going to be able to get over our father's betrayal so we can become a semi-functional family? Or will we remain distant allies at best? So many scenarios play over and over in my head as I come to terms with the news.

"So Loki is a quarter of each race, which is how you were able to create children with all four women, but how did each of them turn out as the supernatural race they need to be? Colbie is definitely all shifter with no other traits." Hunter raises a questioning eyebrow at the goddess, who shrugs unapologetically.

"Remember, they only have the potential to be supernaturals, so when they are exposed to the right magic, it triggers the change. Had Colbie been subjected to Eryx's magic instead of mine, she would have been a vampire. Loki is the only one in the Chaos Kingdom who has all four bloodlines running through him."

"That doesn't seem like a coincidence," Gem points out dryly, and the goddess blushes.

"We did what needed to be done."

I focus my attention on the man who sired me. "My mother told me you were a cheating bastard who left when he found out she was pregnant."

He scoffs and rolls his eyes. "Your mother always had a propensity to tell lies. I'm sure that narrative fit her perfectly. In fact, she was only ever a brief fling, one I knew she would get pregnant from, but the goddess told me you would have to be raised alone to become the person you were meant to be. I entranced her and her parents to believe I was around longer than I was, but that the relationship went south, and we split up. In truth, I never saw her again after the week we spent together. I did it so she wouldn't come looking for me. Anything she told you about me is a lie and made up to fit her own needs. As much as I wanted to be in your lives, the goddess forbade it. If I had my way, you would have been raised here in the kingdom with me, spoiling you all rotten." He sounds desperate, like he needs me to believe what he's saying, and I kind of do. That may be my own desperate need for a loving parent grasping at straws, but in this moment, I don't care.

I glare at the goddess, furious that she took away my chance to be raised by a more stable and caring environment, but she just stares back at me. "We did what needed to be done. You are the person you need to be because of your upbringing and have unbiased views of supernaturals. Had you been raised in your father's care, you could have picked up prejudices."

"What a load of crap," Liam spits out, and I feel a rush of love at his support, even though she is probably right. "Being raised in Chaos Kingdom would have been the best place for all of them. It would have made them neutral."

She vehemently shakes her head. "Not if Loki's grandfather had gotten his hooks into them. Remember, Loki only succeeded the man just over ten years ago. The girls would have been fully under his influence."

"What happened to him?" Brodie asks, unable to stop his curiosity.

"I killed him," my father said flatly. "He was throwing around words of war, no longer content to be hidden from the humans or ignored by the other supernaturals. He was stirring up trouble for the kingdom, and I wasn't about to see all of our people die for his delusions."

"You know a lot of supernaturals, especially the wealthy and influential, are not going to be thrilled that all four kingdoms have rulers so closely linked to the

Chaos king. They are going to think he will be able to manipulate them," Micah points out thoughtfully.

Loki shrugs, but the goddess shakes her head. "He will not be the ruler who will see Chaos Kingdom into the future, though I don't doubt he will continue to guide the one who will."

Loki narrows his eyes and growls at the goddess. "What did you do?"

She winces. "There is a fifth child who has been raised by a woman in the Chaos Kingdom. You will step down, and she will take your place."

He stiffens and jumps to his feet. "What do you mean? I have not had a relationship with another woman in years. Not since…" He trails off, and the goddess nods, her eyes glistening with unshed tears.

"Not since you thought you found your mate, but she turned out to be someone else's. I know. I'm sorry we did that to you, but we masked the mate bond for all of you so our plans could move forward. We needed you to do what we required without the burden of guilt. Both Camila and Wyatt are your mates. She was already pregnant when they met. They have been raising the child together."

Loki looks furious. "Why? I did everything you asked for. I gave up my chance to be a father five times over for all of your machinations. When is it going to stop?" I hear the anguish in his tone, and I can't help but feel a sense of kinship for this man. These goddesses have been manipulating all of us for too long, and he got the worst of it.

"I'm so sorry, Loki, but now you get your reward for having served us so well," she says as she stands, affectionately cupping his cheek, and my eyes widen.

"Did you and him…" I trail off, wondering if my father has a relationship with the goddess, but they both blanch.

"Hell no!" he exclaims vehemently. "They are like annoying, interfering older sisters."

"We each have our own mates. They just choose not to get involved in our kingdoms," she tells us, and I heave out a sigh of relief. I'm not sure why, but the thought of them together felt wrong.

"We will unmask the bond as soon as the other queens are all in place," she assures Loki. "I'm sorry you have to wait a little longer, but use this time to build relationships with your other daughters. All of them will venture to the Chaos Kingdom for this news. You will send out your other assassins and have them bring them here," she explains.

Titus, who has been quiet this whole time, frowns thoughtfully at the king and goddess. He opens his mouth like he's about to ask a question, but his phone pings, alerting him to a message. He looks at it before slipping it into his pocket then stands up. "Ah, it seems the final player has arrived. I will escort him in," he says, and without waiting for a response, he puts his hooded cowl back on and disappears in the blink of an eye. My mouth drops open.

"What was that?" I point at the now empty space.

"Titus's fae genes give him the ability to sift," Loki says absently, lost in his own thoughts. It looks like our family is having bombshells dropped on all of us today.

"Sift?" I ask, not familiar with the term.

"It's like teleporting. They move through ley lines, which run through each of the kingdoms, allowing them to travel long distances in a blink," Gem explains.

"Who is here?" Hunter asks, smoke drifting from his nose as he looks between the goddess and the king. I can feel his agitation and worry that we are going to be ambushed with something else.

"If I had to hazard a guess, it would be Colbie's final mate," the goddess replies absently. She's still watching Loki carefully, like she's expecting him to explode at any moment.

"Nox?" Gryffin asks, looking toward the door. "But he isn't Colbie's final mate. One is still missing."

"No, there isn't," the goddess retorts, her eyebrows rising with surprise. "They are all gathered here now. Once she seals the bond with the last two, she can return to Aramis and finally claim the crown and face anyone who may challenge her." Aramis's words send my mind reeling. If what she is saying is true, then that means the assassin is my final mate.

THIRTY-SIX

Colbie

"But… that would mean…" Before Brodie can say his name, Titus returns, and he's accompanied by none other than Nox. He blinks unsteadily but recovers quickly then looks around the room. The pleasant albeit polite smile that is on his face drops, and he gapes at me in shock.

"Colbie?" His gaze shifts to the men around the room before settling on King Loki and Aramis.

"Your Majesty." He bows his head the smallest amount before glaring at him. "I was under the impression you were bringing me here for a job offer, not to ambush me with a past I have worked hard to put behind me."

Ouch. I flinch at his words, and he must see the reaction, because he shakes his head at me.

"I meant about being a shifter, not being with you," he explains in a hurry, and I keep my face neutral, even though I am desperate to grab hold of him and never let go.

"It's one and the same really," I tell him flatly before switching my attention to the other asshole in the room.

"Were you ever going to tell me?" I ask him, and his eyes widen ever so slightly. If I wasn't looking for a reaction, I probably wouldn't have noticed.

"I was undecided," he tells me bluntly, dragging that damn hood off and tossing it over the back of a sofa once more. His green and silver wings burst free, and he shakes his head, tossing his long, green hair back over his shoulder.

The goddess scoffs. "I call bullshit. Your innate curiosity would have outed you, even if the mating bond isn't driving you nuts."

Nox stares at Titus now that he has removed his hood. "I know you." He points a finger at him, and Titus smirks.

"I'd say you know me intimately," he purrs suggestively, and Nox glares at him. What the fuck are these two talking about? Do they know one another? And how?

"Where did you go? What did you want with me? I'm assuming you were just scoping me out for your king?" He stabs a finger in my father's direction.

Titus ignores him, and Nox looks to me for help. "Colbie, what's going on here?" He sounds desperate, and I sigh, deciding to put him out of his misery.

"Nox, this is the goddess Aramis," I say, "and my dad, Loki." Nox's eyes widen at my words, but it's Loki's reaction that has me feeling all emotional.

"You called me Dad." His voice is choked up with

emotion, and he moves across the room in a blur of speed. He's so fast, I can barely see him, but then he appears in front of me, throwing his arms around my shoulders and pulling me against him.

This close, I realize he's quite a bit taller than me, and my ear rests against his chest where I hear his heart beating a million miles an hour, much like mine. I return his embrace, and tears stream down my cheeks at how right this feels.

"My precious girl. Can you ever forgive me for what happened?" he murmurs.

"Ah, Dad, I don't blame you. You were as much of a victim as all of us. Let's put the past behind us and move forward from this point," I reply, making a split-second decision to let everything that has happened go, and his whole body shudders with relief.

"Seriously, what the fuck is going on? I came for a job interview, but I have a feeling that's not what is happening here." Nox sounds pissed off. Well, he can join the fucking club. I'm the reigning president.

My father and I pull apart, and I glance around the room, a wave of exhaustion rolling over me. My stomach rumbles like a hungry bear, and my father snaps his fingers.

"Let me send for dinner. We can at least get some food into you while we talk a little longer," he offers, and I gratefully accept. I'm starving and would dearly love to have a shower and go to bed, but I know we have a few more issues to deal with before that can happen.

I turn my attention to one of the issues, whose fists are clenched and wears a look of fury on his face.

"Nox, there are a few things we need to tell you," I start, but he interrupts me.

"How did you find me? I deliberately left my home after I found out you were the incoming queen because I didn't want to be found," he snaps, and his words feel like a stab in the heart.

"Actually, your parents told us where to find you," Hunter drawls, sounding deceptively casual, but his eyes show his dragon, and I don't doubt he's seconds from shifting and teaching Nox a lesson. He does not like the way he is speaking to me. I send calming, soothing vibes down our bond, and I watch as he relaxes somewhat.

Nox's eyebrows jump, and his lips purse in surprise. "They did?" He sounds hurt, and I'm sick of beating around the bush.

"Yes. When they found out that this is your bond group and I am your mate, they thought we had the right to know, especially since I can't become queen without sealing the mating bond with all of you," I say flatly, and the room is silent as Nox absorbs everything I just said. His golden tan is pale as his eyes dart from me to the guys in panic.

He stammers, but doesn't get a chance to form any words before he is cut off.

"If you are Colbie's mate as well, then why hasn't the telepathic bond clicked into place?" Liam glares at Titus, breaking the awkward silence covering the fact that Nox hasn't said a word about the big revelation. I can feel that my mates hurt as much as I do at his lack of a response.

Titus waves a gloved hand. "I wear a ring much like the pegasus's necklace that blocks the telepathic bond. As soon as the mark appeared on my chest, I conjured it up. I was in the palace at Aramis at the time, and I couldn't risk being found there. I wasn't sure who wore the matching bond marks until I spoke to Lucas a little later." He turns his attention to me. "I wasn't sure if I was going to do anything about it until I realized the queen wore the matching mark, and I didn't have much of a choice," he admits without taking his eyes off me.

My creatures snarl internally. Part of me wants to say, "Fuck you, I don't want you either," while the other part of me wants to chase him down and make him submit. I can't stop the low growl that leaves my mouth, and he has the nerve to smirk at me.

"Don't be an asshole," the goddess snaps at him. "You pretend to be cold and calculating, but I know deep down you've always longed for a mate. Well, I gave you one. Don't spit on the precious gift just because you think you need to keep up an aloof front." I don't know if he's brave or stupid by risking her turning her wrath on him.

"You're my bond group, and Colbie is our mate?" Nox finally finds his tongue, and we can practically see the longing in his eyes before it fades and they become shaded with fear.

"Yes, and we don't give a flying fuck if you're a pink pegasus or a pink flying pig, so how about you pull your head out of your ass and prove you belong with us by stepping up and doing the right thing," Gem says bluntly, and Nox's eyes widen in surprise.

Brodie chuckles darkly, so unlike his usual happy-go-lucky persona. "Though if you continue to hurt our mate, maybe we will appeal to the goddess to fix this clusterfuck. I don't know why we need either of you."

There's a knock on the door, and Loki stands, holding his hands up. "Hey, whoa, how about we all take a moment to calm down? Let's have something to eat. We don't need to figure this all out today."

"Actually, we do. I have other shit I need to focus on," I reply as he lets in the staff who wheel in six carts covered in all kinds of food. We are silent, and the tension in the room is thick as they lay it all out on a large dining table farther in the room. It's big enough to seat all of us, and when they leave, Loki gestures for us to move over to it. My mates get up and head in that direction, ignoring the two elephants in the room. I turn to the goddess.

"Can you fix this? These two obviously have no desire to be my mates, and I don't want to be with anyone who is being forced. As it stands, I can't be crowned with them still a part of the bond, so can you sever it?" I ask frankly, and she gapes at me, looking slightly horrified.

"You want me to sever the mate bonds? That will cause you immense pain," she warns, though she doesn't admit if it's something she can do.

I shrug. "Probably no worse than what their emotional detachment is doing right now. My chest hurts with the need to bond with them, and it hurts even more every time they say something against it."

"No!" Nox exclaims, lunging toward me. Titus does the same thing. When the three of us collide, I feel a lurching motion, and I squeeze my eyes shut, my stomach rolling with nausea.

When it stops, I open my eyes and don't recognize where I am. Gone is the dining room and my mates, Father, and goddess, and in its place is an opulent bedroom with elegant furnishings and a massive bed with luxurious bedding and a mountain of pillows. It's surrounded by gauzy curtains and so many plants, it's like a tropical greenhouse in here. I don't even know where to look, but then something catches my eye. In the plants, at the top of the four-poster bed, I see something slither. It's bright blue with beady eyes and a tongue that flicks in and out, and it's definitely not a vine.

"Where the fuck are we?" Nox asks, grabbing his head.

I point to what I think is a snake amongst the foliage. "What the fuck is that? And why the hell are we here?" I demand, taking a step away from the bed.

"My room. I thought it would be better if we discussed this privately without any interference from anyone else." Titus brushes past us, peeling numerous weapons from his body and placing them on a cluttered desk on one side of the room, as well as tugging off the gloves covering his hands. "And that is Fluffy, my Shaylian tree viper." He reaches out to run a finger over the top of the snake's head. The snake arches into him just like a cat, his eyes slitted with pleasure. I wrinkle my nose.

"You named your snake Fluffy?" Nox asks incredulously.

"You know, I was willing to put up with Stormheart and his psychotic ways, but I draw the line at a pet snake," I tell them flatly, crossing my arms, and Nox's eyes brighten at the mention of his blasted cat. "Why are we here?"

"You asked the goddess to sever our bond," Titus growls, facing me and crossing his arms.

I scoff. "Both of you have made it perfectly clear that neither of you want to be mated to me. So what if I asked her to remove the bond? I thought you'd be happier that way, and what was that comment before? How do you two know each other?" I ask him, and Nox stalks up to Titus and stabs his chest with a finger. I have a feeling Titus is letting him. I doubt many get to lay a finger on the assassin spy.

"Did you know who I was when we hooked up?" Nox asks, and my eyebrows jump in surprise. Well, this just got interesting, but I keep the scowl on my face for now and stay quiet. I don't want to interrupt.

"Of course I did. I wouldn't disrespect my mate by cheating outside the mating bond. I assumed since Gem and Gryffin hook up, she wouldn't have a problem if others did." He tilts his head to the side, staring at Nox with cold eyes. "But you didn't feel the same way. You were happy to go outside the mate bond."

"Hey, whoa, no. My necklace blocks most of the bond. I didn't know for sure if our mate had been marked. All I knew was my bond mark throbbed more than usual. I put it down to the magic of the necklace wearing off," he claims, panic in his tone. Nox looks at me with imploring eyes. "I swear."

I shrug, not feeling sympathetic to his plea. "You're kind of preaching to the wrong person. You already slept with me before you knew I was a shifter. You weren't interested in saving yourself for your mate." I sigh, deciding to give him a little grace. "But don't sweat it. None of the others were celibate either. I wouldn't have expected any of them to be until their mate appeared and they knew for sure."

He heaves out a sigh of relief.

"But none of that matters if neither of you want to be mated to me. I can't be crowned with unsolidified bonds, which is why I asked Aramis to sever them. I refuse to give up my crown," I explain unapologetically, and they both frown. I know my tune has changed since I was first marked, but I'm grabbing my destiny with both hands now.

"I want to be your mate, Colbie," Nox says, taking one of my hands in his. "It's a dream come true. All I could think about as I drove away was the fact that bond groups don't get to be with queens and kings. I didn't care about my past trauma, I would have run headfirst into bond group life for you, but I thought it wasn't possible. Had I known, I would have accompanied you to the shifter zone then and there." His eyes beg me to believe him, and I think I do.

"Take off your necklace," I order him, and he drops my hand to comply, reaching up and tugging the cord, which snaps, then he tosses it onto the cluttered desk with all of Titus's weapons. My chest is flooded with the same, needy aching feeling I felt when I first met Nox, only it's ten times stronger. Somewhere inside me, I always knew this man was mine. I stagger slightly, and Titus jumps forward, putting a hand out to steady me.

"Easy," he croons. "Give it a moment for the bond to settle." My creatures thrash inside me, and my head spins, but my gaze catches on the ring on his finger now visible without his gloves.

I clear my throat and lift my head, meeting his eyes. "What about you? Do you want this bond?" I ask him, and without removing his gaze from mine, he reaches for the ring on his finger and yanks it off before tossing it onto the desk to join Nox's pendant.

I stagger again, and this time, both of them catch me. "I want you more than I want my next breath,"

Titus tells me, making my heart skip a beat. My creatures thrash harder, pushing me to bite both of them so they can't get away, but I'm still cautious. If they are only telling me what they think I want to hear and I bite them, there is no reversing that. I would hate for both of them to grow to resent me, but before I can voice my concerns, I see them exchange a glance over my head.

"I can feel you," Nox murmurs into my ear, pressing his body into my back and pushing me closer to Titus who puts his hands on my hips, tugging me against his own body. "Your soul is reaching for mine. My mouth waters at the thought of biting you and adding my mark to the ones already on your neck. I've never hoped this could happen to me, and I've never wanted anything more."

My spine tingles, and my heart thumps harder inside my chest. A finger presses against my chin, lifting my head for me to look at the fae in front of me. "The goddess was right. I have always wanted a fated mate. I couldn't ever hope for one because it's rare for hybrids to get them. I would never spit in her face or turn my back on my dream, but it is hard for me to trust. I can count the number of people I do on one hand. Be patient with me," he asks, and it's the most serious I've heard him since we met.

"What are you? Fae and…" I trail off, but I'm pretty certain I know what he is.

"Fairy shifter," he says, confirming my thoughts. "I actually still have family in Aramis, though it's been a while since I visited them. Not since my teen years."

"How do fairy shifters bond?" Nox's words brush past my ear, and goosebumps erupt across my skin.

A wicked grin crosses Titus's lips as he slides a hand

into the back of my hair and tilts my head to the side before taking my lips. He tastes like chocolate and chili, both sweet and spicy, and he kisses me with enthusiasm. His tongue plunders my mouth, caressing my own and licking like I'm the best thing he's ever tasted. My mind goes to what it would feel like for him to kiss my pussy the same way, and I shudder in their arms. When he pulls back, I'm breathing heavily, but he hardly seems affected. His hand slides out of my hair and yanks Nox toward us, and I turn my head as he treats Nox's mouth to the same decadent kiss he gave me.

Holy shit. My core throbs, and my nipples pebble. Nox is breathing as heavily as I am when Titus pulls away again, and they both rub raging hard-ons against my body.

"Apart from the mer and phoenix, all shifters bond through biting. Same with the rest of the supes, aside from witches. They do some weird sex ritual." He smiles, and I feel my eyes widen when I catch sight of his fangs.

"Holy shit, were they there the whole time?" Nox mutters as I reach out to press my finger against the tip of a fang, but he pushes his tongue to the roof of his mouth, and they retract into his gums before I can.

"Don't you think you would have felt those on your cock if they had been?" Titus replies dryly, and I feel Nox shudder behind me, but I'm not sure if it's from disgust or lust. I certainly know what I feel.

"Do you drink blood?" I ask him.

"Not for sustenance like a vampire, but it is enjoyable for both parties during sex," he tells me.

"Right, well, ah, okay." I slide out from between the two men, trying to wrap my head around everything I just learned. Just when I thought I was getting a handle on everything, this threw me for a loop. I just need some space from the two of them to clear my head. Nox's scent of cinnamon and sugar blends so well with the decadent scent of chocolate with a hint of spice that comes from Titus. Combined with the way my body is screaming to bite these two and lock my final mates down, I just need a moment to get my bearings and make sure they actually want this.

"So, uh, what you're both saying is that neither of you were rejecting me, you're just assholes with a whole load of issues?" I ask, pacing back and forth in front of the giant bed. Both of them are watching me, Titus with cool amusement and Nox with a sort of desperate concern, like he fucked up everything and is certain I'm going to reject him much like a whole heap of people in his past.

"Yes, but when you put it that way, it sounds really bad." Titus's gaze swings upward, and his eyes widen. "Fluffy, no!" He moves faster than the eye can see, but he's not fast enough. I feel something drop down onto my shoulders, and I freeze, a very unladylike squeal barreling up, but I clamp my lips closed so I don't scare the viper that just wrapped itself around my shoulders, its tongue caressing my cheek.

"Oh fuck. Is it venomous?" Nox asks quietly, and Titus nods, standing just out of reach, frozen so he doesn't startle his pet.

"Deadly," he mutters, not taking his eye off the snake. "Stay still, love, and let him scent you. Hopefully removing the ring and lifting the block on the bond will help you smell a little like me."

It takes everything that I have not to scream and

fling the snake across the room, but I have a feeling that won't be good for any of us, so I allow Fluffy to become acquainted. He slithers his way around my body, his tongue flicking out constantly like he's trying to taste my essence. He sticks his head into the cleavage of my top, burying it between my breasts, and I narrow my eyes as he makes this very quiet purring sound that I hadn't expected from a snake.

"Well, I guess this is a nicer greeting than the one I got from your pet," I hiss quietly at Nox, and he just chuckles and nods, though his eyes are still shadowed with worry.

"Stormy will get used to you," he tells me as Titus steps closer and gathers his pet in both hands. The viper happily lifts his head out from between my boobs, and he kind of looks like he is smiling.

"Seriously? Your pet is a perv," I snap at Titus as he takes Fluffy to another plant on the far side of the room, far away from the bed.

"On a more serious note, are you sure you want this?" When he turns to face me again, his eyes are clouded with doubt.

"What do you mean? Of course I want this, you're my mate," I tell him, wondering where the doubt is coming from.

"Yes, but you will be the first queen with a crossbreed mate," he tells me. "I'm not sure how well that is going to go down with your subjects."

I shake my head. "Changing the law that outlaws crossbreeds is at the top of my to-do list. I don't care and nor should anyone else. You can't help who you love, and you shouldn't be punished for it. That's just as bad as punishing people for loving the same sex. I won't stand for it, and I will be proud to be the first queen with a fairy fae hybrid as her mate, so screw what anyone else says."

"And anyone who says anything to either of you will have to deal with the rest of us," Nox agrees firmly. I knew he wouldn't have any problems with it. His own experience with prejudiced assholes would make him completely sympathetic to Titus.

Titus studies us with serious eyes. I guess he's trying to gauge how genuine we are. Do the fae have mental powers I don't know about? Can he read my mind? His lips quirk up on one side, and my eyes widen as he lifts a hand and snaps his fingers and my clothes disappear. Nox shouts, and when I turn, I find his have disappeared as well.

I let my eyes wander his naked body and smirk. "Well, that is certainly handy. Will I be able to do that in fairy form?" I ask Titus who stalks toward us and waves his hand, and both of us go flying backward, tumbling in a tangle of limbs, onto his bed. "Telekinesis too."

"Sorry, my pretty little mate, but those are from my fae side. The plants and snake are my fairy gifts." He snaps his fingers, and his own clothes disappear. I swallow down any retort I was going to make.

"Holy shit," I murmur quietly, and Nox chuckles.

"I know, right?"

Titus is all glittery pale skin and elegant, sleek muscle, and his wings shimmer behind him, drawing my eyes.

"Will I have wings?" I ask absently, distracted by all the naked flesh as Nox pushes me onto my back and leans over me, blocking my view of Titus.

"Probably," I hear him reply, but I've lost interest as my hands skim over Nox's beautiful, familiar body.

"I missed you," I tell him quietly, and he smiles.

"You have no idea. I was so close to coming after you. It's why I came to the Chaos Kingdom. I figured a little more distance may make things easier, but it didn't. I'm so glad I'm your mate."

THIRTY-SEVEN

Colbie

He kisses me, and it's like coming home. I melt into his body, wrapping my arms around his back and dragging him against me. A finger trails up my calf, tickling the back of my knee, before continuing its upward path. I gasp into Nox's mouth when Titus replaces his finger with his lips and presses a kiss to my inner thigh a few inches below my opening. I thrust my hips up and hear him chuckle.

"Settle, pretty lady. Patience is a virtue in a queen," he mumbles against my skin, but my attention is quickly dragged back to Nox as he slides his lips down my throat and swipes his tongue across my other mate marks, sucking sharply on each of them.

My body floods with desire as the other guys' lust flows into my bond. "You are wicked," I murmur to Nox, and he grins at me.

"I didn't want them to feel left out."

"I'm sure they are going to be thrilled to suddenly have raging hard-ons in the company of Loki and the goddess." I feel Titus shake with amusement as Nox's own chuckles fill the room. He moves lower, sucking sharply on both the heart scale beneath my skin and the living flame inside my chest, and both start to pulse in time to the beat of my heart.

I groan as every single one of my nerve endings feels like they are coated with sparkles, snapping and spitting with energy that has my body buzzing with heady desire.

Nox licks a path over my left nipple before using his teeth to scrape it, the sharp bite of pain sending the buzzing need into a frenzy. Titus pushes my thighs farther apart, and his long hair brushes against them as he leans in and presses a gentle kiss to my clit.

"Fuck," I groan, desperate for more, and I roll my hips up into his mouth, grinding against him.

His moan is music to my ears as he slides his hands under my thighs and holds me in place as he licks and sucks my cunt like a starving man, finally giving me the pressure I need. I slide my hand between Nox and me, and wrap it around his length, stroking it with a tight grip I know he likes.

He mutters a curse and thrusts into my hold, and I smirk, happy to get that kind of reaction from him. I push him back and coax him farther up the bed until he's kneeling at my head, then I wrap my lips around it and try to give him as much pleasure as Titus is giving me, but he makes it very difficult to concentrate. Nox doesn't seem to care, and he mutters words of praise as I sloppily suck his dick.

Titus slows slightly, and when I drop my gaze to

him, I find him watching us with intense need in his eyes, completely distracted by what I'm doing to Nox.

"Get up here," I growl with a sudden need to have my mouth on both of them. His eyes widen at the command he can't ignore, my queen energy forcing him to do what I want. He prowls up the bed, his beautiful wings fluttering behind him, and kneels on the opposite side of Nox. I scramble to change positions to make it easier for me to move back and forth between them.

I alternate between them, lavishing attention on their delicious lengths. Their taste floods my mouth as their cocks drip with precum. I look up and find the two of them kissing, and it's so fucking sexy, I moan as my pussy throbs with excitement.

I'm done waiting, my creatures whining for me to finish sealing all of my mates to me, and I am done denying our needs. My jaw shifts, and I lurch forward, sinking my teeth into Nox's thigh, waiting until his red-hot life liquid fills my mouth. His shout of surprise turns to a guttural moan as I swallow the blood and instinctively run my tongue over the wound. It closes, leaving behind a perfect imprint of my hydra's teeth. I growl with delight before turning my head and doing the same thing to Titus. Titus grunts but holds perfectly still. Once his bond mark seals, I look up at them, allowing my need to shine in my eyes.

"Fuck me, please," I beg, wanting to feel them both inside me. They look down at me with matching sinful smiles.

"As our queen commands." Nox bows a head as a bottle of lube appears in Titus's hand. I watch, feeling breathless, as he squeezes some into his palm before wrapping it around Nox's length, covering him before doing the same to himself.

"How do you want us?" he asks bluntly when he's done. "Both in your pussy or one in your pussy and one in your ass?"

I groan as images flood my mind of each scenario. I'm not sure if it's Titus's magic or Nox's power of illusion that is showing me my options, but I'm too far gone in my desire to choose.

"I don't care. You decide," I reply, sliding my hand to my pussy where I rub a finger over my clit, trying to ease some of the desperate ache.

They must have a private conversation, because Nox quickly slides onto his back, and Titus lifts me to straddle him, holding me just above his cock, which Nox is angling so it's an easy slide for me as Titus allows me to lower.

Nox and I groan in unison as I force his cock into my tight channel in one go. He shudders as my pussy walls flutter around him, and I throw my head back and squeeze my eyes closed.

"So good," he groans as I rise and fall a couple of times, enjoying the sensation of feeling full. He massages my breasts and tweaks my nipples, pushing my aching need higher.

"Lean forward for me," Titus murmurs in my ear, pressing a hand to my back and coaxing me down so my breasts are squashed against Nox's pecs.

Nox kisses me, keeping me distracted, but I feel Titus line up his length and push in next to Nox. Nox grunts, and a high-pitched keening sound comes from my mouth as Titus thrusts and retreats before pushing in again until he is buried deep in my cunt alongside Nox.

"Holy fuck," he mutters, but I'm a sobbing, desperate mess, and I beg them to move.

"Fuck me, please. Mate me, I need you." My words come out garbled, but they get the idea, and Titus starts to retreat before driving his cock in again hard, doing all the work as Nox pins me in place, giving small little thrusts with his hips.

The room is filled with the sound of our pleasure—moans and groans and grunts as well as me begging for more. They work my body like experts, and it's not long until I'm on the edge of an orgasm. Nox turns his head and presses his lips to a gap on my neck as Titus curves himself over my body without stopping his onslaught, placing his mouth on the opposite side. I tense with anticipation, but nothing could have prepared me for the sensations when they both sink their teeth into me. Nox's bite is blunt and painful, whereas Titus's is a sharp, searing prick, but together, they send me flying over the cliff, screaming their names in praise as my orgasm explodes through my body.

My cunt clenches down, making it difficult for them to move, but it doesn't matter. Nox pulls away and shouts his joy as I feel his cum fill my pussy. Titus continues to suckle the blood on my neck, and a second later, his whole body stiffens, and he, too, fills me with his seed. The bonds snap into place, and a wave of power explodes out of me, washing over both of them. They seize before they pound furiously into me, then another wave of heat tells me they are both coming again. My creatures croon with joy as my mates fill me with their seed once more. My own orgasm seems to be never ending as my brain and body short-circuit and I lose consciousness.

y stomach rumbles so loudly, both guys look at me with shock. "What? I'm starving. I have barely eaten all day," I defend.

It's late into the evening now, and I know we missed the big meal my father put together. I feel a little guilty, but for the first time since I walked through the palace gates, I feel balanced and whole, like everything is right with the world. I feel kind of invincible, to be honest. I still haven't shifted into my phoenix or fairy forms, though, and I definitely need to give my pegasus and wolf forms a trial run, but I feel like everything is going right—at least with the possibility of being crowned queen. I know there are other issues we need to deal with, but it's like a weight has been lifted off my shoulders.

"Apologies, my mate. I was thoughtless when I dragged you away from dinner with your family." Titus throws the covers back and climbs out of the bed the three of us had been basking in during our after sex glow. He pads naked across the room, and it's no hardship for Nox and me to watch him go. His wings frame his ass perfectly when he holds them against his back.

A hiss in my ear has Nox shrieking and launching himself off the bed as Fluffy slithers down and makes himself comfortable against my naked body. I guess he's drawn to my body heat.

"No, no, no. I draw the line at a snake in the bed." Nox puts his hands on his hips and glares at the serpent. I run my hand over his triangular head, and he leans into it as I stare at Nox's naked body this time. Damn, the goddess blessed me with what must be the most beautiful men in the whole of the shifter kingdom.

"I bet Stormheart sleeps on your bed," I argue stubbornly, "and he has a violent vendetta against me. I think Fluffy should come along because then it might keep Stormheart in line." I pick the viper up and carry him back to his tree branch perch, stroking a finger over his head, before turning my attention to Nox.

"But Stormheart won't murder us all in our sleep." He looks between me and the snake.

"Maybe not you, but I bet he'd slit my throat and eat my face if he could."

Titus disappeared into what must be the bathroom, but he hears our conversation. "Colbie, you can literally change into a big cat and eat him. I bet if you roared in his face, he would never bother you again."

Nox's mouth drops open, his eyes wide. "You wouldn't!"

"I so fucking would, so make sure you have a word with him if he is going to live in the palace," I warn him.

"Maybe I will just leave him with my parents… or maybe my sister. Her kids love to spoil him." He looks around for clothes, but Titus magicked both of ours off, and there is nothing for us to wear.

He returns, and his hair is brushed back and tied in a ponytail at the nape of his neck, and his wings are away. He's wearing a pair of sweatpants and nothing else.

"Wow, you look casual," I comment, running my gaze over his naked chest.

"I still prefer the little black pair of hot pants." Nox

winks, and I laugh. They explained their first meeting to me while we were coming down from all the amazing orgasms.

"Make sure you pack them when you come to the castle," I say lightly, and he frowns, and my heart sinks.

"You aren't coming to the castle?" I ask him, and he rubs his head awkwardly.

"I am one of Loki's assassins and spies. I'm not sure he will allow me to leave."

"We'll see about that," I say stubbornly, crossing my arms and tapping a foot, but then something occurs to me. "Unless you don't want to come?"

He looks torn, and my heart aches. He winces and rubs a hand against the bond mark on his chest. "Oh, baby, don't do that. I can feel how hurt you are. I didn't mean for you to think that. I want to come, but I trained all my life for this position. It won't be easy for him to find spies and assassins he trusts as much as me and my brothers."

"But surely he won't need you all anymore, not if the goddesses' plan comes to fruition and five sisters rule the continents." I feel hopeful, but Titus scoffs.

"Five sisters who know nothing about one another. Hell, it is one of the best kept secrets because although I know of their existence, none of us know their identity. Loki only shared yours with me once the magic passed to you. I certainly didn't know I was your mate, and at that stage, I wasn't. I think the goddesses are hoping you all get along, but what are the chances of that? Who knows what kind of upbringings the others had? Yours certainly wasn't all roses, but you did have the steady presence of Jenny and Joseph."

Titus has a point. "Well, no use speculating," I say,

trying to be positive. "How about you dress us? As much as our other mates may enjoy us coming to dinner naked, I doubt my father and the goddess want to see it."

Titus flicks his hand, and Nox and I are fully clothed again. He put us both in comfy lounge clothes, Nox's sweats matching his own, and he has a fitted shirt. I wear a soft pair of pajama style pants with a tank top, and none of us are wearing shoes.

"Shouldn't we dress more formally around the king?" Nox asks, looking down at the tight shirt that hugs his beautiful body.

"Pfft, some days it's a struggle to get Loki to wear pants. He prances around in his boxers more often than not, especially in his private living quarters. We will be fine." Titus waves off Nox's concerns.

He holds out a hand to each of us, and we both grab hold. I squeeze firmly, not wanting him to lose me somewhere along the ley lines. In a flash, we rematerialize in the family living area we were in before this started. Nausea rolls through me, and I grimace, struggling to get my bearings.

"Fucking finally," Liam grumbles, speeding over to me and snatching me away from the others. "I missed you." I lean into him, breathing in his scent to calm my racing heart.

I can hear my other guys and Father congratulating Nox and Titus and welcoming them to the family. The goddess remains seated on one of the sofas, her eyes soft when I meet her gaze.

"Finally. You are ready," she says triumphantly, but before I can answer, my stomach rumbles again. I blush and press against Liam's chest, trying to get him to put me down.

"I need to eat before we do anything else. I'm starting to get hangry," I warn him, and he pales slightly, but instead of putting me down, he hurries over to the table and dumps me into a seat before piling a plate full of food that is conveniently warming on a sideboard.

Both Nox and Titus join me as the others take seats around the large table. Each of them have drinks in hand, but it's just the three of us who are eating.

"So you're mated to all of us now," Gem points out, looking between the three of us. "That's good. It means we can return to Aramis, and you can be crowned. That will secure your position, and then we can focus on going after the people who took the children and are raising a shifter army."

"I also need to inform the council of my decision and face challenge day," I remind him around a mouthful of food. Sure, it's not very queenly, but I am seriously starving. I have expended a crap load of energy today, and I'm feeling the fatigue. Shifter mating is no fucking joke.

"Pfft. The shifters are going to take one look at the nine of you crowned, and no one will step forward to challenge you," my father says wryly, looking at me with warmth and pride in his eyes. It makes me feel warm and tingly, and I hope that with whatever will come that I can cultivate a relationship with this man and my sisters.

"Don't be so sure. Shifters are nothing if not stubborn. I'm sure she will get a few contenders, because no one knows what she shifts into yet," Hunter tells him, not taking his eyes off me. I can see the possessive, greedy light of his dragon in his gaze. I blow him a kiss, and he slowly winks at me.

"So now that I'm fully mated, the crowning can take place at any time?" I ask, and Gryffin nods.

"Yes. The average time between a human being marked, gaining their magic, finding their mates, and being crowned is two weeks. You're a little inside that, but being given a bond group saved you from having to pick from a group of random strangers."

I wrinkle my nose and shudder. "Yeah, not sad I missed all of that," I admit.

"You're welcome," the goddess tells me. "These men were picked for you from your birth. There was never going to be any other option."

"Even us?" Micah points to himself and Titus, and the goddess purses her lips.

"No, not originally, but I'm nothing if not flexible. My magic saw an opportunity and grabbed it. Having her mate with not only the strongest shifters of their generation, but three of the shunned breeds, is actually a genius idea, and I'm not sure why I didn't think of it from the beginning. I always knew there was potential for more for Colbie and—" She breaks off, biting her lip like she's reluctant to admit something. She sighs. "The magic actually got away from me, took over, and marked both of you, but it all worked out for the best." She stands up and brushes her hands over her pants. "Now I'm going to get back to my own mates. I'll see you tomorrow at your coronation."

"Tomorrow? That soon? Surely it will take a day or two to get back to Aramis. We also need to check in with Nox's parents to see how they are doing with tracking the children." A wave of intense nerves floods my body with adrenaline, and my hand starts to shake as I lift it toward my mouth again. Everything that was on my fork falls back to the plate, so I lower it until I can get control of myself.

"Titus will portal you all back to the palace, and yes, I will not risk anything happening to you before we can get that crown on your head. Get a good night's sleep, and by this time tomorrow, you will be the undisputed queen."

"But challenge day?" Brodie argues, and the goddess turns her gaze on him. He flinches.

"Challenge day is a ridiculous shifter custom that has nothing to do with any of my instructions. I'd like to see them challenge her in front of me." Her voice has gone cold, and Brodie blanches, nodding his head.

"Of course," he agrees solemnly, but then he grins and rubs his hands together. "Tomorrow is going to be fun."

With a wave goodbye, the goddess disappears without another word.

Another rush of nerves swirls in my stomach, and the food I just ate threatens to reappear. I grab my glass of water, take a big sip, and breathe deeply.

"Baby, are you okay?" Nox reaches out, and I grimace.

"Yeah, it's just a lot, you know?" I explain, giving his hand a squeeze. My nerves are replaced with a rush of emotions that barrel down my connection with the guys —love, pride, and fierce support flood through me, and I straighten my back and shoulders. "But as long as I have all of you beside me, I'm sure I will be fine." I send them my own wave of emotions—love and thanks and utter joy at having them as my mates.

"Right, I think everyone needs to go to bed. You will all need a good night's rest. I have assigned a family suite for you, Colbie. It will be yours whenever you visit my kingdom, and I hope you know you are welcome anytime."

I smile at my father, hiding my amusement at his very dad-like suggestion.

"Thank you. I promise once we have the council sorted and rescue our missing shifter children, I will come back and spend time with you."

"Ah, Colbie. I don't think I have to warn you, but I would appreciate it if you didn't tell your mother who I am. She only knew me as a human male. I have a feeling if you tell her I am Chaos Kingdom's king, I may find her on my doorstep, trying to rekindle something."

I frown. "You're not wrong, but I don't think my mother is talking to me at the moment. She did much the same thing to me and was subsequently evicted from the shifter zone."

"Your mother is a piece of work. I shadowed her for a few weeks before I approached her, and she was constantly hitting on rich and influential men, even ones who had partners. All it took was me flashing around a bit of wealth, and she was attached to my hip like a barnacle. It was like shooting fish in a barrel," he admits reluctantly, looking at me with worried eyes.

That sounds familiar, but I don't feel sorry for my dad. There were obviously no feelings involved, and although he gave my mom and grandparents a different narrative to remember, my mother has never been one to be loyal to a man.

"I'm sorry. I know what I did is unforgivable, but I hope that someday, we might have a normal father daughter relationship. It's my greatest wish for all my daughters." He glares at where the goddess had been standing. I have a feeling their relationship might be a little dented since his discovery of his blocked mate bond and his other child he knew nothing about.

"I'll show them to their suite," Titus offers, seeing that I've lost my appetite now that the crowning is imminent, and my nerves are wreaking havoc with my stomach.

"If you need anything or get hungry in the middle of the night, there is always someone on duty in the kitchen. Call down, and they can bring anything up," my dad tells the guys as we push back from the table. "And there's a fully stocked bar, but again, anything you need can be requested." He sounds kind of frantic, like he needs to please us.

"Loki, they will be fine. I've got them," Titus assures my father, and I wonder about their relationship. It kind of feels close. Hell, Titus has a room in the palace. If I had to hazard a guess, they are more than just employer and employee. It kind of feels familial. I wonder what his relationship is like with his own family.

"Thank you, my boy. Have you seen your brothers? I wanted to fill them in on everything that is happening."

Titus shakes his head. "None of them are in residence at the moment. Each are in their respective kingdoms, and Luka is chasing down a lead in one of the gambling dens in the city. He's trying to figure out who put the hit out on Colbie."

"The what?" I ask, snapping my head around to look at my fairy mate.

"My assassin guild was offered a job to remove you,"

Loki explains. "Of course we turned it down, but it didn't mean others didn't."

"I guess that explains the attack on the way to Zalfari," Liam grumbles, rubbing his chest where the arrow pierced him.

"You were attacked?" Titus growls. "By who?"

Micah and Hunter take turns explaining what happened, and by the end, the assassin, as well as my father and Nox, are looking at me with wide-eyed awe.

"Holy shit. Challenge day certainly wouldn't be a problem, even if the goddess wasn't going to put a stop to it," Nox says admirably.

"Yeah, I'm not so sure about that. I'm still not particularly coordinated in hydra form," I admit, and Titus snorts with amusement.

"I noticed. We will work on that tomorrow morning before we leave. The goddess can wait a few extra hours. You need to gain control of every one of your shifts. You never know when you might need them. Even with the crown on your head, those factions are still creating an army, and despite my and my brothers' attempts, we still haven't worked out who is behind it all. They have been very successful in hiding themselves."

"Hopefully when Lena tracks down the missing children, we'll find more clues," Gem points out.

"My mother is very good at her job. She will have the location for the children before you know it," Nox assures me. I didn't share her hostility when we first met with him because she quickly came around to the idea of helping us, even if it was just for the children. I have hope going forward that our relationship won't be so rocky.

We take our leave, and Titus directs us to my new

suite. We don't do much there but get ready for bed, our conversation avoiding any of the serious topics and just sticking to getting to know you kind of stuff. The others grill Titus and Nox, and the two are good sports and allow the interrogation. I think the guys realize I have reached my limit for the day, so they keep the focus off me. The bed in this suite is huge, big enough for all of us to climb in together. A sneaky goddess definitely had a hand in creating something this big. It's basically one big mattress built into a sunken base in the floor, kind of like Hunter's dragon nest. His smile stretches wide when he sees it, and he quickly shucks off all his clothes except for his boxers and throws himself into it. I blink, stunned to see him roll around in it.

"Ah, what is he doing?" I ask Liam.

"He's covering the bed in his scent. The others will do it too, watch." He's right. Gem, Gryffin, Brodie, and Nox all strip down to their underwear and join Hunter on the bed. Liam follows them down, leaving Titus, Micah, and me on the side.

"Animal shifters," Titus scoffs. "Ruled by their baser instincts. To be honest, mer and fairy shifters are most definitely the higher beings of the shifter race. We aren't reduced to animal instincts and retain our logic when we shift," he whispers quietly.

"Shh, don't let them hear you," Micah hisses, and I giggle. I think they are messing around, but I'm not entirely sure.

"Come, our queen. Let's join the riffraff. It's going to be a long day tomorrow." Micah holds out his hand, and I strip out of my pants, then he helps me step down into the bed.

My animals poke their heads up for the first time

since we left Titus's room, and I get the sudden urge to roll around on the bed too, but I grit my teeth and clench my fists, trying to control it.

"Just go with it, baby." Brodie tugs me down into the pile of bodies. "Despite what those two assholes say, there is nothing wrong with giving into your baser instincts."

I give in and throw myself onto the puppy pile, a feeling of contentment and pure happiness replacing all my worries. For now, I'm going to enjoy this. I'll save the worries for tomorrow.

THIRTY-EIGHT

Colbie

I sleep like the dead. Everything that has happened since I was marked, as well as mating with eight men, has taken its toll. Not even their bickering about who was going to sleep next to me could keep me from falling asleep. They are big boys and could sort it out between them with no input from me.

It's the feeling that I'm baking in one of my own ovens that finally wakes me. Being surrounded by eight of them has me dripping with sweat. This will be great in winter back in Aramis, but it's way too freaking warm in Chaos to be dealing with this. I look around the room, and in the filtered light peeking through a curtain over a window, I see an AC vent. Note to self, it goes on every night if we are all in bed together.

I turn my head to the side and find the main culprit. Hunter has one arm thrown over my waist, his body pressed against my side, and he is snoring softly, smoke drifting out of his nostrils every now and again. His skin is scorching against mine, like his dragon is working overtime to keep me warm. On my other side is another snorer. Liam is a lot louder than Hunter though, and I grimace and pray that I am the first to fall asleep every night, otherwise I may ban them from the room. Goddess, I hope the rest of them don't snore, but I won't be able to find that out today, because none of the others are still in bed. I hear voices out in the living area of our suite, and I also hear water running somewhere.

Ugh, a shower to wash off all the sweat would be amazing. I carefully slide out from between the two guys and smirk in amusement when Hunter reaches for me but finds Liam instead and tucks him against his body. Liam is so deeply asleep he doesn't even notice. He just mumbles my name and presses a kiss to Hunter's cheek before snoring again.

As much as I want to stick around and see their reactions when they wake, I want a shower more. When I get into the bathroom, I find Brodie singing quietly under his breath as he runs a loofah all over his body. I lean against the wall and watch for a moment, admiring his form, which I really didn't get a good look at originally. Brodie is not quite as covered in muscles as Micah, Hunter, and Gryffin, nor is he as sleek as Gem or Titus. He has a very similar build to Nox—wide shoulders, a tapered waist, like a swimmer, and an eight pack on his stomach. When my gaze drops lower, I find his hand wrapped around his sizable cock, stroking it languidly. When I bring my eyes up, I find he's watching me with a smirk on his lips.

"See something you like?" he asks, and I strip off my tank and underwear and stalk toward him, desperate to get my mouth on him, but his eyes widen in panic, and he holds his hands up.

"No, no. Shit, I can't believe I'm saying this, but the others will kill me if we start anything, because if we do, my wolf won't stop until you smell thoroughly of us."

I shrug, taking a step closer. "I'm okay with that."

He yelps as he steps backward and his back hits the cold tiles. "No. Unfortunately we have too much going on this morning." He pouts before stepping around me, giving me a wide berth and getting out of the shower. He grabs a towel, swiftly drying off his body. "I need a goddess damn medal for my restraint," he mutters. "Wash up and come out to the living area. Nox, Titus, and Gem are all waiting to work with you on their respective shifts, and there is some breakfast on the table. My job is to wake the sleeping beauties and get them ready to leave. We can work on your wolf shift when we return to Aramis. It doesn't need as much open space as the other three."

"Fine," I grumble, and my creatures roll in complaint, but I do as he instructs. Washing my hair and body, I enjoy the warm water rushing over me, but I don't take too long, and when I get out, I find a watch uniform on the counter for me. I didn't even hear anyone come in and leave it.

When I emerge from the bathroom, the bedroom is empty, so I follow the voices out to the living area and find everyone having breakfast. Gryffin hands me a mug of coffee and gestures for me to take a seat at the table. I give each of my mates a quick kiss on the way past, and when I sit, my skin buzzes like there is a swarm of bees sitting beneath the surface.

"Whoa," I mutter, rubbing my arms.

"Your power is astronomical," Titus observes. "Now that all bonds are sealed, it may take a little while for you to get used to it, but eventually, you won't even notice anymore."

"I never knew it would be like this," Gem murmurs. The fire in his eyes is bright today. In fact, all of them seem to be buzzing with their own aura of power.

"I don't think it ever has been before," Gryffin muses. "Dad and my moms certainly never felt like she does."

"It's the mate bond. I'm not sure anyone else will feel what we feel." Micah passes me a plate of pastries, and I take a couple, smiling my thanks.

"Make sure you eat plenty. Shifting frequently burns through calories." Nox adds a couple more to my plate before taking some for himself. My heart wants to burst out of my chest at all the careful care they are giving me.

"Are you ready to shift?" I ask him, assuming this might be a sore subject for him.

He blanches, and his gaze flitters around the others before resting on me.

"I was always teased for being a pink pegasus, but I did shift and fly here. It was nighttime, and I wasn't risking running into any ferals in the rift before the tunnel. It was so nice to fly again. I'm looking forward to joining you in the sky," he admits.

"There is nothing better," Hunter rumbles. "I will join the three of you to keep watch as you practice."

"That would be great, then Nox and I can concentrate on Colbie while you keep a lookout for anyone who might show a little too much interest in us. I'm sure there are quite a number of beings who can fly in Chaos

Kingdom," Gem agrees, looking at Titus for his thoughts.

"There are, but I doubt any of them will be brave enough to bother us if we're escorted by both a dragon and a phoenix. If I remember correctly, pegasus are quite lethal as well. Control of lightning, am I right?" Titus asks Nox, who nods, his cheeks turning a little pink.

"Yeah, control of all weather really, and I can cast illusions, which isn't very helpful." All of us hear the self-doubt that I'm sure has plagued him for years. It's something I'm familiar with, my mother's passive-aggressive tendencies causing the same mental and emotional damage to me.

"Like hell it isn't. You will be a major asset. Imagine being able to show our enemies one thing when we are really doing something else," Micah argues.

"Not to mention getting my sisters off my back when they are nagging me. You can help me escape and leave them arguing with an illusion of me." Gryffin chuckles at the idea. I plan on staying far away from that one. I'm not getting caught in the cross fire.

"I'm sorry," Nox blurts out, and we all frown.

"For what?" Brodie asks, taking a sip of his coffee.

"For not searching you out in the first place. I should have trusted the goddess. I shouldn't have assumed the worst, and I should have put my faith in the team I had been blessed with."

The guys all murmur words of reassurance, and I smile, feeling all warm and tingly. "I love my new family so much." They freeze and stare at me with wide-eyed shock. "What?" I ask, patting at my hair and wiping my mouth. "Do I have something on my face?"

"You said you love us," Liam replies, smiling broadly.

"Well, duh, of course I do."

"We love you too, cookie," Gryffin tells me, his eyes glassy with emotion.

"We sure do. Now how about you get your cute ass moving, and we can do some flying on this beautiful morning?" Titus looks happy. I haven't seen him look quite this way since I met him. Shit, was that only yesterday? Is a side effect of the mate bond the feeling of having known them all your life? Until now, I've only seen the slightly sarcastic, stoic assassin version of him, as well as the sexy, seductive, lusty version, which I'm kind of partial to, but this is nice as well.

I drink my coffee and scarf my pastries down before standing up. "Are you coming?" I ask the non-flyers, but they shake their heads.

"No, we're going to go hang out with your dad for a little while. He said he has some intel on the humans in the various zones we should investigate as being involved with the conspiracy. He's had his assassins keeping tabs on the wealthy and influential as well as some of the politicians. He has some files on the more likely suspects, ones who have been openly verbal of their disdain for supernaturals," Micah explains.

"That sounds like a good use of time. Stall the goddess if she arrives before we get back. If Colbie can get a handle on her physical shifts, we can work on her ability to use the forms' magical properties at another time," Titus tells them.

I make my way to the front door, preparing to leave, but he calls me back. "Colbie, we aren't going that way," he tells me, holding out his hand and gesturing to the others to move closer. "Everyone needs to touch me."

"No, no way." Nox steps back, realizing what's about to happen before I put two and two together. "We are not doing it your way. We have two perfectly good legs to get us from point A to point B."

"I'm with Nox. I don't need to puke up everything I just ate," I protest.

Titus pays no attention to me, and both Hunter and Gem look excited at the chance to sift.

"We are moving halfway across the kingdom to a desert oasis that's out of the way. The king has a getaway place, and there will be no one around to observe us, but it's inaccessible by vehicle, and it would take too long to walk," he explains impatiently.

"We can all fly. How about we do that? Colbie can ride on Hunter or me." I perk up at Nox's suggestion. I would love to ride his pegasus, but Hunter shakes his head, grinning with glee.

"Nope, that would take too long as well. Come on, let's do this. Time is wasting." He happily places a hand on Titus's shoulder, and Gem does as well. I grimace and exchange a wary look with Nox.

"If you're going to puke, do it on his feet," I tell him, pointing at Titus. "He deserves it." I reluctantly take his hand, and Nox takes the other one, and without waiting for either of us to breathe, let alone say another word, we move. That same rolling stomach feeling that is disorienting and nausea inducing hits me, and when we reappear, I slap a hand over my mouth and breathe deeply through my nose, trying to keep my breakfast down.

"Ugh," Nox groans, clasping his head. I hear both Gem and Hunter groan as well.

"Shit, you could have warned us," the phoenix complains, looking paler, the flames in his eyes dull.

"Why do you think we objected?" I retort, taking another deep breath, waiting for the vertigo to ease.

"I thought you were exaggerating. Let's not do that again." Hunter looks slightly green as I turn to see where Titus brought us.

"You'll get used to it eventually," he assures us as I look around.

We are standing next to a tropical oasis of palm trees with a brilliant, ripple free, mirror-like pool nestled between them. On one side of the pool is a small, elegant tent-like structure, which I'm assuming is my father's accommodations when he comes here to stay. Beyond the sanctuary is nothing but golden sandy desert. Sand dunes break up the expanse, making it impossible to see beyond them, but there's no sign of life.

"This is but only one of a few oases that allow navigation of this desert. You could wander for days and not stumble across one, which makes traveling it unwise. That and ward protection set up by the goddesses when they helped the first king create the kingdom is how we've managed to stay off the humans' radars," Titus explains, allowing us to get our bearings.

"Right, well, we have no time to waste. Let's start working on shifting. You have three forms to get through today," Gem tells me. "Let's start with mine. Like the dragon and your hydra, I can adjust the size of my phoenix to suit my needs and environment. We will work in a smaller form today so you aren't too tired to work on the other forms."

"Size matters?" I ask him, and he smirks, and the other three chuckle like schoolboys. I roll my eyes at their behavior. "I mean, which size I choose will affect how exhausted I am?" Again, they snicker at my comment.

"To begin with, yes, but as you get used to shifting and make sure you are filling your reserves sufficiently, you will adjust and size won't matter," Nox explains. "Why do you think shifters eat so much?"

"Is that why there is always a buffet available at the palace? Because you all eat so much? I thought it was a royalty indulging in excess thing," I ask, and Hunter nods.

"Yes, we all have voracious appetites." He pauses, and his eyes heat. "For everything." I hear the suggestion in his voice. Well, that explains why I'm constantly needy. I guess this is my new state of being now. Luckily I have eight mates to take care of those needs.

"Okay, so feel for the fire inside your soul," Gem tells me. I close my eyes and search for my inner creatures. It's freaking crowded inside my mind, but I am easily able to distinguish between each of my forms. They are all different to a certain degree. My mer form has the slightly salty taste of brine as well as feeling cold, whereas my hydra has the same cold sensation but feels like freshwater and has the bitter taste of acid. I find the one that radiates heat. There are two, but my dragon form has a slithery, reptilian feel and is a slow burning heat, whereas the phoenix is an out of control wildfire with the rush of wind from its wings.

"Got it," I tell them.

"Pull it forward," Gem instructs quietly.

I sink into the power, handing control over to that blazing inferno, and it explodes forward like it's been waiting patiently for this exact moment. My own consciousness takes a back seat, though I share their eyesight as we shoot into the sky, a piercing scream leaving our beak. I lose track of time as I dive and glide on the eddies of wind. My vision is so sharp, I catch sight of small, scurrying creatures that move in a rocky outcrop jutting up out of the desert a small distance from the oasis.

Did you know the Chaos Kingdom is known for its precious gems? Those rocky outcrops are entrances to mines all over the kingdom, and it's where the kingdom gets its wealth, Gem says in my head, his own phoenix keeping pace with mine, our wings occasionally brushing.

But where are the miners? I swoop down to take a closer look, Gem on my tail.

Off to the side, I spy Hunter's purple dragon flying parallel to us, and on the opposite side is a magnificent pink pegasus. He's breathtaking, with a huge wingspan and a lush, full mane and tail that flutters around him. I don't see Titus, but I have no idea if his wings would be able to keep up with us. They look elegant but flimsy, and I have no idea how they would hold his body aloft, let alone move speedily.

Possibly underground working, or maybe this mine isn't being harvested at the moment. Loki told us he has the workers sifted in and out every day by fae hybrids. You've done well, baby. Let's return, and you can try one of the other forms now.

I do as he says and spend some time in both my pegasus and fairy forms. My wings are smaller than Titus's, and they are purple, silver, and black. They are so freaking pretty. He said mine are smaller because that's the normal size of fairy shifter wings. His are larger because of his fae heritage, but not as big as full fae wings. Flying as a fairy is way harder than as a pegasus or phoenix. I crash a couple of times, have bruises all over my body, and am bone tired by the time they call a halt to the session.

We head back to the castle, and Titus takes us straight to our room where I have another shower and change into a dress that someone laid out for me. We reconvene in my father's living space for lunch. The goddess taps her foot impatiently as I devour the meal. I know she wanted to go this morning, but what I did was important. I feel so much more confident in my abilities now, and I'm in tune with my creatures. None of the other kings and queens ever had to contend with multiple animals, so I think everyone needs to cut me a little slack.

"I sent a message to my parents this morning," Gryffin tells me as I'm finishing up. "They are preparing for a coronation, but they said it will take time to invite everyone who needs to be there. They suggested we put it off for another few days."

"Nonsense. No one needs to be there, but we need her crowned today," Aramis argues, her face showing signs of stress. Her mouth is pinched, and her eyebrows are turned in. She is obviously worried about something. "As long as there are shifters to witness it, it doesn't matter about any of the other kingdoms."

"Because that's how I want to start my rule, by insulting the other royals," I say dryly, taking a sip of wine my father produced for me.

"It won't matter, because none of them will be

ruling alongside you," she argues, and I guess she has a point.

"What about tomorrow? I'm pretty tired after this morning. That will give Lucas and the queens a chance to put something together we all might be happy with," I suggest, trying for a compromise, and she gives in with a reluctant nod.

"Fine, but I want you crowned by sunrise tomorrow. Make sure Lucas and his queens know this. I will see you then." She disappears in a flash, and I grimace.

"Not sure I'm winning any allies at the moment," I grumble.

"She will be fine. She's not used to having to compromise, and she's definitely not used to someone saying no," my father explains. "But good for you for standing up for yourself. Don't become a slave to their whims like I was."

"Will you be coming to my coronation?" I ask him, and he winces.

"I want to be there more than anything, but I am worried I will run into your mother."

"Shit, I hadn't even thought of her. Do you think your moms and dad will invite her?" I look at my tiger who grimaces.

"I don't think they want to, but it might cause more issues if we don't."

I sigh but nod my agreement. "Okay, but I'm warning all of you, she will get handsy and probably try to seduce all of you."

Liam doesn't look surprised by my words, since he's already experienced her delightful ways.

"She already tried," Brodie says gruffly. "When we

escorted her back to the neutral zone, she offered us sex in exchange for us to look the other way and let her go."

I gape at him, hurt beyond comprehension that my mother would stoop so low, and that was when she didn't even know they were my mates.

"She will be worse now that you are my mates. It will be a game to her," I tell them quietly. "It isn't something she hasn't tried in the past and succeeded in."

I feel their sympathy for me and disgust for my mother inside my chest, and it aches but also reassures me that they have no intention of falling for her games.

"Maybe they won't be able to find her," Gem says hopefully, but I'm probably not that lucky.

Colbie

When we return to the Aramis palace, we arrive in an office. The nausea isn't so bad for me this time, and both Nox and I look on with amusement while everyone else groans and clutches their heads and stomachs.

A throat clearing behind me has me whirling around. Lucas is behind a large desk, his eyes wide with surprise. He stares at Titus, and he gives him a look of consternation. "You really know how to make an entrance, don't you?" he grumbles before getting up and giving Gryffin a hug before doing the same to me. He envelops me in his arms and presses a kiss to my head.

"I'm so proud of you. What an unstoppable queen you are going to be," he murmurs quietly. His praise makes me feel all warm inside, grateful to have his support, and I squeeze him back.

"Though, I do feel sorry for you having to put up

with that one." He nods his head at Titus, who just narrows his eyes at the king. "I've been dealing with that pain in the ass for years now."

"Ah, he's not so bad. Under that dark and deadly facade, he's a big softy." Titus is back in his assassin garb, but Gryffin informed his dad of his mate status.

"Yes, well, it certainly eases my worries knowing you have such a formidable mate to watch your back."

"Hey," Brodie grumbles, throwing himself into one of the chairs and pulling me down to sit on his lap. "We aren't completely defenseless." He scowls at the king whose eyes twinkle with delight.

"No, you aren't," he agrees before turning his attention to Nox, who is the only person in the room he isn't familiar with.

"Hi, I'm Lucas, Gryffin's father." He puts out his hand for Nox to shake. Nox looks a little rattled at the friendly greeting but returns the handshake.

"I'm Nox," he replies, and Lucas nods.

"Yes, I have met your mother a few times. Unfortunately, we aren't as friendly as I hoped, but I'm sure Colbie is going to right everything I couldn't." Wow, no pressure! Before I can respond, the door to the study bangs open, and the already crowded room is filled with chattering, shrieking women, followed by Archie and Adam.

"My sidepiece!" Archie shrieks and throws himself at me, not caring one little bit that I'm on Brodie's lap. Brodie grunts, a whoosh of air escaping his lungs, as Archie's knee makes contact with his crotch. Archie's little arms wrap around my neck, and he has me in a chokehold as I hug him back. "I thought you had gone forever." His little voice trembles, and I rub his back, trying to comfort him.

"I could never leave my favorite little man," I tell him, and he relaxes and spins around so he can see everyone else in the room, waving to the rest of the guys.

"I'm sorry," Gracelin mouths, but I shake my head. I love the delightful little boy.

"Welcome back," Mia says warmly to us, and Gryffin introduces his family to my two new mates. I gave him permission to tell his family everything, so they know of my parentage and who my two new mates are.

"Now, we have issued a kingdom-wide announcement for tomorrow's coronation. It will be held in the colosseum. I just need to know if you have any family you would like to invite," Evie says, her attention on us.

"Evie, just let them catch their breath," Layla scolds, but she glares at her co-mate, so I answer to keep the peace.

"My grandparents, of course, and I guess my mother, but she is still avoiding my calls." I tried to call her from Chaos Kingdom. Cell reception is spotty between kingdoms, but Loki rigged something that makes it possible from his palace. It's how his assassins feed him information if they can't physically return. Not all of them are fae hybrids with the ability to sift like Titus. "There's no one else really." I feel a little sad about that. I might have invited Niles and Brock, but they were banned from the shifter zone, and I can't see Lucas lifting that, especially considering their relationship to the Tidemans.

"Fuck no," Liam grumbles. He has no relationship with his family. Liam was the youngest of four brothers and the only polar bear like his mother. The rest were grizzlies like his father, and he was tormented for it. From what I understand, his family members are not good people, but he doesn't like to talk about it, so I haven't gotten all the details yet.

She nods, sympathy in her eyes. "I can't stop them if they turn up, but I won't issue them a specific invitation."

"I will speak to my father myself," Micah assures her. "He's a stubborn old bastard and holds a grudge like no one else. Unless he knows that I am one of the queen's mates, he will ignore the announcement."

"That would be lovely, thank you. We want Colbie's reign to be a new beginning for shifter relations," Evie says with so much hope. Again, no pressure.

"I would love for my parents and sister to be there, but they are likely to be in danger since they are in a mixed relationship." Titus sounds sad.

Archie's attention turns to the assassin, who had been shadowed against one wall during the conversation. I hear his gasp, and he struggles to get off my lap before darting over to the hybrid.

"Who are you?" he asks, wide-eyed and awestruck. "You look like a warrior. I'm Archie, Colbie is my side-piece." He puffs out his chest and holds out a hand for Titus. "Why are you hiding your face? Are you ugly?"

Gracelin groans and goes to snatch Archie away from Titus, but my mate drops into a crouch so he's the same height as Archie.

"I am a warrior, and I only show my face to those I trust," he tells the boy before reaching up and removing his cowl and cloak. "But I trust you since you have such good taste in sidepieces." His eyes twinkle when he looks at me. I roll my eyes, but I can't stop smiling at seeing how kind the assassin is to the boy.

"Titus?" I hear a gasp and find Violet, who I hadn't noticed, looking at my mate with wide-eyed shock.

"Hello, cousin." Titus smiles at my friend, and it's my turn to gape as I look between them.

"Oh my goodness, you're Colbie's fairy mate! Mom is going to be so happy. Does this mean your parents will visit more often now?"

"I hope so. When Colbie's relationship with the Chaos king becomes common knowledge, and she disposes of the ban on cross mating in the kingdom, it will become a lot more hospitable for them."

Violet beams at my mate and claps her hands happily, and I just kind of shake my head. Aramis is such a meddler, but I'm glad.

"My parents are focusing on the missing children. I spoke to them this morning, and they said they are hot on the trail. If they find them, they will keep watch over them until we can get there to extract them. My sister, her mates, and her children probably won't come either, but I can't wait to introduce you to them," Nox tells everyone.

"What about you two?" I look at Gem and Brodie. I don't know as much as I would like about my mates' families yet. There just hasn't been enough time.

"My parents are kind of aloof," Gem explains. "Both of them have precognition as their gift, so they find it difficult to be around people."

"That's a thing?" I gasp.

"Yeah, it can be for phoenixes. There aren't very many of us. We were one of the races targeted in the great war. As far as I know, they are the only two in existence at the moment. They live in an isolated area and avoid being around big crowds so they don't become overwhelmed. I think it's bullshit. They can block it if they try, but they are also very self-involved, so they don't try too hard. I was grateful when the trait didn't pass down to me."

"Yet," Layla warns. "Sometimes it can take years for mythicals to grow into some of their powers."

Gem grimaces.

"I'd love for my parents and brother to be there. It's been a long time since I've seen them. They are so busy with their wolf pack that we don't see each other as much as I like," Brodie says. "My younger brother should be starting college soon. I wonder if he's been bond marked."

"Wouldn't they call and tell you?" Gretchin asks, and Brodie shrugs.

"I don't know, but probably not. Wolves are kind of funny about bond marks. They think their loyalty should stay with the pack. It's why I'm not as close with them as I used to be, because I put my bond group ahead of the pack. They wouldn't be thrilled if Briden was marked. They'd probably encourage him to hide it, kind of like Nox. So if he is, they might avoid coming to the city in case he runs into any of his bond group. They would have made me hide mine, but I was already at college with Hunter and Gryffin when it appeared." I can hear his disappointment for his parents in his voice. I guess I don't have a monopoly on asshole parents. Well, my mother anyway, because my father is turning out to be quite a blessing.

"Right then, I guess you guys can go do whatever,

but Colbie, we need to have you fitted for your gown." Evie turns her attention on me, and I groan.

"Can't I wear something already in my closet?" I ask, thinking about all the dresses in there.

"Absolutely not," Gracelin exclaims. "We already have the dressmaker working on something fit for a queen. She just needs to fit it to you."

"Damn it," I grumble, and Archie giggles.

"Colbie said a naughty word. She needs a time out."

I look hopefully at Gracelin, but she shakes her head.

"Colbie is an adult who is allowed to say those words," she says. "I've told you that when you're an adult, you can do the same."

I sag back into Brodie, who chuckles beneath me. "Fine," I mutter, and the others laugh.

"Come on, pamper day will be fun," Violet enthuses. I wrinkle my nose, and she laughs.

"Hunter, your dad wanted to speak to you as soon as you arrived regarding the outpost. He said to tell you and Micah to head over to the barracks when I saw you," Lucas tells him.

"Will do," Hunter replies, and he comes over to give me a quick kiss. Micah does the same, then they both leave the room.

"Eww. Am I going to have to do that?" Archie asks. He lost interest in the various knives strapped to Titus's body. I watched Titus gently push his hand away every time he reached for one.

"Do what?" Adam asks.

"Kiss Colbie like that? On the lips? Is that what side-pieces do?"

Everyone chuckles, and I shake my head. "Nope, only cuddles and lots of games," I assure him, and he returns his attention to Titus's arsenal, satisfied with my answer.

"Here." Titus holds out his hand, a small, child-sized dagger appearing on his palm. He hands it to Archie. "Mine are far too sharp and dangerous for a young warrior to learn with, but this one is perfect for you to practice with." He bends it slightly, showing Gracelin and Adam it's rubber before handing it to the boy.

Archie's eyes widen with excitement and glee. He takes it and suddenly thrusts it into the air. "Die, die." He slashes it around, and Gracelin groans again, glaring at Titus.

"You're on my shit list," she tells him, but Adam grins and nods his approval.

"Archie, you will have lessons with me once a week to learn how to use it. You're a warrior now, and that means you need to learn to be responsible with your weapons," Titus explains, and the boy stops stabbing invisible people and nods solemnly.

"Okay, I need to learn how to protect my sidepiece."

"Well, your sidepiece doesn't need protection at the moment. We are going for mani pedis and a massage. The staff is waiting for us." Gretchin holds out a hand and tugs me off Brodie's lap. He releases me reluctantly. I lean in and give him a kiss before doing the same to the other remaining five.

"Jesus, it's not like you won't see them later," Gracelin complains, and before I can say another word, the three girls bundle me out of the office, through the palace, and to a Roman bath style area. I still don't have the whole layout of this huge place, but from the looks of it, I'm going to spend a lot of time in here. There's a large communal pool with statues of women holding jugs with water flowing out of them. I see massage tables and chairs in a separate room with one-way glass for us to see out, but no one can see in. On the other side of the glass is an outdoor pool area, but it's miserable outside, with snow flurries drifting through the air.

"Oh wow, winter has arrived," I murmur as they hustle me into one of the massage chairs, and I stick my feet into the foot spa.

"Not quite. We will have a few days like this before the snow finally sticks to the ground. Thankfully the colosseum has retractable roofing, so if it's like this tomorrow, no one will get wet." Gretchin takes the seat next to me, Gracelin sits on my other side, and Violet takes the one next to her. "Now tell us everything that happened over the last few days, and don't leave out any details."

I watch as four beauticians approach us and take seats in front of the spas. I don't ever remember having taken the time to have a pedicure before, so this will be interesting. I'm also kind of worried about sharing everything with the girls, because I don't really want the four strangers to hear everything.

Gretchin must understand my dilemma, because she pulls out four stones and hands one to each of us. "Privacy stones," she explains. "You can talk, and none of them will hear a thing, but we can still hear if they are talking shit about us," she tells us, and I look at one, trying to ascertain if she heard what Gretchin said, but she doesn't even lift her head.

"Don't worry, this is a common thing for them. Our moms do it all the time," Gracelin assures me, so I let go of my worry and share my very entertaining tale with my girls.

CHAPTER

FORTY

Colbie

The next morning, I'm woken very early by the queens, their daughters, Violet, and a slew of maids. They kick Micah and Brodie out of my bed, the two mates who won the rounds of rock, paper, scissors they played last night. I rolled my eyes as I watched them play rounds and rib each other good-naturedly. Thankfully, there were no hurt feelings when I said I would only accept two in my bed. There's room for more, but if there was ever a day when a girl needs to not wake up drenched in sweat, it's the morning of her coronation.

I'm primped and prodded and stuffed into my gorgeous gown. It's royal blue with short, off the shoulder sleeves, delicate beaded embroidery on the bodice, and a full skirt. I look and feel like a princess when they are finally done with me. My hair is down with gentle waves, and I have blue kitten heels on my feet.

"Okay, so usually challenge day happens before the coronation, but because we want this done as soon as possible, Lucas is going to ask the gathered crowd if anyone wants to challenge you after your crowning," Mia explains as we make our way through the palace to the waiting vehicles.

"Aramis was not happy about challenge day and said it was a shifter thing, not something she condoned," I warn her, and she nods.

"Yes, but if she wants your reign to be successful, then she should allow it. The shifters will respect you more. If someone is brave enough to go against you, then shift into your hydra, and they will quickly concede. Hydras are basically unbeatable," Evie recommends.

"Then you will be asked to appoint your council," Layla advises me, and I wince. Shit, I haven't had a chance to let the others know they will no longer be needed. Oh well, I didn't like any of them anyway, so if they are pissed at me, it's not a huge deal.

"Once you and your mates are crowned, the full power of the shifters will settle over you. It might be painful, but don't show any weakness. The shifters won't respect you if you do," Gretchin tells me as the vehicles travel from the palace to the colosseum on the far side of the shifter city. My mates will meet me there.

"Then you can make any declarations you like to. Now would be a good time to announce repealing the crossbreed ban, as well as announcing your intention to create a more inclusive shifter nation by welcoming members of the mer, fairy, and equine shifters onto your council and into your bed with your new mates, who will be introduced and crowned just before you're crowned."

"Remember, anyone who beats you not only gets to

claim the crown, but they can also claim your mates as well," Gracelin warns me.

"What?" I screech. Have they told me this before? My creatures blaze with righteous fury. There is no way I am losing my mates to any asshole who thinks they can take them. "That's not fucking happening," I growl, and Gracelin smirks like she is pleased with my reaction.

"Hang on to the anger," she taunts me.

"You did that on purpose." I stab a finger in her direction, and she shrugs.

"Whatever works. I know you now, Colbie, and you're too nice. You would end up losing to someone because you don't want to hurt them. I gave you a reason not to lose. Shifters appreciate strength, and if you kill any challengers, you will be seen as that much stronger."

"I don't want to have to kill anyone." My anger fades and is replaced with worry. Will I really be able to do this? It's such a giant change in everything I have ever known.

"Well, they won't have the same hesitation, so think about whether you want this or not."

"And the fight is anything goes, so if the challenger is magical, they can use their powers to attack. Seriously, the hydra will be the best option. Sable discovered an obscure text that says a hydra is impervious to magical attacks as well," Layla explains.

"Okay, hydra it is. Hopefully I can shift quickly enough."

The queens exchange a look.

"Colbie, your shift is a lot quicker than most. You just seem to change in the blink of an eye, while the rest of us take at least a few seconds," Evie explains.

"Once a fight starts, it doesn't finish until one party dies or submits. Hopefully when they see your hydra, they will submit immediately, but a lot of shifters are arrogant and will see you as a major challenge. Be prepared to have to kill someone," Mia warns.

Fuck, maybe I'm lucky Gracelin warned me about the winner getting my mates. The idea of killing someone is abhorrent to me, but my creatures are blood-thirsty little fuckers and are excited about it. There is still definitely a disconnect between my human and shifter sides.

The vehicle pulls into a private entrance to the colosseum. Guarding either side of the door are soldiers Bryson assigned to protect me and my mates until the crown is on my head. They aren't expecting trouble, but it's better to be prepared for it.

We climb out, and the girls and queens fuss around, straightening me out before we move into the building.

"Now remember, you need to be naked for the challenge to make sure you aren't concealing any fae or witch charms on your body." My stomach drops at Gretchin's words. I didn't fucking remember that fantastic little bit of information. Thank God for the waxing I had done yesterday.

"If it's any consolation, so does the challenger," Violet says, trying to reassure me, but it doesn't help.

We arrive at a door, and I hear familiar voices behind it. My mates are just beyond it, waiting for me. I take a deep breath to enter when a voice screeches my name.

"Queen Colbie, a word!" I turn and find Sophia Gardiner beelining toward me, fury in her eyes. She's followed by her daughter, Gianna.

"Fuck," I mumble under my breath. Gretchin, the good personal bodyguard that she is, steps between us, holding up a hand.

"That's close enough," she warns the councilwoman who throws her a venomous glare. The soldiers in our protection detail put their hands on the weapons at their sides. Gianna looks a little wary, but Sophia pays no attention to them.

"How dare you invite members of the rejected species to be a part of the council! I will not be in the same room as those lower species," she sneers, throwing her hair over her shoulder.

"Well then, I guess it's lucky you won't have to," I snap, fury replacing my nerves. "Thank you for your service, but you will no longer be required as a council member," I tell her, and Gracelin hands her an envelope containing her severance package. I was hoping I could do this in one group, but I guess I will need to have someone give Councilors Mason and Altmore their own severance packages. I was going to do this before the coronation out of courtesy, but the queens assured me I didn't owe these people anything.

Sophia's fury turns to shock as she stares at the envelope like it's Fluffy about to bite her. "You can't," she stammers, her cheeks paling. "I've served on the council for more years than you've been alive."

"Yes, and I think it is time for a change, don't you?" I turn my back on her, and she growls, but none of my creatures consider her a blip on our radar.

"You'll regret this. You will be challenged, and everyone will see that the reason no one knows what kind of shifter you are is because you're insignificant and weak."

I ignore her, and Violet opens the door to the room. I move inside, followed by the others, then I look over my shoulder. I see Gianna try to get a look at who is in the room, and her brow furrows when she catches sight of Watch Team One. I wonder if she's smart enough to put two and two together. Her gaze goes to the marks on my neck and then back to theirs. Her eyes light up, and as the door closes, I see her reach for her mom, excitement and calculation practically vibrating off her.

"Fuck, Gianna's going to challenge you," Gretchin sneers as she, too, sees what I saw.

"She wouldn't, would she? She's only a fox, so she has no chance." Violet shakes her head.

"But she's good with a knife." Liam comes over, rubbing his hand up and down my arm in reassurance. "And they think we haven't shared what kind of shifter Colbie is because she's weak."

"Are weapons allowed in a challenge?" I ask, panicking because although we've done a little self-defense, weapons are out of my skill set.

"Anything goes, but you've got this," Lucas reminds me as he approaches. "Colbie, you look beautiful. I'm sure your mates were just too stunned at the sight of you to say anything." He glares at the boys, and they all rush over to give me compliments.

Layla's peal of laughter is musical and lusty. "You are such a charmer," she says to her mate, straightening the lapels of his shirt. "Are you ready for this?" she asks him, and he nods firmly.

"So ready to be done with it all." I frown, worried that asking them to be on my council wasn't a good idea if they really don't want it.

"Ignore them. They can't wait to help you

scheme," Evie assures me, seeing me watch her mates with concern. "They are just trying to keep up appearances." She rolls her eyes, and Layla actually flips her off. She was the last queen I thought would do something like that, but it makes me like her even more.

"Mother," Gryffin scolds playfully, and she shrugs unapologetically.

"I haven't selected the mer, shifter, or fairy council members yet." I bite my lip once the guys stop fussing over me. I can't say it wasn't nice to be adored like that, but I have so much on my mind. "There hasn't been time."

"That's okay. Announce your intentions and tell the crowd your mates will fill those positions until a suitable candidate can be found," Gracelin assures me. She seems to have everything under control, and I am so happy I asked her to be my right-hand gal.

"Okay, yeah, cool, that works," I agree.

"We already have a few nominations. I have dossiers on all of them, and when everything settles down, we will invite them for dinner so you can get a feel for each of them and then make a decision."

"Did your family come?" I ask Titus, who is looking at his phone.

"Yes, they just arrived. General Bryson and Lady Sable are escorting them here and will be with them as their protection."

"That's good." I share a smile with him and feel his relief and joy as if it were my own.

"What about my mother?" I ask, bracing myself for the answer.

Hunter and Liam exchange a glance. "Jenny and

Joseph arrived without her. Jenny says they haven't seen nor heard from her."

Worry niggles at me. It isn't like her to not take the opportunity to try and steal the spotlight from me. I would have thought she would be here, wearing her most scandalous outfit and flirting with everyone.

"Where are my grandparents?" I ask, wanting to see them before all this kicks off.

"They are in the VIP seating," Brodie tells me. "I escorted them there myself. They said to wish you luck."

I consider sending one of the guys to go get them, but before I can, the door opens, and Bryson and Sable enter, followed by three people.

The male is the spitting image of Titus, with the same green hair and pointy ears, as well as similar green wings as his son, but instead of silver accents, his are gold. The woman is slightly shorter and more curvy than her mate. She has pretty, silver and bright purple delicate wings that flutter behind her, and she shares similar features to Violet. The younger girl with them is stunning, with long green hair like the two men in her family, but her wings are purple and gold.

"Daddy, they have wings. Am I going to have wings?" I hear Archie say to Adam, and I stifle a smile. I don't hear Adam's reply though.

"Aunt Calla," Violet squeals and throws herself at the woman who startles before smiling widely and hugging her niece.

"Violet, my gorgeous girl. I didn't expect to see you."

"Colbie is my friend, and she asked me to be her lady-in-waiting," Violet explains as she switches her attention to the younger girl who I'm guessing might be close in age to her or maybe slightly older.

"Hi, Holly." Violet gives her cousin a hug as well, and the girl smiles at her, but her attention keeps shifting to another area in the room. I follow her gaze and find Gretchin staring at her with extreme interest.

"Colbie, these are my parents, Calla and Koa, and my sister Holly." Titus joins me and drags me forward to meet his parents. "Guys, this is my mate, Queen Colbie Karridge."

I greet both of them, welcoming them to our kingdom and assuring them that I hold their safety as a high priority, but the whole time, I hear the rumble of a jungle cat behind me.

"Oh, for fuck's sake, Gretchin." I whirl around to face my bodyguard. "What is the problem?" I demand and find she's moved as close as possible to Holly and is sniffing her.

"What the fuck?" Liam mutters behind me, and one of the queens scolds him for his language, but my focus is on my friend and Titus's sister.

"Does your sister have a mate mark?" I ask him, and he shakes his head.

"Not that I know of, but it has been a while since I went home for a visit." He raises an eyebrow at his parents who are watching everything with closed expressions.

Koa sighs. "One appeared a few days ago," he admits, and I gasp.

Did it happen on the same day the magic activated Titus's and Micah's?

"Can we see it?" I coax gently, but the girl ignores me, focused completely on Gretchin.

Before I can ask again, the two of them collide in a smoldering kiss that has me fanning my face.

"I'm going to go out on a limb and say they are mates," Brodie says, scrunching up his nose. "Gross. I don't want to see my sort of sister making out with someone else."

"Imagine how I feel," Titus mutters as the two girls get a little handsy.

"Pfft, we have to watch all of you with Colbie," Gracelin reminds us, beaming with joy at the fact her sister has found her mate.

Before anyone else can say anything, there's a flash of light, and the goddess appears. The two girls stop making out, and everyone but me bows to the deity.

"Right, we're all here. Let's get this shit show on the road. The sun should be rising any moment," she tells me.

I guess we aren't messing around. A swarm of butterflies swoops in my stomach, and my heart starts to beat so fast I'm afraid it's going to pound out of my chest.

"Just give us a moment to get to the VIP section please." Bryson and Sable wave for Titus's family to join them. We have to physically separate Gretchin and Holly, Titus grabbing his sister and Gryffin his. Holly starts sobbing, and Gretchin snarls at Gryffin. Gracelin steps up and slaps Gretchin across the face.

"Get your shit together. Let's get Colbie safely crowned, and then you can hole up somewhere for days if you need to," she tells her sister who seems to snap out of it.

The goddess smirks, and she meets my eyes, giving me a wink. Meddling busybody, but I am happy for Gretchin. Aramis waves her hand, and they disappear in a flash, aided to their seats by her magic. I hope it's not as disorienting as Titus's sift is.

"Right, let's just make this a little bit more of a spectacle than it already is. I do enjoy drama." She waves her hand again, and my mates are all wearing black cloaks with hoods concealing them from the rest of the audience. She rubs her hands together. "This is going to be so much fun."

FORTY-ONE

Colbie

When the goddess transports us into the main arena of the colosseum, the noise is deafening. The crowd roars with excitement as they notice us on the center stage. I look around, and behind us are the crowns encased in their display cases. Each of the mate crowns are black with different colored gems and flourishes on them, but they are a matching set. The middle crown is a shiny, silvery white and doesn't look like any metal I have ever seen before, with blue green gems the same color as my hydra. Lucas and his queens join the others in the VIP box to the side of the stage. I see my grandparents sitting in there. My grandpa waves, and my granny dabs at her eyes with a tissue. I smile at seeing them, pleased that at least some of my family was able to attend. I'm pissed because my father deliberately avoided coming because of my mother, and she couldn't even be bothered to appear.

I turn my attention to the goddess, who has stepped forward. As one, the shifter population gets down on one knee and bows their heads. I guess it's hard to dispute the existence of gods when they appear in front of you. Aramis has this otherworldly glow around her, obscuring her from the crowd. I guess she doesn't allow just anyone to see her true form.

I don't really pay attention to her words, instead scanning the crowd for possible threats. Are any of these people going to challenge me for my position? Are they going to make me possibly kill someone at the start of my rule? I don't want to be a queen who rules over her people because they fear her, but I do want their respect, so if it's going to take a challenge to get it, then I guess I'm okay with that. I will take the queens' advice, though, and shift as quickly as possible.

Most of the expressions in the crowd are a combination of awed and excited, and while the atmosphere is tense, it doesn't feel aggressive, just anticipatory.

"I have blessed Queen Colbie with eight mates in hopes to usher in a new age in shifter relations. They are all fully mated, and I have the pleasure of crowning your new kings. Please step forward and remove your hoods so I may place your crowns on your heads." The goddess gestures for my mates to come forward.

Almost like they rehearsed it, they move forward together, removing their hoods and letting their capes drop dramatically to the ground. The guys are in full warrior mode, strapped with weapons on every part of their body, and they wear fierce expressions on their faces. They are a formidable bunch, and the crowd ripples with surprise and awe at the sight of them. I hear mutterings of surprise as they recognize most of Watch

Team One, but I also hear questions about who the other three are.

Aramis steps in front of Gryffin, and he ducks his head as she places his crown on it. "I give you King Gryffin, white tiger." She moves down the line, repeating her actions with each of my mates. "King Jeremy, phoenix. King Hunter, dragon. King Liam, polar bear." There is a noise of discontent, and my eyes go to the source. I see four men, one slightly older than the others, and I can tell these are Liam's father and brothers. They all look a little like him despite his shock of white hair and piercings. They are broader, almost overweight, which is not something I have seen in a shifter before, and they all wear scowls of disgust. I see a couple of soldiers moving through the crowd in their direction, but they don't do anything, just position themselves in case they are needed.

The goddess pauses and looks in the same direction. She glares at Liam's family, and two of the brothers visibly shrink back into the crowd, but the father and remaining brother cross their arms and stupidly stare down the goddess. Are they brave or just fucking dumb?

She must decide they aren't a threat, because she continues. "King Brodie, wolf." I brace myself for the reception of the next three. I'm sure there is going to be some sort of reaction. "King Lennox, pegasus." There are ripples of movement and murmurings from the crowd, but nothing outwardly hostile yet. I look around the arena and notice a crap load more soldiers. Bryson is prepared to subdue a riot if need be. "King Micah, mer, and finally, King Titus, fairy-fae hybrid and Chaos Kingdom assassin." Aramis drops that final bombshell, and the crowd starts to shout.

"Hybrids are outlawed in Aramis."

"An assassin? Holy shit."

"What the fuck?"

"Wow, I can't believe the queen has an equine, mer, and fairy as mates. That's amazing."

Positive and negative reactions echo all around us, but Aramis ignores them before turning her attention to me.

"Colbie Karridge. Do you promise to honor and protect your people from any who may wish to do them harm, and uphold the values of Aramis Kingdom from now until the end of your reign?"

"I do," I reply as she approaches me, sparkly crown in hand.

"Then I crown you Queen Colbie, ruler of the shifter nation, until your death or you choose to step down and hand the crown to one of your descendants." She places the crown on my head, her voice ringing out over the crowd. "I decree that Colbie will be the final human chosen as a shifter ruler, and her bloodline will now carry the responsibility." This announcement has everyone forgetting about what species my mates are, and they are stunned into silence.

"Long live Queen Colbie, may she reign in peace and prosperity." Aramis's voice thunders through the colosseum, and as one, the people get down on one knee.

"Long live Queen Colbie," the crowd responds, and the magic slashes across my body, burning into my very soul. I grit my teeth and clench my fists as pain like no other spreads through every nerve ending as the final bit of ruler magic assaults my body.

"Almost there," Aramis whispers to me, and my

mates send me reassurance, pride, and love through our bond, but there is also a sense of pain from them. I pry my eyes open and see that they are also battling some kind of power influx, their bodies glowing like stars in the sky. A ripple of surprise flows through the crowd, and there are more shocked reactions and comments, but I can't focus on any of them. I'm gasping for air, and my body is coated in a fine sheen of sweat when the pain finally recedes, but I didn't fall or falter, and as I lift my head and look out over the crowd, my body starts to glow with power.

"Although the queen challenge has nothing to do with anything I chose, I will honor shifter tradition, and I ask you this—is there anyone who considers themselves more worthy than my chosen who wishes to challenge Queen Colbie for her crown?" Aramis glares out into the crowd, almost daring someone to go against her.

The crowd still murmurs, and I watch as it parts, Liam's remaining brother stepping forward. "I challenge King Liam to his mate position," he calls out, and I jolt in surprise.

"Is that allowed?" I mutter out of the side of my mouth to the goddess, and I feel her own surprise.

"It's never happened before," she replies, glaring at Liam's brother. We both turn to look at Liam, who grins with undisguised joy. He gives the goddess a small nod, and she shrugs throwing her hands into the air, looking exasperated.

"Why the fuck not. Anyone want to challenge the actual queen?" The crowd looks around, some even look hopeful that someone is brave enough to challenge me.

Again, the crowd parts, and Gianna walks through, looking smug. "I will challenge the queen who usurped a ready-made bond group who was meant for one of us instead of picking from her marked potentials, and when I win, I will take the crown and her mates for myself, and I'll keep the spare." She points at Liam's brother, who blows her a kiss and gives her a wink.

"Eww," I mutter childishly. "Those two deserve each other."

"You dare to question my decrees?" The goddess's voice reverberates around the arena, her gaze laser focused on Gianna. I have to give Gianna credit. She either has big lady balls or is completely batshit crazy, because she just shrugs and nods.

"Yes."

"So be it, but I'll have you know Colbie wears the matching mate mark for this bond group. It is as it should be," the goddess announces. The crowd, which had been looking a little rebellious after Gianna's state-ment, settles when the goddess tells them this.

"Well then, clear a space. You will strip and fight until someone either submits or dies." Bryson moves from the VIP area, taking control of the challenges. "The king challenge will be first."

Liam steps out of the line and starts stripping off his clothes. I grit my teeth and begin to growl under my breath. I do not like all those thirsty female and male eyes on my mate. I glare at the crowd, and anyone who meets my eyes drops their gaze to the ground, bowing their heads and submitting to my dominance.

"Aww, baby, you know I only have eyes for you." Liam approaches me, now completely naked, and gives me a quick kiss and a wink. "But hold onto all that aggression, and we can angry fuck later," he promises before jumping down from the stage and stalking into the fight ring. Liam's brother does the same thing, then the goddess waves a hand, and ten thrones appear on the stage.

"We may as well take a seat and be comfortable while Liam eviscerates him," she says, unconcerned, and gestures for me to take one before claiming the seat next to me. The guys join us, but I can't get comfortable despite the cushioned seat under me. I'm too tense, biting my lip as I wait for the fight to start.

"First to kill wins, unless one concedes," Bryson tells them, and they give him short nods. Liam's brother roars and shifts, a huge brown grizzly bear taking the place of his human form. He snarls and starts to run toward Liam, who just fucking stands there.

"What the fuck are you doing? Shift," I scream, forgetting about being the polite and regal queen with my concern for my mate.

The rest of my mates are shouting words of encouragement too, but none of them look worried. Even my new mates are relaxed. Nox even goes so far as taking out his phone and checking his messages.

The grizzly is quick, and he swipes at Liam, who hasn't even shifted yet, with a huge paw that has claws that look like daggers.

Liam just dodges to the side and laughs. "Is that all you have? You've become fat and slow since I saw you last, Lionel," he taunts. "That's what happens when you're a lazy fucker who treats his pack like slaves."

The bear roars again and charges once more, his thunderous stride echoing through the colosseum as he barrels toward my polar bear. Again, Liam dodges to the side, swift and light of foot, his muscles rippling with the movement. I hear a sigh of admiration and find Gianna staring at a certain part of him with longing. I jump to my feet, clenching my fists.

"Shift and finish this," I command my mate, completely done with this shit. He's definitely going to get an angry fuck later. How dare he flaunt what is mine in front of all these women? Especially that fucking bitch.

He chuckles and winks at me, feeling exactly how pissed I am at him, but my glare turns into a look of surprise when, unlike his usual shift, which has his body contorting, he is enveloped in a cloud of purple magic, and when it clears, we see his polar bear.

"Holy fuck," Gem mutters as we take in Liam's shifted form. I guess the magic must have enhanced my mates as well as me. His polar bear is almost double the size it was before. He rears up, pawing at the air while roaring loudly. The crowd shrieks and moves farther back as Lionel charges once more, undaunted by the monster polar bear in front of him.

"Fuck, Lionel's animal is in the driver's seat. No rational thought, just pure instinct. He's going to die," Gryffin, who is on the throne on my other side, mutters.

Lionel rears up onto two feet and lunges at Liam with his front paws extended. I scream when Liam doesn't move, just swipes at him with one of his massive paws and sends the bear flying backward, blood splattering the crowd as he lands heavily on the sandy ground. A puff of dust forms around him before it settles back down.

When it clears, Lionel is still, a pool of blood staining the sand ruby red as he bleeds out from the massive claw mark across his chest. I can see muscle and sinew in the gaping wound. His chest shudders as he takes a final breath before it stills, his sightless eyes staring up at the sky.

Liam killed his brother!

He lets out a bone-shuddering roar and rears up, pawing at the air in a frightening display of dominance. Shifters all around the cleared area drop to their knees in submission. I search the crowd, looking for Liam's father, and when I find him, I don't like what I see. Instead of the expected grief, his father looks furious, and there's a calculating gleam in his eye. He melts into the crowd without a backward glance for his fallen progeny.

"King Liam is the undisputed winner," Bryson declares loudly, and the crowd shouts and stomps their feet in approval. There's a flash of purple light, and Liam shifts back to his human form. Brodie jumps up and runs over to him, slapping him on the back and wrapping his discarded cloak around his shoulders. I send him a wave of gratitude through our bond for covering Liam, and he gives me a playful wink. They move back and take seats on their respective thrones.

"Queen Colbie?" Bryson gestures for me to stand.

The goddess gives me a nod of reassurance. "Kill her. You don't need to be constantly looking over your shoulder," she recommends, and I grimace. That's not the kind of advice I was hoping for, but what more can I expect from a primal deity?

I step forward, and Gem moves with me, assisting me by drawing the zipper down on my dress.

"You've got this. Just shift immediately. You're faster and way more powerful. You should get her to submit instantly," he coaches, but I'm laser focused on Gianna and don't respond to him. My creatures are baying for blood. I don't want to kill her, but I will if I have to.

My dress pools at my feet, and I feel my cheeks heat with embarrassment. I'm left standing in my panties, as there was no need for a bra in this dress. All eyes are on me as I peel my underwear down my legs. I hear murmurs of admiration, and there is a spike of lust from our bond. My mates' gazes are on me, and this seems to infuriate Gianna. She makes a show of stripping, throwing her dress off to the side with a flourish before doing the same with both pieces of underwear.

"Same rules apply. There is no conclusion until someone submits or dies," Bryson warns us. We both nod our acknowledgements, and Gianna doesn't even wait for him to say anything else before she shifts. The crowd shouts in encouragement, and I see money exchange hands, but there are many more looks of disappointment at Gianna's behavior, and this gives me confidence. Gianna finishes her shift, and she stands there, a small red fox, snarling at me. I can't stop the snort of laughter that leaves my mouth.

"She's a fox?" I turn to look at my mates, feigning surprise at her creature. We were just talking about her before the coronation, after all. "You could have told me she wasn't anything challenging." I see the amusement in their eyes at my comment.

Naughty girl, you just pissed her off, Hunter warns me telepathically, sounding amused, before his voice turns anxious. *Shift now.* I turn forward and see her running toward me.

I let my hydra take control, and she bursts out of my skin in a flash of light, towering over the cleared area. The crowd falls into awed silence as my hydra's eight heads let out an ear-shattering roar that has the whole stadium full of shifters falling to their knees in submission. Gianna's fox skids to a stop not far from me.

You could hear a pin drop, but when my hydra focuses on the tiny terror that was charging toward us, we find her cowering with her head beneath her paws, a puddle of urine staining the sand beneath her. She yelps, jumps up, and flees through the crowd, which is still on their knees, and no one stops her retreat.

I hear Nox chuckle behind us. "I guess that means Colbie wins."

"I'm still going to make sure she can't come for her again," Titus growls, and I understand that Gianna's days are numbered if my assassin has her in his crosshairs.

"Long live Queen Colbie," a voice calls from somewhere in the crowd. I recognize it as my grandpa's, and when one of my heads turns to look at the VIP area, my grandparents are the only people not on their knees. As humans, they wouldn't be subjected to the alpha dominance within me. I lean in and give him a lick on the cheek.

"Get away, you," he says, laughing and pushing my head away from him as the crowd takes up the chant.

The goddess stands and gestures for me to shift back. I do, and I redress, and once again, Gem helps me with the zipper.

"Now that we have established she and her mates are the right shifters for this position—something I already knew," the goddess says sarcastically, "she will announce her council."

FORTY-TWO

Colbie

When we finally leave the colosseum, I'm exhausted and relieved but relatively pleased with how everything went. The majority of shifters were delighted when I lifted the ban on interspecies matings, announcing that all interspecies relationships and hybrid children were welcome in the kingdom. I don't expect to have an influx of people moving here, since I'm fairly certain the ones who live in Chaos Kingdom are happy where they are, but it makes visiting family and friends a distinct and safe possibility.

My new council was met with enthusiasm, as was the news of the three vacant spots that will be filled with mer, fairy, and equine representatives respectively.

The goddess then made the proclamation that all humans would be offered the chance to transition to shifters. This was met with a fair amount of skepticism and suspicion, but no one was brave enough to call the goddess out on it. I'm sure they will adjust eventually. Sable and the queens will be taking the names of volunteers who are happy to bite any humans who would like to be a specific shifter type, but screening will be carried out. A human who is a psychopath is not suddenly going to change when they become a shifter and have the possibility to be even more dangerous. According to Sable, who is a doctor as well as the chief archivist, shifters with psychopathic tendencies tend to go feral and need to be put down.

There are a lot of adjustments coming to Aramis, but that is a future Colbie problem.

It is midday by the time the ceremony wraps up and we go back to the palace for a meal with my mates and their families. I'm exhausted and feeling a little shaky as my grandparents surround me for a group hug when I arrive at the dining room.

"We are so fudging proud of you," Grampy says, squeezing me tightly. Tears well in my eyes as my granny cups one of my cheeks.

"You were magnificent. I only wish your mother had been there to see how amazing you are," she tells me.

"I'm sure she would have tried something underhanded to steal the spotlight," Grampy grumbles as we take a seat at the table.

I'm introduced to Brodie's mother and father, who give me a slight nod of their heads but are not particularly warm. Brodie's brother is more enthusiastic and gives me a hug and a kiss, congratulating me on my spectacular display of dominance.

As he pulls away, there's a slight tug in my chest, and I get the urge to put my hand over his sternum. Allowing it to happen, I press my hand down, feeling a lump beneath his shirt, kind of like a pendant hanging from a chain. My hand warms, and I feel magic flow out of me and into him. He flinches and tries to pull away, but the magic holds him in place. He grimaces, and when the magic finally releases him, he reaches in and pulls out what I touched. A pendant, very much like the one Nox used to wear, hangs from a chain, but it is split in half. I instantly recognize it for what it is—a bond blocker.

"What did you do?" Brodie's father growls, jumping to his feet.

"I… I don't know," I mutter, looking to the goddess for help. She smirks at Brodie's father, but I see the wicked glint in her eyes.

"She righted a wrong. Messing with my will is a sure-fire way to get on my bad side," she tells the wolf, who pales and sits back down.

We look at the goddess, hoping she will share what she knows with the rest of us.

"Lift your shirt please," she asks Briden, and when he does, he stares in surprise at the mark above his heart.

"I have a bond mark," he says with astonishment.

"Yes. Your parents gave you that pendant when you were younger in the hope they could stop the mark from appearing," she explains, and Brodie growls.

"You gave him that just after I got my mark," he snarls at his parents.

"We already lost one son, we weren't losing anoth-er," his mother snaps, and I whine as Brodie is filled with sorrow. Jesus, what assholes.

"That's the same as my brother's mark." Hunter waves Talon forward. Talon is beaming, and he pulls

Briden into a hug and ushers him away from the table so they can talk. Brodie stalks over to his parents and grabs each of them by the arm before forcefully removing them from the room.

"Well, I guess we won't be celebrating Christmas with them," I murmur to Nox as he puts an arm around my shoulders to comfort me.

Micah's father is slightly warmer, and I get a positive response regarding the council position. He promises he will send his nominations as soon as he returns home.

Gretchin and Holly disappeared as soon as they congratulated us. I doubt we will see them anytime soon, but I am happy for them. I don't really need a body-guard attached to my hip at the moment with eight attentive, clingy mates to see to my every need.

We eat our meal, and the conversation around the table is lighthearted and joyful, but it kind of feels like it's the calm before the storm. Nox keeps looking at his phone, and I know he received a message from his parents.

I sigh, aware this celebration has come to an end. I will not wait a moment longer to go after the children. The power flows through my veins, and short of my death, no one can take the crown from me, and consid-ering I regenerate, my death is not likely to happen anytime soon.

"Tell me," I encourage him. I know he's been keeping quiet for the whole meal out of the need for me to enjoy myself, but I'll be a lot happier once those chil-dren are reunited with their parents. They must be frantic with worry.

"My parents have a location. They said they are in an underground compound deep in one of the mountains of the rift. They said that not only can they feel the children, but there are hundreds of feral shifters there as well. They can't get any closer, though, because there are wards and guards set up around the perimeter."

My heart sinks. Hundreds of ferals, and I don't have the book with the spell to fix any of them.

"And the Tidemans? Any sign of them?" Lucas asks.

He shakes his head. "They don't know. They say people come and go, but they are all wearing hoods and capes, so they haven't been able to identify any of them."

"I'll assemble the teams." Bryson jumps to his feet.

"No." I wave him back into his seat. "I can't do anything about any of the ferals at this stage."

"And it will be too dangerous to bring all of them back to our prisons to wait for the cure," Micah adds, agreeing with me. "This will be a straight extraction. Titus can sift us into the mountain, we'll grab the kids, and sift back out."

"I'll go back and sneak around once the kids are safe," Titus promises. "It will be easier if it's just me. I can move around without anyone knowing, and I can nullify any fae wards I come across."

"What if they have witch wards?" Mia asks, and I frown.

"I don't want you going without backup and end up stuck there," I argue.

"Fine, I'll ask my assassin brother who is part witch to come with me," he compromises, and I'm satisfied with his response.

"The kids will probably be traumatized. They have been stuck in their animal form for a long time. Command them back into human form, but be prepared for them to become unconscious. It will be a shock to their system. Transport them back to the med bay here at the palace, and I will be on standby," Sable instructs Titus.

"What about the people responsible? You're not going to let them get away with this, are you?" Gracelin asks angrily, hugging Archie. I don't blame her, she almost lost her son to those monsters. I would want revenge too.

"Not at all. We will poke around while we search the compound for the kids. If we come across anyone who seems to be in their right mind, and it's safe, then we will apprehend them, but for now, our focus needs to be the children," Hunter tells Gracelin, who seems to accept this.

"You should stay here," Liam suggests to me, and I glare at him. I'm still boiling mad about him being naked in front of everyone. I'm aware it's hypocritical, since I was just as naked, but this comment just makes me feel even angrier at him.

"I will not. I am coming too," I tell him stubbornly. I expect him to argue, but to my surprise, he accepts it without complaint.

"We need to change. Will you excuse us?" Gryffin pushes back from the table, and the rest of my mates follow suit.

"Be careful." My granny squeezes my hand. "Come to the bakery once you rescue those poor babies, and when you get a free moment, let us know how it goes."

I promise them I will, and the nine of us leave to get ready for the mission.

We arrive in a clearing that Titus got from a picture Nox's parents sent us. It's bitterly cold, and snow swirls around as we get blasted by frigid wind. Nox's parents step around a rock they sheltered behind and point out the carefully hidden entrance to the facility. They wish us luck before the three men put their hands on Lena, and then they disappear from sight.

"Unicorns can teleport?" I gasp, and Nox nods.

"Yes, that's why they make such good trackers. Once they have a location, they can usually head straight to it. It took Mom a little while to get a lock on the area because of the wards, though, which is why it took so long."

"I can sift us in once I deal with the wards." Titus puts his hands up like he's scanning the area.

"Will whoever set them feel you break them?" Brodie asks.

"It depends if the wards are cast by an actual person or if they are set into rocks surrounding the area. If they have been cast, then yes. If they are just using ward stones, then no," Titus says absently, and the rest of my guys gather around me to keep me warm while we wait.

It takes Titus about ten minutes to work out the wards. He explained that if he were full fae, it would have been quicker, but his ward powers aren't as strong because he's a hybrid. They finally fall, and he winces.

"Shit, they definitely have a fae on their team, and

they are going to know we're here. Hopefully the fae isn't in the facility, otherwise there is going to be a welcoming committee," he warns.

"Liam, Gryffin, and Brodie, you should shift, because you'll be able to move quicker in your animal forms. The rest of us aren't as agile in enclosed spaces," Hunter suggests, and they quickly comply.

"How are you with a weapon?" Micah turns his attention to Nox, who shrugs.

"I'm acceptable, but I'm much better with technology. I should be able to get us through any security in the place, and I can wield illusions in this form as well."

"Okay, you and Colbie stay together. It will make it easier for us to protect both of you," Micah tells him.

"Kill anyone who attacks us, but if they stand down, just incapacitate them. We want to question them," Hunter orders, giving Titus a hard look.

Titus pouts but reluctantly agrees. "Fine, but it goes against my training to leave anyone alive. Let's go."

Everyone places a hand on the hybrid, and he sifts inside the compound. When we arrive, it's pitch black, and I can't see despite my enhanced eyesight, but there's no way to miss the cacophony of snarls and howls.

He has brought us into the cells. A flame flares to life in Gem's hand, and I blink against the sudden light. I look around, thankful we aren't in an actual cell but a hallway between two rows of them. I shudder at the sight of all the deformed humans stuck between shifts, foaming at the mouth. They become super agitated at the sight of my three shifted mates and start throwing themselves at the bars of their cells. Some of them eye us with eager hunger, while others ignore us completely and randomly attack one another in their crowded cell.

"Oh my god, this is awful." I shudder and step back as one of them lunges at the bars, reaching for me with a gnarled, claw-tipped hand. "How are we even going to find the children?" I ask, feeling helpless because I can't help any of these people.

"It would be too difficult to move a feral from one floor to another. I bet they are down here on this level somewhere," Hunter says, holding out a piece of cloth for Brodie to scent. Brodie does before putting his nose up, then he starts sniffing the air. His ears prick, and his tail starts to wag as he bounds down the hallway. The rest of us follow him, keeping Nox and me between them. Gryffin and Liam bring up the rear. Anyone who wants to get to me is going to have to go through both of them to do it.

We move swiftly, and I am stunned by the number of cells, each of them containing way more feral shifters than they should.

"Where did all the humans come from? There weren't that many reported missing by the human authorities," Gryffin says, voicing the same thing I was thinking.

"Probably the other kingdoms," Gem suggests, his flame lighting the way. The ferals are kept in a pitch-black environment, and I can only pray they were kinder to the children.

"This is a bigger problem than we ever knew," Micah mutters as we come to a closed door. Brodie scratches at the gap at the bottom, and the others part to let Nox through to do his thing.

"Why don't we get Titus to sift us on the other side?" I ask as Nox pulls out a portable tablet and plugs it into the console on the wall.

"Because we don't know what is on the other side. We don't want to risk running across an armed assault team," Titus answers.

"But we didn't know that before we sifted here either," I argue.

He shrugs. "We got lucky. I don't want to take the risk we get lucky again."

It doesn't take Nox long before the panel glows green, and we hear a click. He unplugs his unit and steps back, allowing Titus, Micah, and Hunter to move to the front, their guns at the ready as they peek through the door to see if there is a force waiting for us.

"Clear," Hunter calls and throws the door open. Brodie pushes through and takes the lead again. There aren't any barred cells in this corridor, but there are a number of closed doors. We pause, and Micah tries one of the handles.

"Locked," he says, but our attention switches to Brodie. He's scratching at one of the doors and whining.

"Whoever is behind these doors is terrified and exhausted, and they are beginning to lose hope. We need to open them." Gem sounds pained, the empathic phoenix sensing their feelings.

Nox does his thing again, and before long, he has the first door open. As he moves on to the next one, I reach to open it, but Hunter stays my hand.

"Let me go first. They are probably expecting whoever is holding them captive, and their animal will be in protection mode. I don't want them to hurt you."

"I have a tranq in case they are feral." Micah raises his gun, and I gape in horror.

"They might be feral?" I hadn't even considered the possibility. I need to get that damn book back. "Poor babies. Is there a way to erase their memories of what happened?" I ask Titus, and he nods.

"Yes. A full fae could probably do it. If they need it, we can appeal to the fae for assistance."

Hunter slowly opens the door, Micah sticking close to him, as the two of them enter the room. I peer in behind them, and thankfully, it isn't dark, but it's no better than the cells. There is nothing in the cement room but a pile of hay, a dirty old blanket, and a small, very agitated white wolf pup. It snarls at the sight of Hunter and yips, snapping its little jaw at my mate.

"Shift," Hunter commands like he did to Archie that first time in my bakery. The command rolls over me, and I barely feel it, but it works on the pup. It freezes and whines as its body starts to painfully reshape itself. By the time it's finished, a young, naked, sobbing girl has replaced the white pup.

"Help me, please," she begs, and Gem rushes in and scoops her into his arms, wrapping the dirty blanket around her.

"I've got you. You're safe. We're going to get you back to your parents," he promises. Her chest heaves as she sobs uncontrollably in his arms, and my heart fucking breaks. Tears well in my eyes, but before they can fall, my grief turns to fury. My creatures roar inside my head, and the need to create bloodshed and chaos begins to ride me hard.

"They will pay," I swear out loud.

A shout has us leaving the room, and we find Nox has opened two more doors and commanded the two children inside the rooms to shift. Two small boys are carried out by Titus and Micah, while Liam and Brodie remain on alert. Both are sobbing as hard as the little girl and are wrapped in the same dirty, smelly blankets she is.

"Alright, I can't sift all of us, so we will take the kids, and then I'll come back and get you. I'll be no longer than five minutes," Titus says, holding the boy against his chest. Gem and Micah each put a hand on him while keeping a tight hold on their respective charges, and they disappear.

Hunter and I breathe a sigh of relief now that the kids are free, but Nox is staring down the hallway, frowning.

"What is Gryffin doing?" He points to where the white tiger is crouched in front of another locked door, snarling and scratching at it.

"Do you think it's another kid, one we didn't know about?" I ask Hunter, and he shrugs.

"Only one way to find out." Nox does his tech magic, and the door unlocks. He steps back, and Hunter takes point with Gryffin on his heels. The door swings open, and when I peer inside, I'm stunned into speechlessness.

FORTY-THREE

Colbie

"Colbie? You're alive! They told me you were dead." My mom looks as surprised to see me as I am to see her. I look around, trying to make sense of what I'm seeing. This room is completely different from the ones the kids were kept in. It's luxurious and spacious in a way that doesn't surprise me, knowing my mother. It has all the amenities of a fancy hotel room, but it's a prison nonetheless.

"Oh my god, Mom, are you okay? Are you injured? Come on, let's get you out of here." I run in, holding out my hand for her to take, but her surprise turns to fury, and her face twists as she snarls.

"You stupid girl, you always ruin everything."

I flinch like she physically slapped me. Gryffin lunges, snarling, but Hunter is quick to grab him by the scruff and haul him back. Mom screams and kicks out, thankfully missing.

"What do you mean? What's going on?" I'm so

fucking confused, but before she can reply, a howl and a growl from Liam and Brodie has us exiting to find we have company.

Vallen Tideman is standing at the end of the corridor with a number of guards, all with their guns pointed at us.

"Ah, Colbie, so nice of you to join us. I guess we won't be needing your mother after all."

"No!" she shouts, hurrying out of her room to join us. "You promised that you would change me if I helped you. You promised I could be queen if I used my blood to open your stupid book. You said the power and her mates would transfer to me when she died because we have the same blood. I will rule over all shifters, with you as my prime king."

As her words register, my heart feels like it cracks in half. My mother basically condoned my death as long as she got what she wanted. I thought she hurt me in the past, but every past infraction pales in comparison to this ultimate betrayal.

A tear slides down my cheek as she clings to Vallen's arm, but I see the calculation in her eyes. She's saying what she thinks he wants to hear, when I know she has no intention of making him her king. He's a handsome man, but if she thinks she can have my mates, then she'd dispose of him in a hot second.

"Yes, but why would we use you when we have the original here now?" He waves a hand in my direction, and she snarls and lunges for one of the guards, pulling a knife from a sheath on his thigh before she spins and runs at me, screaming.

"I hate you! You ruined everything, just like you did when you were born." Fuck, I thought I couldn't hurt any more, but I was wrong. I can't stop the sob that escapes my mouth as I put my hands up to defend myself. I'm so broken that even my creatures are cowering in despair.

I grab her wrist with both hands, stopping her from jabbing the dagger into my heart. I think even my guys were shocked into inaction, because none of them moved to stop her, but that only lasts a split second before they lunge toward us. Nox grabs me, tugging me away, as Hunter grips her wrist, squeezing hard. I hear the bone break as she cries out in pain, dropping the knife. Before she can be restrained further, Gryffin lunges at her, tearing her throat out. She lets out a garbled scream before she topples over, clutching her ruined throat. She looks at me with pleading eyes as Titus, Gem, and Micah reappear.

"Holy fuck," Gem mutters, seeing the blood staining the white fur around Gryffin's mouth before he makes a move to heal my mother, but I know it's too late.

I turn away so I don't have to watch the woman who gave birth to me die. I harden my heart and refuse to feel grief. She never deserved any of my love. I just resent the fact that I'm going to have to make Grampy and Granny sad when I tell them of her passing, but I make the decision to keep her actions to myself. They don't need to hear what a horrible person she turned out to be.

"God, he's never going to forgive himself," the phoenix mutters, tearing his gaze away from my mother to look at the snarling, pacing tiger that almost looks like he wants another go.

"Don't hold it against him, it was instinct," he pleads, and I shake my head.

"There is nothing to forgive," I assure him.

"Well, shit." Vallen watches with detached interest as my mother takes her last breath. "I guess we really can't let you escape now. Get her," he orders his men, who move past him in a wave of force. My guys are ready, and despite the guards having weapons, not many of them get any shots off, and the ones who do come up against a protective barrier that Titus must have woven around us.

"Remember, leave a few alive," I shout, reminding Titus as he goes on a killing spree, looking as excited as a kid in a candy shop to spill the blood of his enemies. He gives me an absent wave, which I hope is acknowledgement, as Nox and I are pushed against one of the walls and nobody is able to get past any of the others. I consider shifting into hydra form, but there really isn't any need. The guards don't seem like they are well trained, and my guys easily overpower them within a few moments, killing most of them while leaving a couple knocked unconscious for us to take with us to interrogate when we leave.

The fight is over within minutes, and the ground is slippery with blood, but I don't look in the direction of my mother's remains.

"Do you want to take her home to bury her?" Nox whispers in my ear as the others tie up the three unconscious guards.

"No, leave her. She deserves to rot," Liam says, shifting and dragging me into his arms. "I'm so sorry, but she is not worth your tears." He dries the tears I didn't realize I was shedding.

I lean into him, absorbing the warmth of his naked skin and support.

"Where did Vallen go? He had a book in his hands. I bet it's the one we need," Hunter growls, and Titus looks around before disappearing, probably in search of the councilor.

"Shall we go look for them?" Gem asks Micah who shrugs, shaking his head.

"Nah, the man is a paid assassin, so he should be fine. Let's wait here. I'm sure it won't be long."

The guys gather around me, Gryffin and Brodie staying in their animal forms to guard our backs while the rest try to give me words of comfort and reassurance, but I'm numb. I have no emotions to give at the moment, just complete apathy toward what just happened.

It doesn't take long before Titus reappears, scowling with disgust. "He got away. I searched the whole facility, and it's abandoned. Even the cells are empty. They must have a very powerful fae or witch working with them to transport that many beings in such a short span of time."

My heart sinks at the thought of all of those twisted ferals. Without the spell to fix them, they will be permanently stuck in that form. Even if they could use the spell, without me or apparently my mother, they won't even be able to open the book.

"We found them once, we will find them again. My mother will help us," Nox assures me, but I have my doubts.

"Titus, why don't you transport Colbie, Nox, Gryffin, and Brodie home, and then come back for the rest of us? We will watch over the prisoners until you return," Hunter suggests, and the assassin approaches us.

"Gem, burn Malina's body so they don't come back and try to use her blood on the book," Micah says, but I don't hear Gem's response as Titus puts his hands on me, and we reappear in my bedroom in the palace.

"Why don't you help Colbie clean up? I won't be long," Titus murmurs to Nox, who scoops me up and moves to the bathroom, the wolf and tiger trailing behind us. My eyelids drift closed. I kind of want to just block everything out for a minute and see if I can finally catch a breath. I don't even see Titus leave again.

The next thing I notice is the sound of water running as Nox steps into the shower with me, both of us still fully clothed. Brodie is naked and starts to pull my ruined clothes off my body.

Despite not actually being in the fight, there was no shortage of blood splatter, and Nox and I are both filthy. Once I'm completely naked, my bloodstained clothes turning the water in the bottom of the shower red, Nox passes me to my wolf as he strips his own uniform off.

"I'm going to go tell everyone what happened, then I'll bring some food back," Gryffin says, but I don't lift my head from Brodie's chest.

Nox mutters some response that I miss because all I can hear is a loud keening sound. It takes me a moment to realize it's coming from me. Brodie holds me tighter against his chest and whispers words of condolences and reassurance, but it does nothing to stem my grief—not grief because the woman who gave birth to me is dead, but grief over the fact that the one person in the world who was supposed to love me unconditionally didn't care about me at all. My whole life has been a lie. First, there was the truth about my father, and now this.

My body shudders as I sob loudly, while Brodie and

Nox work to get me clean. They wash my body and hair with gentle hands as I allow my grief to flow down the drain with everything else that has been staining me. When they finish, and we step out, I pull myself together and tuck the past into a box, burying it deep within my soul. I will not allow my mother to affect my future like she did the previous twenty-six years of my life.

I find myself dried and bundled into warm sweats before I'm carried once more, this time by Brodie, out into our living area. He places me down on the sofa in front of a roaring fire before leaving, taking Nox with him to find some clothes.

Gryffin, who has returned in the time it took for me to cleanse my body and soul, shoves a mug of hot chocolate into my hand then places a steaming plate of something that smells delicious on the coffee table in front of me, and that wakes my stomach up with a roar.

"Eat, cookie, you'll feel better if you do, and then you can sleep."

I give him a wane smile of thanks before taking a sip of the sweet beverage. It's the perfect temperature and taste, and I smile at the little marshmallow hydra floating on top.

"Where did this come from?" I ask him, looking up to see the rest of my guys enter through the door. They must have transported the prisoners to the cells beneath the palace first.

"Your grandpa made some for you as a coronation gift," my tiger explains before placing a kiss on the top of my head.

"We're going to get cleaned up in our own rooms.

We will be back shortly," he tells me, and everyone but Titus leaves.

"I'm going to help General Bryson interrogate the prisoners," he says, his eyes filled with worry. "Are you going to be okay? I'll come back as soon as I can."

"I'll be fine. It's important for us to get all the intel we can from them." I put the good of my kingdom before my own selfish wants, because if it were up to me, I would grab hold of him and beg him not to leave me.

Brodie and Nox, who are now dressed in their own sweats, return as Titus takes his leave.

"Gryffin asked everyone to give you space tonight, and we will debrief in the morning," Brodie explains, holding his own cup of hot chocolate with a little wolf floating on top. Joe made me a wolf!" He grins, not hiding his joy when he sees where my gaze is.

I look at Nox's mug and find another hydra floating in his.

"Joe promised he'd have a pegasus marshmallow the next time he sees me," Nox tells me enthusiastically, and a small ray of light cracks through the grief and sadness that seemed to have encased my heart and soul.

"He said the same thing to Micah and Titus too, though he was a little worried about how he was going to create marshmallow fairy wings. I suggested he create mini bloody daggers instead. He liked that idea," Brodie shares cheerfully, poking at his wolf and chortling when it bobs back to the surface, and that crack widens, letting a little more light in.

Everything is not right in my world, but I have a feeling it will be again soon.

FORTY-FOUR

Colbie

When I went to bed, only Brodie, Gryffin, and Nox were with me. Liam returned just before we turned out the light to let us know the others were going to be delayed. Gem was in the med wing, helping Sable and the healers with the children we rescued. They are going to have to be questioned, but we aren't ready to push them yet. Hunter and Micah were going to join Titus and General Bryson with interrogating the prisoners.

I'm restless, and I don't fall into a deep slumber until I hear the others return, their familiar scents filling my nostrils as they all climb quietly into my bed. I needed them all, needed to know they were safe before I could finally relax.

When I open my eyes the following morning, I'm all alone. I have no idea what time it is, but when I reach out to feel the sheets, they are cold. My mates have obviously been gone for a while. I frown and sit up, discovering a note on the bedside table.

Cookie, meet us in the conference room. We are gathering to discuss what we learned from the prisoners last night. There will be food. XOXO, your mates.

I feel a broad smile cross my lips for the first time since lunch yesterday. My mates think they are funny, trying to bribe me with food. I mean, it works, but I don't want to encourage them too much.

I throw the covers back and make my way into the bathroom to take care of an insistent bladder. Looking over at the shower, I expect to see the mess left behind by us yesterday, but there isn't a spot of blood or ruined clothes to be seen. Someone has been busy this morning, because I know it didn't get done last night. How did they manage it without waking me? I was obviously completely exhausted not to hear it.

Once I pee, I wash my hands but don't bother with a shower. I just run a brush through my hair and decide I'm good. I am not donning queen clothes today, and anyone who doesn't like me in sweats can suck it.

I wander through the deserted hallways, pleased that I don't have to speak to anyone right now. I bet my guys warned everyone to stay clear of our wing. When I get to the rest of the palace, though, it seems just as deserted. Maybe they gave the staff the day off. I can't say I'm unhappy about it.

Although I'm still sad, I made peace with my mother's death last night. I'm sad for the missed opportunity of being loved unconditionally by my father who I'm pretty sure would have been an amazing parent if he had been allowed to be a part of my life, but I had and will continue to have my grandparents in my life for years to come. Although I don't believe they will choose to become shifters, they may surprise me. They aren't too old, in their late fifties, as they had my mother when they were still very young, so they might make the change, and I won't stop them if that's what they choose. They would be extending their lifespan, so they would be able to be with me much longer.

When I reach the conference room doors, I can hear voices behind it but can't make out exactly who is there. Taking a deep breath, I push the doors open, and all conversation stops as everyone looks at me. I find the usual cast of characters, the ones I have come to call family, waiting for me—Hunter's and Griffin's parents, as well as Gracelin, Adam, and Violet. Neither of Hunter's siblings are here, but that's fine, as neither of them are involved in the day-to-day running of the kingdom. Gretchin isn't here either, but again, I hadn't expected her to be since she so recently found her mate. The two unexpected guests are the Coldicotts, but it makes sense that the rest of my council members are here for this debriefing.

"Colbie!" The three queens, Gracelin, and Violet jump to their feet and swarm me, fussing and cooing and generally loving on me like it's been months since they've seen me and not a matter of a day. They basically shepherd me into a seat, placing food and drink in front of me, then return to their own chairs. My mates watch on with amusement, sending me feel-good vibes through our bond.

"I'm fine," I tell them before anyone else can say anything. "I've processed my trauma and tucked it away, and I am ready to focus on the future."

Gem and Sable eye me skeptically, and I allow them that, but my words seem to reassure everyone else.

"We were just discussing what we learned from the prisoners we captured," Lucas explains, looking more relaxed than he's been since I met him. I guess having the pressure of his position removed has lifted a huge weight off his shoulders. I should know because that weight is now firmly on mine.

I pick up my fork and start eating, waving a hand for them to continue.

"The most important thing we learned is Tideman is not the mastermind," Bryson announces, leaning back in his chair and steepling his fingers together.

I blink in surprise, the fork halfway to my mouth. "He's not?"

"No, apparently he's nothing more than a lackey. There were others involved, but the guards didn't know their identities. They said there were five or six who would visit the facility regularly, but they wore masks and kept themselves covered with cloaks. They even had voice modulators so they would be harder to identify. One of the prisoners said he didn't think they were all shifters, though, because he saw them do things no shifter, even a mythical, could do." Titus sounds annoyed. "It makes sense, considering the wards surrounding the facility—no shifter could have set them —but we're no closer to finding out who is involved than we were yesterday."

"What about their plans? Were the prisoners able to tell you why they were trying to change all those humans?" Audrey Coldicott asks, leaning forward.

"Just that an army of warriors would be needed, and humans were easy cannon fodder. Once they are feral, they lose all inhibitions and are happy to kill indiscriminately," Micah answers. "They had high hopes that they could use Malina to open the spell book to access the spell to fix the ferals, because she shared the same blood as Colbie."

"But without the shifter queen magic, it isn't possible to use the spell," Mia argues.

"One of the prisoners said that the rumor floating around the complex was that maybe any one of the other kingdoms' royals should be able to use the book, since they all have access to goddess magic." Bryson looks disturbed at the idea, and once again, I stop eating.

"What do you know about the royals in the other kingdoms? Would any of them entertain this idea?" I ask Lucas, but it's Titus who answers.

"As soon as I heard that, I reached out to my assassin brothers in the other kingdoms. The witch and fae royals are already in their transition phase, so the majority of their magic is in flux until their new queens can be crowned. As of yet, neither of them have been identified or presented themselves to the palaces. I informed my brothers to be wary of possible assassination attempts when the new queens become known."

My heart skips a beat at the mention of my half-sisters. I haven't even wrapped my head around that little nugget of information that my dad imparted on me. That was a future Colbie problem, but I guess future Colbie is now.

"And the vampire kingdom?" Evie asks, wrinkling her nose. "The king is an alright person, but his wives are fucking vicious. I don't like them at all. He kind of lets them push him around. I think they are the true ruling faction in that kingdom."

"But their sons are hot." Gracelin fans her face, and Violet giggles, which lightens the atmosphere in the room.

Lucas scowls at his daughter, but she just shrugs. "What? They are. It's a pity they are all so fangy and drink blood. I bet their breath smells rotten." She mimes fangs with her front fingers in front of her lips, and Lucas shakes his head in exasperation.

"I don't know, being bitten isn't so bad," I murmur absently, looking at Titus, and the room falls dead silent.

"I said that out loud, right?" I feel my cheeks heat with embarrassment as Nox chuckles and nods. "Crap! Ignore me and carry on."

"I wasn't able to get a hold of my brother in the vampire kingdom." Titus is looking at me with a smirk. "But as far as I know, the transition phase hasn't started there. They were supposed to have another year, I think."

"But Aramis said her sister Eryx was going to change that. What about reaching out to the kingdom's ambassador?" I suggest.

"Because we rushed your own crowning, there wasn't time for the royals or their new representatives to arrive. We don't know who they will be, and the previous vampire ambassador has gone radio silent," Mia says, worry in her tone.

"And the prisoners couldn't tell you why? They were shifters, right? What cause could be so profound that they would betray their nation for?" Emmett Coldicott asks.

"Money. They were guns for hire with no morals

and were happy for an easy payday. They were too low on the totem pole to know why. They just followed orders and got paid." Bryson sounds disgusted. "All three of them were rejected by the shifter army because none of them passed their mental evaluation. They were holding a grudge."

A new set of concerns plagues me. The sisters I have only recently learned about are going to be in as much danger as I was until they can get their crowns. I only hope all of them are incorruptible. If this rogue faction can get their hands on one of them and turn them to their cause, then we will be in for a world of hurt.

The table falls silent as we all contemplate the possibilities. I wonder if we can send teams into each kingdom to help guard the new queens when they surface.

"We can't interfere in other kingdoms' politics." It's like Gryffin plucked the thought directly out of my head, and I give him a look of surprise.

"Did you read my mind?"

He chuckles. "No, I think I'm just starting to know you. I would want to do the same thing if my family was involved."

I had given the guys permission to share Loki's story with anyone they deemed relevant, so I'm guessing everyone at this table is considered such.

"For now, we are going to monitor the situation. Titus is in constant contact with his brothers, and your father has the rest of his assassin's guild gathering information. There is nothing we can do until they surface once more, but I have a feeling when they do, it won't be here in the shifter kingdom. They've blown their chance," Bryson surmises.

"And my parents are going to continue their search, this time focusing on the Tideman family. General Bryson had soldiers grab some of their belongings from their abandoned rooms to make it easier for them to be tracked. If we can find them, hopefully we can get our hands on that book," Nox tells me.

"What if he doesn't have it? What if he gave it to whoever is in charge?" Liam asks, playing devil's advocate, but Layla shakes her head.

"Vallen is a weasel. I bet he will hang on to the book and use it as leverage, because the minute he gives it up, he becomes dispensable."

"That's very true," Evie agrees.

"So what now?" I ask, looking around the table.

Gem stands up. "Now, we let the rest of these people run the kingdom, because we are owed a honeymoon period." All of my mates get to their feet, but I frown.

"As much as I want to, I can't drop everything and let others deal with it because of a biological need to spend time with all of you. I would be failing my first few official days as queen," I argue.

"Actually, you can. It is expected. It's why the council is announced on the same day as the new royal is crowned. They take care of the kingdom during the royals' honeymoon period, which *is* a biological need that can distract them from making smart choices." Lucas smiles at me. "Go and enjoy your mates. All of this will be here when you return, but you only get to enjoy the new bond frenzy once."

"Let me get this right. You are giving me time off to go fuck?" I ask bluntly, and he winces but inclines his head.

"Yes, although I would rather not think too hard about it."

"Quick, let's go before they change their mind." Brodie grabs my hand and pulls me to my feet before dragging me out of the room.

"But my food… I haven't eaten," I complain half-heartedly.

"Trust me, we made sure to have plenty of food on hand where we're going. You're going to need every single bit of energy you can get," Liam says behind me. Our bond suddenly blazes, and I feel my core clench and the need to clamp my legs together.

"Holy shit, what is that?" I mutter as my skin erupts in goosebumps and my nipples become rock hard.

"We all agreed to block the lustier side of our bond since we mated so you could focus on everything that needed to happen. We don't have to do that anymore, and you are finally feeling what newly mated shifters feel," Gryffin explains as we make our way through the palace to our living quarters.

"Micah made sure our wing was cleared of all staff this morning, telling them they couldn't return until they were advised to do so, which means we are going to worship you like the queen you are," Nox says, his voice husky with desire.

Hunter chuckles wickedly. "And no one will be around to hear you scream and beg."

Although there is so much still up in the air and a lot we don't know about the plot against us, it seems like it might not be restricted to a shifter thing. I think the next step involves me reaching out to my sisters once they are crowned, and for the four kingdoms as well as Chaos to work together.

None of that can happen immediately, though, so I am going to take a moment to breathe and enjoy my mates and my newfound status as shifter queen. The rest is a future Colbie problem, and now Colbie is very, very interested in exploring her mates' attributes a little more thoroughly.

I snatch my hand out of Brodie's and start to run, looking back at the surprised expressions on my mates' faces. "What are you all waiting for? Last one to our room has to clean the toilet for the rest of the month."

I giggle and run faster. I hear them shout as they begin to give chase.

"But we have staff for that," Brodie says, sounding confused. I just laugh and don't look back, a feeling of immense joy filling my chest. I never wanted the job, but it's good to be queen.

Hello and thank you so much for your patience. This
blew out longer than I had expected but I'm really
pleased with the way Colbie's story wrapped up. I hoped
you enjoyed it too.
Of course not everything was answered, but the story
will continue with Colbie's sisters in future books. For
now I'm heading back to another series and will come
back to the Kingdoms once I tie up a few loose ends
elsewhere.

In the mean time why don't you check out one of my
other series. You can find everything you need to know
here.

www.lexiewinston.com

To my cover designer Laura, of Aura Covers. Thank you for making me the second cover it was much appreciated and is perfect..
My ever faithful and patient editor Jess at Elemental Editing. You are the best and I appreciate you soooo much.
Thanks to Tegan and Amanda for the beta reading brilliance.
I've really enjoyed writing this duet, even though it was unplanned and definitely not on my schedule. But a girls got to be flexible when the muse takes her places.
And lastly to you guys the readers. I love what I do, and probably would do it regardless if anyone read them or not, but you guys make it that much sweeter so thank you.
Until next time, happy reading

Lexie